NEANDERTHAL OPENS THE DOOR TO THE UNIVERSE

NEANDERTHAL OPENS THE DOOR TO THE UNIVERSE

PRESTON NORTON

HYPERION

Los Angeles   New York

First Edition, June 2018
10 9 8 7 6 5 4 3 2 1
FAC-020093-18110

Printed in the United States of America

This book is set in 11-pt. Adobe Garamond Pro/Adobe;
Buntaro/Hanoded; Johnstemp/Monotype

Library of Congress Cataloging-in-Publication Data
Names: Norton, Preston, 1985– author.
Title: Neanderthal opens the door to the universe / Preston Norton.
Description: First edition. • Los Angeles ; New York : Disney-Hyperion, 2018.
• Summary: Nearly a year after his brother's suicide, sixteen-year-old Cliff
"Neanderthal" Hubbard gets recruited to make life better at Happy Valley
High by the school's quarterback, who claims he had a vision from God.
Identifiers: LCCN 2017032265 • ISBN 9781484790625 (hardcover)
Subjects: • CYAC: High schools—Fiction. • Schools—Fiction. •
Visions—Fiction. • Grief—Fiction. • Coming of age—Fiction.
• Family problems—Fiction. • Humorous stories.
Classification: LCC PZ7.N8253 Ne 2018 • DDC [Fic]—dc23
LC record available at https://lccn.loc.gov/2017032265

Reinforced binding
Visit www.hyperionteens.com

To Shannon
who I've never met
but who I know so dearly through the hearts of others

There are three rules to high school irrevocably inscribed within the interstellar fabric of the universe.

Rule number one: It's all bullshit.

Now before you go thinking I'm some angsty little teenage shit, you should know that I'm *not* little. In fact, I'm a behemoth. Sixteen years old and somehow miraculously shattering the 250-pound barrier. Holy crap, you say. Get the hell out of town, you say. You think *that*'s nuts? Let me rephrase it for you:

I'm a quarter of a thousand pounds.

Sometimes *not* sucking at math is a curse all its own.

It's not that I was *completely* fat; I was just big in general. Six foot six, to be exact. I was like this semi-evolved humanoid porpoise standing as a solemn warning of Darwinism gone wrong. I was like the immaculately conceived Force child of Jabba the Hutt and Chewbacca. Someone like me didn't need to look for the bullshit; it found me like a lard-seeking homing missile. Here were just a few shining examples:

"Hey, Cliff!" said Kyle Dunston on September 17 of last year, after I dropped my pencil in Mr. Gunther's Algebra 2 class. "Did you know that when you bend over, your butt crack is big enough to put the Grand Canyon out of business?"

"Easy, Neanderthal," said Lacey Hildebrandt on December 2, while I was making my way to the lunch line. "I'm pretty sure the cafeteria is all out of Twinkies and small children."

"Excuse me, Mr. Hubbard," said the aforementioned Mr. Gunther last month after school—March 23—while he was looking over my make-up assignment on polynomials. "Could you try *not* to sound like a jetliner when you breathe? I can't hear myself think."

That was me, Clifford Hubbard—the Grand Canyon–assed, Twinkie-and-small-children-eating jetliner-breather. Known more commonly by the Happy Valley High School population as Neanderthal.

This was all very pertinent to the second rule of high school:

People suck.

And not just the students, as Mr. Gunther so abundantly demonstrated. Everyone. Such as:

1. Vice Principal Swagley, who always eyed me like I was an escaped convict masquerading as a minor. Surely I just hid my orange jumpsuit in the woods, close to where I buried all the bodies.

2. My guidance counselor, Mr. Gubler, who suggested the possibility of a career in sanitary engineering. Now, stereotypes aside (sanitary engineer = garbageman), sanitary engineering is *actually* a respectable engineering field, a career with a decent salary and a crucial emphasis on environmental safety not to be scoffed at. Unfortunately, my dad was an *actual* garbageman— before his career in professional unemployment, anyway—and

Mr. Gubler knew it. Which therefore made him the Grand Vizier of Douchebags.

3. The lunch lady, Miss Prudy, who glared at me like she was wondering what I was doing in her lunch line and not that other one at the local Satanist compound that served Twinkies and small children.

The list went on and on. And that brought me to Aaron Zimmerman.

The Aaron Zimmerman.

It wasn't that he was more or less douchey than anyone else. Really, his level of douchebaggery was rather average. He was simply the most *popular* douchebag at Happy Valley.

I mean, let's face it. He was cool.

How cool? Imagine that *Ferris Bueller's Day Off* was based on the real-life story of Aaron Zimmerman—this human being whose will the universe miraculously obeyed. Except instead of Matthew Broderick, Aaron would be played by this genetically engineered teenage clone hybrid of Brad Pitt and Tom Cruise. Quarterback? Check. Four-point-oh GPA? Check. I hadn't seen the guy's ding-dong, but I imagine it was the size of a small nuclear warhead. I mean, why not? Everything else in the world was conclusively in his favor.

But before the List happened—more on the List later—I'd only had one real encounter with Aaron Zimmerman. Why would anyone as popular as him have had any reason to even acknowledge my existence?

Why, if my head intercepted his football, of course.

April 12 (12:50 p.m., if you wanna get specific).

I was wearing my "lucky hoodie"—plain black with a four-leaf clover printed on the front—which was really more of an ironic name because bad things always happened to me while I was wearing it. My older brother, Shane, gave it to me for my birthday, although I was pretty sure he bought it from some kind of witch doctor, because it was definitely jinxed as fuck. There was a hole in the inner fabric of the front pocket that I liked to stick my right thumb in—ripping it just a little bit bigger each time. I couldn't help myself. A nervous tic, I suppose, when you're essentially wearing a kismet time bomb.

Meanwhile, Aaron was chucking said football across the crowded hall to his crony, Kyle Dunston—yes, of "Grand Canyon–assed" fame—the trajectory of which was well over everyone else's heads.

Unfortunately, my head was *also* well over everyone else's heads. The football connected with my face. Two hundred and fifty pounds or not, that football nearly sent me flying into last Tuesday. But instead of shattering the space-time continuum, I merely collided into the nearest locker, leaving a perfect, Neanderthal-shaped fossil imprint. For about five discombobulating seconds, I had no idea what happened. My mental processing was going something like this:

Guh...

Uggghhhhh...

Blleeeaaaarrrrrgggghhh...

I was still prying myself out of the locker crater when Aaron Mosesed his way through the crowded hall like it was the Red Sea. He extended a helping hand. I took it.

"Whoa, are you okay?" he said, half laughing, half sounding like something resembling genuineness. "You really did a number on that locker."

I was still struggling to operate the English language, so I just kept blinking, failing to grasp that ever-elusive thing we call reality. Aaron was smiling as he eyed the crushed locker, and in my befuddled state, it could have passed as a real smile.

"Man, what do you eat for breakfast? Twinkies and small children?"

I know I was big, and in the world we lived in, big usually equaled stupid. But I wasn't stupid. I had three realizations instantaneously:

1. That line was a Lacey Hildebrandt original.
2. Aaron Zimmerman had dated Lacey Hildebrandt. (This might have seemed like a grand coincidence, but really, it wasn't. Aaron was like James Bond—always got the girl; never the STD. Or maybe he had all the STDs! Who knew?)
3. During that brief relationship, the two of them had obviously had a great big laugh at Neanderthal, the Twinkie-and-small-children eater.

And that brings me to High School Rule Number Three: Fists speak louder than words.

TWO

My fist was a wrecking ball, and it was swinging to excavate Aaron's genetically engineered Brad Cruise clone-ass face.

That's when I learned that I had made a dire miscalculation. He wasn't just a Brad Pitt/Tom Cruise clone. There was also Bruce Lee in there somewhere because he *limboed* backward, narrowly missing my blow. And then he popped right back up like a jack-in-the-box, guided by his fist, which nailed me right in the jaw.

Now I was obviously a big guy, bordering on Brobdingnagian . . .

. . . but damn!

I staggered backward, nearly into my Cliff-shaped crater, but caught myself with my hands. Aaron held his ground. His good friend, Kyle Kiss-Ass Dunston, however, was under the impression that Aaron was the president of the United States, and he was a member of the Secret Service, and this was suddenly a matter of national security. Kyle flew in, limbs flailing, with all the killer moves of an inebriated octopus.

I was smiling on the inside. I'd been waiting for this since September 17 of last year.

Grand Canyon, my ass.

My fist was a battering ram, straight and true, right into the word-spouting orifice of Kyle's face. You know that scene in *The Matrix Revolutions* when Neo punches Agent Smith in the head, and his whole face just kind of ripples?

Yeah. I was pretty sure that just happened.

Kyle went all Raggedy Ann across the hall—right into the circle of human vultures flapping in to feed on the action.

I lurched, veering my heavy momentum toward my remaining opponent. Aaron took off like a jet toward me. We crashed into each other—two raging, stormy tides of human fury. I may have had the body mass of a baby whale, but Aaron's reflexes were lightning. His left uppercut caught me on the other side of my jaw—*THWACK!*

At least my face would be proportionately fucked.

Fortunately for me, gravity was a cruel mistress. I was already on top of him, only slightly derailed by his blow. We rolled across the hall like some swollen, lopsided ball, roughly the size of a Prius. I had my hands around his throat, but Aaron decided to play prison rules and grabbed me by the nipples. Not that they were hard to find. I reckon I was a solid B cup, preparing to enter the solid realm of C if those Brown Sugar Cinnamon Pop-Tarts didn't stop being so damn delicious.

Aaron was gurgling, and I was screaming. We let go simultaneously. At this point, I just wanted to curl into the fetal position and cry.

We both staggered upright, groaning and drunk on pain like a pair of zombies straight out of a Romero film.

"Son of . . . a bitch," said Aaron between breaths. He sounded as exhausted as I felt. "You fight pretty good . . . for a beached whale."

"Thanks," I said. "You too . . . for a narcissistic . . . pantywaist . . . little ass-taxi."

Aaron actually laughed at this. "Wow ... the Neanderthal knows ... words and shit."

"Please ... the English language ... is my bitch ... you gaping cockmuppet."

And that's when my spidey-sense activated, and I sensed a terrible disturbance in the Force. Or maybe it was just the droves of students scattering like trouble was swiftly approaching.

"CLIFFORD HUBBARD!"

Shit.

This exclamation came from the only woman at HVHS wearing a power suit. Her hands were on her hips, never a good sign. Ever. Her hair fell in straightened curtains of black over her face, contorted into the Scowl of Death.

Principal McCaffrey was pissed.

———

Note that McCaffrey didn't yell Aaron's name. Just mine. Do you know why that was?

Remember High School Rule Number One? Remember Rule Number Two?

Still, that didn't exclude Aaron from being escorted with me to McCaffrey's interrogation chamber. Kyle would have joined us, too, if his borderline-comatose ass wasn't being examined in the nurse's office.

"Take a seat, you two," said McCaffrey.

Aaron sat politely. I sort of collapsed into this flimsy plastic piece of shit masquerading as a sitting apparatus. It released a long, drawn-out squeal. I imagined it desperately reciting the Lord's Prayer before it died under my ass.

To the untrained eye, Principal McCaffrey's office glowed of cheerful professionalism. But I wasn't fooled by the wall of award plaques or the bookshelves lined with inspirational bullshit titles like CHILDREN ARE THE FUTURE or LEARNING WITH LOVE. And don't even get me started on the mug:

WORLD'S GREATEST PRINCIPAL.

I had been waiting *years* for McCaffrey to take her hawk-eyes off me for one goddamn second so I could puke in that thing.

McCaffrey sat down behind her desk and pretzeled her arms and legs together into a fierce knot.

"What happened?" she said.

The words were already springboarding out of Aaron's mouth. "Well, you see, Principal McCaffrey, Kyle and I were just joking around, and I guess something we said must have offended Cliff 'cause he—"

McCaffrey was already shaking her head, eyes closed, one hand on her temple so as to prevent her Bullshit-O-Meter from sending her migraine into nuclear-meltdown mode. The other hand rose, slicing off Aaron's words.

"Okay, stop," said McCaffrey. When her eyes opened, they were firing on me. "Cliff, I want *you* to tell me what happened."

All the muscles in Aaron's face seemed to atrophy instantly. I wanted to take a picture and save it as the background screen on my iPhone. Except I didn't have an iPhone. Or any variation of smartphone. Or even a stupid phone for that matter. My family was the special sort of poor that couldn't afford a phone for their kid if the dude at T-Mobile gave us a brick with buttons for free because, according to my dad, talking to people costs money, too.

But back to Aaron's face...

Ah, screw it. The fact of the matter was that I didn't want to talk to McCaffrey, I wouldn't, I refused to, and she couldn't make me, and that was that.

But boy, could I stare.

McCaffrey and I glared laser beams at each other for a solid minute. Her stare demanded subservience. My gaze was like, *Oh yeah, woman? I can fall asleep with my eyes open. For all you know, I'm already unconscious.*

Aaron's eyeballs ping-ponged between the two of us, unsure what to make of the spectacle.

"Aaron, could you excuse us for a moment?" said McCaffrey.

"Uh . . ." said Aaron. "Sure. Should I just wait outside in the . . . ?"

McCaffrey's brow scrunched impatiently.

"Yeah, I'll just wait outside," said Aaron. He stood up all-too-eagerly and started for the door.

But not before flipping me off.

His arm and erect middle finger were tucked close to his chest—*completely* out of McCaffrey's view, the sneaky bastard. He walked slowly and held it for a long, tense moment until he opened the door and exited.

Before he closed the door, he winked.

Something ignited inside of me. It flashed and burned and billowed—filling me up—and suddenly, I had a purpose.

The next time I saw Aaron Zimmerman, I was going to beat the figurative *and* literal shit out of him. I was going to kill him with my bare hands.

But that was later. Right now there was only McCaffrey, me, and the metaphorical elephant.

"You know," said McCaffrey, shattering the silence like a sheet of glass, "I'm *really* sick and tired of this shit. You not talking to me?

What's that supposed to accomplish? Just who the hell do you think you're helping by giving me the silent treatment? Because it's not you, that's for damn sure."

I actually kind of liked it when McCaffrey swore at me. At least I knew she was being real. None of that "Children Are the Future/ Learning with Love" nonsense. No, deep down beneath the plaques and WORLD'S GREATEST PRINCIPAL mugs, Joan McCaffrey was a hard-ass chick who liked coffee and weekends and speaking her mind, and she hated kids like me. I could respect that. If I was her, I'd hate me, too.

Hell, I *was* me, and I still hated myself.

"Is this about Shane?" said McCaffrey.

My desire to be a part of this conversation plummeted from zero to negative eleventeen gazillion.

"I know it's been hard on you, Cliff," said McCaffrey. "But it's been almost a year. I think your brother would want you to move on. Do you think this—?" She pointed at me. "Whatever the hell *this* is—do you think that's the person he wanted you to be?"

Shane probably spent more school hours *in* McCaffrey's office than outside of it. She knew Shane Hubbard—the pot-smoking, hell-raising juvenile delinquent.

But she didn't know *shit* about the only real friend I ever had.

I leaned forward in my chair, and the words clawed out of my teeth. "Go. To. Hell."

THREE

I was suspended from school for a week. This might have been a big deal *if* I gave a shit about anything. But I didn't. Not one single shit. If it was possible for me to give negative shits, I'd distribute *those* like a six-year-old flower girl at a wedding.

Negative shits! Negative shits for everyone!

No, there were only two things I gave a shit about right now:

1. kicking Aaron's ass, and
2. Shane.

I would always give a shit about Shane.

I left school, but I didn't go home. I had a very important detour to make.

The Shannondale Cemetery wasn't the prettiest thing on God's green earth. I mean, it wasn't even really green, and it certainly didn't look like God had any part in its making. It was this brown-patchy, weed-ridden field of trailer-trash blah, because apparently people like my family had to bury their dead somewhere, too. Tombstones stuck out of the rain-drenched earth every which way like a mouthful of broken, crooked teeth.

Shane's headstone was a tooth that hadn't grown in yet; a tooth that would never grow in. It was a horizontal slab of cheap marble with the fewest words possible chiseled into its empty surface, because words apparently cost money, too:

SHANE LEVI HUBBARD

IN GOD'S CARE

Beneath this were tiny, almost invisible dates that were way too close together. Sixteen years and one month.

Today—April 12—was his birthday.

He *should* have been seventeen today. But he wasn't. He never *would* be. He was frozen—a permanent, chronological fixture in the annals of time.

I was now older than Shane by weeks.

There was something deeply unsettling about becoming older than your older brother. Like you were disturbing the natural order of things.

It had stopped raining a while ago, but I could feel the storm inside of me. Not a raging thunderstorm or anything like that. Just this endless downpour. Filling me up. Drowning me.

"Hey, bro," I said.

Shane didn't respond. Because he was dead, obviously.

Shane had always had the answer to everything. Even when he didn't *really* know. It was the confidence behind the answer. I would have followed that confidence to the end of the world.

Unfortunately, the end of the world was sooner for Shane, and here I was, left with nothing but this gaping hole. Nothing but rain and drowning and slowly dying, but never death, because that would just be too damn easy.

"So I don't know if you're in heaven or hell or some sort of weird purgatory-limbo-thingy," I said, "but it sure as hell has to be better than here."

Shane didn't say anything.

"Is there anything there? I mean, I know this stupid rock says 'In God's Care,' but headstones are supposed to say shit like that to make people feel better. But, like . . . is he there?"

Nothing.

"Even if there isn't a God or a heaven or anything," I said, "if you could just, like, haunt me or do some of that freaky ghost shit and scare the crap out of me every once in a while, I'd totally be okay with that."

Shane gave the obvious response.

"Think it over," I said. "Maybe I'll steal a Ouija board."

I left Shane in the crooked, broken mouth of the Shannondale Cemetery. Somehow, I felt a little less alive leaving this home for the dead.

———

I lived in Arcadia Park, which was, in fact, not a park at all. It was a trailer park. The funny thing about trailer parks is that all the stereotypes—that trailer parks are low-class, trashy, cockroach-infested little shithole excuses for homes . . .

They're all true.

I walked in the door—this sad, rectangular thing barely hanging by its hinges. The first thing people usually noticed was the cat-piss smell, which, fortunately, I'd gotten used to years ago. We didn't have any cats. The second thing people usually noticed was the nicotine stains on the walls—this ghastly yellow splotchiness that *looked* like cat piss. None of us smoked. My dad quit smoking ten years ago, but I had a theory that it was only so he could afford his drinking problem.

And boy, did he drink.

He was the third thing people usually noticed—sitting in the recliner wearing a mustache, a camouflage trucker hat, and a bottle of Bud Light in his hand, hooked to the football game on TV like it was his iron lung. It was his way of vicariously reliving his own football glory days that ended after his own stint at HVHS. He wasn't as big as me, but what he lacked in size, he more than made up for in dangerous levels of drunk-ass mean.

The bad news beat me home. Principal McCaffrey called about my suspension.

Normally, my mom picked up the phone. God gave my dad two hands—one for the TV remote and one for his Bud Light. He didn't have a third pick-up-the-phone hand. And even if he did, there was still the issue of getting his lethargic ass off the recliner.

Every time my mom got the bad news, she scolded me in private. She never told my dad, because she preferred me alive rather than dead. I listened, mostly because I cared about her, and I told her I'd never do it again, even though I had no such intention. I didn't want to break her heart, but at the same time, remember High School Rule Number One? Remember Number Two?

Remember High School Rule Number Three? *Something* has to speak louder than words. Words didn't do shit.

But all this was aside from the point. The point was that my mom wasn't home. And naturally, my dad didn't pick up the phone. But

Principal McCaffrey *did* leave a message on the answering machine—this ancient, telephonic mechanism used by poor people to record messages and dodge calls from debt collectors.

My dad heard *that*, all right. And he'd had plenty of time to get copiously drunk and stew over it.

"You know what pisses me off the most?" he said.

This wasn't a rhetorical question. My dad didn't ask rhetorical questions. And if you waited long enough to figure that out on your own, it'd probably be through an ancient Chinese martial art known as *zui quan*, or "drunken fist."

Okay, not really.

But really.

"What pisses you off the most?" I asked. My tone was flat—undisturbed—but there was a cloud of dread wafting beneath the surface.

"No," said my dad. He raised a dangerous finger, pointed it at me. "I want *you* to tell me what pisses me off the most. You're a smart kid, Cliff," he said. "You inherited my vast intellect, after all. Tell me: What pisses me off the most?"

He didn't ask rhetorical questions, but he sure as hell liked to play mind games.

"Having to see my ugly face every morning for the next week?" I said. (Sometimes, self-deprecating humor worked in my favor.)

"Hey, hey, hey!" he snapped. "You inherited half that face from me, you ungrateful shit. If you've got a problem with your face, take it up with your mom."

Despite appearances, my dad was actually a razor-tongued smart-ass. I suppose I inherited *that* from him. However, most smart-asses use sarcasm as a weapon because it's universally understood that the alternative—violence—is morally wrong.

For my dad, it was merely foreshadowing.

"I called your principal back," he said. "Asked how the Zimmerman kid looked. You know what she said? She said not to worry, he doesn't have a *scratch* on him."

Shit.

"A scratch! How the hell does a kid your size get suspended for a *week*, and not even lay a *scratch* on the other guy?"

"I dunno. He's a quarterback on the football team."

In retrospect, this was one of the dumber things I could say. It brought up a centuries-old argument that I was not ready to have again.

My dad stood up, which meant shit was real.

Even though he was smaller than me, it was scary when he stood up. There was something in the way his entire body tensed—like his veins might pop and he'd literally explode. More important, his hands were fast. If ass beatings were playing cards, he was a Vegas dealer.

"You see, *that's* the problem," he said. "If you'd stop watching all those goddamn sci-fi movies and join the football team like I've told you a hundred thousand times, you wouldn't fight like a little queer."

"I don't fight like a queer," I said—a little too defensively. "There were *two* of them. I punched Kyle Dunston's face inside out."

"Man, I don't give a shit about the Dunston kid. He's a skinny-ass bitch. He was collateral damage. The fact of the matter is that you picked a fight with the Zimmerman kid, and he walked away completely unscathed—which *wouldn't* have happened if you'd *join the fucking football team*."

My dad stepped away from his recliner. He was straight up, tense, and ready to deal.

"What do you have to say for yourself?"

I'd been in this situation before. He was giving me an ultimatum: either join the football team or get my ass kicked. He did the same thing to Shane, and Shane's answer was always the same. I felt Shane's words in the back of my throat.

"Football's dumb," I said.

My dad stopped. He stopped the way the world stops and the air goes silent before the sound waves catch up with the atomic mushroom cloud exploding in the distance.

"What did you say?"

He knew what I said. There was no going back. But I didn't *want* to go back. Not today.

This was when the true Clifford Hubbard came out. Not the Neanderthal. Not the juvenile delinquent. This was the person who was nothing but emptiness. He was only this eggshell. Hollow. Cracked.

"You heard me," I said.

Or at least that's what I tried to say. I didn't get a chance to finish the sentence.

———

My mom came home at eleven. As usual.

I heard her talking with my dad in the living room. She laughed at something he said. She always laughed, whether or not what he said was actually funny. I heard my dad bring my name up, but it was so casual—so *dismissive*—I might as well have been laundry or a random item for the grocery list.

She came straight to my room. As usual.

She was still wearing her Hideo's Video uniform—baby blue, matching her soft eyes. Hideo's Video—owned by this Japanese retro-philiac, Hideo Fujimoto—was the only video store in Happy Valley. It was the last middle finger saluting to Netflix and Redbox, and you know what? It had business! Because sometimes people *want* to watch that awesome movie from way back in the day, and sometimes those assholes at Netflix cycle it out of their rotation, and then what are you supposed to do? The truth is that people *like* going to video stores. Especially ones where the clerk happens to know everything there is to know about every movie ever filmed in the history of ever.

That was my mom.

It was actually thanks to her job at Hideo's Video that Shane and I had a pretty sweet setup in our room. We inherited an ancient thirteen-inch TV/DVD/VCR combo, and Hideo let us have our pick of everything that cycled out of inventory and hadn't been purchased from the discount bin within X amount of time. We had three whole bookshelves filled with the Hollywood greats—Ridley Scott and James Cameron, Martin Scorsese, and Quentin Tarantino. If we had to pick a favorite genre, it would probably chisel down to a solid tie between sci-fi and gangster films. Jim Carrey was a close third place. (Yes, Jim Carrey is totally a genre in and of himself.)

"Hey, sweetie," said my mom.

Not *We need to talk,* or *I thought you said you weren't going to get in any more fights,* or anything like that. Just this . . . love. This love that hurt because I knew I was disappointing her, and her heart was just too big to tell me the truth.

"Hey," I said. I was lying on my bunk bed—bottom bunk, of course, because the top belonged to Shane, and I respected his space. I pretended to read my book. Mostly to hide the right side of my face. It was easier to pretend like nothing was wrong. Because, like, when *everything* is wrong, where the hell do you even start?

My mom sat down on the corner of my bed that *wasn't* covered in Cliff. "Whatcha reading?"

"A book."

"Oh, please. Stop. Spare me the details. I can't. I just can't."

I couldn't help snickering. I was defenseless. I closed the book and showed her the cover.

"*Speaker for the Dead*?" said my mom in her worst attempt at not sounding impressed. "Dang, we're busting out the *heavy* Orson Scott Card. That's some pretty philosophical sci-fi. You reading that for school?"

"I'm suspended, remember? And I don't do schoolwork."

"Oh, right. Because my rebel son only reads American literary classics for fun. Sorry, I forgot."

"It's science fiction."

"Hey, only a snob sticks his nose up at science fiction. The best sci-fi tells us the truths about ourselves that we're too afraid to hear. What part are you at?"

"I'm at the part where they talk a lot. I mean, one guy got gutted by these piggy aliens, and they laid all his organs out like lawn ornaments, so that was pretty intense. But now everybody's just talking. I think that's the point of this book—talking without getting to the point."

"I'm on the edge of my seat just thinking about it."

"You should be."

"I am."

"Well, good."

"Fine."

I was smiling. I didn't even realize it until my guard had already dropped. Hell, my guard fell to the floor, broke through the floorboards, and went twenty feet underground. And that's when my mom's smile faded.

I forgot to hide the right side of my face.

Not that the left side of my face was a basket of roses. Aaron had given me a pretty even facelift on both sides.

But my dad swung with his left arm. My mom knew that.

This was the part where she was supposed to say she was sorry. That things would change. That she would divorce that bastard and get us out of this shithole, so we could start a new life—far, far away from everyone and everything. But that's not what she said.

I'd heard this speech before, and it was bullshit.

"I have to believe that the man I fell in love with is still in there," she said. "Somewhere. I just . . . I can't give up on him."

Normally, I had a filter for my mom. But today was no "normal" day. Between the fight with Aaron, my meeting with Principal McCaffrey, getting suspended, *and* my dad beating the Western Hemisphere of my face into the prime meridian of my skull, my filter was crushed and shattered and all but turned to dust.

"Did you know that Shane died hating you?" I said.

I didn't think about the words. They just came out. My words were like my dad's fists—hard, fast, and uncompromising. He never hit my mom, of course—Shane and I were his punching bags—but if he *did* punch her, this was probably how she would look. Like a scared, wounded animal.

And yet, I continued.

"He *hated* you," I said. "And for the longest time, I didn't understand why. But now . . . I think I get it."

Unlike Shane, I *couldn't* hate my mom. But I could sure as hell ignore her. In some distant corner of reality, I heard her give the same old excuses like they meant something. But they didn't. Not even remotely. Sooner or later, she would get the hint that this conversation was over. She would go to bed with the asshole whose memory she couldn't fall out of love with, and I would be left alone.

Hell, I already was.

FOUR

It was amazing how fast a week went without school. Naturally, I stayed as far away from home as possible. My happiness depended on it. Actually, *happiness* was a strong word. My willpower to not smother myself to death with my own pillow depended on it.

I had a favorite place in town. A special place. With a week of vacation, I had a lot of time to spend there, meditating and deliberating upon the Meaning of Life, or the staggering lack thereof.

Shane called it the Monolith.

Basically, it was this abandoned, unfinished seven-story office building. It was *meant* to be the new headquarters of the Happy Valley Ale Company, founded in 1968, but fate had a funny way of fucking things up.

It all started with the original Happy Valley Ale factory, located on the outskirts of town. In the beginning, everyone in town worked at the factory. Happy Valley *was* the factory. The entire town was built on a single idea: Happy Valley Ale was going to *revolutionize* beer. With its state-of-the-art ale-brewing technique, it came in a wide variety of flavors, including apple, pear, pineapple, banana, plum, cherry, and prune.

What the company failed to realize was that this was motherfucking Montana—the manliest state in the Union. A land where men shaved with axes, head-butted bison, and chopped down trees with their humongous dicks. Montana men didn't drink anything less than *real* American beer. None of this ale bullshit. The hell'd they think this was? Middle-Earth?

And one thing was for damn certain—Montana men didn't drink *anything* fruity.

The Happy Valley Ale Company collapsed a couple years later. The town essentially died with it.

The unfinished office building—the Monolith—was a skeleton. It was all bone-colored concrete floors, window frames like empty eye sockets, and unsealed walls with rib cages of exposed support beams. It was a labyrinth of pseudo-urban decay.

My and Shane's favorite place in the Monolith was near the peak of the building—this concrete lip jutting from an open, gaping mouth, overlooking all of Happy Valley. Once upon a time, I'm sure it was supposed to be a balcony with a sliding glass door and a fancy railing, probably for some high-and-mighty business executive—some Charles Foster Kane of booze—who would walk out in his double-breasted pinstripe suit, smoke his Cuban cigar, and observe his alcohol empire.

But that future was never to be. There was no sliding glass door. No balcony railing. Just this slab of concrete sticking out like an ancient spaceship landing pad.

Shane and I used to chill up there. From that vantage point, you could see the mountains encompassing Happy Valley in a cereal bowl of Shitty Puffs. A river ran straight through it—east to west—dividing the slums and the nice part of town. It was like Mother Nature herself understood the elitist concepts of class and segregation. The Monolith towered on the edge of the south side of the river—the slummy side—along with the factory, which was now a sprawling, industrial coffin left to rot.

That was my side.

The nice part—the part that had nothing to do with Happy Valley Ale, the part that was economically reborn—was where people like Aaron Zimmerman and Kyle Dunston and Lacey Hildebrandt lived, with their cars and their allowances and their beautiful *Modern Family*-esque dysfunctional families. The sort of dysfunctional that always had happy endings and a moral to the story.

Nice part, slummy part—it didn't matter. It was all Shitty Puffs.

Except for the Monolith. The Monolith was more than just an abandoned, unfinished building. It was a symbol. A metaphor. It meant something. I wasn't even sure what that *something* was; all I knew was that it *meant* it, and it meant it fiercely. Desperately.

I know what you're thinking.

Monolith? The hell kind of weird-ass name is that?

From the outside—*especially* when the sun was setting just right—the Monolith was an ominous black rectangle. Shane was *convinced* that it looked just like that black rectangle thingy in *2001: A Space Odyssey*—this enigmatic extraterrestrial anomaly appearing in different locations throughout space and time.

Shane was obsessed with *2001: A Space Odyssey*.

He was obsessed with the Monolith.

He said the movie only made sense when you were high. I *wasn't* high when I saw it, and—as expected—it was confusing as hell. I just had to take Shane's word on it. But occasionally I'd pick his brain.

"So in *Space Odyssey*," I said, "is the Monolith, like, an alien spaceship or a wormhole or something?"

"I like to think of the Monolith as a door," said Shane. "Like, *the* door. Like, the Door of Life."

"A door to what?"

"That's the question, isn't it?"

Cryptic bastard.

That Door of Life bullshit became his catchphrase. He'd pull it on me every time he tried to convince me to do something stupid like enter a creative writing contest or ask a girl on a date.

"Life isn't just existing," he would always say. "It's a door. Don't you want to know what's on the other side?"

And then he died—leaving me all alone in this world of doors. Except it felt more like a world of walls. There was just me, and Shane, and the Great Wall that separated us.

This was my unfortunate train of thought on Friday, the last day of my unpaid vacation courtesy of Principal McCaffrey, as I sat on the edge of the overlook. The sadness and the pain and the hurt—there was so much of it. It was overwhelming. The only way to cope with it was to not cope with it.

I glanced down at my legs dangling over the edge—a seven-story drop. Would a drop like that kill me or just break my legs? Because breaking my legs would suck.

That's when I heard the screaming.

It wasn't bad screaming—like, *Help me, I'm being murdered by a psycho in the shower* screaming. It was fun and laughter and hormones and maybe just a little bit of alcohol screaming. And these screams were accompanied by the scream of tires. A silver SUV rounded the corner of Gosling and Gleason, slowed only by the ginormous boat it was hauling. It roared over the bridge, clearly on a one-way destination to Flathead Lake for a weekend filled with delinquent partying, hangovers, and sandy, vaguely unsanitary beach sex.

And then the SUV—and boat—screeched to a nerve-racking halt.

"Holy shit, Kyle!" said an unmistakable voice. "What the hell?"

The driver's side door opened, and *pop!* There was Kyle Dunston—like a literal nursery rhyme weasel—standing on the running board, gripping the crossbars for balance.

"Dude, Aaron, look!" said Kyle, pointing directly at me. "It's Neanderthal!"

And that's when I saw Aaron—sitting in the passenger seat.

For a brief, infinite second, we made eye contact. Even seven stories down, I could see his eyes swell. The second passed like a season.

Aaron blinked. Shook his head, ever so subtle. Just like that, he was over it.

"Riveting, Kyle," he said, not even looking at me. "Can we go now?"

However, Kyle had already garnered the attention of the backseat.

"You're shitting me."

"No freaking way!"

I recognized Lacey Hildebrandt's voice, as well as this tool-bag, Desmond Steinmetz, who only wore shirts when it was required by dress code or refusal-of-service laws. Kyle's SUV, however, was no such place.

Desmond rolled down his window. "Hey, Neanderthal. You wanna come to the beach with us? I'm sure one of these beautiful ladies would love to have wild caveman sex with you. Ride 'em dinosaur-style! *Jurassic Park*–style!"

"Ew," said Heather Goodman, who typically wore more makeup than clothes. "You have dinosaur sex with him, Desmond."

"Hey, Neanderthal," said Kyle. "When we get back, I'm going to kick your ass so hard, it's gonna fall off!"

And that, my friends, is a Kyle Dunston original. Let's all give him a round of applause before he hurts his brain and tries another one.

"Can we *go* already?" said Aaron.

"Dude, what's your problem?" said Kyle.

The conversation had dropped several decibels, but lucky me, I had the ears of a bat—a giant, diurnal, eavesdropping bat.

"My *problem* is that I want to be on a lake already, not gawking at Neanderthal," said Aaron.

"I dunno, man," said Kyle. "You're acting weird."

"You *are* acting weird," Lacey agreed.

"Well, you guys are acting like a bunch of fucking assholes," said Aaron.

The SUV went silent. The whole *corner* went silent. Not that Gosling and Gleason was the epicenter of civilization. Like I said, once you crossed the river, Happy Valley became Mildly Apathetic Valley. The only thing missing was a drought, some tumbleweed, and maybe a sweeping, desolate score by Ennio Morricone. But the usual Montana sounds—the cicadas, the wind, the diesel trucks roaring on some distant highway—all hit the brakes on their usual activity. Even *my* breath caught in my throat. Thank God I was seven stories up, well out of conversational reach.

Aaron seemed to realize that this could only go one way. So he did what he had to do. He stuck his head out the window, looked me dead in the eye, and flipped me off.

"This is for you, Neanderthal. Take good care of it."

The universe was once again in balance. Everyone laughed, shoving their hands out the windows, saluting me with their middle fingers.

"Happy Birthday, Neanderthal!" said Desmond.

"Merry Christmas!" said Heather.

"No return policy, sorry!" said Lacey.

"Your ass is gonna fall off!" Kyle screamed.

That was the last thing I heard as he hit the gas, and they sped off.

On Monday, rain came down in silver sheets. Purging the grimy walls of HVHS. Bathing the dirty, broken concrete at the corner of Gosling and Alpanalp. Residue drizzled like snot into the gutters—many of which were choking in weeds growing through the cracks. Frankie and his gang of skeezy drug dealers were leaning against the chain-link fence, smoking some shit that was possibly legal, but only because it hadn't been officially canonized in the DEA's bible of Shit That Will Get Your Ass Thrown in Juvie for Possessing.

There was only one dealing machine at HVHS, and Frankie's gang was it.

I wasn't afraid of them. Frankie Robertson and his two buddies, Jed and Carlos, dressed tough—milking the gangsta façade for all it was worth—but like everyone in Montana, I knew that their parents were *Duck Dynasty*–level rednecks. Frankie mostly kept to himself, and Jed and Carlos knew better than to start something with a guy who looked like he clubbed wooly mammoths for lunch.

However, Tegan Robertson—Frankie's little sister and the fourth and final member of the gang—delighted in my torment.

"Hey, Neanderthal baby!" said Tegan. "Where's that ass been all week? You ain't been cheatin' on me, have you, honey? You ain't been unfaithful, have you, sugar-bear? You know that big, curvy ass is mine."

I usually came mentally armed to verbally bitch-slap anyone who acknowledged my existence. And if that didn't get the point across, then I would physically bitch-slap them. With my fist. Or possibly my skull if I wanted them to die instantly. Really, the nickname Neanderthal wasn't completely unwarranted. I think the only reason I had never been expelled completely was because of Shane's death. And that was certainly enough reason for me to hurt people.

Unless that person was a girl.

Tegan was in a category all her own. She dressed like a rapper and was built like she could kick Lara Croft's Tomb-Raiding ass. She also had big chocolate eyes framed in heavy eyeliner and these full lips that were always twisted into a sexy smirk. There were rumors that she made out with Crissy Cranston from the cheerleading squad. How did I hear these rumors?

Two Weeks Ago:

Tegan: "Hey, Neanderthal, me and Crissy Cranston were making out in the girls' locker room the other day. You should join us sometime. I bet you rock the lacy underwear, am I right? Crissy likes that lacy shit."

Tegan and I had something special. It was called catcalling.

I power-walked my fat ass around that corner. Tegan slapped her own ass and did this weird, snarling thing at me.

"Hey, Teg, how come you never check out my ass?" said Jed. "Mine is bigger and curvier than his."

Tegan looked at Jed like he was an actual disease. "Jed, your ass prolly has gonorrhea or Ebola or some shit."

I kept walking, hoping that Tegan would be too preoccupied with Jed's Ebola to notice.

Nope.

"Mmm, you been workin' out, Neanderthal? You been workin' that bench press, honey? That chest is voluptuous."

Jesus Christ on toast! I was indirectly coming to terms with what it was like being a waitress at Hooters.

Tegan grabbed her breasts, plumping them up for me. "Neanderthal, if you let me cop a feel, I'll let you touch mine."

"C'mon, Teg, leave the brother alone," said Carlos.

"*I'll* touch your boobs, Tegan," Jed offered.

The great thing about Jed was his learning curve. It was nonexistent.

"Jed, keep your dirty, fat little claws away from my tits," said Tegan.

Carlos was laughing in spite of himself. Jed had his chubby head hung low, discreetly looking at his "fat little claws." Tegan was still showcasing her breasts for me like they were the next thing up for bid on *The Price Is Right*. Frankie didn't even look at me. He was much too preoccupied smoking his souped-up joint and looking like a badass. Which, let's be honest, he looked like the baddest-ass motherfucker of them all. If Tegan was built for a girl, her brother had every muscle sculpted and tatted like he was a white 50 Cent. He even shaved his head, just to make room for the tattoos that didn't fit on his vast, ripped frame.

Frankie glanced at me.

"Unless you wanna buy something or touch my sister's titties, you better keep moving," he said.

I hadn't even realized I stopped walking until now. Awkward.

I kept moving.

"Woooooo!" said Tegan. "Shake that ass."

———

"That's a nice Game Boy," said Niko Kaliko, at the other end of the hall. "Lemme see it."

Niko wasn't talking to me, though. He was talking to Jack Halbert, who was clutching his 3DS so close to his chest, it might have been attached to his heart. The annoyingly peppy theme music of *Animal Crossing* downplayed the dire nature of this encounter.

Jack was what you would call a nerd. He weighed about a buck-ten, wearing glasses that I *swear* he stole off of Harry Potter's face, and T-shirts that said things like CURSE YOUR SUDDEN BUT INEVITABLE BETRAYAL! or NOW WE SEE THE VIOLENCE INHERENT IN THE SYSTEM! HELP, HELP, I'M BEING REPRESSED! He was also the one and only black kid in all of HVHS—one of the few in all of Montana, actually. Montana was about as diverse as the Republican National Committee.

Niko was what you would call the Antichrist. His evil was legendary. Like this one time in fifth grade? He stole his little sister's Barbie dolls and turned them into "voodoo dolls." He dressed each one up (cut hair, made personalized outfits out of paper, drew on facial hair with Sharpie, etc.) so that they resembled several of the teachers and faculty at Happy Valley Elementary School.

And then he held a "public execution" on the playground.

Now he was a junior in high school. His sadism had evolved, and so had his body. Now he was the size of a small mountain. No shit, the guy was almost as big as me. Almost. Oh, and Kaliko was only an abbreviation of his last name. The real thing was a doozy—Kaleoikaikaokalani.

"Um . . ." said Jack. He seemed to consider correcting Niko that it was, in fact, a 3DS and not a Game Boy. Then he reconsidered and handed it over.

"Thanks, buddy," said Niko. He pocked the handheld gaming device in his fake leather jacket, messed up Jack's hair with his biker-gloved hand, and strolled away.

Was Niko actually going to play *Animal Crossing*? Hell no. He probably didn't even *like* video games. He simply fed on the misery of the human race.

Fortunately for him, there was a lot of misery to feed on.

I had a checklist:

1. Find Aaron.
2. Kill Aaron.

Once my hands were around his throat, I could decide if shit was figurative, literal, metaphorical, or whatever.

Our classes didn't intersect until after lunch—fifth period English with Mr. Spinelli.

Fact: the supposedly fictional characters of Ebenezer Scrooge and the Grinch were *actually* based on the real life story of Mr. Spinelli. (Yes, I realize this would mean that Charles Dickens and Dr. Seuss were, in fact, time travelers.) Mr. Spinelli was the grouchiest, meanest, nastiest, evilest, Christmas-eating old fart in the history of evil old people. And it goes without saying that old people are generally evil by nature.

But as with all Forces of Evil, Spinelli had once met his match. The yang to his yin. The Luke to his Vader. Only one student had ever dared to stand up to Spinelli's reign of terror.

Shane.

Except in all actuality, Shane was more like Han Solo, because he was really a selfish asshole, and everyone loved him for it. He and Spinelli had this *Breakfast Club*–esque "John Bender meets Assistant Principal Richard 'Dick' Vernon" sort of relationship. They hated each other's guts, and it was epic. Spinelli ruled with an iron fist, and Shane rebelled like he was upending a fascist police state. His pranks were legend. Such examples included:

1. When Shane attached an air horn to the bottom of Spinelli's swivel seat.
2. When he covered the floor of Spinelli's classroom with Styrofoam cups of water. (Yes, the *whole* floor. Every inch.)
3. The granddaddy of them all: When they were reading *King Lear*, Shane raided the theater dressing room and came to class dressed as the Earl of Kent. What happened next went something like this:

SHANE: (*pointing at Spinelli*) *A knave! A rascal! An eater of broken meats!*

SPINELLI: What in the . . . ?

SHANE: *A base, proud, shallow, beggarly, three-suited, hundred-pound, filthy, worsted-stocking knave!*

SPINELLI: Out! Get *out* of my classroom!

SHANE: *A lily-livered, action-taking knave! A whoreson, glass-gazing, super-serviceable finical rogue!*—

It goes on—evidence that Shane had too much free time (he actually memorized those lines), and Shakespeare was an incurable smart-ass.

But this was all aside from the point. The fact of the matter was Spinelli's insatiable evil could be tolerated today because I was going to kill (figuratively/literally/metaphorically) Aaron Zimmerman, and then everything would be right in the world.

I walked into fifth period. Aaron's seat was empty.

I sat down. I waited until the bell rang.

Aaron's seat was still empty.

Mr. Spinelli commenced his lecture on our weekend reading of

The Old Man and the Sea. Clearly, Spinelli did not realize that Aaron's absence had thrown the whole world off its galactic track, and the entire universe was collapsing in the wake of this interstellar disturbance. Suddenly, the sense of purpose and fury and determination and bloodlust that had been accumulating within me—like stormy tides—defused. My purpose melted into a disorienting, unsettling, disappointing puddle of blah.

And I felt lonely again. Because I didn't have someone to kill.

What.

The.

Hell.

And that's when I noticed Lacey Hildebrandt, sitting one seat ahead of me to the left. Lacey was all blonde hair, blue eyes, and fair skin, and she dressed like her life was one ongoing photo shoot, wearing avant-garde things like "one-sleeve tops" or "cropped crochet vests" or "cold shoulder jumpers." Which made the current situation all the more jarring.

She was wearing sweatpants and a hoodie—emphasis on the "hood" because it was pulled all the way over her head. Probably to hide her bloodshot eyes, emphasized by deep purple circles.

She had been crying.

She had been crying *a lot*.

She was looking straight ahead at Mr. Spinelli as he spoke of the crucifixion imagery in the text, but at the same time, she *wasn't* looking at him. She was looking through him.

On the opposite side of class, Lacey's best friend, Heather Goodman, wasn't much better. Heather had rich brown hair, freckles, and typically wore eyeliner like a superhero wears a mask—bold, dangerous, mysterious. Today, however, her face was zombified beyond the point of makeup repair.

And then I saw it—the note that left Heather's hand. It slipped inconspicuously from Mary Smith to Patricia Johnson to Danny Stern to Linda Jones.

It was on a direct path to Lacey.

Spinelli, oblivious to the floating note, read aloud from the novel, "'Ay,' he said aloud. There is no translation for this word and perhaps it is just a noise such as a man might make, involuntarily, feeling the nail go through his hands and into the wood."

I intercepted the note from Elizabeth Darley—just one seat away from Lacey. I wasn't exactly subtle about it, either. Since my arm was roughly the size of a small tree trunk, my hand snatched it midpass like a shark leaping out of the water.

And now I had successfully garnered the attention of the entire classroom—Spinelli included. He rested the book on his waist and hit me with this look that could best be described as the fiery Eye of Sauron.

"I'm sorry, Cliff," said Spinelli. "Is my lesson not capturing your vast attention?"

I ignored him and read the note.

Kyle says he's still not awake. Doctors are saying it's a coma.

I wasn't just reading now. I was absorbing it. My eyes scrolled over the words again and again, trying to make sense of it. He? Who the hell was "he"?

My gaze slowly shifted up from the note to Aaron's empty desk.

"MR. HUBBARD!"

This was the part where Mr. Spinelli was going to tell me to get my punk ass the hell out of his crib and march my shit over to Principal McCaffrey's office, stat.

I stood up from my seat and marched to the door before he could say anything.

I was out the door, down the hall, and strolling through the main offices.

I opened the door to Principal McCaffrey's office and marched right in.

Sure enough, she was on Facebook. Watching a cat video. Her laughing smile did this awkward, flustered transition—like, *surely* no one ever had the nerve to interrupt a cat video—before transforming into her trademark authoritative scowl.

"Dammit, Cliff!" she said. "I swear, if you punched another kid in the face—"

"What happened to Aaron Zimmerman?"

That was probably the last thing in the universe she expected me to say—ranked only slightly above *I like eating hair.*

McCaffrey's eyes narrowed. She paused her cat video.

Shit was real.

"Take a seat, Cliff."

I took a seat.

She interlocked her fingers, squeezing her hands into a tight ball. "Aaron Zimmerman is in a coma."

Well yeah, I had already gathered that much. McCaffrey didn't say anything else for a long, seemingly eternal moment of silence. So I prodded her along with an "Okay..."

"He and some friends took a boat out to the lake. They were water-skiing or wake boarding or something. I don't know. Anyway, Aaron fell in the water—right as another boat was coming along. They didn't see Aaron and..."

McCaffrey didn't finish. She didn't need to finish.

"Shit," I said.

"Shit is right," said McCaffrey.

I didn't know what to feel. Which was weird. I mean, I *should* have felt happy. I came to school with one purpose today—revenge—and I didn't even need to do anything. The universe served him up a nice, steamy bowl of karma. Aaron got what was coming to him. And yet . . .

I didn't feel anything.

Actually, that wasn't true. I did feel something. I felt emptiness. This tangible nothingness billowing inside me. This black hole in the fabric of space-time, bending gravity and sucking everything, even light, into its infinite, abysmal event horizon.

I felt alone.

"Are you okay, Cliff?"

I blinked. McCaffrey was looking at me, head cocked slightly.

"Yeah," I said.

It sounded like a *no* coming out of my mouth.

I didn't give the conversation one more second to continue. I stood up and escorted myself out.

I didn't go back to class.

———

A psychologist named Abraham Maslow once created a pyramid chart that ranked the stages of human need. This chart became known as Maslow's Hierarchy of Needs. The foundation of the pyramid started with the most basic human needs necessary for survival—food, water, air—and advanced to more evolved stages of need such as "self-actualization" and even "transcendence."

Alas, I was just a lowly Neanderthal. I was hardly *that* evolved. Right now, I just needed to get high. The need was rudimentary. Physiological, even. I needed it to survive.

I didn't have any money, but I was willing to negotiate.

"What?" said Frankie. He blinked because *surely* I did not ask what he thought I just asked.

"Do you have any free samples?" I said again.

Carlos snorted, stifling his laughter. Jed responded with this sort of confused and inquisitive look, as if to ask, *Uh, do we?*

"Free samples?" said Frankie. "*Free* samples? Does this look like Costco?"

"Uh…"

"Does this look like some Asian food joint at the mall? Do you see Tegan out here with a tray, handing out little joints on toothpicks?"

Tegan laughed a little too hysterically at this remark. "Toothpicks! Little joints on *toothpicks*!"

She was clearly baked like a three-story wedding cake. I was jealous.

"Well, how do I know your stuff's any good?" I said.

The corner went silent. Tegan blinked her glazy eyes, and Jed and Carlos exchanged glances that deserved to be canonized in the Archives of Holy Shitdom.

Frankie looked like I had just insulted his dead grandmother, the Virgin Mary, and Tupac all in one breath. He stepped toward me until we were just a breath apart. Then he lifted a little joint, pinned between his fingers, and stuck it in my face.

"You see this?"

Actually, I couldn't see it because he was holding it right in between my eyeballs. I refrained from pointing this out.

"This ain't no normal marijuana. We call this Stairway to Heaven. My cousin Zack is a chemical engineer. Graduated from Stanford. And he grows this shit in his basement. Do you know how much a chemical engineer makes?"

I didn't know if this was a rhetorical question, but I shook my head anyway.

"A shit-ton. Do you how much a chemical engineer would have to make selling pot to decide it was worth farming in his basement?"

"Uh . . . a shit-ton?"

"Damn straight. This shit has thirty-three percent THC. That'll send you through the roof and to the moon, bro. Send you up to Jupiter."

"THC?"

"Tetrahydrocannabinol, man," said Frankie. Now *he* sounded like a chemical engineer. He stopped and studied the cluelessness written all over my face. "Do you even smoke, Neanderthal?"

Had I smoked? Yes. Shane got ahold of some joints every now and then, and we got roasted in the Monolith. I could probably count the number of times on one hand.

Okay. One finger. I got roasted once. Leave me alone.

"Yeah, I smoke," I said. "So you gonna give me that free sample or what?"

"I've got your free sample," said Tegan.

This turned everyone's heads.

Tegan lifted the Magic Dragon she'd been Puffing all afternoon. She then turned it so the lit end was facing her lips. She pinched it delicately between her teeth. And then she started slow-dancing her way over to me. Her hips were a pendulum, and her arms were swaying in sync.

I was hypnotized. It was the weirdest, sexiest thing I'd ever seen in my entire life. And apparently I wasn't the only one mesmerized. Jed and Carlos both stared, slack-jawed, like they had stepped into a real-life porno.

Frankie just scowled.

Tegan grabbed me by the shoulders, and pulled me down to her level—a solid twenty inches. She leaned into me on her tiptoes, her face hovering inches from mine. Her whole *body* was inches from mine. She gently nudged the joint into my mouth. Her lips were so close, I couldn't even process whether or not they brushed mine, but I felt her breath caress my face, and I breathed it in.

It smelled like McDonald's. Somehow, even *that* turned me on.

"There's your free sample," said Tegan. "You know where to come for more."

Remember when I told Aaron the English language was my bitch? Well, currently, I didn't know a verb from a noun. And, like, prepositions and shit? Forget it.

I got the hell outta there.

———

I thought smoking a used joint would be low-key. Like Tegan might have smoked half the "high" out of it or something.

I had made a dire miscalculation. Whatever the hell that THC stuff was that Frankie was talking about...

Merciful Jehovah.

It came in three phases:

Phase One: Coughing—I couldn't stop. I probably sounded like I had asthma or whooping cough.

Phase Two: The details! Like, when did the world suddenly become so intricate and shiny and beautiful and, like, shit, have you ever looked at a concrete sidewalk up close? It's composed of all these tiny little bumps and air pockets and imperfections that form together into this mosaic of modern art that people just trample under their *feet*— the uncultured bastards! (Naturally, I was observing this on my hands and knees.) And leaves! Oh, don't even get me started on leaves. They're so beautiful and unique with their own personalities—like flat, green people growing on trees, aging and dying the same time every year.

I couldn't. I just couldn't. I'd cry.

Phase Three: I was a superhero.

BAM! I was at the Monolith—so fast, I didn't even remember why I came there to begin with.

Not only that, but my *brain* was superhuman. Every thought that had ever been conceived in the history of the universe was orbiting my posterior cingulate cortex, bouncing around like bingo balls, each one falling perfectly into place, and the answers made sense. The glass was half-empty because water was in a constant state of evaporation. The Meaning of Life was to find out what things gave your life meaning, duh! So cake was definitely up there. And the CIA was *obviously* covering up the existence of aliens because the world was so damn bigoted, how the *hell* were we supposed to handle beings from another planet?

I walked out onto the concrete lip overlooking Happy Valley. The sun was a fiery sliver, retreating behind black silhouetted mountains. Shadows elongated, forming bars of darkness, trapping the town in a metaphysical prison. As the flow of Supreme Omnipotent Consciousness flowed through my elevated state of mind, I took one look at the crumbling architecture around me—one look at the meaning behind everything—and I knew what I had to do.

I ran out of the Monolith.

I ran down Gleason.

I turned left at Randall.

Considering my superhuman speed, this took a lot longer than I anticipated. But it didn't matter because I was *there*. It glowed before me in neon red like the fiery bowels of hell. Except the opposite, because hell is bad, and this place was good because it contained the answer to Life, the Universe, and Everything, and it had nothing to do with the number forty-two—no offense, Douglas Adams—and not to mention my mom worked here.

Hideo's Video.

I walked inside. Except my walking was more like running. The doors flew open, and I ran to the front register where my mom observed me like I was some psycho druggie off the street.

"Mom, I need to watch *2001: A Space Odyssey* RIGHT NOW!" I said calmly. Except my voice came out kind of loud like I was screaming.

Why was she still looking at me like that? Didn't she know how important this was?

"Cliff," she said. "Are you high?"

Of all the audacious accusations.

"What the hell, Mom?" I said. "Of course I'm not high. I just ... I smoked a little pot, but I'm fine. I need to watch *2001: A Space Odyssey*. You know, the one Stanley Kubrick made? Stanley Kubrick ... he's the guy that made *The Shining*. You know, with Jack Nicholson? Anyway, I need to see *2001: A Space Odyssey*."

My mom was still looking at me like I had antlers growing out of my nipples. "Cliff, you're high. I can smell it."

I couldn't take it anymore. Why couldn't she just understand?

I started crying.

"Shane wanted me to watch *2001: A Space Odyssey*," I said/cried. "It's the last thing we watched together before he killed himself, and I know he was trying to tell me something, and the Monolith is the Door of Life, and I need to know what's on the other side, and I just need to watch it because I want to know, I need to know, why we weren't good enough for him, why I wasn't good enough for him because I can't keep living like this, I can't, I can't, I can't, I just can't do it anymore."

It's funny how we try so hard to hide from the truth. We tell ourselves that it didn't happen. We say it enough times that we start to believe it. We live in a lie that exists only for ourselves. But the Truth is still there—dangling above us, hanging on a very weary thread. Out of sight. Out of mind. Until the thread of our self-denial breaks, and the Truth comes crashing back down. Shane found his Door of Life in the Monolith. Our Monolith. He found it when he stole a gun, brought it into our old hideout, and blew his brains out the top of his skull.

If life was a door, Shane opened that son of a bitch wide open and stepped into the darkness.

My mom was crying now. That's when I knew I was screwing up magnificently. But it didn't stop her from hugging me. She hugged me and hugged me and kept hugging me as I fell apart completely—this six-foot-six, 250-pound thing unraveling in her arms. And somehow, she held it all together.

"It's okay," she said. "Everything's going to be okay."

I knew she was lying. *She* knew she was lying. But it was okay. I needed someone to lie to me right now. I needed someone to make me believe, if only for a little bit, that everything was going to be okay. Even if it wasn't.

Especially because it wasn't.

FIVE

I didn't go to school the next day.

SIX

Or the day after that.

SEVEN

On the third day, a miracle happened.

Whispers filled the halls of HVHS like misty vapor—seeping into every social crack and crevice, sticking to every surface.

"Aaron's back!"

"He's awake?"

"He's here, he's here!"

A miracle—that's the word that the *doctors* were using. Apparently, after eleven years of premed, med school, and residency, doctors didn't have a better medical word to explain it. Despite what was typical for a coma victim, his brain was no worse for wear. They MRI'd, but there wasn't even a hint of damage. Nothing. So they released him.

As if all this wasn't enough, Aaron had the audacity to say that he felt "fantastic."

Apparently, there was a long, epic debate between Principal McCaffrey and Coach Slater concerning whether or not he should still be allowed to play football again. Principal McCaffrey was reluctant.

Coach Slater, however, was of the opinion that Football Is Life, and if you don't play, what's even the point?

Ultimately, it came down to parental consent. And let's just say that Mr. Zimmerman and Coach Slater shared the same sentiment.

Just like that, HVHS's quarterback reclaimed his throne.

It was like the stars had aligned. We both came back to school on the same day.

So I could kick his ass.

Just kidding. I was pretty sure there was a rule in the High School Ass-Kicking Handbook that says: *No ass is to be kicked within twenty-four hours of the ass-kickee leaving the hospital. And kicking the ass of one who has just awoken from a coma is an act of the utmost douchebaggery.*

I'd kick his ass next week.

Everyone was mobbing and paparazzi-ing him. They came in droves, hugging him, patting him on the back, ruffling his hair. I even saw one or twelve people slap his ass. Not that I was looking or anything. It's just hard to focus on the empty half of the hallway when the other half is involved in a fully clothed, sexless orgy. He was the sun of the Happy Valley galaxy, and everything within fifty thousand light-years was in his gravitational orbit. People cheered and applauded as he rounded every corner and entered every room. Hell, even a teacher or two stood up and clapped. The only thing missing was the signed autographs.

There was only one problem. Actually, it wasn't so much a problem as it was a strange detail—a detail so peculiar and near invisible, nobody seemed to notice.

Aaron kept looking at me.

I mean, yeah, I was looking at him, too. But still. We kept doing that awkward "make eye contact/look away/make eye contact again" thing. Yeah, he was hugging people and high-fiving and fist-bumping and everything else you do when you're being assaulted in the friendliest way possible. But then, in the midst of it all, I'd catch him looking at me again.

Still, that didn't stop me from actively contemplating his demise. At the moment, I was thinking about hitting him with a school bus, Regina George–style.

Everything changed when I sat down for lunch.

Let me tell you something about lunch—it's like the perfect metaphor for my life. Here you are, surrounded by hundreds of beautiful people. They are all so happy and talkative, blissfully absorbed in their own social spheres. And then there's me, smack-dab in the middle of it. All by myself. There was always this barrier of empty chairs around me, like I was surrounded by this invisible quarantine force field. Watch out, everyone! You might catch Neanderthalitis!

I left the lunch line with two chimichangas, corn, custard, fruit salad from a can, and chocolate milk—all of which I was rather fond of—and sat down at my usual spot.

By myself.

As usual.

And that's when Aaron Zimmerman sat down at my table.

He didn't just sit down at my table. He sat down *directly* across from me. This was a clear barrier breach of my invisible quarantine force field.

"Hey," he said.

Hey. Just like that. Like we were bros or something. He was smiling like he knew the greatest secret in the world.

My whole body tensed up. A long time ago in a galaxy far, far away, Admiral Ackbar was surely spinning in his swivel space chair, proclaiming, *It's a trap!* I had no doubt that Kyle cock-waffle Dunston or some other football asshole was sneaking up from behind to dump custard on my head.

I looked to the left. I looked to the right.

Nobody was sneaking up. On the contrary, everyone seemed well aware of my invisible quarantine force field. However, the whole cafeteria became quieter. Because everyone was watching the resurrected Aaron Zimmerman sitting next to the caveman kid. That left only one option:

Aaron Zimmerman was here to mock me.

My head turned back to him like the slow rotation of a cannon. Screw the High School Ass-Kicking Handbook. I was going to stab Aaron to death with a chimichanga.

"It's Cliff, right?" said Aaron.

This question completely defused my offense.

"Huh?" I said.

"Cliff—that's your name, right? You know, the thing on your birth certificate that people call you by? I mean, unless your parents actually named you Neanderthal."

Something was definitely up. Admiral Ackbar was probably shitting lobsters at this point.

"What do you want?" I said.

Aaron's smile flinched. "So I don't normally do this," he said, "but, um...sorry?"

I blinked.

"Jesus, I suck at apologizing," he said.

I blinked again.

"You should say something," he said. "This is awkward."

Was I still high? How long did it take for marijuana to wear off?

And that's when Kyle dick-for Dunston breached the invisible quarantine force field. Maybe I wasn't so high after all. He was holding his lunch tray and wearing this curious half smile, as if wondering why his best friend hadn't let him in on the joke.

"Hey, man," said Kyle. "We eating with Neanderthal today?"

Shit got weirder. Aaron's face flinched. His eye twitched.

"Can you give me a sec, man?" said Aaron. "I need to talk to Cliff."

"Uh..." said Kyle. "Okay...?"

But Kyle stood there for another ten seconds, waiting for the punchline. Aaron waited. I waited, watching the awkward standoff like I had inadvertently ventured into the Weird Part of YouTube.

Finally, Kyle left.

"Sorry about that," said Aaron. "Listen. Um. I know this is weird, but I need to tell you something important. Maybe the most important thing I've ever told anyone in my entire life. Just don't freak out, okay?"

Pro Tip: Telling someone to *not* freak before you tell them something usually has the *opposite* effect.

I just kept staring, waiting for this delayed marijuana hallucination to disappear.

"Are you familiar with near-death experiences?" he said.

Aaron waited for me to answer the question.

Near-death experiences?

If he was referring to the phenomena associated with out-of-body experiences, some sort of wonky afterlife, and a whole lotta light at the end of the tunnel, then yes, I was familiar with near-death experiences.

I was also of the opinion that they were bullshit.

"Yeah..." I said. "What about 'em?"

"What if I told you that I had one?"

"I would probably tell you to go see a psychiatrist."

"Cliff. I had a near-death experience."

"You should go see a psychiatrist."

"I don't need to see a psychiatrist. I need to talk to *you*, Cliff."

"Me? What the hell for?"

"Because you were a part of it."

Okay. My Weird Shit-O-Meter was currently off the scale.

"I mean, you weren't *in* it, per se," said Aaron. He hesitated, suddenly looking self-conscious. "I didn't *see* you. But . . . listen. This is going to sound crazy, okay?"

It was a little late for that.

"I need to tell you this," said Aaron, "and I know I don't know you, but you're just gonna have to be okay with that because this is real, okay? Like, realer than football."

Marijuana my ass. That joint was laced with mushrooms.

"Okay, here it is."

Aaron's face went rigid with a laughable amount of seriousness, his eyes narrowing on me like mini-cannons. He was apparently mentally bracing *himself* for whatever bomb he was about to drop on *me*. And that's when he said the craziest shit I had ever heard.

"I saw God."

EIGHT

Welp. Didn't see that one coming.

"You saw *what*?" I said.

I was secretly hoping that I had heard wrong. That I had somehow switched the letters around in my head, and he had actually said "dog." *I saw dog.* Yeah, that was it. Aaron was just an illiterate moron who saw this really cool dog, and he thought that Neanderthal was the only one who could appreciate his awkward canine fetish. Anticlimactic, yes, but I could swallow that.

"God," Aaron repeated. "I saw God."

Dammit.

"Also," said Aaron, "God told me that Happy Valley High School needs to change. He gave me a list of things to do. And he told me I need your help. And yeah. So that's why I'm talking to you."

My jaw unhinged.

"So . . ." said Aaron. "That was about as awkward as expected."

Aaron waited for a response from me. Something. Anything.

And then I did the unthinkable.

I stood up. I turned around. And I walked out. I abandoned my entire uneaten chimichanga lunch—and Aaron—in the cafeteria. I wasn't hungry anymore.

Have I mentioned how fond I am of chimichangas?

———

Here is an in-detail account of my entire religious history:

1. During elementary school, my parents, Shane, and I went to Christmas/Easter Mass at St. Matthew's Catholic Parish in Kalispell a grand total of four times—two back-to-back years.
2. Shane and I watched *Bruce Almighty* approximately fourteen infinitrillion times.

The end.

But seriously, *Bruce Almighty* was our movie. We could quote that thing backward and forward and upside down—not just a figure of speech. We would *literally* hang upside down by our legs on the monkey bars at Meyer Park and quote the movie. We would go back and forth, back and forth, back and forth, until so much blood had rushed to our heads, we couldn't even think straight.

As far as we were concerned, God looked and sounded exactly like Morgan Freeman.

And then Shane died.

Now obviously I wasn't religious to begin with. But when Shane died, God did too. And if God *wasn't* dead, I hated his guts, and I wanted to punch him in his Great Omnipotent Face.

But now the heavens had opened and the Prophet Aaron Zimmerman had been given a divine mission. And apparently I was his Holy Sidekick.

I felt sick.

I barreled into the very first bathroom stall I could find, dropped to my knees, and puked my guts out. Niagara Falls would have been jealous. When I was done, the aftermath looked like it could have been chimichangas once upon a time.

The cruel irony.

That's when I heard the shoes scuffling in the handicap stall beside me.

"The hell are you doing?" a voice whispered with not-so-whispery panic.

"It's okay," the other voice whispered. "Just chill."

Due to the extreme nature of their whispery-ness, I couldn't attach the voices to faces. But I knew one thing:

They were both dudes. In a stall together.

I had a formidable suspicion as to whom one of them was.

The neighboring stall door opened and closed. Whoever was still inside made sure to lock it.

I glanced up from my barf just in time for Noah Poulson to peek around the corner.

I actually knew Noah a little more personally than I knew most kids at HVHS because he tutored Shane in Algebra. Not Shane's first choice—being tutored by a gay kid a year younger than him. But then again, Shane actually *cared* about his grades because he wanted to go to college. That would have been a first in the Hubbard family tree. And he never would have passed Algebra if it wasn't for Noah.

And honestly, I don't think Noah was what Shane expected at all. He dressed mostly in earth tones, his moppy hair looked like it had never seen the likes of a comb in its follicular existence, and he always wore band shirts. Lots of band shirts. Kick-ass band shirts like Nirvana, Led Zeppelin, and Nine Inch Nails, with the occasional softie like Death Cab for Cutie. Currently, he was wearing a badass Tool shirt featuring this large peering eye with two pupils.

"You okay, Cliff?" he asked.

I gave a thumbs-up. "Yep. Just . . . trying out the . . . bulimia thing," I said between exhausted breaths.

"What? Are you serious?"

Noah's brow furrowed in concern. My sarcasm was obviously far too advanced for how depressingly huge I was and how catastrophically I was puking.

"Bulimia is a dangerous eating disorder," said Noah. "Not to sound preachy, but if you're having body image issues, and you feel like bulimia is the only answer, you need to talk to someone. There're people who help with this kind of—"

"Noah?" I said.

"Yeah?"

"I'm not bulimic."

"Oh," said Noah. He seemed to consider this for a considerably long moment. "Are you sure?"

"Painstakingly."

"Oh. Okay." Again, Noah hesitated. "Do you need to talk?"

I glanced at Noah. Then I glanced at the wall separating me from the dude in the adjacent stall. Back to Noah. Not to be rude, but I wasn't keen on having a heart-to-heart in front of Noah's mystery make-out man.

Noah followed my gaze and blushed. "It's not what you're thinking."

I tilted my head down, eyes still trained on Noah. My skepticism amplified tenfold.

"It's not!" said Noah. "We're just having a coming-out pep talk."

Actually, I believed him. Despite being openly gay, I'd never seen him with another guy. Hell, I'd never even seen him *flirt* with another guy. That wasn't really his style. Honestly, his coming out seemed more like a friendly girl deterrent than anything else—which he probably needed. I knew for a fact that Elizabeth Darley spent the better part of middle school shamelessly crushing on him. In the small capacity that I knew Noah, he was the sort of genuine friend who would give a pep talk to the sexiest guy at school, expecting nothing in return. He'd do it simply because it was the right thing to do.

"I'm good, Noah," I said. "But thanks for the offer."

Noah nodded. He started to turn. Then he stopped again.

"I know it's old news, but . . . I'm sorry about Shane." He paused. Apparently he was trying to think of the most outrageously nutty thing he could say to me. Because that's what came out of his mouth. "God loves you, you know."

The end-of-lunch bell rang.

"Dammit!" said the guy in the stall. The lock unlatched, the door exploded open, and he dashed out of the boys' bathroom—so fast, I didn't even catch a glimpse of him.

"Hey," said Noah. "Wait!"

Noah was gone. It was only me and my floating pool of vomit.

———

For the remainder of school, teachers' mouths moved, but I only heard one line:

God loves you, you know.

To fully fathom what a stupid thing this was for Noah to say, you had to know his sister, Esther. Esther Poulson was the leader of the resident Christian clique, the JTs (Jesus Teens). And I use the term *clique* generously, because really they were more of a malevolent cult.

As I left school, I crossed the Quad and watched the cult leader herself, ending another day in Babylon. She was elevated above the crowd of her congregation—fifty or so teenagers circled around her, holding hands—standing on what I swear to God was a portable pulpit. As always, she was spewing her usual sugarcoated vitriol.

"God loves everyone," said Esther. "Therefore, it is *our* job to love everyone. Even the people who don't deserve it. *Especially* the people who don't deserve it. Unfortunately, we don't have control over the sinners and the million ways they know how to sin. It's God's job to judge them. It's our job to be *better* than them. As I like to say . . ."

Apparently this was a verbal cue, because then every one of the JTs chanted with her:

"SINNERS GONNA SIN; WINNERS GONNA WIN."

Esther was beautiful. Esther was popular. Esther was smart—equipped with top-notch grades and razor-sharp wit. Not to mention, she was the student body president. When you coupled all those things with religion-fueled elitism, she was arguably the most dangerous person at school.

The fact that the JTs were a social group composed of *other* social groups only amplified their power—Zeke Gallagher, who was in with the rockers; Roy Porter from the football team; Lacey's friend Heather Goodman, who was a cheerleader *and* a member of the Fashion Club. Really, the scope of their grasp on the HVHS social sphere was staggering.

On the opposite end of the spectrum was Noah—the only person who openly recognized the JTs as a problem.

Noah was the *only* out kid at HVHS. Had been his entire stint here. Sure, there were other gay kids—like whoever that was in the bathroom with Noah—but they seemed to have no intention of coming out. Who could blame them?

Noah was confident. Noah was smart. Noah *knew* that something needed to change. So, over the course of his almost three years at HVHS, he had been fighting to implement a Gay-Straight Alliance.

"I think a Gay-Straight Alliance only works if there's more than one of you," Esther had said. "Seems a little narcissistic, wanting a whole club devoted to yourself, don't you think?"

"I'm *not* the only one. That's the *point*."

"Whatever. We all know you just want a place to hit on dudes. As the Babylonians say: Keep it in your pants, bro."

The JTs heckled Noah endlessly. But at the end of the day, they couldn't stop the formation of a GSA. Even the student body president didn't have *that* sort of power.

But they could sure as hell complain to their parents.

That's where Mr. and Mrs. Poulson came in.

You see, Mr. Poulson was a pastor at the local Church of (insert long line of ostentatious and yet mildly ambiguous Bible buzzwords here—seriously, I can't remember the name). But it was big. The sort of big that is less a church and more of a franchise. And when the words *gay* and *straight* and *alliance* were injected into the rumor mill, the entire congregation went on the offense, because *clearly* Jesus did not eat with sinners.

Of course, there were laws regarding this sort of thing. Banning an extracurricular club like this was not only discriminatory. It was illegal—unless you banned *all* extracurricular clubs.

That's what HVHS did.

Principal McCaffrey was hardly homophobic. But when an angry mob storms the castle waving torches and pitchforks, well . . . not all of us can be Joan of Arc.

Of course, getting rid of *all* extracurricular clubs was insane. Parents were well aware of this. But fortunately for them, they had a very sneaky student body president on their side. One who would claim that a certain club wasn't *extra*curricular, but rather, curriculum *related*. The Glee Club, for example, was related to choir. All sports-related clubs were an appendage of PE.

Remember Heather Goodman's Fashion Club? Apparently that was related to Home Economics.

Esther drew these obscure lines between *every* club and its "related" curriculum. Every club except the GSA.

Still, Noah kept fighting.

God loves you, you know.

That was the oddest thing about Noah—he didn't *just* believe in God. He was, like, full-on, level-80 Christian. As far as I could tell, it wasn't just a phase for him. I'd seen Shane confront him about it on multiple occasions.

"The Bible teaches you to hate gay people," Shane had stated once—so matter-of-factly, you'd have thought he'd read it out of a textbook or a dictionary. "So why the *hell* would you believe that shit?"

"Does it?" asked Noah, feigning cluelessness.

"Well, yeah. Duh. Have you heard your sister talk?"

"Love your neighbor."

"Huh?"

"Love your neighbor as yourself—that's the second most important commandment."

"What does my neighbor have to do with anything?"

"It's a phrase. It means *love everyone*."

"Oh. Well, what's the most important commandment?"

"Love God."

Shane snorted, and rolled his eyes, and shook his head. "That's a little egocentric, don't you think? Why should I love God more than everyone else?"

"It's not about loving God *more* than everyone. It's about loving someone whose sole purpose is *for* you to love everyone. That's what God is—the embodiment of love."

God loves you, you know.

I respected Noah. I really did. But all this "love your neighbor" bullshit was going to get his ass kicked. The Rules of High School (One, Two, *and* Three) applied to everyone.

———

The stress must have been getting to me. My walk home was derailed as I clutched my gut, bent over, and barfed *again* on some poor bastard's well-kept lawn. Like, where the hell was it all coming from?

"Damn," said the last voice in the world I wanted to hear.

I jolted up. Aaron was standing only a few feet away, head tilted. His mouth was pulled in a grimace.

"You okay, man?" said Aaron. "That's a lotta puke."

"What do you want?" I said.

"Um . . ." said Aaron. "Well, I guess I kind of gave you the CliffsNotes version of what I want. But if you really want to know what I want, it'd be helpful if you listened to what I have to s—"

I turned around and started walking.

"Cliff!"

I kept walking.

"Dammit, Cliff!"

I could hear him jogging after me. I walked faster.

Yeah, I may have been a semi-evolved humanoid porpoise, but I was one with humongous legs. When I wanted to walk fast, I traveled a couple Machs short of light speed.

And then, because the universe hated me, I heard a car approach. It slowed down, only to pull up beside us at a leisurely roll.

"Aaron, what are you doing?"

It was Lacey. I recognized her voice but turned my head anyway. Her silver Camry was rolling in perfect synchronization with Aaron's determined jog.

"Oh," said Aaron. "Hey, Lacey. I'm just . . . talking to Cliff."

"Cliff?" said Lacey. Her questioning tone made me grit my teeth. "You mean Neanderthal?"

Lacey looked at me. We only maintained eye contact for a brief second. I turned away, glaring with furious determination on the path ahead.

"His name's Cliff," said Aaron. "But yeah."

"It doesn't look like he wants to talk to you."

"Thanks for your input, Lacey. We're fine."

I walked even faster, just to prove how not fine this was.

"Is this a joke?" said Lacey. "Like, is this some kind of prank? Because Kyle says he has no idea what the hell you're doing."

"Maybe Kyle doesn't need a status update on every little detail of my life."

Aaron stopped. The car stopped. I *almost* stopped—then I remembered that I was trying to get the hell out of here. I did glance back, however, as I kept walking.

Lacey looked speechless. Which, to the extent of my knowledge, was a new look for her.

"Just . . . let me talk to Cliff, okay? I'll explain everything later."

That was as much as I heard. I rounded the corner of Gosling onto

Gleason, swallowed in the shadow of the Monolith. The moment I was safely out of view . . .

I ran.

———

I was already daydreaming about Brown Sugar Cinnamon Pop-Tarts and reading Orson Scott Card until I passed out due to sci-fi pseudo-philosophy overexposure when I finally reached Arcadia Park.

Aaron Zimmerman was sitting on the front steps of our trailer home.

I stopped. Although "stopped" was putting it generously. I probably looked more like one of those Star Wars AT-ST chicken walkers tripping over Ewoks and shit.

Aaron stood up. "Hey. You're fast."

I looked at Aaron. I looked behind me—where he should have been—a mile away. And then I looked back at him.

"How'd you beat me here?" I said.

"Lacey gave me a ride. We actually drove right past you, but you seemed like you were pretty in the zone. I would've offered you a lift, but . . ."

I started marching directly at him—mostly at the door behind him—which sort of threw his conversational skills off-balance.

"Whoa, hey!" said Aaron. He frantically backed up the steps. "Chill, man, chill!"

I stepped up the first step, second step, until he was pinned on the third step between me and the door. Though he was a step higher, our eyes were level.

"Get lost," I said.

"No," said Aaron.

"Do you want to die?"

"Actually, I almost did. But I'm not dead. That's why I'm here, genius."

"Stop!" I screamed. "Stop it with this God bullshit, okay? Do you realize how insane you sound?"

"Well, my family's atheist," said Aaron. "So yeah, I'm sure I sound bonkers."

"Then why are you doing this?"

"Because it's the truth."

"No."

"Dude. I saw God."

"Shut—"

"He gave me a list of things to do."

"—the—"

"And he wants me..."

"—hell—"

"...to recruit you."

"—up."

"You're important, Cliff."

That last line. Oh boy. The last strand of my sanity snapped. I laughed. I laughed hard. I couldn't stop laughing. It erupted from my gut and fried the nerves in my face. I was the Joker, this hysterically laughing psychopath, and there was no Batman to beat the hysterics out of me.

"Um...Cliff?"

I pushed Aaron off the stairs, opened the front door, and walked inside. He fell like a delicate autumn leaf—tied to a bowling ball. Fortunately for him, he landed in the brown-patchy bullshit pretending to be grass.

"Son of a bitch," said Aaron, crawling on the grass. "I'm not going anywhere, Cliff. Not until you agree to help me."

"Then I hope you like being a lawn ornament," I said, and I slammed the door.

———

The next day, my morning started the way mornings always should. My alarm clock was set to the radio, which was set to the Blaze, which blasted the Beastie Boys screaming, "*So, so, so, so listen up 'cause you can't say nothin'/You'll shut me down with a push of your button*," and I hit my Snooze button, and I proceeded to hit it another six times until Rage Against the Machine played "Wake Up," and, like, who the hell am I to argue with Rage Against the Machine? So I got up, showered, fell asleep in the shower, woke up again when the water started getting cold, scrubbed all seventeen square acres of my body, dried off, and got dressed.

I stared scrutinizingly at my "lucky" hoodie.

"Ah, what the hell," I said, and I pulled it on.

I slinked my ratty backpack over my shoulders and ventured into the kitchen, charting a direct course to the Pop-Tarts. As soon as I stepped around the corner, there was my mom, filling her thermos to the brim with coffee, black as the new moon. Our eyes made contact. The tension was more than palpable; it was a whirlpool. It was swept underwater, the oxygen sucked out of my lungs. I felt an apology in the back of my throat. In that same moment, I noticed my mom's lips hover apart, searching for words.

And then the moment passed.

I didn't even know who let it pass—her or me. It was most likely a joint effort. My mom screwed the cap on her thermos, and I grabbed a silver-wrapped rectangle out of the Pop-Tart box. We parted like well-acquainted strangers—her, to the bedroom to collect her purse and things. Meanwhile, I determined to make a quick exit.

In an effort to defuse the tension, I immediately unwrapped my Pop-Tarts, stuffed one of those diabetes-filled bastards in my mouth, inserted my right thumb in the hole of my hoodie pocket, and walked out the door.

Aaron Zimmerman was sitting cross-legged on my lawn. The Pop-Tart fell out of my mouth.

Damn you, lucky hoodie!

"You're awake, finally!" said Aaron. "Have a nice hibernation, Papa Bear? We gotta hurry, or we're going to be late to school."

"What the—? Why are—? How did—? Did you sleep on my lawn?"

That already didn't make sense because he was wearing different clothes.

Aaron laughed. "I'm not that crazy. I just woke up early and walked over. I live on the other side of HVHS. I timed it, and it's a little over forty minutes from here to school. That should be plenty of time for me to tell you everything. Whaddaya say?"

I walked back inside and locked the door.

"Cliff!" Aaron shouted.

I couldn't do this for one more second. My brain was short-circuiting. I shuffled to my bedroom and dropped my backpack on the floor. No school today.

"Dammit, Cliff. Just listen to me!"

I spun and flopped on my bunk bed like Shamu the Whale doing his showstopper.

"Life isn't just existing," said Aaron. "It's a door."

What the hell?

I rose from my sinking mattress like a shark.

"Don't you want to know what's on the other side?"

WHAT THE HELL?

I exploded out of my bed, across my entire forty-foot home, out the door, and down the stairs. Aaron's hands flew up in his defense, but I already had him by the throat. I slammed him into the nearest tree.

"Who told you that?" I said.

"*Gahh ... ack ... urp ... gluck,*" said Aaron.

I released his windpipe, but only slightly. "Who the *hell* told you to say that?"

"Told me to say what?"

"'Life is a door,' you bastard! Who the HELL told you to say that?"

Aaron was blinking, irises quivering, as he absorbed the fury and saliva flinging out of my mouth. "Um. God?"

"DAMN YOU!" I screamed.

I threw Aaron aside, and I punched the tree, and I punched it again, and bark was flying, and my fist was screaming, and I could see blood on the tree, and I knew it was from my knuckle, but I pretended it was the tree bleeding, because right here, right now, this fucking tree needed to die.

And then I collapsed—a broken heap on the brown-patchy trailer-trash grass. I was crying. I was crying for the whole world to see—particularly for that asshole Aaron Zimmerman to see—but I didn't care, because when you want to die, it doesn't matter who sees anything.

And then the storm subsided.

The calm enveloped me.

I stared up at the canopy of the sympathetic tree I attempted to murder. The tree leaned over me and seemed to understand. It glowed with compassion against the teal-painted sky, and for a moment—just a moment—that tree reminded me of Shane.

Everything was eclipsed by Aaron's head as he hovered over me. "Are you okay?"

I raised the thing that used to be my hand but was now just a bloody, pulpy mess with fingers. "I don't think anything's broken."

"Oh. Good."

I sat upright. I breathed in a nice, clean breath of oxygen, and let it out nice and slow. I could breathe, and it felt good.

"I'm going to go grab my backpack," I said. "You have a little over forty minutes to tell me about your bullshit near-death experience."

Aaron's mouth twitched, creeping into a grin. "Brace yourself."

NINE

"**S**o this boat hits my head," said Aaron, "and the next thing I know, I'm on this tropical beach, and Morgan Freeman is standing over me."

My speechlessness was a placid crystal lake without ripples. I was drowning in my own inability to form words.

"Only it wasn't Morgan Freeman," said Aaron. "It was God. I only knew this because he says to me, 'Hi, Aaron. I'm God.' Only he *sounded* exactly like Morgan Freeman, too. So yeah, it was weird."

I kept staring at Aaron like he was the Easter Bunny or Adolf Hitler or Barney the Dinosaur. My inner skeptic/conspiracy theorist was almost convinced that Aaron had somehow extracted every precious detail of my relationship with Shane, and he was now using it to manipulate me into his twisted little scheme. But how would he know about our obsession with *Bruce Almighty*? There was no way.

"And I had to believe him," said Aaron, "because, like, what's weirder? Waking up on some obscure island and randomly discovering God or Morgan Freeman? Anyway, it doesn't matter what he looked like. It only matters what he told me."

"What did he tell you?"

"Basically he said that Happy Valley High School sucks."

Wow. Maybe Aaron *did* talk to God.

"He told me that things need to change," said Aaron. "And that I was the messenger who would set these changes into motio— Son-of-a-bitch-don't-talk-I'm-not-done!" He said this with a raised, silencing finger as I opened my mouth, wearing the most cynical look since Scully met Mulder. I closed my mouth. "And he said that I needed *your* help. You, Clifford Hubbard. He put a lot of emphasis on you actually, and how we needed to do this together. And then he gave me the List."

"List? Like, he actually wrote a list out for you? Like a shopping list?"

"Yes. Like a shopping list. Because he wants us to go grocery shopping for him. *No, not like a shopping list!* It was weird. He touched my forehead, and I saw the list. I can still see it. It's like it's ingrained in my brain. I wrote it out, though, so you could see it yourself."

Aaron reached into his pocket and pulled out a folded, slightly crumpled piece of paper that looked vastly unspectacular. He handed it to me and I unfolded it to Aaron's deplorable handwriting:

1. *Put an end to Niko's bullying.*
2. *Call the JTs to repentance.*
3. *Remind Mr. Spinelli why he chose to teach.*
4. *Show Frankie's gang a better way.*
5. *Find and stop HAL.*

I folded up the sheet of paper and handed it back to Aaron.

"Well?" he said. "What do you think?"

"I think that is the stupidest thing I have ever read in my entire life."

"Which part is stupid?"

"The part where these letters come together to form words."

Aaron paused to mull this over for a moment. "So . . . you don't like the List."

"I feel like the stupidity of the whole thing is burning a hole in my cerebral cortex. I'm trying to figure out which part is the dumbest, but the levels of stupidity for each point are so astronomical, I wonder if two of these ideas bumped together, the universe might implode in a reverse Big Bang, and life as we know it would vacuum into a supermassive black hole and disappear from existence."

"Do you write a script every morning of all the weird shit you're gonna say?" said Aaron.

"One," I said, ignoring him. "Niko is the Antichrist. You can't put an end to his bullying unless you cast him down to hell where he belongs, which probably involves incapacitating him with a crossbow, holy water–dipped arrows, and an ancient exorcism that must be recited in Latin."

"I'll take that as a yes."

"Two," I continued, "the JTs will call *us* to repentance. And then they will crucify us. And then they will set the crosses on fire. And then they will scatter our ashes in Esther's breakfast cereal, which she will *enjoy* eating."

"Ah."

"Three: Mr. Spinelli became a teacher to ruin teenage lives. Four: If you try to 'show Frankie's gang a better way,' which I assume involves *not* pushing drugs, they'll probably laugh at you. And then Frankie will disembowel you with his bare hands."

Aaron's mouth became a very thin, straight line.

"FIVE!" I exclaimed. "HAL IS FREAKING AWESOME."

Heretofore, I have not explained the greatness that is HAL, so here's the skinny. Nobody knew who the hell he (or she) was, but one thing was certain: HAL could hack *anything*. Like when he hacked into the report card files and gave the entire student body failing grades. Or when he erased the faculty from computer records and gave their jobs to the most unqualified students. (I am proud to announce that for three and a half hours, I had replaced Ms. Lipton as the instructor for Dance.) And then there was the yearbook. Right before it went to print, HAL Photoshop-replaced everyone's face with that of Nicolas Cage. It was the most beautiful thing I had ever seen in my entire life. HAL was a hero.

"I refuse to believe in a God who doesn't find HAL absolutely hilarious," I said.

"So you're not going to help me?" said Aaron.

"No, I will."

"What? You will?"

My sudden agreement surprised even me. But I played it cool and shrugged. "I don't have anything better to do."

"Oh," said Aaron. "Okay."

"So where do we start?"

"Um. I dunno. I wasn't expecting you to be so agreeable all of a sudden. Where do *you* think we should start?"

"We could start with the easy one," I suggested.

———

Fun fact: the pseudo-evil sentient computer in *2001: A Space Odyssey* is named HAL 9000. Shane and I were in agreement—if that title alone didn't make this hacker a complete badass, nothing did.

Okay, so I didn't *really* know who HAL was. In the same sense that the judicial system didn't *really* know that O.J. killed his wife.

However, there was a preponderance of incriminating evidence.

Mr. Gibson's computer lab was closed before school. Unless you were one of his two student tech-support lab monkeys: Jack Halbert (the most recent victim of Niko's 3DS theft) and Julian Jeffries. Julian was the Ron Weasley to Jack's Harry Potter. Not just because they were best friends *or* because Julian was so ginger that the existence of his soul was questionable, but because, even for a genius computer nerd, he was bafflingly stupid. But this wasn't about Julian.

No, we were here for Jack *HAAAAALbert*.

See what I did there?

"You're sure it's him?" said Aaron.

"I'm sure," I said. "Are you sure you know what you're doing?"

"*Psh!* Please. I'm God's Messenger, bro. Am I sure that my left testicle hangs lower than my right?"

"Well. That's . . . hmm. Okay."

Aaron waltzed into the computer lab like he owned the place. I followed a little more reluctantly behind him. Jack and Julian were seated at Mr. Gibson's desk when they noticed us. They jolted up from their seats.

"Hey, guys," said Aaron.

"What are you two doing?" said Julian. "You're not supposed to be here."

Aaron raised his arms in the air. "We're on a mission from God, bitches. Ain't that right, Cliff?"

"Uh . . ." I said. "I don't think . . ."

"So here's the thing," said Aaron. He crashed his weight down on the computer table with two heavy hands. The impact caused them both to jump, and Julian yelped. His gaze narrowed on Jack. "We know you're HAL."

"What?" said Jack. "I'm not HAL."

"Sure you are. You're a computer genius."

"Well, that's flattering, Aaron, but I'm not HAL. Besides, Julian knows just as much as I do about computers."

"Unless we're talking about shitty, overpriced Macs," said Julian.

"You can shut your oral cavity, Julian," said Jack. "The ghost of Steve Jobs will *Paranormal Activity* your ass."

"Sorry, I don't think his ghost-iPhone has an app for that."

Aaron slammed the table with his fist. This brought the *oh shit* back to their eyes.

"Your last name is Halbert," he said to Jack. "*HAAAAALbert.*"

"Yeah, and Cliff's last name is Hubbard," said Jack. "That doesn't mean his dad wrote *Battlefield Earth* and created Scientology."

Aaron's cool composure was in a rapid state of disintegration. He turned to me. "He's HAL."

"I'm not HAL," said Jack to me, because apparently I was now the Supreme Court Justice in this hearing.

"Uh..." I said.

Aaron grabbed a pencil out of a pencil holder on Mr. Gibson's desk. He snapped it in half with one hand. Tossed the severed halves across the room.

Jack and Julian both swallowed, their Adam's apples bobbing in sync.

"Aaron?" I said.

Aaron grabbed another pencil. Again, he snapped it with one hand. Tossed the pieces.

Ohhhhhh boy.

"Okay, Aaron," I said. "I think we need to—"

Grabbed another pencil. Snapped. Tossed.

"—talk this over?"

"Look," said Jack. "You can't just use scare tactics to make me confess to being someone I'm not."

Grab. Snap. Toss. A graveyard of dismembered pencil corpses was accumulating on the other side of the room.

"AARON!" I said.

Aaron looked at me, eyes wide, the left one slightly twitching. Clearly, the pressures of his Divine Calling were weighing heavily on his sanity.

"Can I have a word with you?"

We left Julian and the alleged HAL-in-denial, stepping just outside the lab and into the hall.

"I take it back," I said. "I don't think he's HAL."

"What?" said Aaron. "Of course he is."

"Even if he *is*," I continued, "I feel like this is completely the wrong way to go about it."

"Well, alrighty then, Cliff Almighty. What's the *right* way to go about it?"

"I don't know, but for being God's Messenger, you're kind of acting like a raging asshole."

"Hey! I'm just trying to figure this out as I go along, okay? It's not like God gave me an instruction manual or anything, like, *Making High School a Better Place for Dummies*. I mean, aside from the fact that I *saw* God, he didn't really give me shit to go on. So instead of being a dickwipe, how about you try to help me?"

Okay. My Nice-O-Meter was maxed out.

"You know, that's another thing," I said. "Is God's Little Messenger allowed to use potty language like that?"

"You know what? Screw you."

"Screw *you*, Moses."

74

This was the moment when Aaron and I would turn around and storm off in opposite directions. We would never talk to each other again because someone like me could never be friends with someone like him. And someone like him could never see God. What the hell was I thinking anyway?

Except that didn't happen because, at that exact moment, Jack and Julian entered the hallway.

Jack took the lead, stepping forward with his fingers interlocked. He cleared his throat, and said, "We have a business proposition."

"You have a what?" I said.

"Like I said, I'm not HAL. But we *can* find out who HAL is. However, I need you to do something for me first."

Did this kid comprehend the number of shits that I did not give anymore?

"What do you mean?" said Aaron.

"It's simple, really," said Jack. "We have a program that allows us to see all of the current TCP/IP connections in the HVHS network."

"And if we can get HAL's IP address," said Julian, "we can trace him down with this geographical location IP tool site I know."

"I also know a site where we can use his IP address to find out his ISP, and if we hack into *their* network and peek into their customer files, we can find out his name, address, bra size, you name it."

They might as well have been speaking Klingon.

"I was just joking about the bra part," said Jack. "No legitimate Internet service provider would ask for that."

"Okay-okay-okay," I said. I closed my eyes, because doing that seemed to hold the inevitable brain aneurysm at bay. "So you're saying you can find out who HAL is?"

"That is correct," said Julian.

I looked at Aaron. Aaron looked at me. Our argument had all but dissipated in the wake of this new plot development. We were fish, and the worm was squirming on a hook, and we could see it in each other's eyes—neither of us could help nibbling just a little.

"What do you need us to do?" said Aaron.

Jack turned his attention solely on me. "Cliff, you may have noticed the other day that Niko stole my 3DS. I want it back."

"I'm also tied into this fiasco," said Julian. "Because I let Jack borrow *my* copy of *Animal Crossing* that happened to be inside his 3DS at the time of thievery."

"You guys get us our property back," said Jack, "and we'll give you HAL's identity on a platter. But you have to make sure that Niko doesn't target us again. Otherwise it defeats the whole point. Do we have a deal?"

Jack and Julian were already extending their hands to shake on it.

It seemed a little more than coincidental that, in exchange for HAL, Jack and Julian were asking us to do yet *another* thing on Aaron's goddamn List.

Again, Aaron and I exchanged glances. Neither of us had to say a thing.

We knew that we were in.

TEN

We had a plan. Sort of.

We had a Plan B. Sort of.

My stomach was churning. Completely.

"C'mon," said Aaron. "What's the worst that could happen?"

"In third grade," I said, "I *distinctly* remember Niko finding random insects and pulling off each of their legs. He collected all of them inside a jar. Like, fifty of 'em. These squirming little peanuts that used to be insects. And then he snuck into the cafeteria and microwaved them. And then he poured the contents of the jar into the lunch lady's coffee. She took one sip and spewed. When she found out what Niko did, she spent the rest of the day in the nurse's office. I think she started going to a shrink after that."

"Jesus," said Aaron. "Is this your way of telling me you want to back out?"

"Nah. I'm just thinking out loud."

It was kind of unnerving how Niko lived up to every bully stereotype. It's like he had a checklist that he was marking off. Big, nasty, and violent? Check. Dress like a biker in spite of not owning a motorcycle? Check. Put a special emphasis on bullying the only out gay kid? Check.

I only bring this up because Niko was currently making said kid's life a living hell. Noah was holding his books close to his chest, trying to walk away, and Niko kept walking in front of him, cutting off his path.

"Where ya goin', Poulson?" said Niko.

Of course, Noah didn't respond. He stood still for a moment and attempted to walk in a different direction—only to be intercepted again with a push and a "Hey, Poulson, where ya goin'?"

Eventually he'd get bored. Or he'd grind Noah's bones to make his masturbation lubricant.

"I'll do the talking," said Aaron.

This was going to be good. And I meant *good* in the most ironic, disastrous way possible.

"Hey, Niko," said Aaron.

Niko looked up at Aaron like he had just insulted his mother.

Noah took full advantage of the distraction and made a silent escape. Niko didn't seem to care. His predatory gaze shifted from Aaron to me—it stayed on me for a little bit longer, just because I was so obscenely gargantuan—and then back to Aaron.

"Hey, fellas," said Niko. "Can I help you with something?"

"Yes, actually," said Aaron. He was smiling, and as far as I could tell, it was genuine. "So I realize this is none of my business, but I understand that you may or may not have Jack Halbert's Nintendo 3DS in your possession?"

"3D-what?"

"It's like a Game Boy."

"Oh. Yes. Yes, I do."

"Okay, perfect. So I've experienced an interesting turn of events lately. You're probably aware of the boating accident I had last week that put me in a coma?"

Niko nodded. For a violent sociopath, he seemed to be absorbing this bizarre conversation rather well.

"Here's the thing," said Aaron. "It wasn't just a coma. While I was out, I had a vision. More than a vision actually. I *saw* God."

Niko raised an eyebrow.

"I know that sounds crazy," said Aaron, "but it's true. God actually *spoke* to me. He gave me a very specific List of things to do. Things that would make Happy Valley High School a better place. And my good friend, Clifford Hubbard"—he gestured elaborately to me; I waved awkwardly—"and I are on a mission to accomplish the things on this List. And God mentioned you by name, Niko. He said your bullying needs to stop."

I basically cringed through that entire monologue.

"Did he now?" said Niko.

If there was a Richter scale for sarcasm, the little needle would be drawing a horizontal tornado right now.

"The point I'm trying to make is that God is aware of you," said Aaron. "I don't think God wants the bullying to stop just for everyone else's sake. I think he cares about *you* too and the quality of *your* life. I think God has a plan for you. A better plan. One that you can't even comprehend right now. That's why I'm extending you a personal invitation. I would be honored if you would join us. Help us complete this List and make this school a better place."

I guess I had a lot of confidence in Aaron because, in my head, this conversation sounded a lot more mentally stable.

And then something weird happened to Niko's eyes. They got

all screwy. And by "screwy," I mean they appeared kinda . . . I dunno. Genuinely touched? It was a new look for the guy, and I didn't know how to process it.

"You think God cares about someone like me?" said Niko.

Holy shit-kittens. Was this actually happening?

"You think someone like *me* can change?" Niko's voice wavered.

No. No no no no no. Something was up.

"I think so," said Aaron.

Except that Niko's fist was in Aaron's face on the last word, and it turned into: *I think s—SMACKKKKKKKKKK!* Extra emphasis on the *KKKKKKKKKK* because I swear, Niko had punched a hole through Aaron's skull. Aaron spun 180 degrees. I managed to catch him before he performed a stunning 360. Fortunately, his face appeared to be mostly intact.

"If you wouldn't mind, could you pass the word to the man upstairs?" said Niko. "Also, tell him to eat shit."

Aaron blinked, and his face was sharp. A razor. He gritted the blades of his teeth together, and here was *the* Aaron Zimmerman of legend. The forecast was cool with a hundred percent chance of kick-ass. God's Little Messenger had left the building.

"Should I give you ladies a moment?" said Niko.

Aaron's face was a twig, and it snapped. "Let's Plan B this son of a bitch," he said.

I shoved Aaron forward, and he rolled with the momentum—so fast, his fist was slicing atomic particles. He nailed Niko in the face. Hard. Like, for a second, I almost expected Niko's face to fold inside out like a sock.

Niko spun the full 360.

But he didn't fall. His thick legs splayed out and he regained his footing—balanced and deadly. And then, just to reaffirm the theory that he was the Antichrist, he smiled.

Niko grabbed Aaron by the shoulders and kneed him in the gut.

Aaron's eyes became wide and distant as he mumbled a feeble "Sonuvabitch." His voice sounded like air being let out of a balloon. And then he crumpled to the floor.

Niko looked at me next, and oh shit.

I felt the impact—like I was being tackled by a moving Volvo head-on. Our shoulders interlocked as we crashed into each other. The fire exploded in my clavicle, but screw clavicles, who needs 'em, and screw Volvos too, because I was a Hummer. I slid one foot back to brace myself and stood my ground.

And that was my mistake.

I was all pushing and no balance. Niko twisted and shoved me down.

I hit the ground hard. And naturally, Niko's motto was kick 'em while they're down, because his foot punted me in the gut. I buckled into the fetal position and wished I could cry, because maybe crying would make it hurt just a little bit less.

And then Niko said the most words he'd ever spoken to me.

"Piece of shit," he said. "You should go kill yourself like your dumb-ass brother."

That single sentence caused my humanity to dissolve. Hate swallowed me whole.

You should go kill yourself like your dumb-ass brother.

I screamed and kicked my leg out, blasting Niko's feet out from under him. He had barely hit the asphalt before I was on top of him, punching his face. Punching, smashing, wrecking, destroying—

"Son of a bitch," said Aaron, breathless. "Cliff!"

Aaron's voice registered in some distant cubicle of my brain. At least it got me to stop punching. But I wasn't done. I was so far from done. I was on my feet, scouring the schoolyard. A perimeter of students had formed a wall around us. Behind the wall of their heads, the sunrise had left its last bloody streaks on the cloudy horizon.

I marched up to some chump on the baseball team with this aluminum bat sticking out of his bag. I took the bat. Babe Ruth tried to protest, but I palmed his face like a basketball.

You should go kill yourself like your dumb-ass brother.

I marched back to Niko, dragging the bat against the asphalt.

Aaron was still crumpled on the floor, clutching his gut. But he was looking at me. His eyes were huge, absorbing the vastness of my hate.

"CLIFF!" Aaron screamed—or at least he tried to. His voice came out soft and strangled.

I ignored Aaron. I reached Niko, still on the ground, his face a bloody mess. But his one halfway-open eye saw me. He saw my hate. It caused the bat to tremble as I raised it over my head.

Niko swallowed. But no words came out.

You should go kill yourself like your dumb-ass brother.

And then, suddenly, Niko's bloody face became Shane's bloody face. The penetration wound beneath his shattered jaw.

The top of his skull blown open.

I screamed—long and hard, until I was breathless. I chucked the bat as far away from me as possible. It was like a rogue helicopter blade—spinning, sailing, careening.

It clattered on the high roof of HVHS.

And then everything was still.

ELEVEN

The first-period tardy bell rang while I was sitting my voluminous ass on the curb. School wasn't exactly in my plans anymore. As for God and his To-Do List, they could both eat it in the nearest paper shredder.

"Don't take this the wrong way," Aaron said, "but have you talked to a therapist? About your brother, I mean?"

Oh, nuh-uh. The guy who thought he saw God was gonna tell me I need to see a therapist?

"Don't talk to me about my brother," I said.

Aaron didn't push the matter.

"Anyway," he said, "I'm sorry about Shane."

"Don't be. It's nothing."

"It's not nothing—" Aaron started to say, but I cut him off.

"IT'S NOTHING."

Jesus. I was sure doing a stellar job proving the nothingness of the matter.

"Look," I said. "I really appreciate"—I hesitated, fumbling for a word that fit—"this. Everything. Whatever it is that you're trying to do. But I think I'm the wrong person for the job."

"What do you mean?"

Was he serious? Did I have to spell it out for him?

There were countless reasons why I was a bad choice. But as I paused to consider my vast unqualifications, all I could think about was my mom—the only living human being whom I loved and who loved me—and the thing I said to her the day of my suspension. That Shane died hating her. Shane might have said it, but that didn't necessarily qualify it as "truth." Shane said a lot of things that he didn't mean. I still threw it in her face like a vat of acid. I felt no satisfaction, only the lingering aftertaste of venom.

"You can't fix something," I said, "when you, *yourself*, are not fixed. Yeah, this school is fucked-up, but I'm probably the most fucked-up thing about it."

"I dunno. You *are* competing with the likes of Esther and Niko."

"Okay. Third most fucked-up. I get the bronze medal."

"What about Spinelli? He's on the List too."

"Yeah, but his evil is probably a product of old age. Like, *you* try not being evil when your saggy balls touch the toilet water."

Aaron laughed.

I couldn't help it. My defenses cracked, and a smile splintered across the hull of my face, from port to starboard.

"What about me?" said Aaron.

My smile faltered. "What *about* you?"

"Are you more fucked-up than me?"

I wasn't exactly sure what to say to that. If I'd been asked this question a couple days ago, Aaron might have ranked number one. I mean, I *hated* him. Maybe I hated him because he was perfect, and he had it so fucking easy, but still. Hate is hate, and assholes are assholes, and Aaron was an asshole supreme, regardless of social standing.

"I don't like myself very much," said Aaron. "Bet you didn't know that."

I looked at Aaron. Like, *really* looked at him. Somewhere, deep beneath his perfect tan that he didn't have to work for a day in his life, and his perfect face—probably shaped by God himself on his Holy Pottery Wheel—I could see it.

The self-loathing.

"You're probably wondering why I do it," said Aaron. "Act like such a tool to everyone, I mean."

I shrugged awkwardly. What was I supposed to say? *Yeah, why ARE you such a tool?*

"Have you ever said something—*done* something—that you instantly regretted? But it's out there, and you don't know how to take it back, so you try to justify it because now there's one more person who doesn't like you, and you think: *Good! They* shouldn't *like me.*"

"Doesn't like you?" I said. "Is there a single person at school who doesn't like you?"

"You'd be surprised."

"Name one person."

"Lacey."

"Lacey," I repeated dubiously.

"Definitely Lacey."

"How can Lacey of all people not like you? You guys dated, didn't you?"

"Dude," said Aaron. "Dating is the *surest* way to get someone to not like you. Lower their defenses. Make them vulnerable. Then fuck them over like you always do."

"Don't you sit at the same table?"

Aaron shrugged. "I'm friends with Kyle, and Lacey's friends with Heather Goodman, and Kyle and Heather are friends. That's just the dynamics of our group. And I don't *not* like Lacey. She's just good at coexisting. Some people are silent in their dislike."

Even as Aaron spoke, I could already smell the bullshit in his hypothesis.

"I'm pretty sure she doesn't *not* like you," I said. "I mean, she chased you down in her car, didn't she?"

"Yeah, well," Aaron stammered, "only because Kyle *told* her to."

"Dude," I said. "She *cried* while you were in that coma."

Aaron's mouth opened. It closed. He lowered his head, glaring at his shoelaces.

"Yeah, well," he said. "She *shouldn't* like me."

Of all the tough nuts to crack, Aaron was steel-plated. Impenetrable.

"Face it," I said. "Everyone *loves* your tool ass."

"Whatever," said Aaron. "Doesn't change the fact that I'm still a tool. What I'm trying to say is, if *you're* not qualified for the job, a tool like me sure isn't."

"Yeah, but you're the sort of tool who goes to college, gets a master's degree in success, and marries a supermodel. Who am I? I'm *nothing*."

"Cliff," said Aaron, "you *are* the right person for the job."

"Why?"

"Because God *chose* you, dickwipe."

"But WHY? I mean, is he stupid?"

"Maybe God sees something in you that you don't."

"Ugh. You sound like a Poulson."

"Maybe Shane put in a good word for you."

And that stopped me. I met Aaron's gaze, long and hard—digging for the bullshit in his eyes. The quiver of a lie in his irises.

His gaze was unwavering.

It didn't matter if it was true or not. Not really, anyway. Aaron *believed* what he was saying. Who was I to argue?

———

I was in drastic need of escapism, so I walked directly to Hideo's Video after school—something I *shouldn't* have been able to do because I beat another kid half to literal death. This was the part where I got suspended—possibly expelled—for being a juvenile delinquent psychopath.

Except I *didn't* get suspended. I didn't even get sent to Principal McCaffrey's office.

Because no one said anything.

This was mind-boggling to me. We basically had a balls-to-the-wall MMA double brawl in front of the school. This shit was public, free admission. Not to mention the fact that I turned Niko's face into a piñata.

And no one said anything.

Maybe they were afraid I was a real-life Michael Myers or Jason Voorhees or Leatherface, and if they ratted me out, I'd grab my trademark weapon of choice, the Baseball Bludgeon of Death, and beat their weasel faces into Dimension X. But even the faculty refrained from confronting Niko about the added girth to his face. He was one ugly stick beating short of the Elephant Man. Everything was bruised, swollen, and disproportioned.

And no one said anything.

This made me both relieved and sad. Relieved that I was off the hook.

Sad that people could care so little.

As fate would have it, I arrived at Hideo's Video just as my mom was getting off early. Hideo Fujimoto insisted she take the evening off—on the grounds that she looked like shit.

Not even kidding. I was at the checkout counter, about to rent *Pacific Rim*, when it happened.

"You look like shit," said Hideo to my mom.

"Hideo!" said my mom—smiling, not even remotely offended.

"You look like scary zombie. Eat customers' brains."

That was just how Hideo talked. I used to think it was hilarious and teased him about it relentlessly. Once, I tried to get him to say the iconic botched video-game phrase "All your base are belong to us," to which Hideo responded, "All your ass I am going to kick, mother-fucker. Now go pick your damn movies." Afterward, my mom said to me, "I hope you know, that was kind of a racist thing to say to Hideo." That startled me. I mean, I wasn't trying to be racist. When I told my mom this, she said, "Most people don't *try* to be racist. It's prepro-grammed in our culture. Most people will think, 'Oh, he speaks bad English, he should move back to Japan or wherever' rather than 'Wow, he can speak two languages; that is so impressive.' Did you know that Japanese is the most difficult language for a native English speaker to learn? If you moved to Japan and tried to learn their language, how would you feel if they made fun of the way you speak? Because believe me, it would sound ridiculous."

Leave it to my mom to call her smart-ass son on his own bullshit.

"Zombies good in movies, not good in movie store," Hideo told my mom. "Go home. Take nap. Come back tomorrow. I take care of store today."

Suffice it to say, Hideo was a stellar human being, cleverly dis-guised as an asshole. To be completely fair, my mom was so over-worked, she looked absolutely like shit. She had dark circles under her eyes, her skin looked clammy, and her hair was a slapdash rat's nest, pinned up in ways that didn't even make sense.

Hideo seized control of the register, took my movie, and scanned it. Then he did a double take, staring at the cover. He shot me a scathing glare.

"This movie is shit," said Hideo. "Power Rangers for big kids. Watch *Neon Genesis Evangelion* instead. Better robots, better aliens, better show."

"I've seen *Evangelion*," I said. "Not really in the mood for convoluted existential psychodramas."

Hideo snorted as he finished checking out my movie. He handed me *Pacific Rim* along with the receipt. "Lucy, take your big, dumb teenager home with you. His shitty taste in movies is pissing me off."

———

Some people clear their minds through meditation. Some do yoga, some go running, and some sip a relaxing cup of chamomile. I, Clifford Hubbard, clear my mind via watching giant robots and monsters beat the shit out of each other, Gundam-style—hence *Pacific Rim*.

I fully intended to walk home, but now that my mom had the day off work, I had a ride back.

I almost would have rather walked.

Needless to say, things were still weird between us because (1) I felt terrible about what I said to her, and (2) that didn't change the fact she was married to a monster. Even if he *was* my biological father. It was hard to separate my feelings between the two of them. They were kind of a package deal.

"I'm sorry about what I said."

Apparently, those were words that came out of my mouth just now.

My mom looked at me. "About what?"

"About Shane hating you."

She returned her focus to the road.

"Maybe I deserved it," she said.

I shook my head. "I don't think anybody deserves to be hated. Not really."

My mom fidgeted her grip on the steering wheel.

"He just wanted to be noticed," I said.

"I noticed him," she said, almost defensively. But her eyes wavered, harboring regret.

"Not when it mattered," I said. "Not when he needed to be noticed."

I didn't have to bring up my dad to make it explicitly clear who or what I was talking about. When he beat Shane, my mom was always conveniently absent. It wasn't until after the fact—after the damage was done—that she always made her magical reappearance, in full mother mode.

Always loving. But never defending.

My mom sniffed. She hastily wiped away the evidence of sadness.

"It's okay," I said. "I didn't notice him, either. Not when it mattered."

TWELVE

On Monday, Aaron sat with me at lunch—which, I'm not gonna lie, surprised the shit out of me.

"Uhhhhhh," I said, like it was the *actual* alarm sound of my invisible quarantine force field breach.

"What?" said Aaron. "Am I not allowed to sit at your table?"

"No, I just . . . It's lunch. Don't you want to sit with your friends?"

"Oh, so I'm not your *friend*, is that it?"

"No, no, it's just . . ." But I had run out of arguments. I didn't even *know* what I was arguing. All I knew was that Aaron was Aaron, and Cliff was Neanderthal, and we weren't supposed to sit at the same table. It might upset the cosmic order.

I glanced over at Aaron's table, and—rest assured—we were getting all sorts of stink eye from the likes of Lacey, Kyle, Heather, and other esteemed members of Team Aaron. Their captain had abandoned ship to mingle with the savages. A mutiny was surely in the works.

"Look, it's simple," said Aaron. "Lunch is valuable List-strategizing time. Forgive me if I'd rather talk about the List than the latest god-damn episode of *The Walking Dead*."

"Dude, I hate that show," I said. "It's so depressing."

"I know! Like, I get that it's the zombie apocalypse, but can we cut these characters a break for once? I want to see a Christmas special where they all have a nice turkey dinner, exchange presents, and learn a heartwarming lesson about the importance of family. No zombies. I'd watch the shit out of that episode."

If Aaron didn't shut up, I was going to start thinking he was a really good guy.

"But, no," said Aaron. "No *Walking Dead*. We need to talk about the List—namely, how to fix everything we've screwed up so far."

No arguments there.

"So how about this," said Aaron. "We apologize to Niko."

"What?" I said.

"Of course, we have to be tactical about it. If we apologize to his face, he'll definitely beat the shit out of us. But maybe if we hire someone to apologize for us? Like a telegram?"

"What?"

"But that could get expensive. And I don't even know if telegrams are a thing in Montana. And I don't know about you, but I suck at writing apologies. So how about this: we buy a Hallmark card in the Apology section, and we stick it in his locker. It's not much, but that's gotta mean *something*, right?"

"What?"

I knew all my *what*s were grating on Aaron's nerves, because his eyeball started twitching. And then something snapped inside of him, and he said something brilliant:

"Say *what* again, I dare you," said Aaron. "I double-dare you, motherfucker, say *what* one more goddamn time!"

"Holy shit," I said. "You just quoted *Pulp Fiction*."

"You've seen *Pulp Fiction*?" said Aaron, surprised.

"Are you kidding me? Quentin Tarantino is a filmmaking god."

"Well, have you seen *Reservoir Dogs*?"

"I LOVE *Reservoir Dogs*!"

So much for the List. Any attempt at planning disintegrated as our conversation derailed into the realm of schlocky, bloody neo-noir that is everything Quentin Tarantino.

Not that it mattered. Because five minutes later, Esther Poulson sat at our table.

"Hello, Aaron," she said. "Hello, Clifford."

Heretofore, I have spent a great deal of time elaborating on the sociopath that is Esther Poulson. However, I may have left out the superficial detail of just how *hot* Esther is. I mean, it's not exactly the first thing that comes to mind when you're describing an evil, puritanical genius. So here it is:

Esther Poulson was a babe.

Nice boobs, nice ass, but the kicker was her face. It had this perfect symmetry that would have made Leonardo da Vinci marvel.

I had to blink a couple of times to remind myself that Esther sitting at our table was a bad thing.

"So there's a rumor circulating," said Esther. Her eyes shifted to Aaron. "A rumor that you *claim* to have seen God."

Hmph. Apparently HVHS hadn't kept *completely* quiet about the Niko fiasco.

"Here's the thing," said Esther. "You're either lying—"

"I'm not lying," said Aaron.

"—*or*," she continued, raising a silencing finger, "you're physically delusional. Considering the timing, I'm putting my money on the latter. You *did* hit your pretty head rather hard on that boat after all. I imagine that tiny jock brain of yours probably bounced around like a pinball. Got scrambled like a tiny little hummingbird egg omelet."

Aaron's lips were sealed air-lock tight. Mounting pressure aboard the USS *Zimmerman* caused his nostrils to seethe, and his face turned a healthy shade of magenta.

"Do you know what blasphemy is?" said Esther.

"No," said Aaron. "But I have a feeling you're going to tell us."

"Blasphemy is the act of speaking offensively against God. That's what your"—Esther's face contorted, like she was physically regurgitating the word—"*List*...is. I'll be honest: it's kind of sick."

"What exactly are we saying that's offensive?"

"It's not what you're *saying*. It's who you *are*." Esther's gaze shifted to me. "Who *both* of you are. Don't think I didn't see Clifford nearly beat Niko to death. And correct me if I'm wrong, but this was an agenda on your so-called List?"

Neither Aaron nor I had a response to this.

"Interesting," said Esther. "You *say* this List is from God; however, I'd wager it's from the other guy. Maybe you know him? Red pajamas, horns, pitchfork, embodiment of all evil—you guys seem like his type."

"Why are you here?" said Aaron. "Because if you're trying to convince us to give up on the List, you're wasting your breath. I know what I saw."

"And *I* know the type of people who God shows himself to. Suffice it to say, you two aren't it. You're the sort of delinquents who get first-class tickets to hell—VIP box seats—and your only options are original recipe or extracrispy."

"Ooh," I said. "Extracrispy, all the way."

"I'll take either as long as there's no coleslaw involved," said Aaron. "God, I hate coleslaw."

"You think this is a joke?" said Esther. "I'll tell you a joke: you two pretending to be servants of God."

"That's funny. God basically told me the same thing about you."

Esther glared. The perfect symmetry of her face tweaked as her jaw tensed. "Fine. You want to play that game? You want to put your false prophethood to the test? Then I invite you to a Sermon Showdown."

Aaron blinked. I blinked. Between our two brains, I'm pretty sure we didn't have half a clue what the hell a Sermon Showdown was.

"Two weeks from Friday," said Esther, "after school, we will both give sermons to my congregation. Whoever gives the better sermon—whoever proves to my congregation that *they* are God's true spokesperson here at Happy Valley High—wins. If I win, you publicly renounce yourselves."

Admiral Ackbar was surely at it again, assessing the traptacularness of the situation. Of course Esther would win. They were *her* congregation! We would be preaching to the most biased group entity on the planet Earth.

"If we win," said Aaron, "you resign as student body president."

What?!

"Deal," said Esther. She stood up and smiled, like she'd already won. "Four p.m. at the Quad. Two weeks from Friday. I look forward to seeing you then."

Translation: I will devour your immortal souls.

Esther left. I redirected my look of utter whatness to Aaron.

"What just happened?" I said.

"I know, right?" said Aaron, chuckling. "Sermon Showdown? Who came up with that? Sounds like a shitty Southern Baptist reality show."

"Are you out of your skull? Esther is going to eat us for breakfast."

"Well, *technically* we're doing this thing in the afternoon. So she'd be eating us for lunch."

"It is my medical opinion that you are an idiot."

"It's cool, man. We got this!"

"No, we most certainly do not *got* this. I have two great fears, Aaron. Number one: little people. Number two—by like a *centimeter*—is public speaking."

"What? Seriously?"

"Oh yeah," I said, kind of breathless. "Just the thought of . . . speaking in front of . . . a large group of people . . . makes it hard for me to"—I actually had to stop and inhale and exhale deeply—"breathe."

"You're afraid of *little* people?"

"Horrified. But that's aside from the—"

"Dude," said Aaron. "That's messed up. Those are actual people with a real medical condition."

"Can we just not talk about little people? My heart is beating so fast right now, and I can barely breathe." True story. I was on the verge of a panic attack. "The point I was *trying* to make is that public speaking is my second-greatest nightmare."

"Okay, let's talk about it."

"Actually, I don't want to talk about that either. I feel like I'm going to hyperventilate. Or pass out. Or hyperventilate and *then* pass out. There's no way I'm doing this with you. No. Way. The line is in the sand, and I'm standing on the other side—far, far away."

"C'mon, man. This is number two on the List. It's like the door's already been opened for us. All we have to do is walk through!"

"No," I said. "If this is the metaphor I think it is . . . Just. No."

"Don't you want to see what's on the other side?"

"*Guuuuuhhhhhhhhhh.*"

"Is that a *Yes, Aaron! I would love to walk through this Door of Life and give a co-sermon with you at Esther's cult gathering?*"

"Not all doors should be walked through," I said. "You know that, right? Like, sometimes you'll come across a door with a biohazard symbol? That means deadly bacteria and viruses are on the other side."

"If your pessimism could be turned into optimism, you would be the most optimistic person in the world."

Here was the thing: Aaron *knew* I was in. *I* knew I was in. Aaron knew that I knew that I was in. So he wasn't so much asking me to do this as he was asking me to stop bitching about it, because how often do you get to speak your mind to a malevolent cult of psycho zealots?

I sighed. "I'm in."

THIRTEEN

The next day, I didn't even make it to my first class before I got jumped. But not by Niko. I could at least *fight* that asshole.

I got jumped by Lacey Hildebrandt.

She shoved me against my locker with both hands, grabbed my wrists, and pinned them to my side. Her Manic Pixie Dream Girl face morphed into a Don't Fuck with Me scowl. Lacey was on a mission, and there were only two items on *her* list:

1. Kick ass.
2. Take names.

"I'm done with the bullshit," said Lacey. "Everyone's talking about how Aaron *says* he saw God, and that God gave him some list of things to do, and that *you're* helping him. So you're going to tell me—right here, right now—what's *really* happening, or I'm going to rip your testicles out of your scrotum with my bare hands and wear them as earrings."

This confrontation was so simultaneously terrifying and sexy, I didn't even know what life *was* anymore.

"What if I told you that that *is* what's happening?" I said.

"No," said Lacey. "Don't even."

"Lacey," I said, "that's what's happening."

Lacey let go of my wrists, and her arms fell and dangled flimsily at her side.

"Yeah," I said. "I know it's insane. There's basically nothing you could say to make me think this is any crazier than I already think it is."

Lacey was a sponge, struggling to soak it all in, but mostly just dripping in WTF.

"So that fight you guys had with Niko . . ." said Lacey. "That was something on the . . . List?"

"Yeaaaaah, that didn't exactly go according to plan," I said. "The original plan involved more talking and peaceful feelings. And less beating each other to death."

"And . . . now you're friends with Esther because of this List?"

"Ha!" I said. "No. Esther is to Jesus what ISIS is to Muhammad. She is a terrorist against the human spirit. And she has to be stopped."

"Okay . . ."

"The List told us to call the JTs to repentance or whatever. So we arranged with Esther to do a Sermon Showdown."

"A *what*?"

"We're basically giving sermons to Esther's congregation, but it's a face-off. If Esther wins, we publicly renounce ourselves and the List. If we win, she resigns as student body president."

Lacey just kept looking at me, waiting for the part where I exclaimed *APRIL FOOL'S!*

"And this is supposed to make them . . . change?" she said, finally.

"Basically."

Lacey went right back to staring at me. She was really good at making me feel like I had something growing on my face—like a wart, or a tumor, or a leprechaun.

"Aaron has a concussion," she said.

I shrugged. "Maybe. Or maybe he saw God."

"You cannot be serious."

"Aaron seems pretty serious."

"Because he has *brain damage*! Shit. We need to tell someone. We need to tell a doctor!"

"Um. I don't think Aaron will..."

"Will *what*? You don't think Aaron will like us getting him the medical attention that he needs?"

I shifted uncomfortably.

"What if there *is* something wrong with him? What if it gets worse? Are you going to let Aaron ride the crazy train all the way to the psych ward? Or do you consider yourself his friend? Because a *real* friend would get him the help he needs."

"What do you need *me* for?" I said. My tone was a little too defensive for someone who supposedly didn't think Aaron was nuts. "If you're so worried about him, go tell everyone he's crazy yourself."

"You've been with him," said Lacey. "You know all the details of what he's doing and thinking. Doctors will want to talk to *you*."

I hated every syllable of this conversation. I hated that this was somehow *my* responsibility now. I hated how much I still questioned Aaron's sanity.

But more than anything, I hated hated *hated* the idea that Aaron was only my friend because he had brain damage.

It wasn't until that moment that I realized Aaron and I really *were* friends. This epiphany was reinforced when Aaron passed a note to me in English. In any other class, this might have been a casual thing. In Mr. Spinelli's class, however, this was the equivalent of High Treason. But Spinelli was too absorbed in the excerpt of the text he was reading aloud to notice. All that mattered was the Old Man, the Sea, and a Big-Ass Fish that unfortunately didn't make it into the title.

"*Then the fish came alive,*" said Spinelli, "*with his death in him, and rose high out of the water showing all his great length and width and all his power and his beauty.*"

The note was folded into a tight little mock envelope, labeled in Aaron's remarkably shitty handwriting:

For Cliff

(If you are not Cliff and you open this, you will die)

Naturally, nobody had a hankering to die. The note passed from hand to hand to hand to me.

I opened it.

Aaron wrote: *If Mr. Spinelli loved students as much as he loves this shitty book, he would be the best teacher ever.*

I wrote below Aaron's message: *If Mr. Spinelli loved students as much as he loves this shitty book, he would be a pedophile.*

I passed the note. The same chain of hands were waiting for the pass, and it was delivered smoothly. Aaron opened the note and read it.

You know that snorting/choking/raspberry sound people make when they're trying *not* to laugh, yet somehow it becomes just as loud—if not louder—than the laugh itself?

Aaron did that.

Spinelli was a falcon. He swooped down the aisle and snatched the note from Aaron's hands.

I was hoping and praying that Spinelli refused to read anything less than classic literary works. That student notes need only be inter-cepted for the little heathens to be sent promptly to the stocks. I would gladly go to the stocks. Just please, Lord God Almighty, do not read that note.

Spinelli read it.

His face turned red.

And then slightly purplish.

I doubted Aaron would rat me out, but he didn't need to. The incriminating evidence was written on the back of the note: *For Cliff.*

"CLIFF HUBBARD AND AARON ZIMMERMAN," said Spinelli. "COME WITH ME RIGHT NOW."

Now obviously I'm heavier than most things that aren't measured in tons. But wow did my body and the air and gravity all feel denser than ever as I stood up. Each step was like trying to walk through water. Aaron and I followed Spinelli out of the classroom.

Aaron shot me a *Sorry, dude* look. I noticed it, but I didn't really look at him because I was too busy looking at every inch of Spinelli's taut body. His arms were straight lines to his fists—curled white balls of fury. There was no question. Every muscle, every follicle, every fiber of his being said that he hated us.

There was something about being hated *that much* that made you sort of hate yourself too.

"Mr. Spinelli—" I said.

"SHUT," said Spinelli, his voice a sonic boom, "UP!"

I think Aaron sort of felt what I was feeling now. He stared at his shoes. So much for point number three on the List. Operation: Remind Mr. Spinelli Why He Chose to Teach had progressed approxi-mately eleven steps backward.

Spinelli escorted us through the main offices. Directly to Principal McCaffrey's office. Unlike me, he knocked. But his knock was more like an AK-47 unloading its clip into her door. McCaffrey opened it just as fiercely.

"What in God's name—?" she said.

Spinelli shoved the note in her face. "This is the note Cliff and Aaron were passing in my class."

McCaffrey had to pull the note a foot away from her face before she could read anything. Her eyes scrolled, and her mouth pulled into a grim line.

"I want these two expelled," said Spinelli.

Aaron and I both whipped up straight like metal tape measures. The only person who seemed more alarmed than us was McCaffrey.

"Roger," said McCaffrey, because apparently Spinelli had a first name. "That's not how disciplinary action works at this school. This is neither the time nor the place for—"

"Don't give me that shit, Joan," said Spinelli. "I'm tired of you covering for these little assholes. Just the other day, I saw them in a fistfight with Niko Kaleoikaikaokalani."

Yes, he *actually* said Niko's last name and seemed to pronounce it correctly. English teachers, Jesus!

"Cliff here turned Niko's face into pudding," Spinelli continued. "Has anybody bothered to do anything about this?"

"You and I both know that Niko isn't a victim when it comes to fights. Besides, Aaron has a relatively clean record. We can bring this issue up in the next school board meeting, but—"

"Fine," said Spinelli. "Just Cliff then. I want Cliff expelled."

My stomach bottomed out.

"Roger, please."

"He's just like his brother. He's not a *student* here. He's not here to *learn*. He's a goddamned anarchist."

"Roger!"

"Shane didn't belong here. He belonged in a mental hospital."

"*Roger!*" exclaimed McCaffrey. "That is out of line."

Everything inside me imploded—sucked into an infinite emptiness. I couldn't even breathe.

"But *nooooo*," said Spinelli. "We kept treating Shane like he *wasn't* a problem."

"Roger," said McCaffrey. "Be rational."

"Be rational? I'll give you rational, Joan. Either you see to it that Cliff gets expelled, or I resign right here and now."

"I can't do that."

"Then consider this my official resignation."

Spinelli rotated 180 degrees and marched the *hell* outta there.

"Roger?" said McCaffrey.

Spinelli veered into the copy room. And then he popped right back out with a cardboard box in hand. He exited the main offices.

"Roger!" said McCaffrey. She shoved her way between Aaron and me and chased after him.

Aaron looked at me, and I looked at him, and we chased after them as well.

Spinelli was heading back to his classroom. But not to finish his lesson. Not even close.

Fifth period English had unraveled into its natural order of chaos—students standing, sitting on top of their desks, one kid flinging a crumpled-up paper ball at another kid's head. Spinelli stormed into class so fast and furious, students tripped over themselves trying to get back into their seats. Silence fell like a shroud. But Spinelli didn't care. Spinelli didn't give a microscopic fuck, because he immediately went to work cleaning off his desk and emptying the contents of the drawers into his box.

"Roger, please don't do this," said McCaffrey. "Talk to me. We can work this out."

But there was an invisible wall between Spinelli and McCaffrey. Her words bounced off the surface. There was only Spinelli, his box, and the shit that needed to get into said box. Everything else was just white noise.

It was like Mr. Spinelli had it rehearsed. Like he'd been planning this for weeks. Years, even. He was leaving HVHS, he was leaving with a bang, and he was leaving forever.

Wasn't this the sort of thing that teenagers dream of? Their asshole teacher quitting in the middle of class? So why did this feel like a special kind of nightmare?

In less than a minute, Spinelli had his box filled. Aaron and I barely stepped out of the way as he barreled out the door. McCaffrey followed him all the way to the front entrance of the school asking, begging him, *pleading* for him to reconsider. They disappeared on the other side of the doors.

Aaron and I didn't follow.

FOURTEEN

I turned down Aaron's offer to drive me to school the next morning—something that was becoming a ritual. Not that I didn't appreciate his company. I just needed time to think. Or not think. I wasn't sure which I was doing. In the forty-something minutes it took me to walk to school, all I could see was Niko's pulverized face. Raising the baseball bat above my head. Spinelli cleaning off his desk. McCaffrey chasing desperately after Spinelli.

Lacey telling me that Aaron had a concussion.

"Hey, Cliff. You okay?"

This came from Tegan. Oddly enough, it wasn't prefaced with "honey" or "sugar-bear" or commentary on my "big, curvy ass." I must've *really* looked like shit.

I blinked myself out of my dead-zone haze. Apparently I was running on autopilot, because I had nearly passed Frankie's corner in completely detached oblivion. I was all but sleepwalking.

Carlos had pulled out a nudie magazine and garnered Frankie's and Jed's attention.

But Tegan didn't seem to be feeling it. Her hands were in her pockets, mouth pressed in a straight line.

My instinct was to keep walking. But I didn't. I stopped, and I looked at her.

"Have you ever had the feeling that there's this"—I struggled for the word—"this *thing* that you're supposed to do? This really weird but really important *thing*? But the harder you try to *do* that thing, and the more you care about it, the more it feels like you're moving backward? Like, maybe everything you're trying to do—your entire *purpose*—is bullshit?"

The moment I said it, I realized how stupid it sounded. Especially to Tegan of all people. I thought of attempting some sort of verbal recovery, but that would probably only make things worse. So I turned and kept walking.

"Sometimes," said Tegan, pausing almost thoughtfully, "we get so caught up in the *things* we gotta do . . . that we forget about the *people*."

That stopped me in my tracks. I turned and looked at Tegan. Like, *really* looked at her.

Who knew she could be so . . . eloquent?

"Don't forget about the people," she said. "And don't stop caring. Ever. Only assholes stop caring. Stop caring, Neanderthal, and I'll kick that big, sexy ass of yours. But only 'cause I care."

I didn't know what to say. So after a long, awkward moment, I nodded.

When I finally turned and left, I felt more confused than miserable—which I guess was an improvement.

Tegan's words were etched in my mind, a monolith in my head. There was no room to think anywhere else.

Sometimes we get so caught up in the things we've got to do . . .

. . . that we forget about the people.

Also, sometimes I get lost so deep in my own thoughts, I'm approximately a gazillion percent oblivious to my surroundings. That was the only way I could have collided with the second-largest human being at HVHS.

Niko.

There was a brief moment in which I was convinced that I had just been hit by a Volkswagen. I staggered backward, and by some miracle of God I managed to stay on my feet. Niko seemed to mirror my *I just got hit by a Volkswagen* reaction. And then we stared at each other for the longest six seconds of my life. Well... I stared. It was hard to tell what Niko was doing since he had two black eyes and his face was so swollen, he could have been either pissed *or* happy to see me, and I wouldn't have been able to tell the difference.

Once the six seconds ended, Niko walked past me.

A part of me was relieved. That could have ended *sooooo* much worse. And by *worse*, I'm referring to my homicide.

The other part of me opened my mouth.

"Niko," I said.

Why? Why did I do that?

Niko turned around.

"I'm sorry for..." I said.

And then I struggled to fill in the blank. I'm sorry for turning your face into a real-life Picasso? I'm sorry for nearly busting the candy out of your piñata head?

"Just," I said, "I'm sorry."

And then I walked away as fast as I could without looking like I was trying to escape.

Sometimes...

...we get so caught up in the things *we gotta do...*

...that we forget about the people.

By the time lunch rolled around, I could barely contain myself. Aaron and I met at the table and we exploded verbalization all over each other simultaneously.

I said, "We're forgetting about the people!" while Aaron said, "Dude, Tegan totally has a thing for you!"

"Huh?" we both said.

"You go first," said Aaron.

"No, no, no, you go first," I said.

"You sure?"

"Please . . . say whatever the hell it was that you just said."

"That Tegan has a thing for you?"

"Yes. That. Why would you say that?"

"Um . . . other than the fact that it's super obvious? C'mon, I just *saw* you two talking. Something about 'Don't stop caring' and your 'big, sexy ass.' I would've said hi, but then I saw the way she was looking at you. Three's a crowd—I know the bro code. So I kept walking."

"The way she was *looking* at me?"

"Cliff," said Aaron. "It is my professional opinion that when it comes to the opposite sex, you are a dimwit. That girl is nuts for you."

"No," I said. I shook my head to emphasize the utter no-ness of the matter. "I mean, I'm pretty sure she's, like, lesbian or bisexual or something."

"Okay, for starters, being lesbian and bisexual are completely different. If she's lesbian, she wouldn't have a crush on you. If she's bisexual, you're fair game, buddy! *If* she's one of the two, I'd put my money on the latter. Because she totally wants you."

"But WHY?"

"Oh, c'mon. You're a good-looking guy."

"Is that a joke? Have you seen how fat I am?"

"Dude. Shut your doughnut hole. You're like . . . what? Six five?"

"Six . . . six."

"Six six!" Aaron exclaimed. "I'm pretty sure there's a rule that says it's impossible to be fat when you're six six. Chicks dig big guys. And Tegan is super-tough, so she needs a guy who's built like a refrigerator."

I raised my eyebrow.

"The fact of the matter is that the hottest girl at school likes you, and if you don't ask her on a date—like ASAP—I will."

Lacey was right. Aaron had a concussion.

"Did you just call Tegan the hottest girl at school?"

"Hell yes, I did. She's totally got this badass, slightly emotionally damaged warrior chick thing going on. *Sooooo* hot."

"And you'll ask her on a date if I don't."

"Hell yes, I will."

I paused a long moment, trying to assess whether or not he was being serious. Was this just some clever tactic to get me to ask her on a date?

Because it was working.

I mean, she *was* cute—in her weird, vaguely threatening sort of way.

"What about Lacey?" I said.

"What *about* Lacey?"

Seriously? Did I really need to explain myself?

"You guys dated, didn't you?" I said. "I'm thinking that about one hundred percent of Happy Valley High would agree with me that she is the hottest girl here."

"Ninety-nine-point-nine percent," said Aaron. "Because *I* think that Tegan is the hottest. Don't get me wrong; Lacey *is* pretty. She's just not my type anymore."

"And Tegan *is* your type."

"Good God, Cliff. What's so difficult to understand about this?"

I felt like I needed to invite another human being or twelve into this conversation to emphasize that I wasn't the crazy one here.

"So are you going to ask Tegan on a date or not?" said Aaron.

I sighed. "Fine. I guess."

"Good. She's sitting two tables behind you."

"Wait, what?" I said. I turned around, and sure enough, she was there, two tables away, sitting with Frankie, Jed, and Carlos.

"We've still got nine minutes until the bell rings," said Aaron. "That should be plenty of time to ask her on a date and get her digits."

"Her what?"

"Her phone number, dumb-ass. Now hurry!"

"Okay, one: I just barely agreed to this. Two: I am *not* going to ask her on a date in the most public place in the whole school. Three: I don't even own a phone."

"You don't have a phone?" said Aaron. "What are you, Amish?"

"Also, I don't have any money. And I've heard rumors that dates cost money."

Aaron pulled out his wallet.

"No," I said.

He pulled out two twenty-dollar bills and threw them on the table in front of me.

"Put that shit back in your wallet," I said. "Right now."

"It's not for you," said Aaron. "It's for Tegan—the girl who will never know I had the hots for her. Because *you*, my friend, are going to take her out on a nice date. And then you will kiss her, and make her your girlfriend, and when you graduate, you two will get married and have twenty-seven gigantic babies, and you will name them all Aaron—even the girls—after your good friend, Aaron Zimmerman, who funded your first date. Deal?"

I stared at the two twenties like they were cleverly disguised mousetraps.

"You have seven minutes before the bell rings," said Aaron.

"Damn you," I said. I shoved the twenties in my pocket, stood up, and started toward Tegan's table. With each step, I practiced lines in my head.

Hey, Tegan. Ever since you put that joint in my mouth with your lips, I can't stop thinking about how high you make me. Like metaphorically high. Without the drugs. Wanna go on a date with me?

Dammit.

Hey, Tegan. Remember that offer to let me touch your boobs if I let you touch mine? Maybe both of those things will happen if you go on a date with me.

Shit.

Hey, Frankie. I really like your sister, and I was wondering if I could have your permission to ask her on a date.

This was destined to be the worst seven minutes of my life.

The cafeteria was a human beehive—the chatter and laughter and yelling and clatter of silverware joined together into a mind-numbing buzz. I suddenly felt very claustrophobic, like this human hive was closing in on me. Or maybe that was just me having a panic attack. Whatever the case, I was already thinking about flipping a U-ey, but by the time that thought even processed, I was standing at Tegan's table. Frankie and the gang were having a riveting discussion about herbology (of the illegal variety) when they apparently noticed the human skyscraper eclipsing the sunlight pouring through the window behind him.

Suddenly, herbology wasn't as fascinating anymore.

"Hell no," said Frankie. "You ain't getting no more free samples."

"Oh. Um, that's okay," I said. "I don't want your weed."

"What?" said Frankie. "My weed ain't good enough for you?"

"Huh? No. *No!* Your weed was fantastic! I've never been so wonked in my entire life."

"Oh," said Frankie. Now he just looked confused.

"You wanna sit down?" said Tegan.

Tegan was wearing a white Death Grips T-shirt, baggy sweatpants, and a bandanna around her head—a look that was simultaneously intimidating and adorable. I couldn't tell if her expression was curious or pitying, but I didn't even care. Standing up was making me dizzy.

"Yeah," I said. "Yeah, that'd be great."

I sat down. Right next to Tegan. Which I immediately realized was a bad idea because my overwhelming body mass was brushing up against her.

Carlos's eyebrows were making a serious attempt at touching his hairline. Jed's face was pinched, looking slightly jealous that my fat was touching her and his wasn't.

"So..." said Tegan. "S'up?"

"Not much," I said, which was a total lie because my dick was at twelve o'clock and harder than advanced Calculus.

"Oh. Okay. Cool."

And that's when I had the worst kind of mental breakdown. The kind that is worse than not talking. This was the sort of mental breakdown where you say anything—*anything!*—to backtrack your way out of the pit you just walked into.

"Aaron wants to go on a date with you," I said.

"Huh?" said Tegan.

Carlos's eyebrows reached even higher, which didn't even seem anatomically possible, but whatever.

"I know, right?" I said, laughing nervously. "He said he thinks you're really cute, which was surprising to me too, but he wants to go on a date with you because he's really not into Lacey anymore. You should totally go on a date with him though because, I mean, c'mon, it's Aaron Zimmerman."

Tegan blinked. Her face was the most indecipherable thing since the Dead Sea Scrolls.

"He doesn't know that I'm telling you this, though," I said. "But, like, you should ask him on a date. He'll totally be flattered. And. Um . . ."

I dug my hand into my pocket, pulled out the crumpled twenties, and set them on the table in front of her.

"There. You can even pay for it. It's actually Aaron's money, so technically, it's like he's paying for it . . . except you have the money instead of him. So now he *has* to go on a date with you."

I laughed, mostly as a tension reliever. No success.

For the record, I had about zero mental comprehension of the words coming out of my mouth. It was like they were a river, and the dam had busted, and now here comes the flood and several million dollars' worth of damage.

Tegan glanced from the balled-up twenties, to me, back to the balled-up twenties, and back to me. Each time her gaze shifted, her eyes narrowed further.

"Is this some kinda joke?" she said.

Tegan stood up. This was made slightly more difficult because she was wedged next to a mentally stagnant Neanderthal, but she battled her way up, shoving me out of the way because surely anything was better than sitting next to me.

"Go to hell, bitch."

She said this while walking backward with both middle fingers extended—suddenly cool, indestructible, fearless—like a total badass. Like she was the Queen of Not Giving Shits.

But as she turned around, I caught the glimmer of a tear. She walked fast, her arms straight, and she rounded the corner out of the cafeteria.

And that's when I realized that everything I touched was meant to fall apart.

"Damn," said Carlos. "That was screwed up."

I didn't say anything. I felt exhausted—like I had just run a mile with my mouth, only to find out that I'd been running the wrong direction.

"You *do* know that she has a thing for you, right?" said Frankie.

"*Thing?*" said Carlos. "*Thing* doesn't even start. That girl is in love with you."

"It's true," said Jed, glumly.

I already had a wound. Frankie, Jed, and Carlos were the salt, lemon juice, and steel wool brush to scrub it all in.

"Yeah," I said, miserably. "I heard."

"Seriously?" said Frankie. "Well, what the hell, man?"

"I came over here to ask her on a date," I said. "And then I panicked."

It took several seconds for the sheer idiocy of it all to sink in. And then they laughed.

"Oh man," said Frankie. He lifted a beefy, tatted arm and proceeded to wipe an actual, legitimate tear from his eye, he was laughing so hard. "Oh man, oh man. That's too funny."

"Can you talk to her?" I said. "Tell her that I'm a dipshit, and I'm sorry?"

"Oh, hell no. I ain't touching that. You wanna fix it, you're gonna have to talk to her yourself."

My gaze shifted dejectedly to my size fourteen shoes. They might have passed as clown shoes if I wasn't roughly the size of three small clowns stacked on top of each other.

"*But*," said Frankie, "I will give you a hint."

I glanced up.

Frankie pulled his backpack up, removed a pen and a notebook, and began scribbling on the first page. "This is our address. Any guy that comes to our house to apologize is gonna get her attention." He ripped out the sheet and slid the paper to me.

735 Golden Row Dr.

The bell rang. With profound reluctance, I grabbed the crumpled twenties—mousetraps, indeed—and shoved them back in my pocket.

"Oh, and Cliff..." said Frankie.

I met his gaze.

"My pop's crazy. Just so you know."

Great. As if I didn't already have one of *those* to worry about.

FIFTEEN

I knew something was wrong when the address Frankie gave me—735 Golden Row Drive—took me to the north side of the river.

The nice side.

Tegan and Frankie's house was *waaaaaaay* north. Past the shiny new businesses that were keeping Happy Valley alive. Past the fancy new subdivisions on the outskirts of town. Past anything that even remotely *resembled* civilization. I soon found myself wandering out of the last neighborhood, walking down a gravel road in the middle of nowhere. If Tegan and Frankie lived with the Blair Witch, I was done.

But this was still Golden Row Drive (according to the last street sign I had seen fifteen minutes before), and the numbers were in the early seven hundreds and going up. So I kept walking.

And then I saw it.

It was impossible not to see it.

Frankie and Tegan's "house" was not a house at all. I wouldn't go so far as to call it a *mansion*. It was more like a big, swanky-ass log cabin extraordinaire. It was about the same size as one of those neighborhood mini Walmarts. Every inch of the vast, ribbed log exterior had a glossy sheen, gleaming in the floodlights. A dozen triangular arches jutted over fancy window frames, peering into the warm coziness inside.

I *knew* it was Tegan and Frankie's house because of the large stone mailbox with the number 735 carved into the surface.

My first thought was: Frankie and Tegan live *here*? Why the hell are they selling drugs?

My second thought was: Shit. I'm here.

My awe melted into dread. I didn't know what to say, and I didn't know how to say it.

All I knew was that I *had* to.

When I reached the door, I took a deep breath, raised my unsteady hand, and rang the doorbell. From inside, I could hear the obnoxious: *ding-dong-dang-DONG . . . dang-dong-ding-DONG!*

"Goddamn!" said a twangy male voice from inside. "Who in the hell? If this ain't the goddamn Girl Scouts sellin' 'em Thin Mint cookies, I'm gon' shoot the fool."

Crap.

My fight-or-flight response was currently telling me to get the hell outta there. Except that my fight-or-flight response had a third, less-evolved option called deer-in-the-headlights.

The door opened. On the other side of the door was an explicitly hairy man—hair on his back, his shoulders, and other ungodly places. He was like a Chia Pet experiment gone wrong. He was also wearing nothing but socks, boxers, and a Bass Pro Shops ball cap to emphasize the hair factor. The man was tall but built like a summer squash—long neck, deflated chest, wiry arms, and a *humongous* gut. His face was mostly engulfed in an impressive, ZZ Top–esque beard, but it hardly hid the scowl on his face.

"You ain't no Girl Scout," he said.

"No, sir, I am not," I said. "You're Mr. Robertson?"

Mr. Robertson's eyes narrowed on me. "The hell you know my name? You with the IRS or somethin'? 'Cause I don't owe a goddamn penny."

Was this guy for real?

"Actually, I'm here to see Tegan? Your daughter?"

"Tegan? What you want with my baby princess? You her boyfriend or somethin'?"

"No, I just wanted to apologize to her."

"Apologize for what?" Mr. Robertson leaned forward, grabbing both sides of the door frame. His summer-squash build became tense and dangerous. What he said next came out in a whispering growl. "You didn't knock up my baby princess, did you?"

"What? No! No, no, no! We've never..." I just shook my head because I suddenly felt uncomfortable even verbalizing the *S*-word around this guy. "I mean...we haven't even kissed! I just wanted to apologize for saying something stupid. That's all, I swear."

Mr. Robertson turned his head slightly and glared dissectingly at me with his left eye—like this was the eyeball that meant business.

"Okay, kid," he said, finally. He stepped aside and gestured me inside and toward the living room. "Come on."

I came inside and followed Mr. Robertson into the living room—which I could've easily parked my house inside and had room to spare. An honest-to-god antler chandelier hung from the tall, vaulted ceiling. The walls were adorned with mounted fish and mounted animal heads, and the Grizzlies were getting their asses kicked on all sixty inches of an LED flat-screen HDTV—also mounted on the wall.

Mr. Robertson turned the game on mute. "Take a seat...uh... what you say your name was again?"

"Cliff."

"Right," he said, as if he'd known this all along. And then he shouted, "Frankie! Get your ass out here!"

Frankie appeared around the corner of what I assumed was the kitchen. He had a half-eaten sandwich in his hand. Like his dad, he was also shirtless, except his upper half was pure, taut muscle, graffitied in badass tattoos.

"Yah?" he said through a full mouth. *"Wash hup, Popsh?"*

And then Frankie saw me. He smirked—a little too amusedly—and he swallowed. "'Sup, Neanderthal?"

"You know this gigantic kid?" said Mr. Robertson.

"Yeah, he's Tegan's boyfriend."

Mr. Robertson turned his left-eyed death stare on me. "I thought you said..."

"I'M NOT HER BOYFRIEND, I SWEAR!" I said.

Frankie had made the mistake of taking another bite of his sandwich. He barely had a chance to chew before he was laughing and choking on it.

"All right, all right," said Mr. Robertson. "No need to get your big-ass panties in a knot. Frankie, go tell your sister that her boyfriend that ain't really her boyfriend is here."

"You got it," said Frankie—sounding way more excited about this than I was comfortable with. He started up the nearby staircase, leaving me alone...with Mr. Robertson.

"Take a seat."

I sat down on the leather sofa—positioned precariously beneath the heads and bodies of every dead animal known to the northwest. Mr. Robertson sat down in the adjacent armchair—which also happened to be beside a glass display gun cabinet.

Like, who in the hell keeps a gun cabinet in their living room?

"So...what do you do for a living?" I said—because making light conversation with this guy was better than being stared down by his evil left eye.

"Construction," said Mr. Robertson.

"Seriously? Wow. So you...uh...make a lot of money doing that?"

"I don't *do* the construction. I *own* the construction. W and W Construction Company. Run it with my brother, Wade."

"Ah. That...makes sense."

Silence proceeded to fill the room.

"So what you wanna be when you grow up, Clinton?"

"Uh, it's Cliff."

"That's what I said, ain't it?"

"Right. Um, I dunno. I haven't given it much thought."

Again, Mr. Robertson was laying the lefty stink eye on me thick. "Well you better figure that shit out if you're gonna date my baby princess. She deserves somebody that can take care of her, not some ho-hum bum who don't know what he's gonna do with his life."

"Tegan and I aren't dating."

"Right. You're just the nice guy that comes over to her house in the middle of the goddamn evening to 'apologize.'" Mr. Robertson air-quoted the word *apologize* with his middle and index fingers. "My mistake."

I shifted uncomfortably.

That was when I heard an upstairs door open and close and footsteps storm over to the balcony overlooking the living room.

It was Tegan. And she did *not* look happy to see me.

"Cliff?" said Tegan. "What in the *hell* are you doing here?"

"Clinton and I were just discussing you two's future and all," said Mr. Robertson. "You need to tell your boyfriend to figure out what he wants to be when he grows up."

"Daddy, stay the *hell* outta this!" said Tegan.

Mr. Robertson chuckled lovingly but made no attempt to argue further.

Tegan's gaze narrowed back on me. "Well?"

I should've written down an apology speech, because I was drawing a special kind of blank. I had nothing.

But I was *really* good at gaping like an idiot with my mouth open.

"Know what?" said Tegan. "I don't give a shit. Get lost, Neanderthal."

With that, Tegan stormed back into her room and slammed the door.

"*Daa-aa-aamn!*" said Frankie from the balcony. I didn't even notice he was there until his exclamation echoed across the tall living room, and he doubled over, laughing. "Neanderthal, your girlfriend's pissed!"

I couldn't even get mad at Frankie. I deserved this. I was a grade-A, first-class dipshit.

"I should go," I said.

I stood up slowly from the sofa and started shuffling to the door.

"The hell for?" said Mr. Robertson.

I stopped awkwardly and gave Mr. Robertson a confused look.

"You came here to apologize to Tegan, di'n'tcha?" he continued. "'Cause far as I seen, you ain't done shit."

"What am I supposed to do?" I said. "You heard her. She won't talk to me."

"Okay, first off, stop feeling so damn sorry for yourself. Secondly, if you really wanna apologize to her, you're gonna march up them stairs, knock on that door, walk into that bedroom, and give her the best goddamn apology ya got. And then, if she still don't feel like forgivin' ya, you can at least walk outta here like a man."

"You want me to just walk into her *bedroom*?" I said, genuinely shocked.

"Well, like I said, knock first. This ain't the goddamn Stone Ages."

I stared at Mr. Robertson. Slowly, I closed my sweaty palms into determined fists, and I nodded. I marched up the stairs, across the hallway, and up to Tegan's door. And then I knocked.

I didn't have to wait long for Tegan's response—maybe a half millisecond. "FUCK OFF."

I opened Tegan's door and closed it behind me. I was swallowed in the dim neon glow of lava lamps.

Tegan's room was decorated in the intellectuals and poets of the hip-hop scene—Saul Williams, Illogic, Aesop Rock, even that asshole genius Sage Francis. Her desk was cluttered in sheets of scribbled paper, and her nearby trash can was overflowing in crumpled-up paper balls. I could only guess what she was writing. Her own lyrical prose, maybe? Whatever it was, she seemed determined to write it.

My gaze shifted to Tegan's bed. Her body was curled up tight, completely submerged beneath the blankets. The blanket lump was trembling.

She was crying.

"Tegan?" I said, timidly.

The blanket lump froze. The sobbing stopped. And then her blanket flew off, and she bolted upright. Her mascara was an inky mess at the corners of her eyes, but that didn't stop her from glaring the hell out of me.

"Jesus, Cliff!" she said. "What the hell are you doing in my room? Get out!"

I opened my mouth to respond, but the fear was rolling back into my throat, choking me.

"Look, I don't *care* what you have to say, okay? I DON'T CARE!"

"When I came over to your table today, I meant to ask you on a date."

And just like that, the Tegan-storm dissipated. She stared at me for a long, hard moment.

"What?" she said.

The silence that followed was pervasive. The silence needed to be stopped.

"Can I just say everything that's on my brain right now?" I said. "Like, one hundred percent honesty? All judgments on hold? No questions, comments, or concerns until I'm done?"

Tegan continued to stare, but her gaze softened—at least by Tegan-standards. She scooted to the foot of her bed. "Fine."

I took a deep breath. "I think I like you. I think I like you *a lot*. And I didn't think you liked me until Aaron said that you did, and then he was telling me that he thought you were the hottest girl at school, and at first I thought it was some kind of weird reverse psychology, and maybe it was. But maybe it wasn't. Maybe he really *does* like you. I can't get the possibility out of my head."

"What? Seriously?"

"Not done. Anyways, he gave me that money to take you on a date, and so I came over to your table and, as you know, did the exact opposite of asking you on a date. But the stuff I said came from somewhere, and in some stupid, backward sort of way, it made sense to me."

"Wait. What made sense?"

"I'm getting to that. I want to date you, Tegan. I really do. But at the same time, Aaron is like my best—and only—friend in the world. I feel like my life suddenly has *meaning* ever since that asshole stumbled into it. And as much as I want to date you—and maybe do *more* than just date you—well, if I'm being completely honest, I feel like you deserve someone better than me. Aaron, on the other hand . . . well, he's Aaron Zimmerman! And I mean this from the very deepest chamber of my beating heart when I say that Aaron could be the best thing that ever happened to you." I exhaled climactically, indicating the finale of my rant. "Okay, I'm done. You can talk now."

"Hundred percent honesty?" said Tegan.

"Yes," I said.

"No questions, comments, concerns or shit till I'm done?"

"Yes?" I said, a little more hesitantly.

Tegan stood up from her bed, grabbed me by the shirt collar, and pulled me down—simultaneously raising herself on her toes. We met halfway, and she kissed me. She kissed the *hell* out of me. I breathed her in, and she didn't smell like McDonald's this time. She smelled like spring and summer and autumn and winter having a seasonal orgy on my olfactory receptors.

Our lips parted, only inches away.

Our animal instincts and hormones assessed the height situation, and we compensated. Tegan leaped onto me, and I caught her by the thighs, and we tangled into each other. Our lips melded together— kissing like we were drowning, and the only way we could breathe was through each other's mouths.

I lost my balance and fell backward—fortunately, onto her bed. We laughed, and she rolled off of me, but not too far. She was still touching my side. Our fingers brushed, and her index finger inter-locked with mine.

"So . . ." I said, breathless. "I guess that's a 'no' on the Aaron idea?"

Tegan's smile was an infinite curve, pushing two infinite dimples into her cheeks. "Well . . . it ain't exactly a secret that I have a thing for that big, curvy ass o' yours."

This made me laugh.

"What about *you*?" she said, jabbing me with her finger. "What does the Neanderthal want?"

"Well, now I'm feeling really selfish and I want you all to myself."

"Hmm," said Tegan. Her smile's infinitude increased to impossible proportions. "I don't think I would be terribly opposed to that."

SIXTEEN

The next morning, I woke up to something buzzing outside my bedroom window.

I glanced at my alarm clock, which wasn't set to go off for another four minutes. Normally, I would have *loathed* those four minutes. Waking up for school was generally ranked among my least favorite things to do—right up there with *going* to school and *doing* schoolwork. However, I wanted to go to school for two reasons:

1. Tegan.
2. Telling Aaron about Tegan.

Oh man, did I need to tell Aaron about Tegan.

The thing outside my window kept buzzing and vibrating and rattling against the window. What the hell *was* that thing?

I lurched out of bed and shuffled over to the window, rubbing and blinking the sleep out of my eyes. And then I glanced outside.

It was a cell phone. There was a fucking cell phone—a basic, archaic flip phone—sitting on the outside ledge of my windowsill. It continued to vibrate against the window, gradually sliding across, as if begging to be let inside.

I opened the window and glanced at the name of the caller:

Aaron Zimmerman

I flipped the phone open. "Aaron, why the hell am I talking to you through a cell phone that I found outside my window?"

"Because," said Aaron, "you are now the proud owner of a no-contract, cheap-ass cell phone which I am currently paying for with my college fund. My parents don't know that yet. But let me put an added emphasis on the cheap-ass nature of this cell phone. Like, I'm pretty sure AT&T is *giving* me money to take this piece of shit off their hands."

"You bought me a phone?"

"Um, yeah. How are we supposed to do the will of God and bring balance to the Force and shit if you don't have a cell phone? Teamwork is all about communication, and communication is all about teamwork."

I had no response to that.

"I stole that last line from Coach Slater," said Aaron. "He said that before every game. I hated it. I don't know why I said it." In a detached, commentary tone, he added, "That awkward moment when you realize you've been brainwashed."

"Wow," I said. This was a genuine sort of *wow*, not the sarcastic *wow* that I used liberally to elucidate the stupidity of mankind. I was completely, utterly, majestically *wow*ed. "Um . . . thanks."

"Don't thank me just yet," said Aaron, "because the best part is yet to come!"

"Oh no."

"Tomorrow, Friday night, you are cordially invited to my house for a—Wait for it. *Waaaaait* for it.—A SLUMBER PARTY!"

I blinked, slowly trying to wrap my brain around this.

"Are we going to watch rom-coms and paint each other's nails?" I asked.

Aaron laughed. "Okay, maybe *slumber party* is the wrong term. But I figure we've been trying so hard with the List, and failing so epically, we need a night to regroup. I still wanna talk about the List, but we're going to have fun tomorrow. That's why I currently have Quentin Tarantino's entire filmography on Blu-ray, we're gonna order a large stuffed-crust pizza of your choice because I will *only* eat the stuffed crust, and we will stuff Twinkies with Reddi-wip, deep-fry them, and binge on the greasy little bastards, because tomorrow will not be a success if we finish watching *The Hateful Eight* before dying of cardiac arrest."

"Aaron, if I wasn't so completely in love with Tegan right now, I would marry your ass."

"Okay, no bullshit—what *happened*?" said Aaron. "You talked to her for, like, one second, and she stormed off! And then *you* disappeared from school before I could give you a ride. Like, seriously, this is why you need a cell phone!"

"I may or may not have kissed Tegan Robertson," I said. "On the lips."

"What?"

"It was big and fat and sloppy and amazing."

"Shit. I'm picking you up, and you better tell me the whole story in the car."

"CliffsNotes version in the car, Peter Jackson Extended Edition during our slumber party." I cringed just saying *slumber party* out loud. "Um, can we *please* call it something other than a slumber party?"

"How about Testosterone-Filled Man Party of Supreme Mantacularness?"

"Yeah, never mind. It's a slumber party."

———

Contrary to plan, I managed to give Aaron a rather sprawling, epic, Peter Jackson–ish retelling of last night. Aaron was pretty good about keeping his eyes on the road, but they got bigger with each detail.

"Son of a bitch," said Aaron. "Cliff, you are a hero to mankind."

"Whatever," I said.

"And I am so jealous of that kiss. Like, don't take this the wrong way, but I'm a little bit horny right now."

"Dude. You *do* know that you can have any girl at school, right? *Any* girl! I bet you could drop down on one knee and propose to the first girl you see, and she would say yes. You wouldn't even need a ring. You could have a Ring Pop, or an onion ring or, like, ringworm even. She would still say yes."

Aaron didn't say anything. In fact, his smile faded a little bit.

I shot him a slanted glance. "What?"

Aaron forced his smile back into place. "Nothing. I'm just happy for you."

Not that I'm an expert on happiness or anything—my experience has usually been associated with the *other* thing—but this was definitely not nothing.

But I wasn't a nosy bastard. I let it go.

And then I started having a mild panic attack. About Tegan. About what a boy and a girl do the day *after* they've kissed. Were we boyfriend/girlfriend now? Was I supposed to just walk right up, say,

Hey, beautiful, and kiss her right on the lips again for the whole world to see? Put my arm around her like I owned the place?

Aaron parked, we exited, and started the long walk along the chain-link fence to the entrance of the HVHS school grounds.

Frankie, Tegan, and the gang were at their corner, right between us.

"Help me," I said.

"Huh?" said Aaron.

"What do I say to her?"

"Who?"

"Tegan!"

"I dunno. Whatever you want to say to her. Whatever comes naturally. You guys obviously had a connection yesterday. I seriously doubt that all just disappeared overnight. Follow your instinct."

"Right now, my instinct is telling me to run away."

"If you even try that, I will follow you with my car and I will hit you. And I will keep hitting you with my car until you talk to your girlfriend."

"But *is* she my girlfriend? We never really had that talk. We just kissed. Aaron, I don't know how this works. You know girls. Tell me something useful."

"Be yourself?"

"That's the sort of bullshit advice they give on the Disney Channel!"

It wasn't until now that I realized how hard my heart was beating, like a V-12 engine, hammering blood through my veins like the shit was nitrous oxide. I was breathing so frantically, the oxygen only seemed to be making it halfway to my lungs, never quite getting there. I felt dizzy.

"I can't do this," I said. "I think I'm hyperventilating. I need a paper bag. I can't breathe."

The chain-link fence rattled behind me. First, I noticed that Aaron wasn't walking beside me anymore. Then I saw him scaling the fence like he was a spider monkey or Spider-Man or just a regular old spider. He dropped down on the other side and grinned at me.

"What are you doing?" I said.

"I'm helping you out," said Aaron. "It's always easier to talk to a girl when you don't have a third wheel cramping your style."

"Third wheel? She's with her brother and their two drug-dealing friends! This is already a five-wheeler!"

Aaron winked—like he was some sort of friend and not the biggest traitor in the history of friendkind. And then he walked away.

"Aaron!" I said. "Dammit, Aaron. Get back here!"

Aaron entered the glass double doors of HVHS and abandoned me to the cold, harsh world of girls and talking to them.

I approached the corner until I was standing a good, safe conversational distance away from Tegan. She was laughing at something Carlos said. And then she noticed me. My mouth opened, like I might actually have something more thought-provoking to say than *Phluuughflamphbloooeeeaarrrghhh*, which was all that was really coming to my brain at the moment.

And then Tegan said the most Tegan thing she could possibly say.

"Heya, *Neanderthaaaaaaal*. Ow ow! Mmm, I like me a slice of that caveman ass. That hunka juicy man meat."

Some things never changed. And that was hardly a bad thing.

I couldn't help laughing as she stroked her invisible goatee, leaned to the side, and proceeded to scope out "that caveman ass" in the most conspicuous way possible.

"Why you always playing hard to get, baby?" said Tegan. "You wearin' them panties Mama likes? You wearin' that Neander-thong?"

So much for playing it cool. I was laughing so hard, I was practically hyperventilating.

And then Tegan's eyes lit up and she smiled that infinite smile with those two dimples that were irrationally sexy.

I didn't have a chance to say *Phluuughflamphblooooeeeaarrrghhh* or any variation of it, thank God, because Tegan gave me a hug cleverly disguised as a flying jump attack. Her arms wrapped around me, and her legs wrapped around me, and I didn't have time to catch her anywhere but by her butt, and she didn't seem to mind that at all.

"Hey," she said with her face inches from mine.

"Hey," I said back.

I didn't realize how much I was smiling until I kissed her. *I*, Clifford Hubbard, kissed *her*!

It was the only thing I could do. The universe demanded it.

Maybe Aaron knew what he was talking about after all.

———

It wasn't that the List wasn't as important to me anymore. It was. It was my purpose. My lifeline. I may not have fully understood the List, but what it lacked in comprehensibility, it made up for in the simple fact that it *felt* right.

But suddenly, my life purpose was being distracted by my hormones.

I didn't have any classes with Tegan. This resulted in my introduction to a form of torture I didn't even know existed. When the lunch bell finally rang, I had a weird thought:

Whom would I sit with?

I was funneling with the student cattle into the lunch room, and by some weird chance, I happened to spot Tegan and Aaron simultaneously—Tegan standing by the wall with Frankie, Jed, and Carlos—and Aaron sitting by himself in the spot that used to be equipped with an invisible quarantine force field.

Okay, here were the facts as I knew them:

1. I *had* to sit with Tegan, otherwise I was just inviting awkwardness into whatever it was that we had going on. Also, I would die because I already appeared to be experiencing a severe case of Tegan withdrawal.
2. I would be the Supreme Overlord of Assbutts if I didn't sit with Aaron. I mean, he was kind of the reason Tegan and I even had a thing to begin with.

And then Tegan saw me. And her face lit up all over again, and then she pointed at Aaron, which was weird, until I realized that she *wasn't*, in fact, pointing at Aaron, but rather she was pointing to the extra lunch tray at his table, kitty-corner from him, right next to where I always sat. And then Aaron saw me, and he proceeded to give me the most obvious wink in the universe.

Here was the thing. Even though Tegan was sitting with us, small talk didn't even *exist* in the Aaron Universe.

"So I'm sure Cliff already told you that I saw God," said Aaron, "and that he gave us a List of things to do to make Happy Valley High School a better place."

I was eating a taco. This was only a pertinent detail because I immediately proceeded to *choke* on said taco.

Tegan stopped chewing. She swallowed awkwardly. And then she nodded—slowly, like she was still considering her answer. "Yeah, I mighta heard something 'bout that."

Well, shit on a stick.

"The whole school's kinda talking about it," said Tegan as an afterthought.

Shit. On. A. Stick.

Aaron didn't seem fazed. He didn't even blink.

"Good," he said.

"I don't know if *good* is the word I'd use," said Tegan.

"What word would you use?"

"Um. *Crunk*, maybe?"

"Oh, c'mon. You don't believe in God?"

"I mean . . . I don't *not* believe in God. If Tupac can come back to life, I'm sure Jesus can too."

"Wait, what?" I said. "Tupac *is* dead, isn't he?"

"Oh nuh-uh," said Tegan. She shook her head and shot me a deadly serious look. "Tupac is alive. Trust me."

Aaron and I exchanged confused looks.

"Anyway, it's cool," said Tegan. "People believe some crazy shit, but if it doesn't hurt anybody, I don't got a problem with it. Carlos, for example? He believes that God is actually part of an alien race called the Annunaki who came here from Planet X to mine for gold, and, like, their only purpose for us is to be their slave mine workers. Although Carlos only talks about that shit when he's torched. When he's not high, I think he's a Protestant."

"Hey, everybody's gotta believe in something," said Aaron—*still* unfazed. "We're all like Rice Krispies Treats, and having something to believe in is the marshmallow glue that holds us all together."

"Hells yeah! That's what I'm sayin'!"

I didn't know how these two became my friends, but it was so simultaneously weird and awesome, I couldn't even.

"Also," said Tegan, "any list that tells you to stop Niko or to put that uppity bitch Esther in her place is all right by me. So if you guys need help or whatever, count me in."

"What?" I said.

"Seriously?" said Aaron.

Aaron and I *did* need help with the List—namely writing our speech for the Sermon Showdown, which sure as hell wasn't going to write itself. And, as I had learned less than twenty-four hours ago, Tegan was something of a writer herself. I mean, they were probably rap lyrics and this was a Sermon Showdown—but those were better qualifications than Aaron and I had combined.

"Tomorrow," said Tegan. "Same time, same place. We plan like hell. Then we kick this List in the ass."

SEVENTEEN

The next day at lunch, Aaron, Tegan, and I came ready to get down to business. I had to hand it to Tegan: she gave one helluva pump-up speech.

Unfortunately, she also had the focus and attention span of a toddler gacked out on Halloween candy.

Aaron had barely even *mentioned* the Sermon Showdown when Tegan saw Jack and Julian pass by wearing matching Marvel Comics shirts (yes, *matching*), and she started raving about the new Avengers movie, and oh my God, Iron Man is the greatest Marvel superhero ever, blah-blah-blah.

Oooooooh boy. So much for the List. Ten minutes later, this was the conversation that ensued:

"Superman is *easily* the best superhero," said Aaron. "I can't believe we're even having this conversation."

"Superman is *easily* the most two-dimensional superhero," I said. "I mean, he's this all-powerful alien entity who's basically invincible *except* that he has an all-crippling weakness to Kryptonite. One second, he's kicking ass and taking names, the next, 'Oh no, Lex Luthor has alien rocks!' Sorry. Not buying it."

"But he shoots lasers out of his eyes!"

"Yeah," said Tegan. "And he wears red undies over his blue tights. Kinda sketch."

"Who wears red underwear anyway?" I said.

"I'm wearing red panties," said Tegan.

"Yes. And that's awesome."

"It *is* awesome."

"Um," said Aaron, "how did we go from Superman to Tegan's panties?"

"The fact of the matter is that Tegan's red panties are awesome," I said. "And Superman is overrated."

"You two aren't American."

"Whatev, man," said Tegan. "Everyone knows that Batman is the best superhero."

Aaron and I groaned simultaneously.

"What?" said Tegan.

"Batman isn't even a superhero," said Aaron.

"He doesn't have a superpower," I said. "Thus disqualifying him from the hall of fame of superherodom."

"Shut your whore mouths," said Tegan. "Of course Batman has a superpower."

"Really?" said Aaron. "And that would be . . . ?"

"Justice. And money."

"Okay, this conversation needs to end," I said. "Because Spider-Man is the best superhero, bar none."

"Spider-Man is the best at kissing upside down," said Tegan. "That's it."

At this point, I was basically ready for anything to end this conversation. It was all fun and games until someone insulted Spider-Man. Then a shadow fell over us.

It was Niko.

He just stood there. Like a literal mountain, motionless and immovable.

"'Sup, bro," said Tegan. "Can we help you with something?"

But Niko wasn't looking at Tegan. He wasn't looking at Aaron, either.

His eyes were locked and loaded on me. I suddenly felt very naked. And for a six-foot-six, 250-pound mass of flesh, that's a lotta nudity.

And then the mountain moved. He extended his beefy arm—I may or may not have flinched—and he set an object on the table in between Tegan and me.

A Nintendo 3DS. With a game cartridge inside.

I stared. Aaron stared. Tegan, meanwhile, glanced between the awestruck expressions on our faces and the weird Nintendo thingy on the table, possibly wondering if she had just witnessed some sort of rare symbolic male initiatory ritual.

And then Niko turned and left. Just like that. Like this wasn't a big deal. A *huge* deal!

"Hey, Niko," I said.

Niko stopped and turned around.

"Superman, Batman, Spider-Man," I said. "Who's the best super-hero?"

If Niko thought this was a random, borderline-idiotic question, it didn't show on his face.

"Wolverine," he said. "Duh."

"*Hmm*," said Tegan. She nodded approvingly. "With his healing power, he *is* basically invincible. But in a cool way. Not like Superman."

"And," said Aaron, "the fact that he's had adamantium surgically bonded to his skeletal structure not only makes him *double* invincible, but it also makes him a total badass."

Niko didn't seem to know how to react to our positive appraisal of Wolverine. He nodded awkwardly. And then he started to turn and—

"Hey, Niko," I said. "Do you want to sit with us?"

Niko paused to consider this. "Yeah, okay."

Niko sat down a seat away from me, leaving an empty seat between us. I could have interpreted this as social hesitation, but really, it was just common sense. Even Lacey Hildebrandt's skinny ass would have a hard time squeezing into that empty seat against the immensity of our combined girth.

I glanced at Aaron, and he glanced at me, and something passed between us. Something that defied words. Something that defied logic. I didn't know what it was, and I didn't know if God had anything to do with it, and I didn't even know if Aaron had a concussion, but I knew one thing for damn certain:

The List wasn't crazy. The List was bigger than Aaron. It was bigger than Tegan, it was bigger than Niko, and it was bigger than me. And I'm HUGE.

It was bigger than all of us.

———

There are certain conversations that should just never happen, ranked among the likes of "How many squares of toilet paper should you wipe your butt with?" (the Environmentalism vs. Sanitaryism Argument) or "Is it okay to have sex with your cousin if she's, like, really, really, really hot?" As Aaron and I entered Mr. Gibson's computer lab, Jack and Julian were embarking on a Level 5 Is This Conversation Seriously Happening?

"Dude, it's not even a question," said Julian. "Boa Hancock from *One Piece* is *easily* the hottest anime chick."

"Wow, what a sellout answer," said Jack. "Do you even anime, bro?"

"That's like saying Kim Kardashian is a sellout answer. Are we analyzing her media overexposure, moral integrity, and overall depth as a human being? No. But her body's so hot, it could start forest fires."

"Scientifically impossible."

"It's called hyperbole, Jack. There's a very real fire in my heart, and it burns for Hancock."

"No, man. It's all about Yoko from *Gurren Lagann*. Not only is she a babe and a half, but she's more emotionally mature than the entire male cast combined. Also, she has a sniper rifle that shoots lasers."

"Oh, snap. I forgot about Yoko." Julian clutched his chest dramatically. "Ah, my heart! It's being torn asunder!"

Aaron cleared his throat. "Are we . . . interrupting?"

Somehow, Jack and Julian were just now noticing us. And then they noticed the 3DS in Aaron's hands.

"Holy shit," said Jack.

"Holy apeshit," said Julian.

And as they gaped in awe at the Holy Grail of handheld gamedom radiating celestial light from Aaron's hand, he walked over and set it on the desk in front of them. But he didn't let go. Not right away.

"You two are going to find out who HAL is for us," said Aaron. "Right?"

Jack met Aaron's gaze with an earnestness that he probably only reserved for anime porn. "We will give you HAL's identity on a silver platter."

·EIGHTEEN

It was just me, Aaron, and the List.

And Quentin Tarantino's entire filmography.

And a plethora of deep-fried things.

It may have seemed like these *other* things were distracting from our main focus—the List—but I liked to think of them as moral support.

Mr. and Mrs. Zimmerman were just heading out the door when I arrived. They had a reservation at Auberge de l'Ouvre. Which was a restaurant, apparently.

I didn't know how old Mrs. Zimmerman was, but she *looked* like a Victoria's Secret model. But, you know, fully clothed. And Mr. Zimmerman looked and walked and even *smelled* like the sort of guy who married Victoria's Secret models—like he was the perfect genetic zenith of success.

In other words, a forty-something version of Aaron.

"So you're the famous Cliff Hubbard," said Mr. Zimmerman. "Your dad's Hank Hubbard, am I right?"

My dad did, indeed, have a first name. And it was Hank. And holy shit. How did this guy know my dad?

I just nodded stupidly.

"Hank and I used to play football together at your high school. He was one heck of a running back, but then he tore a tendon...um... his senior year, I think? Shame, too, 'cause he was fast. Your dad was lightning."

He might have lost his ability to run, but one thing was for damn certain: his fists were still lightning.

"So are you on the team with Aaron?"

There was no need to make this weird. So I lied.

"Yup," I said.

"Great! What position do you play?"

"The one that hits people."

"Ah," said Mr. Zimmerman, unfazed, because his genetic code did not allow him to be fazed or confused by sarcasm. "Lineman. Gotcha. One of my best friends growing up was a lineman. That guy could eat a whole buffalo if you let him."

He chuckled at his own joke that wasn't really a joke.

"You two have fun," said Mrs. Zimmerman. "Money for the pizza is on the fridge."

And with that, Mr. and Mrs. Zimmerman departed for their reservation at Le French-Ass Restaúrant.

Aaron looked at me. "Twinkies?"

I reciprocated the look. "Twinkies."

There is a deep, dark secret in the culinary world, and that is this: everything is better deep-fried.

Everything.

Do you like cookie dough? Deep-fry it. Watermelon? Deep-fry that healthy shit. Bacon? Those wonderfully delicious strips of juicy pork ecstasy saturated in oil and grease and fat with the power to end wars and cure vegetarianism?

Deep-fry it.

Aaron had just paid the Pizza Hut delivery guy and decided that our Meat Lovers Stuffed Crust masterpiece wasn't nearly greasy enough to stop our hearts by the end of *The Hateful Eight*. So we were going to deep-fry a few slices of that, too.

At long last, we evacuated the kitchen with our deep-fried delicacies, popped in *Reservoir Dogs*, bombarded the sofa with our butts, and watched the aftermath of a diamond heist that had gone horribly, horribly wrong. It was right about the time that Mr. White was driving a speeding car while trying to comfort Mr. Orange, who was bleeding profusely in the backseat, when Aaron said:

"Did you know Mr. Spinelli won the Montana Teacher of the Year award?"

So much for watching *Reservoir Dogs*.

I turned to Aaron with a half-chewed deep-fried fudge-covered Oreo in my mouth, and said "*Whaaaaaghhh?*" And then I made an awkward attempt to swallow. After nearly choking, I retried: "WHAT?"

"Yeah," said Aaron. "I googled him, and that's the first thing that came up."

"Why in the holy name of Quentin Tarantino would you google Mr. Spinelli?"

"I thought it would pull up his e-mail from the school directory or something. I was going to write him an apology letter."

"Oh," I said. And now I felt shitty all over again. But I felt shitty *and* curious, which was at least mildly distracting from the shittiness factor. "Teacher of the Year?"

"For the whole state of Montana! Do you know how big of a deal that is?"

I'm sure my face was ninety-eight percent cynical and two percent something else. Indigestion, maybe?

"Where did you read that?" I said. "How do we know this is a reliable source?"

"I didn't read it. It was on the news. Well, technically it was on YouTube. But yeah, that news. Here, look."

Aaron whipped out his phone and pulled up the video. He then shoved it in front of my face and pressed Play.

"We're here at the small town of Happy Valley," said Sandra Shelley of KXLH, "where the Montana Professional Teaching Foundation has awarded their annual Teacher of the Year award to fifty-one-year-old Roger Spinelli."

Video footage of Spinelli appeared on the screen, in action, teaching in the classroom, but something was staggeringly wrong because he was smiling, and he was using all these wildly captivating hand gestures, and the students were smiling, and they were even laughing.

"Spinelli has taught ninth- through twelfth-grade English at Happy Valley High School," said Sandra offscreen. "And his teaching method is always an adventure."

"The fact of the matter is it's not about the teaching," said Spinelli in a standing interview outside of a slightly newer, cleaner, and overall *happier* HVHS. "It's about the learning. Too many teachers get so caught up in the mechanics of the lesson plan that they lose sight of *who* they're giving it to. I make it a goal not to get comfortable in my curriculum. I experiment with new things because I *can*. I teach because I love it, and I care about these kids. They make me smile, they make me laugh, and they always keep me coming back for more."

"But don't take Spinelli's word for it," said Sandra. "The students speak for themselves."

"I always hated English," said a girl with braces, grinning so wide that nearly every single bracket was unsheathed. "But with Mr. Spinelli...I don't know, it's weird. You know that he cares about you and that makes you want to hear what he has to say."

"Mr. Spinelli is tight," said an olive-skinned kid. "Spinelli is the bomb. He's funny, he's smart, he's loving...It's like he's family. It's like *we're* a family. I'm actually gonna be sad when school ends."

"And there you have it," said Sandra. "It just goes to show the difference one teacher can make. Back to you, Ron."

The video ended.

"What. Was. That," I said. It wasn't a question. It was the breathless declaration of one who had witnessed the unthinkable. It wasn't a question because there couldn't possibly be an answer. But Aaron tried anyway.

"Apparently he used to be a good teacher," said Aaron.

"Montana Teacher of the Year!" I said. "I mean, Montana's a big state. You can fit a lot of teachers inside Montana. And for one year, Spinelli was the best? I can't even wrap my brain around that. Next to my dad, he's probably the most evil old quaffle I know."

"Well, it was an old interview. A lot can change over time."

"A lot? As in, *everything* about Spinelli?"

Aaron shrugged. "Maybe Google will have the answer."

I rolled my eyes. "You and your Google. While you're at it, could you ask the Googles how many deep-fried fudge-covered Oreos it takes to kill a person? Because I'm on number thirteen."

Aaron ignored me, opting instead to scroll and click and scroll and click. I decided to take my chance with death and ate another Oreo.

Suddenly, Aaron's eyes went wide as his mouth fell apart. "Holy shit."

"What?"

Aaron's eyes darted from side to side as he continued reading. "Oh my God."

"AARON, WHAT?"

He handed me the phone. The headline sucker-punched me in the eyeballs.

WOMAN KILLED BY TEENAGE DRUNK DRIVER

KALISPELL, MT—A 16-year-old driver was indicted last Monday for a first offense underage DUI and vehicular homicide after allegedly slamming into another vehicle in a high-speed crash, killing the driver.

The late-night crash occurred Saturday as the teen was driving south on Sunset Boulevard. He ran a red light at the corner of Center Street and hit a car driven by Helen Spinelli, 50. By the time the ambulance arrived, Spinelli was pronounced dead.

"It's a small town," said Gary Lamar, who witnessed the scene. "I know both families. It's an unfortunate tragedy, and really, all you can do is pray for everyone involved."

Though it is currently uncertain whether or not the teen will be tried as an adult, police have stated that possibility is "not likely."

"We're well aware of everyone's suffering in a situation like this," said Chief of Police Rodney Bassett. "We're conducting a very thorough investigation, taking all factors into consideration. We intend for the justice system to work in its most meaningful capacity."

Helen's husband, Roger Spinelli, is an English teacher at Happy Valley High School.

I stopped reading.

"No wonder he hates teenagers," said Aaron. "A teenager killed his wife."

I looked at the top of the article. It was dated December 22.

"Three days before Christmas," I said.

"Jesus Christ," said Aaron.

Jesus Christ, indeed. Most people didn't know what death did to a person. But I did. If I was Spinelli, I would hate teenagers. I would hate God. I would even hate myself. Because why not?

"Well, we know what the problem is," said Aaron. "So what the hell's the solution? How do we remind Mr. Spinelli why he chose to teach?"

I tried to consider the question. But I didn't. *I couldn't.* Maybe I didn't know the *solution* per se, but I knew something that superseded the formula of what we were trying to do.

"It's not about reminding him why he chose to teach," I said.

"What do you mean? That's what the List says."

"I know what the List says. But forget the List for a sec. Mr. Spinelli is broken, okay? And when something is broken, it doesn't work."

"Okay . . ." said Aaron. "So what do we do?"

"Living things always repair themselves. Plants regrow. Bones heal. Cells regenerate. What we need to do is remind Mr. Spinelli that he's still *alive*. Once we do that, the rest will take care of itself. Mr. Spinelli will remind *himself* why he chose to teach."

Aaron gave me a skeptical look. "That's the most Freudian-ass shit I've ever heard in my entire life. What does that even mean?"

"Whatever, I just know how that feels, okay? I thought I was broken beyond repair. And then someone reminded me that I was still alive."

"Really? Who?"

"You, asshat!"

Tagging *asshat* at the end was supposed to make it funny. But Aaron just stared at me with this weird look on his face that I couldn't even begin to discern.

"What?" I said.

"It's strange," said Aaron. "I feel like I've spent the last sixteen *years* in a coma, and I'm just now waking up."

———

Aaron was sprawled on the couch, and I had the La-Z-Boy kicked back in full horizontal, watching *Pulp Fiction* past the summit of my gut. It was right about when John Travolta and Uma Thurman were doing their dance-off at Jack Rabbit Slim's that I drifted into semiconscious oblivion.

"Cliff?"

I blinked. And then I blinked another dozen times. Finally, I registered that the end credits were rolling.

"Whoa," I said. "Alrighty then. *Jackie Brown.* Bring it on."

But Aaron didn't move, and my brain was failing to send the necessary electrical impulses to the rest of my body.

"Have you ever done something really bad?" said Aaron.

Huh?

I turned my sleep-intoxicated head to Aaron. His eyes were wide open—beyond sleepless—trained on the ceiling.

"Um . . ." I said. I blinked again, trying to comprehend the question. "You do know who you're talking to, right? I don't think I've ever done a thing that *wasn't* really bad."

"No, I mean *really* bad. Something you can't forgive yourself for. You *want* to forgive yourself for it, and you *need* to forgive yourself for it . . . but you just can't."

My thoughts inevitably drifted to Shane—that he killed himself and that he must have killed himself for a reason. But a part of me knew that *I* wasn't the reason. At least not directly.

"I still like Lacey," said Aaron.

"What?"

"I think . . . I dunno. Maybe I even love her."

My hand fumbled for the lever on the side of the recliner, and I ejected myself upright.

"What are you talking about?" I said. "Just the other day, you were telling me that she's not your type anymore."

Aaron was still staring at the ceiling, studying the popcorn texture like it was a galaxy—a universe—of stars aligned into an indecipherable meaning.

"I cheated on Lacey."

I nodded slowly, processing. Actually, that wasn't surprising at all. In fact, it sounded like the most pre-List Aaron thing that Aaron could possibly have done. Of course he cheated on her! Why else wouldn't they be together anymore?

"Okay," I said. "People screw up. Have you two . . . you know . . . talked about it?"

"It's complicated," said Aaron.

"How complicated could it be?"

Aaron sighed in that way that prefaces the beginning of a long story.

"We were planning a surprise birthday party for Lacey," he said. "Heather Goodman and me. Heather was Lacey's best friend, and Lacey and I had been dating for six months—longer than I'd dated anyone else—so if *anyone* was going to throw a surprise party for her, it made sense for *us* to do it. And it started off great! I told Lacey that football practice would be running overtime in preparation for the next game, and Heather told her that she had family coming into town. Heather's family had this cabin out toward Whitefish. It was big enough, had a sweet fire pit, and was way out in the middle of nowhere so we wouldn't have to worry about noise complaints. Heather had everything mapped out—shopping lists for supplies, ideas for decorations, food and catering, cake—the whole shebang. She even had an older cousin who was going to supply the booze. We spent the first day shopping for decorations and planning where everything would go. Then we get back to the cabin and . . . we accidentally kissed."

"*Accidentally* kissed?" I said. "How do you *accidentally* kiss?"

"And then we accidentally had sex."

Apparently, we were using the word *accident* in the context of poor decision making.

"We did it *two more* times before the birthday party," said Aaron.

"No," I said.

"The thing you have to understand about my and Heather's relationship was that it wasn't romantic. It was purely sexual. Almost businesslike. Except I was cheating on my girlfriend, and Heather was screwing over her best friend, and the guilt was too much for either of us to handle. So, in order to cope with the guilt, we kept . . . you know . . . *doing* it. It was a sort of therapeutic self-destruction. Unfortunately, it gets worse."

"You're kidding. How could it possibly get worse?"

Once again, Aaron gave that tragic sigh.

"The night of the party, I was in charge of Lacey. Heather was in charge of the 'surprise.' We had it all figured out: I would take Lacey out on a romantic one-on-one camping trip. Lacey *hates* camping. Last minute, I would reveal that we were actually staying at a cabin. Meanwhile, Heather would direct traffic and make sure everyone made it to the cabin and got into position in time. When we finally got there and everyone jumped out and shouted 'Surprise!' Lacey started crying. Like, happy crying. Anyway, Lacey got hammered to the point of no return. She was playing drinking games with Kyle and Desmond and some other guys—California Kings, I think. For whatever reason, Heather and I decided to sit out on the same round. I don't know if either of us intended to do that, but at some point, I looked at her, and she looked at me, and there was this sense of . . . completion, I guess. We had set out to plan the best surprise party ever, and it was. Then like five minutes later, we were in one of the upstairs bedrooms."

"What?"

"And then Lacey walked in."

"What?"

"Oh yeah. She just walks in, makes direct eye contact with both Heather *and* me, and then, without saying a word, she calmly walks out and shuts the door behind her. And that was the last that was ever said about it."

"What do you mean, that was the last that was ever said about it?" I asked. "Nothing was said!"

"Exactly," said Aaron.

If Aaron was any less direct, I swear, he'd be talking backward.

"Look," said Aaron. "Heather and I were so freaked-out, we decided to let Lacey bring the incident up herself. Heather offered to drive Lacey home that night. Lacey never brought it up. I pulled her aside at school the next day and asked how she was doing. She said she was great. And if you know Lacey, her sarcasm is so on point, you almost have to be psychic to tell the difference."

"And you kept dating?" I said.

Aaron grimaced. "We kept dating for another month. It was a solid month of hell—mostly because I couldn't relax around her. I felt like I was dating a double agent or something. Like, the moment I let my guard down, she might snap my neck. So I became distant. And my distance made her distant. And then we mutually broke up. Heather and I never screwed around after that. She was going through the same thing as me—interacting with Lacey on pins and needles, waiting for the bomb to drop. But it never did. After all this time, Lacey has never said a word about it."

I nodded silently, taking in Aaron's story. I was a roll of paper towels, tasked with mopping up a geyser.

"So, what?" I said. "Did she see you, or didn't she?"

Aaron threw his hands in the air. "Hell if I know. Either she was so drunk that she didn't process what she saw—which is a definite possibility, one that I might have wrecked our relationship over—or she *did* see us, and just . . . I dunno . . . switched off the part of her brain that deals with cheating bastards and backstabbing best friends."

"And you're still in love with her."

Aaron shrugged hopelessly. "Maybe. I think so. Yeah."

Somebody call the CW. I'd just found their new teen drama.

"Aaron," I said. "You need to tell her the truth. The whole truth. And nothing but the truth."

"Nice try, Judge Judy. But no way. That ship has sailed. There's no way I can tell her the truth now."

"Now that you're not dating? Because if you ask me, now seems like the *perfect* time."

"Oh, c'mon. It's not like there aren't other people caught up in this. Things are finally normal with Heather and Lacey again. If I throw that stick in the spokes of Heather and Lacey's bicycle of friendship, it'll beef."

"Aaron?"

"Yeah?"

"That was probably the dumbest metaphor I've ever heard."

"You know what I mean."

"So, what? You're just going to keep your feelings pent up inside of you forever and ever until you either have a psychological breakdown or you spontaneously combust?"

"Um, yeah, duh. Let's go with door number two."

It was clear I wouldn't win this argument. I let it go. I leaned back in the recliner, and Aaron unspooled on the sofa. His eyes drifted back to the ceiling.

"I think I know why God chose me for this List," said Aaron. "I think he wanted to find the shittiest person in Happy Valley and give him a chance to unshitify himself."

"I guess that explains why I'm your sidekick," I said. "Because I'm definitely the second-shittiest person."

NINETEEN

The next morning, Aaron and I shook off our deep-fried food coma, crawled off our furniture sleeping apparatuses, and staggered into the kitchen. The thing about a night of raging gluttony is that it expands your stomach, leaving you to wake up in a state of starvation.

"Need . . . cereal," I moaned.

Aaron laughed nervously. "About that . . ."

He opened the cereal cupboard. Except it *wasn't* a cereal cupboard. It was the Gateway to Fat Person Hell. He looked at me and added, "Have I mentioned my parents are health nuts?"

"What. Is. That?" I said.

Instead of answering my question, Aaron proceeded to awkwardly rattle off the titles of quote/unquote "cereal."

"Raisin Bran, Fiber One, Quaker Oatmeal Squares . . ."

No. No. No.

"Kashi Go Lean, Peace Cereal with Goji Berry and Chia, Grape-Nuts . . ."

God no.

"And Cinnamon Toast Crunch," said Aaron. He turned and faced me, completely deadpan. "Which would you like?"

I stared at Aaron. "Did you really just ask me that?"

"I try not to make stereotypical assumptions."

"How sensitive of you. Now hand over the Cinnamon Toast Crunch."

I rummaged through the dinnerware cupboard. There I discovered what was either a large cereal bowl or a small mixing bowl. I filled it to the top. When I poured the milk in, the cereal formed a treacherous mushroom cloud over the rim.

Aaron stared at me and my cereal like we were a pair of escaped convicts.

"Don't judge me," I said.

"I'm not judging you."

"I can feel you judging me. I see it in your eyes."

Aaron poured himself a bowl of—heaven help him—Quaker Oatmeal Squares, and sat down across the table from me. Shoved one hefty spoonful in his mouth. Chewed. Swallowed. He then rested his spoon on the side of his bowl, interlocked his fingers, and shot me a deliberating look. His face was a little too serious, countered harshly by his bed hair, sticking up like the Berlin Wall on the right side of his head.

"Show Frankie's gang a better way," said Aaron.

"Hmph?" I said through a mouthful of cereal.

"Number four on the List: show Frankie's gang a better way. How do we do that?"

I swallowed. "Better question: What does that even mean? A better way of *what*? Pushing pot?"

"Yeah, that's definitely what God meant." Aaron rolled his eyes.

"Hey, just . . . thinking outside the box," I mumbled.

I shoved another spoonful of cereal into my mouth so as to shut myself up.

"*I* know how we can show Frankie's gang a better way," said Aaron.

I swallowed again. "What? How?"

"Tegan."

It took a moment for that to sink in. I shook my head vigorously. "No. No, Aaron. Just because she's my, like, *girlfriend* or whatever, that doesn't mean she'll, like—"

"Help us with the List?" said Aaron. "Because from what I understand, she already agreed to do that."

Aaron was right. She *did* agree to help us.

I sighed. "Okay. Maybe you're right."

"I am?"

Aaron seemed shocked that I would agree with him so easily. Surely, there had to be a catch.

"We probably *do* need Tegan's help," I said. "But we can talk to her on Monday. Right now, I want to focus on something else."

"Something else?"

"*Someone* else," I said. "Our Montana Teacher of the Year."

———

After a quick phone call to Jack Halbert, we managed to extract Mr. Spinelli's home address—with one stipulation.

"Don't tell him I gave it to you," said Jack. "That man scares me."

Once upon a time, this seemed like a good idea. But that felt like a long time ago. The moment we hopped in Aaron's car, plugged the address into Google Maps, and set off on the proverbial Road to Redemption, I realized I had no clue in hell what I was doing.

So far, my plan involved the word *sorry* used in excess. I wanted to call it a work in progress. But that implied progress.

Aaron slowed down as we neared his address. Naturally, my heart rate accelerated.

And then I saw Mr. Spinelli.

I actually stared at him for a solid five seconds before I realized who he was. He stood on the left side of the street, three houses ahead, checking his mail. The fact that he wearing nothing but boxers and a bathrobe was almost forgivable. So was the bottle he was carrying—what appeared to be vodka—which was massive enough to make all of Mother Russia nod their *ushanka*-wearing heads in respect.

The unforgivable part was his front lawn. Because it wasn't a lawn. It was the motherfucking Congo.

Seriously, the grass was over a foot tall in places. To make matters worse, it was on Gleason Avenue. The neighborhood was hardly extravagant, but it sure as hell wasn't slummy. This was solid middle-class suburbia, and Spinelli's house, by association, looked like the trashiest POS this side of Arcadia Park.

"Mother of pearl," said Aaron. "That's like a half gallon of Smirnoff."

"The vodka?" I said. "The *vodka* is what you're noticing here?"

"I mean, his lawn is scary, too. But no wonder it looks like shit. He probably can't even mow straight."

Spinelli didn't notice Aaron's car creeping conspicuously up the street. He grabbed his mail out of the mailbox, shuffled up his driveway, and shut the door.

I hadn't noticed the door until now. There were several sheets of paper haphazardly attached to it like a bulletin board.

Aaron parked on the opposite side of the street. I was out of the car before he even shut off the engine. I veered across the street, on a vicious course to Spinelli's house.

"Whoa, Cliff, hold up!"

If someone were to ask me what the hell I was doing, I would have given them a firm *I dunno*. But my curiosity was a missile, and I had to know what those papers were all about.

If one of those was an eviction notice . . .

. . . because he couldn't pay the rent . . .

. . . because he quit his teaching job . . .

. . . because of us . . .

I missiled my ass straight to his front door and ripped off a paper—one of three—on his door. Aaron caught up behind me and silently read over my shoulder. This notice had the most recent date, and was immensely long, and even more immensely boring—despite the threat, which was mildly alarming. I would be doing a great disservice against humanity to quote its monotonous bullshit verbatim, but it essentially said:

> *Dear Home-Owning Bitch,*
>
> *We're the Home Owner's Association, and you're in a crap-ton o' trouble. This is your third warning, in case you can't count the papers still taped to your door. Due to your inability to pull your shitty lawn together, we are charging your raggedy ass a $500 fine. We invite you to a hearing before our HOA Board of Evil Douchemongers where we can negotiate a resolution, and the fine can possibly be waived. But not likely, schmuck.*
>
> *Sincerely,*
> *Your Executioners*

Okay, so the letter exercised a little more social restraint than that, but you could just smell the condescension. I hated these HOA assholes, and I didn't even know them. And Spinelli obviously hated them too and cared about their threats about as much as he cared about wearing pants. He wasn't going to do shit about his lawn.

"Shit," said Aaron.

Shit, indeed. I came to three conclusions:

1. If we tried to talk or apologize to Spinelli, he would slam the door in our faces before we got two words in.
2. If we persisted, he would probably call the cops.
3. We didn't need to talk to him to mow his lawn.

Now, to tackle Problem Number One—where were we going to get a lawn mower?

My gaze drifted to his garage door.

It was worth a shot.

"Cliff?" said Aaron.

I approached the garage door and lifted. There was nothing holding it shut. In fact, the flimsy metal thing practically flew open.

"Whoa, whoa, whoa!" said Aaron. "What are you doing?"

"I'm just looking for a lawn mower," I said.

Aaron rolled his eyes. "Of course you are. What else would you be doing?"

Contrary to the anarchy that was Spinelli's lawn, the garage was actually organized—albeit covered in a blanket of dust.

A push mower was parked in the back corner.

I marched into Spinelli's garage like I was the Queen of Sheba.

"You know," said Aaron, "there's a fine line between being a Good Samaritan and breaking and entering."

I ignored Aaron. I unscrewed the gasoline lid and peeked inside. It was hard to gauge the gas level, but it looked a little on the low side.

Definitely not enough to tackle the jungles of Congo that awaited. However, I didn't need to look five feet to find the portable gasoline container on the dusty shelf beside me. I filled up the tank, screwed the lid on, and pushed the mower out onto the driveway. And then I pulled the starter cord.

Nothing.

"Well, that was fun," said Aaron. "Now let's get the hell—"

I pulled the cord again.

And again and again and again and again and again and—

VROOOOOOOOOOOOOM!

The lawn mower roared victory, and I added my own victory cry.

"Okay," said Aaron. He flapped his arms at his side. "This is happening. Great. Awesome."

I ignored Aaron and plowed into the wild Congo. But the thing about mowing grass this tall...is that lawn mowers can't. They just can't. The mower stalled within five feet.

"Guuuuuhhhhhhhh!"

I backed the mower up, allowing it to regurgitate the mutilated grass chunks it couldn't swallow. Then I pulled the cord again. Fortunately, the engine was warmed up, and it started effortlessly.

"THANK YOU," I said.

I pushed the mower another five feet. Then it stalled again.

"GYEEEAAAAAAARRRGGGGHHHHH!!!!!"

I followed this abominable pattern for another seven stalls. But whether it was the grace of God or the lawn mower finally pulling its inanimate shit together and becoming the Little Engine That Could, stalling didn't seem to be an issue.

Aaron, meanwhile, disappeared rather ominously into the garage.

When he came out, it was with a weed whacker in hand.

He stood there and revved it a couple of times, staring directly at me. I wouldn't go so far as to say he *wasn't* contemplating chopping me up into little pieces and burying me in Spinelli's floorboards (I doubted Spinelli would be terribly opposed), but Aaron didn't. He just weed-whacked—around the trees, corners, everywhere I couldn't reach with the mower.

The mower didn't have a bag attached, so it was just spitting obliterated grass dust out the side. However, that didn't stop the lawn from looking approximately a bajillion times better. With our powers combined, the lawn was shaping up fast—or at least it didn't look like the Ewok planet from Star Wars. I was moving in a diagonal pattern, and once I had annihilated half the rain forest, the visible improvement was its own reward.

Aaron, meanwhile, was apparently a weed-whacking samurai. He was mostly done—just touching up a few rough spots.

That's when the front door swung open and Spinelli burst out. To no one's surprise, he was still wearing nothing but a bathrobe and boxers.

"Who the...? What the...? Aaron? Cliff? Just what in the hell do you two think you're doing?"

I stopped the mower, and Aaron stopped the weed whacker. We looked at Spinelli. We looked at each other. We looked at the lawn. And then we looked back at Spinelli again.

"What does it look like we're doing?" I said.

"Get the hell off my property. No one asked you to mow my lawn."

"Get the hell back in your house, Mr. Spinelli," said Aaron. "No one wants to see you in your underwear."

The mower and weed whacker roared/buzzed back to life, and we went back to work.

Spinelli's face turned reddish-purplish, like the world's largest beet. "IF YOU DON'T GET OFF MY PROPERTY RIGHT NOW, I'M CALLING THE COPS!"

Aaron stopped the weed whacker again. I stopped the mower. We exchanged a meaningful look. And then we laughed.

"You think the police will arrest us for mowing your shitty lawn?" said Aaron.

Spinelli didn't have a response to that.

We went back to mowing/weed-whacking.

Spinelli stood on his porch watching us for a solid five minutes. Once he realized we were going nowhere, he grumbled unintelligible, possibly made-up profanities under his breath and marched into his house, slamming the door behind him. Aaron finished with the weed whacker and returned it to the garage. I continued mowing—sweaty, nasty, my legs covered in shredded grass.

I felt amazing.

I had nearly finished when Spinelli came back out wearing grass-stained jeans and a ratty flannel shirt. He veered into his garage and came back out with a rake and a heavy-duty trash bag. I finished the last unmowed strip of grass, stopped the mower, and watched him march out onto the finished grass.

"What are you doing?" I said.

"What am I doing? You think I'm just going to let some punk-ass kids do whatever the hell they want with my lawn? I'm cleaning up all this grassy shit you left everywhere. What does it look like I'm doing?"

Spinelli stopped.

He looked around.

"Where'd that Zimmerman kid go?"

Actually, that was an excellent question. I thought he had gone into the garage. Didn't Spinelli see him?

At that moment, Spinelli's front door opened. And out came Aaron. As ill-timed fate would have it, he also happened to be zipping up his fly at *That. Exact. Moment.*

Spinelli's death glare caused Aaron to freeze against the closed door—like a pinned insect.

"Oh, hey," said Aaron. "Sorry, I had to tinkle."

Silence—as long and awkward as middle school.

Aaron shifted uncomfortably. So, as a disclaimer, he added: "But don't worry, I got everything in the pot. I have the precision of a sniper."

And he winked—like only Aaron Zimmerman could.

He quietly walked around the house and disappeared into the garage. *Again.* Spinelli's head rotated 180 degrees—like an owl's—following him every step of the way.

"What the *hell* are you doing in there, Zimmerman?"

Aaron exited the garage with another rake and a kooky grin on his face.

"No." Spinelli shook his head. "Put that away. I don't need your help."

"Um, have you looked in the mirror lately?" said Aaron. "You're like a hundred years old. Of *course* you need my help."

Aaron joined Spinelli on the lawn, raking clumps of mutilated grass into small mountains. For a moment, I thought Spinelli might break his wood-handled rake in half. Instead, he raked—furiously—as if to punish the lawn for letting this happen.

I laughed as I pushed the lawn mower toward the driveway. "You guys are funny."

Spinelli grumbled. "Scrape your shoes off before you walk on the cement. The last thing I need is a bunch of green footprints all over my goddamn driveway."

"Yeah, Cliff," said Aaron. "You uncivilized cretin."

"Lick my anus, dickweasel," I said—to Aaron, not Spinelli.

Spinelli just kept shaking his head.

I wasn't exactly sure how to do this, since the only thing I could wipe my shoes on *was* the grass. So that's what I did. Fortunately, I didn't leave any footprints as I stepped out. I pushed the lawn mower back into its corner in the garage.

Then I saw an edger hanging on the wall.

Hell yeah.

I pulled it down, filled up the gas, and started it. The edger was much more cooperative. It buzzed to life on the first go. I tested the trigger, and the little square blade became a sharp, spinning circle of precision.

As soon as I walked back out of the garage, Spinelli had dropped his rake and trash bag, staring at me like I was Leatherface about to go on a Montana Chainsaw Massacre, *Better Homes and Gardens*-style.

"No," said Spinelli. He was shaking his head so hard, I thought it might topple off. "Hell no. Put that thing back where you found it, Cliff."

"Hey, I'm the one with the sharp, spinning stick of death," I said. "I think you better let me edge your lawn."

Spinelli raked even *more* furiously. If he raked any harder, he might have ripped the grass right out of the ground.

I proceeded to edge Spinelli's lawn, and fortunately, it wasn't a complete train wreck. I managed to cut a (mostly) straight perimeter along the concrete. Considering what it looked like before—like some great green tentacled monstrosity spilling out of the ground—I might as well have been the Landscaping Messiah.

Three trash bags later, Aaron and Spinelli finished raking the lawn. They carried them into the garage, one by one. I finished edging around the same time. When we finished, the three of us stopped and stared at our work, and it was good—except for the traces of grass that my edging had left around the curb. I glanced back at the garage and saw the leaf blower. And then I saw Spinelli eyeing the leaf blower. And then I saw him seeing me see him eyeing the leaf blower.

We both raced into the garage.

"It's mine!" said Spinelli.

"No way, José!" I said.

"Hey now, kids!" Aaron called after us. "You can either take turns with the blower, or no one gets to blow at all!"

I got to the blower first. But just barely. I practically swiped it out of Spinelli's old, decrepit fingers. But that wasn't good enough for Spinelli because he started walking at me, hands out, ready to mug me.

"Give me back my blower, asshole!"

"Sure thing, old man. After I use it. Now back off before you dislocate a hip."

"Damn you!" Spinelli's face was a cherry bomb. "You ... you're just like your fucking brother!"

I stopped. Moving, smiling, breathing ... everything. Because how are you supposed to react when someone uses the person you love the most as an insult?

Spinelli stared at me. His eyes were cold, his face was hard, and he just stared—picking me apart with his eyes. Peeling me open.

Aaron, meanwhile, stared at us like we were an automobile accident.

"I'm sorry," I said. My voice was hollow. "This was a mistake. We'll go."

I turned to leave. Spinelli grabbed my arm.

"Wait," he said.

I looked at Spinelli.

"I . . ." he said. Hesitated. "I'm sorry. That was out of line. My wife would kill me if she ever . . ."

His voice drifted. Every tense knot of muscle in his hundred-year-old body seemed to unravel. His shoulders dropped, heavy with the weight of pure emptiness. His fist unspooled—palms open, fingers numb.

"Anyway," he said, "I'm sorry."

I nodded, slowly. But even my nod was a shadow of a reaction.

We parted ways.

TWENTY

We decided to regroup at Aaron's house. Sweaty, covered in grass, and utterly dejected, we showered (again) and got ready for the day (again). Aaron let me use his bathroom while he used his parents' upstairs. As I toweled off, got dressed, and felt every bead of moisture evaporate off my body, contributing to the frigid bathroom mist, I was harshly reminded that it was April in Montana with a high of fifty-something degrees. So I pulled my lucky hoodie on. I figured my luck was already at a low, and I dared an article of clothing to prove me otherwise.

Contrary to superstition, however, my luck seemed to be on the rise. For starters, Aaron beat me out of the shower and decided to do breakfast (again). After all that yardwork, both of our metabolisms had made the jump to hyperspace. Fortunately, he skipped the cereal shenanigans and went straight to cooking bacon on a long plug-in skillet. He didn't even bother with that "balanced breakfast" nonsense. Just bacon on bacon with a side of bacon.

"I was going to ask you how many slices you wanted," said Aaron, "but then I made a stereotypical assumption and decided to finish off the packet."

"You are wise beyond your years," I said.

"But just you know, we're splitting this fifty-fifty."

"Okay. But if you realize your poor little sissy tummy can't handle all that delicious bacon..."

"Please."

When Aaron finished with the bacon, he divvied up the slices judiciously (there was an odd number, so he broke the last piece in half), set the plates on the table, and we feasted.

"We have a sermon to prepare," said Aaron in between bites. "Unless, of course, we want to look like dipshits."

"I am in favor of *not* looking like a dipshit," I said.

"Do you have any sermon ideas?"

"*Hmmmmmmmmmm.*" The sound effect of my thinking was drawn out for an uncomfortable length of time.

"C'mon. If you could say *anything* to Esther, what would it be?"

"I'd tell her that if people wanted to hear from an asshole, they'd fart."

"That...is an idea. Hmm. Maybe if we had a committee for this...?"

"A committee?"

Aaron stood up from the table—a suddenly determined look on his face—and left. He crossed the living room and disappeared down the hall.

"I'm not following you," I said.

No response.

"I'm finishing this delicious plate of bacon, and I'm going to enjoy it."

Nothing.

"Cold bacon makes the heart cold."

Nope.

"Dammit." I abandoned my fried strips of juicy happiness and chased after him.

I followed the noise of shuffling papers. This led me to the bedroom of the legendary Aaron Zimmerman, which could be summarized in four words:

Sports. Illustrated. Swimsuit. Edition.

No kidding, there appeared to be a decade's worth of the thought-provoking literature, and Aaron had wallpapered the walls with it—bronze skin, cleavage, and swimwear that covered the equivalent two-dimensional surface area of a dishrag.

"Nice décor," I said.

Aaron ignored me. He was busy digging through his backpack and pulling out a week's worth of schoolwork.

I'd left my bacon for this. I demanded attention. "When someone inserts the Book of Aaron in the Bible," I said, "I hope they make it illustrated and include a picture of this bedroom. That would *revolutionize* church as we know it."

Aaron transitioned to digging through his backpack with one hand while he casually extended his middle finger with the other.

"Aha, found it!" he said. He raised a rather thick stack of paper stapled together like it was the honest-to-god Book of Aaron made manifest.

"What is it?"

"The Happy Valley High student directory," said Aaron. "Addresses, phone numbers, bra sizes . . . I've got all the confidential info right here."

"Bra sizes? Hold on. You actually got Jack and Jill to print this out for you?"

"Sure. Let's go with that."

"Wait. You didn't *steal* it from them, did you?"

"*Steal* is a strong word. I prefer 'permanent borrowization via stealth tactics.'"

"You dirty thief!" I said. "So, like, what? Are we seriously gonna call a bunch of random people and tell them we're organizing a committee to write a sermon?"

"Not *random* people. Just whoever we wanna call. I bet I know a particular person with a bra size who you might wanna call."

And thus began the calling.

First, I called Tegan. Aaron called Niko. Then I called Jack Halbert, who informed me that he would invite his other half, Julian, as well.

All yesses so far. At this point, we were excited, and the momentum had us wanting to invite even more people.

"You should invite Lacey," I said.

Even as I said it, I realized that Lacey would hardly be a meaningful contribution to our Sermon Showdown planning committee. After all, she was of the opinion that Aaron had a concussion, and the List was just a delusion of his damaged mind. However, first and foremost, I was Aaron's friend. And, as his friend, I knew that he *had* to come clean with Lacey.

"You should invite your mom," said Aaron.

"Come on, I'm serious."

"So am I."

"You don't even know who my mom is."

"And you don't know who Lacey is. There, we've eliminated two stupid possibilities. Moving on."

"What do you mean, I don't know Lacey?"

"You know *of* Lacey," said Aaron. "But you don't *know* Lacey. Tell me, what sort of person pretends they didn't see you cheat on them with their best friend?"

"Someone who wants to salvage relationships?"

"No, Cliff. Someone who wants to salvage relationships tells you the truth—that they *saw* you cheat—and then, after they've had a fair amount of time to be pissed off and process what you've done, they forgive you—or tell you that they can't. The other sort of person—the person Lacey is—is a time bomb."

"Just last night, you said you might still be in love with her," I said. "Now you're saying she's a time bomb? That makes no sense."

"Look, Cliff, I'm not blaming Lacey for anything. This is my fault. I ruined our relationship, I've come to terms with it, and I'm moving on. There's absolutely no reason for me to tell her I cheated on her. With her best friend. At her birthday party."

"Other than that you might still be in love with her."

"Forget I said that," said Aaron. "It was late, and my brain was running through the Greatest Hits of all my fuckups. That just happens to top the chart. Lacey and I didn't have closure, okay? That's all. I'm not in love with her."

I met Aaron's gaze with the highest form of skepticism. Now I was no psychologist, but this sounded like denial, supersized, with a side of fries. But we had both said our piece, and I respected his right to be an idiot. I relinquished the argument.

"Should I call Noah?" I said.

"Noah *Poulson*?"

"Yeah."

"Hell yeah. Shit, he might write this sermon for us!"

I called.

The dial tone lasted for a small infinity. And then it clicked over to the answering machine:

MR. POULSON: *Well howdy there! This is Pastor Poulson!*
MRS. POULSON: *And this is Pam!*
ESTHER: *And this is Esther!*
NOAH: (*grumbling*): *Noah...*
MR. POULSON: *We can't come to the phone right now because we're busy spreading the good Word of God. Have you accepted Him into your heart? Leave your name, number, and a spiritual message if you feel so inclined, and we'll get back to you as soon as we—!*

There was click on the other end as the phone was lifted off the receiver.

"Hello?" said a voice that was distinctly Noah's.

"Hey, just the guy I wanted to talk to!"

"Cliff?"

"That's my name; don't wear it out."

Jesus Harold Christ, did I actually just say that?

"So...Aaron and I are participating in a Sermon Showdown against your evil sister."

"Yeah, I heard about that," said Noah. He laughed uneasily. "Listen, I know you have good intentions and all, but...are you guys insane? She's going to eat you alive."

"My thoughts exactly. Which leads me to why I'm calling. We want your help pulling this sermon together."

Noah laughed. He kept laughing until he realized that it wasn't a joke.

"You're serious?" he said.

"Deadly serious."

"I'm flattered. Really. But hell no."

"Why not?"

"Mostly because I prefer *not* being crucified upside down by my sister and her cult."

"And sitting on the sidelines is going to put her in her place?"

"It has nothing to do with that. It has to do with provoking the one person who can make my life a living hell. You know, aside from my parents."

"Do you believe in God?"

Yes, I actually said that.

"What does that have to do with anything?" said Noah rather defensively.

"If you believe in God," I said, "which I *know* you do, then you have to believe that he gives a shit that your sister is a psychopath bullying in his name. The question is: Are *you* willing to do something about it?"

Noah was silent on the other end. Aaron was in the middle of a conversation with someone else on his phone, but his words were a blur. All I could hear was Noah's silence.

"*Are* you willing to do something about it?" I said.

"Why are you doing this?" said Noah.

"Because my brother is dead. And I have to believe there's someone up there who gives a shit."

I waited for him to say something until finally—tentatively—I said, "Noah?"

"I'm in," he said.

"Oh. Okay."

I was playing it cool on the outside, but I could feel something big inside of me, steadily growing bigger—this enormity that filled every empty spot inside of me, overflowing.

I gave Noah the when and where—Aaron's house, ASAP—and hung up. When I finally turned my big, stupid grin to Aaron, I noticed he had set his phone down to graze through the HVHS directory for names.

My gaze stayed on Aaron's phone far longer than it should have.

There comes a time when one's self-confidence and purpose are so on point, the feeling of unstoppable-ness that usually follows ends up spiraling wildly out of control. That's probably the best way to explain why I did what I did next.

"Hey," I said. "Did you hear that?"

Aaron glanced up. "Hear what?"

"Your mom?" I said. "I think she was calling for you."

"Huh." Aaron stood up and exited the room. I heard his voice grow distant down the hallway. "Mom? *Mo*-om!"

I grabbed Aaron's phone, fumbled through the contacts, and found Lacey's name. I texted:

Hey, lacey, it's cliff. Stole aaron's phone. We're getting people together to plan the sermon showdown at his house. I think you two need to talk.

"Cliff?" said Aaron's voice, down the hall.

Shit. I texted:

Don't reply. Just come.

I hit the Home button, turned the screen off, and set the phone where Aaron left it. I immediately scanned the room for some convenient distraction. Silly me. Every square inch of his walls was a distraction!

"Cliff!" said Aaron, entering the room. "My mom's not even home. Her car's gone."

Aaron caught me staring a little too intently at the nearest swimsuit model. Maybe I was trying a little too hard because my face was like six inches from the wall, level with her breasts.

"Well, then," said Aaron. "Should I give you three a moment?"

"Sorry," I said, feigning embarrassment. "Boobs. You know."

———

Our committee trickled in like the steady drip of a faucet. First Tegan, then Jack and Julian, then Noah. We congregated in the Zimmermans' living space like patients in the waiting room of a scientific study. Expectations were, more or less, incomprehensible.

"So . . . what are we doing here again?" said Jack.

"We're assembling a committee to discuss the Sermon Showdown," said Aaron.

"Ah. Right. That's what it sounded like over the phone."

"You could say," said Julian, "that you're assembling a *team* to combat the forces of *evil*."

"What?" said Aaron.

"Like the Avengers."

I appreciated Julian's enthusiasm.

"*Evil* is a strong word," said Noah. "The JTs are more like a tumor—destructive, but morally disconnected."

"Like Galactus," said Julian.

"Uh . . ." said Noah.

"Dude," said Tegan. "If we're the Avengers, I totally got dibs on Batman."

"Wrong universe," said Jack. "What you want is the Justice League."

"Um, he's Batman. Pretty sure he can be in whatever the hell universe he damn well pleases."

"No, Jack's right," said Julian. "What you're suggesting is interdimensional travel, which is *highly* improbable. If anyone could do that, maybe Doctor Strange could—but even *that's* questionable."

"Your mouth is moving, but all I hear is 'Wah-wah-wah, I wish I was Batman.'" Tegan opened and closed her right hand like a talking duck to help illustrate.

"Cliff," said Julian. "Can you please explain to Tegan that Marvel and DC are nonintersecting universes?"

"I refuse to participate in this conversation," I said.

"Who else are we waiting for?" said Noah.

"Niko!" Aaron exclaimed, all too eager to change the subject. "We are waiting for Niko. But maybe we can go ahead and get started if he isn't—"

Knock, knock, knock.

Everyone in the room appeared visibly relieved—everyone except for me. Because I knew about one more guest whom Aaron was completely unaware of.

"I'll get it!" I said, leaping up from my seat, probably a little *too* anxious. I left the living room and veered into the entryway, which—thank God—was out of the living room's line of sight. If it *was* Lacey, I figured I should take any sort of control over the situation I could get.

I opened the door. It was Niko. And his face actually *didn't* look like an asymmetrical abomination, which was the highest praise I could give, all things considered.

I don't think anyone had ever been so relieved to see Niko.

"Hey," he said. "I'm here for the ... Sermon Shootout ... thing?"

I simply nodded and directed Niko into the living room.

Aaron was sitting in the recliner, and Jack and Julian were on the love seat whispering indiscernibly to each other, although I was pretty positive I heard the word *larping*. Which left the sofa for Niko, Noah, Tegan, and me. Noah decided to take his chances with the larping and moved to the love seat. Tegan scooted *all* the way over to make room for the combined circumference of my and Niko's butts.

"All right," said Aaron, clapping his hands together. "As you all are well aware, Cliff and I are participating in a Sermon Showdown against Esther Poulson."

"Which is suicide," said Noah.

"Which is, in fact, suicide," Aaron agreed. "Which is why all of you are here. Now, contrary to popular belief, Cliff and I are not very good at public speaking."

"Is that a popular belief?" said Julian.

"He's being sarcastic," Jack whispered.

"Not to mention," said Aaron, "we have no *clue* what we're going to say. That's where you guys come in. We need help. *Aaaaand* that's all I've got. You got anything you wanna add to that, Cliff?"

"Help us," I said. "Please."

"Question," said Julian, raising his hand high. "I have a question."

"Yes, Julian?" said Aaron.

"What is a Sermon Showdown?"

Everyone else nodded their agreement/confusion. Even Noah.

"A fair question," said Aaron. "I think the general idea is that we give a sermon, and Esther gives a sermon, and whoever gives the better sermon wins."

"Who determines which is the better sermon?" said Jack.

"Um . . ." said Aaron.

He looked at me. I shrugged.

"You don't *know*?" said Jack.

"I mean," I said, finally, "when Esther proposed the idea, I think it was to deliver the Sermon Showdown to her congregation. Which, I guess, would make *them* the judges?"

There was a long silence in the room. It was only amplified when Tegan whistled like a bomb was dropping.

"Well, when you say it like that, it makes us sound like dipshits," said Aaron.

I doubted anyone would argue that we *weren't* dipshits.

"Okay, here's what needs to happen," said Noah. "You need to clarify the rules with Esther. Tell her that the winning sermon is determined by the *audience*. And the audience is everyone in attendance at the Sermon Showdown."

"Everyone in attendance?" I said. "Won't that just be the JTs?"

"What? No. Of course not."

Aaron and I exchanged confused looks. Everyone else just seemed confused by *our* confusion.

"Oh, come on," said Tegan. "I already *told* you everyone's talking about you and your crazy-ass List. So of *course* everyone's talking about the Sermon Showdown, too."

"Define 'everyone,'" said Aaron.

"Okay," said Jack. "Let's pretend that there's a circle that represents the student population of HVHS. Now let's cut a slice of that circle, color it pink, and say that that pink slice is the percentage of HVHS that *isn't* talking about the Sermon Showdown."

"Okay," said Aaron, nodding.

"There is no pink slice."

"Ah."

"Talk to Esther," said Noah. "Clarify who determines the winner of the Sermon Showdown. It's so public at this point, if Esther tries to throw a stink, it'll only make her look bad. She *has* to agree."

There was a knock at the door—putting our planning session to a grating halt.

"Who's that?" said Aaron. He glanced at me. "This is everyone we invited, right?"

"Uh...yeah," I said.

Unfortunately, I wasn't wearing my lying face.

Aaron's eyes narrowed to a squint. "You're saying *yeah,* but it sounds like a *no.*"

Forget that someone just knocked at the door. Everyone turned to study my face like some progressive art piece at the local gallery.

"Oh yeah," said Tegan. "He's lying. I know. He's my boyfriend."

"Tegan!" I said.

"What, it's true. You're blushing hard-core."

"Am not!"

"Bruh," said Niko. "I could cook a Hot Pocket on your face, you're blushing so hard."

"Cliff," said Aaron. His tone was a channel of controlled suspicion. "Who did you invite?"

The knocking continued. The jig was up.

I sighed. "Look at your recent sent texts."

"My recent...*sent*...?" Aaron's eyes expanded. "You didn't."

He pulled his phone out of his pocket—tap, scroll, tap, scroll—and then—

"You did," said Aaron.

"I'm sorry," I said.

"Sorry doesn't unsend the text, Cliff."

"I know, I know. But I'm sorry anyway. I only did it for your well-being."

Aaron exhaled like he was breathing out sandpaper. "You know what? It's fine. I told you the story, I asked for it. Don't worry about it."

"Should we just not answer the door?" I asked.

"No, we'll answer it. We'll invite her in, and we'll move forward with the meeting, as planned. And we will *not* bring up anything else. If she asks, the Sermon Showdown is the *only* reason you invited her. Is that *clear*, Cliff?"

"See-through," I mumbled.

I didn't notice anyone had left the room until Julian was already walking back. "Jeez, you'd think you guys were talking about Emperor Palpatine or a communist or something. It's just Lacey."

All around the room, everyone groaned and rolled their eyes.

Aaron, meanwhile, looked like he'd just had the wind sucked out of him. "Did you open the door?"

"What?" said Julian. "Nah, I just looked through the peephole. C'mon, this isn't my house."

"Oh," said Aaron, visibly relieved. "Well. Can you open the door?"

"Sure thing, El Capitan." Julian disappeared into the entryway once more.

Aaron looked at me and raised a warning finger. "Not one word."

I nodded, lips ziplocked.

The door opened, awkward greetings were exchanged in the entryway, and Julian and Lacey entered the living room.

"Hey!" said Aaron, jumping up from the recliner, a little *too* amped. "You got Cliff's text. Perfect. Glad you could make it, Lace. Here, take a seat."

He gestured elaborately to the recliner like it was some cleverly disguised trap.

"Oh," said Lacey. She seemed standoffish—understandably so. "Okay."

As she started for the recliner, she shot me a questioning look. I deflected it with a sudden, unbreakable fascination with the carpet.

Lacey sat down and pursed her lips, resigning herself to her current fate.

"All right, all right, all right," said Aaron, clapping his hands together. My God, he was turning into Matthew McConaughey. "Lacey, we were just discussing a plan for this Sermon Showdown we're having against Esther. I'm sure you're well aware of it?"

"Yep-p-p," said Lacey, popping her lips on the *p*. There was zero amusement in her ice-cold stare.

"Good. So, we already addressed one issue: the judging of the Sermon Showdown. Are there any other issues we need to take into account?"

Lacey raised her hand. "The possibility that you have a concussion from the boat accident?"

Oh boy. Shit had just hit the proverbial fan.

Aaron's smile—without moving a millimeter—hardened into something irritated and slightly crazed.

"Well," he said, choosing his words carefully, "I don't think the doctors would have released me from the hospital if they thought I had one. But I appreciate your concern. Now—"

"But do they know you think you saw God?" said Lacey, cutting him off. "Because that's insane."

I shoved my hands under my ass and grabbed the couch cushion. Everyone else in the room was like a gawking bystander, mesmerized in the wake of a horrific collision. Only it was happening in slow motion so you could appreciate every detail. The soft implosion of metal, the spray of glass, smoke pluming into the sky, filling it with gray.

Aaron stood silent for a long moment, but his body language had plenty to say—back rigid, muscles taut, jaw threatening to crush his teeth into his gums.

"I think you should go," said Aaron.

"Really?" said Lacey. She stood up from the recliner, but she was *far* from going anywhere. "Because *I* think I should stay. I think we need to have an intervention."

"Oh, for God's sake, Lacey—"

"No, Aaron. For *your* sake—not God's. God is the *problem*, because you *didn't* see him, because he isn't real!"

"Is that what this is about? You want to have a pissing contest over the existence of God?"

"No. I want you to go to a doctor, because you hit your head on a boat, you were in a coma for three days, and now you think you're Jesus Christ."

"You don't know anything!" said Aaron, throwing his hands in the air. "I'm doing something important. What are you doing with your life? God, you're so fucking oblivious to the world, I don't even know how you survive."

Okay. In the short amount of time that I'd known Aaron and his unfortunate history with Lacey, I would go on record saying this:

That was the dumbest thing he ever said.

Something snapped inside of Lacey. Something big. Something furious. I saw it in the way her fists curled and trembled. In the way her glossy upper lip tweaked and her left eye twitched beneath her mascara.

"I'm oblivious, huh?" said Lacey.

"You done messed up, A-Aaron," said Tegan.

Only Tegan would quote Key and Peele at a time like this.

"So I guess I wouldn't know anything about you cheating on me," said Lacey. "And definitely not with my best friend. And *especially* not at my birthday party."

I had to say, Aaron walked into that one. And unfortunately, he deserved every bit of the shitstorm headed his way.

"Oh," said Lacey, touching her lips. "Did you not know that I knew that? That's surprising. I mean, I did walk into the room while you were *fucking her*!"

Aaron's defense had all but crumbled. His mouth floundered, and his wide eyes seeped with regret.

"So who's the oblivious one?" said Lacey. "Do you think these people believe you? The only reason they're here is because the legendary Aaron Zimmerman is losing his mind, and it's like watching a house catch on fire. It's just so horrible and fascinating, you can't look away. But hey, don't take my word for it."

She glanced around the room, meeting everyone's uneasy gazes.

"Show of hands. How many of you *actually* believe that Aaron saw God? How many of you? Raise your hand if you think that Aaron is one hundred percent sane."

Nobody raised their hand right away. I'm sure that's exactly what Lacey wanted. So without further hesitation, I shot my hand up. I waited for others to join me.

But they didn't. Mine was the only hand that went up.

"Oh, well, congratulations," said Lacey. "Neanderthal believes you. I guess that seems fitting."

I glanced from Noah, who gave a sad shrug, to Jack, who just stared at his shoes, to Tegan, who frowned and mouthed, *Sorry*.

Aaron's face was the last I focused on. His mouth was pulled into a feeble line. Every ounce of fight had evacuated the premises. He looked defeated, and sick, and slightly dizzy.

"Why do I even *care* about your mental health?" said Lacey. "That's the biggest mystery. God, I almost think I'd be better off if you never woke up from that fucking coma."

"I'm s…" Aaron stammered, shaking his head. "Lacey, I'm s… I'm sor… Lacey, I'm sor—"

But the words weren't coming out right. So he kept shaking his head, as if to jar the words loose.

"You know what?" said Lacey. "I hope there is a God—just so you can rot in literal hell."

Aaron's head stopped shaking—but not for the right reasons. No, this was very wrong. His arms went limp. His head wobbled.

And then he collapsed.

"Aaron!" I screamed.

That's when the convulsions started. He was twitching, shaking, jerking uncontrollably. His eyeballs rolled into the back of his head.

There was gasping everywhere. Lacey stood over him, but her arms merely hovered, trembling, immobilized in sheer, untainted terror.

I dropped down, kneeling over him—only to fall into the very same Lacey-paralysis. I wasn't a doctor! What the hell did I know about seizures?

Finally, logic struck. I shoved my hand into my pocket and pulled out my phone—the phone my best friend bought me—and fumbled to punch three numbers. The phone dialed, and then there was a voice.

"Nine-one-one, what's your emergency?"

"I need help!" I said. "My friend is shaking on the floor, I think he's having a seizure, I don't know what to do, oh my God, please help!"

TWENTY-ONE

The Emergency Department waiting room was a well-lit, family-friendly perdition with its freezing tile floor—so glossy clean that every tile was a mirror—and cold blue faux-leather chairs with armrests designed to punish love handles for existing. Even the buzzing light fixtures above us felt chilly, like white, rectangular sheets of ice.

I couldn't stop staring at Mr. Zimmerman—yes, *the* Mr. Zimmerman—no longer the zenith of genetic perfection. His face had contorted into this ugly thing as he cried into his wife's shoulder. Mrs. Zimmerman's eyes were swollen red puffs as she tried to keep her shit together because *someone* in the Zimmerman family had to, and it sure as hell wasn't going to be Mr. Zimmerman.

Niko, Jack, and Julian went home after the ambulance picked Aaron up. Lacey, Noah, Tegan, and I—in that exact order—sat adjacent to the Zimmermans. Really, I had no room to talk about Mr. Zimmerman, because even though I had stopped crying, I was still as emotionally wrecked as Lacey, and Lacey was practically choking on her own tears and snot. If she seemed less than human during the seizure, now she was a mere shadow. Noah and Tegan sat between us like the awkward/solemn glue trying to hold our sanity in place.

A doctor entered the waiting room, clipboard in hand, and approached our sad little corner. Everyone whipped straight.

"You're the Zimmermans?" she asked.

"And friends," I said.

"I'm Dr. D'Souza. As you may be wondering, we believe Aaron's seizure is related directly to the boating accident he was in recently."

My stomach was wrung into a tight-knotted cinnamon twist.

"Now, I've looked at the records, and when Aaron awoke from the coma, his MRI didn't show any sign of cerebral damage. That's not uncommon with traumatic brain injury. Sometimes, signs of damage aren't manifested until days, weeks, or even months later. But his doctors were wrong to send him home so early. They should have kept him and monitored his situation. What our CT scans are picking up now is a subarachnoid hemorrhage. Essentially his brain is bleeding inside his skull."

My stomach plunged into an infinite abyss. I couldn't even breathe. Lacey gasped into her hands.

"Oh my God," said Mr. Zimmerman.

"The good news is that he's currently stable," said Dr. D'Souza. "We've successfully performed what we call a coil embolization—a minimally invasive procedure. We inserted a catheter into his leg and guided it up the brain vasculature to close off the blood vessels. Fortunately, we caught it at a stage where he's in no real medical danger. If all goes well, he'll come home with nothing more than a Band-Aid on his leg."

The tension had been a black, billowing rain cloud, thick and impenetrable. But now it had burst wide open, and relief was pouring like rain. Lacey broke down, crying a small storm into her hands.

"Can we see him?" said Mrs. Zimmerman.

"Of course," said Dr. D'Souza. "He's still groggy from the anesthesia, but I'm sure he would love to see your faces."

Just as soon as Lacey, Noah, Tegan, and I started to stand, Dr. D'Souza stopped us with a gentle hand. "I'm afraid only family is allowed."

My heart dropped. Lacey's head dropped. Tegan just gave this sort of pissed-off snort like she was ready to drop the doctor, Compton-style.

The four of us slumped back down. Mr. and Mrs. Zimmerman didn't look back at us as they followed Dr. D'Souza across the lobby and into the ER corridor. The silence that followed was dark and infinite.

"I should probably go home," said Noah.

———

Tegan left shortly after Noah. This was actually my doing. She looked so miserable seeing me miserable, and the only way that was going to change was if she physically couldn't see me anymore. Of course, that's not what I told her.

"You need to get something to eat," I said.

"Me?" said Tegan. "Hell with that. What about *you*?"

"I couldn't eat a hamburger if it tried to force its way into my mouth."

Tegan bit her lip. "I *am* hungry."

"Go. Seriously. Do it for me."

"You gonna be okay?"

"Aaron's stable," I said, forcing a smile. "I'll be okay."

Tegan nodded hesitantly. She grabbed my face like a basketball and kissed it hard, practically mashing her lips with mine.

"Text me," she said. "I'll kick your ass if you don't."

And then Tegan was gone. It was just Lacey and me, separated by two empty seats and connected by an emptiness that transcended space-time.

"I'm sorry," I said, finally—a meager shout into the void. "You were right. Aaron had brain damage, and I'm a piece of shit. I'm so sorry."

"Cliff..." said Lacey. "You didn't do this to Aaron."

"But I *did*!" I said. "You *said* he had a concussion. You *told* me to tell someone. If I'd reported it when you told me to, this wouldn't have happened!"

"You don't know that."

I didn't. But at the same time, the evidence was so overwhelmingly against me, I felt like I had given Aaron the brain hemorrhage with my own fist.

I didn't look at the time because I didn't care. Time didn't matter, and food didn't matter—nothing mattered except Aaron making it out of this goddamn hospital alive. I stared at my shoes, but all I could see was Aaron's face—talking and laughing over lunch, raving about Tarantino movies, defending Superman, and getting so passionate about his godforsaken List. It filled me with dread to realize it was all a delusion.

But Aaron was alive. *That* was what mattered.

I felt bad for Lacey, though, because the hospital was freezing. Seriously—a couple degrees below Alaska and slightly above hypothermia. It was one thing for someone with enough built-in food storage for a Narnia winter. Another thing *entirely* for a girl with the body-mass index of a large Chihuahua. She was shivering, her teeth chattering, with her meatless arms wrapped around a meatless torso, like turkey-bacon-wrapped asparagus.

"Would you like my lucky hoodie?" I asked.

Really, I just wanted to get the damn thing off my body. I hadn't completely dismissed the possibility that the hoodie caused Aaron's brain to hemorrhage.

"Y-y-y-yes, p-p-p-please," said Lacey.

I pulled the hoodie off over my head and handed it to her. When she pulled it on, it was like she was wearing the actual Barnum and Bailey circus tent. It nearly reached her knees, and when she extended her arms, the sleeves drooped six inches past her fingertips.

"It's big," she said.

"It's also unlucky," I said. "Cursed, maybe. So stay warm at your own discretion."

"Cursed? By who?"

"My guess is either Cthulhu, Pennywise the Clown, or Satan."

"Oh, I hope it's not the clown."

"You think I'm joking, but I'm not. It's seriously a bad-luck charm. One time I was wearing it, and a bird shit on my head. I panicked, and tripped, and landed in *dog* shit."

"Oh my God."

"It was fresh."

"That sucks."

"That's nothin'. I used to have a pet rat named Dirty Harry—he kind of looked like Clint Eastwood. Anyway, somehow he escaped from his cage. I looked everywhere and couldn't find him. Then I remembered that he always liked to burrow in my pile of dirty clothes that I left on the ground. Except I didn't have any clothes on the floor that day because it was laundry day."

"No."

"Yes. My mom accidentally washed Dirty Harry in the washing machine. He died. Guess what I was wearing?"

"Oh. My. God."

"Shane bought me the hoodie for my birthday. Wrapped it up and everything. And then he killed himself—three days before my birthday. I didn't open it until after his funeral."

Jesus Hernando Christ! Where was my filter?

Lacey's mouth was so ajar, I could've inserted a Quarter Pounder with Cheese like a quarter in a slot machine.

"Sorry," I said, avoiding eye contact. "I don't know why I told you that."

Lacey managed to close her mouth. That was the closest she came to a response.

"There's a trick to wearing the lucky hoodie, though," I said, mostly to change the subject. "If you stick your right hand in the front pocket, you'll discover a hole. You gotta hook your thumb in that hole."

Lacey actually stuck her hand in the pocket, digging around for the hole.

"Found it," she said. "Um . . . what's it for?"

"You gotta leave your thumb in there at all times," I said. "I like to think that it defuses the bad luck. Or at least keeps the misfortune to a minimum."

"Ah."

"I'm serious. If Aaron dies because your thumb wasn't in the hole, it's all on you."

If I was weirding Lacey out with the mythology of my hoodie, it didn't show. Instead, I sensed gratitude—in the lines of her weary face, in her broken smile.

"Thank you for letting me wear your hoodie," she said. She paused before adding, "Everything's going to be okay."

I nodded, mostly as a reflex. "Yeah. Everything's going to be okay."

But even as I said it, I knew that I was lying to myself. Everything was not okay. The reasons were a line of dominoes toppling into each other.

The List was bullshit.

Because Aaron didn't see God.

Because God wasn't real.

I breathed the truth in—one nihilistic breath at a time.

Aaron is okay, I told myself. *That's all that matters right now.*

Aaron is okay.

TWENTY-TWO

Lacey and I were never able to see Aaron at the hospital. If we thought the doctors would take pity on a couple of teenagers camping out in the waiting room like Black Friday shoppers in front of Best Buy, we had another think coming. They enforced the "family only" rule with a totalitarian fist. Lacey drove me home. The words we exchanged during that drive were minimal at best.

"Cliff?" she said.

"Yeah?"

"I'm going to hang on to your lucky hoodie. Nonnegotiable."

I nodded—even though I couldn't care less. Good riddance! When we arrived at Arcadia Park, we exchanged feeble good-byes, I exited the car, and Lacey drove off.

———

Going back to school, I felt like I had stepped into an alternate reality. All day, I received looks—weird looks, amused looks, mocking looks, and about two thousand subvarieties of looks in between. These were accompanied by frequent snickers and peanut-gallery commentary like, "Praise the Lord!" or "Yo, dawg, how's Jesus these days?" or "Neanderthal, God should give you a List of things to do to *not* be a fucking idiot."

That last one came from Kyle Dunston.

Now I was more than capable of defending myself against dipshits like Kyle. Obviously. I had a weeklong suspension to prove it.

However, defending yourself is rather unnecessary when you're dating Tegan Robertson, and she overhears said dipshit as she walks you to class.

Tegan one-eightied like a shark in water. "'Scuse me?"

Kyle's cocky smile flinched. "You heard me," he said—although the defiance of his tone kind of nosedived.

It was like the shark had just been challenged by a sea cucumber. Tegan moved in for the kill—strode right up to him, arms swinging, and shoved him hard in the chest. "You got somethin' to say, you little fuckweasel?"

She shoved him again. "Man, I'll fold you inside out and wear your inverted corpse as pajamas!"

Shove. "I'll break you like a Pixy stick and snort your fuckin' remains!"

At this point, Kyle realized his grave mistake as a sea cucumber. He staggered backward and—when that wasn't getting him away fast enough—tucked tail and scampered off.

The scene had not gone unnoticed. Tegan had garnered a sizable audience—all cavernous mouths and bloated eyes. So naturally, she paced down the center of the hall, arms tense and ready to draw invisible pistols, like this was the Wild West and she was Clint Eastwood. The only thing missing was a badass poncho and some tumbleweed.

"From now on, I'm Cliff's personal secretary. You got any questions, comments, or concerns, they come through me." She jammed a thumb at her chest. "So . . . does anybody else got some Howdy Doody bullshit they wanna share?"

Everyone shuffled uncomfortably and averted their gazes.

Tegan adjusted her jacket with a rebellious tug. "That's what I thought."

Tegan extended a gentlemanly arm to me—which I took, thoroughly floored.

And that was the end of the peanut gallery. I didn't hear a single joke after that. Not so much as a snicker.

———

"Aaron's gonna be okay," said Tegan, once she got her feng shui together. It took her all of two minutes. It was like her personality had two intensity levels—amphetamine and benzo. It was like a switch. I didn't know how, but she was totally zenning it now.

When I didn't respond right away, she continued. "Aaron's okay. You're both okay. Everything's okay."

I guess you could say I'd been acting *not* okay lately. I was six feet deep in homework. I hadn't been sleeping well, evident in my raccoon eyes. I wasn't even eating well. I looked like a deflating Macy's balloon. Hence Tegan's sudden need to lather me in reassurances. Which I appreciated; don't get me wrong. It's just that—when you realized my and Aaron's entire friendship was built on the foundation of a cerebral hemorrhage—the *okay*s felt feeble and inept. Like we were trying to patch up the broken hull of a space shuttle with aluminum foil.

"Have you tried calling Aaron?" said Tegan.

I shook my head.

"Why the hell not? He's your friend."

"Is he, though?" I said.

Tegan frowned. I didn't need to explain myself. She knew damn well what I meant.

"Yeah, it complicates your friendship," said Tegan. "But it don't mean he's *not* your friend."

I shrugged. "It doesn't mean he *is*, either."

———

I entered Arcadia Park, and saw my house nestled among the other mobile homes. I dreaded walking in the door, which wasn't an unusual feeling, to say the least. The park was in shambles, our trailer was a metaphor for decay, and somehow it was where I belonged. *That* was the true metaphor—I lived in a shithole because I, Cliff Hubbard, was shit. I deserved this.

That's how I felt when I saw the black, rectangular object lying in front of my door—like a small, handheld Monolith.

A book?

I approached the front steps and picked it up. No cover illustration. No title. Just a thin black book, like a journal. I turned it in my hands. No distinguishing features at all.

I opened the front cover, and read the first page:

Property of Shane Hubbard

The axis of my world snapped in half.

I whipped around on the front steps, glancing left and right and everywhere, anywhere, for any sign of the person or thing or supernatural phenomenon that dropped this book on my porch.

No one. Nothing.

I glanced back at the book. At the name scribbled on the paper in his characteristically neat handwriting.

I turned the page.

Dear friend,

That's how I'm going to start this, because someday, maybe a friend WILL read this, and maybe they'll understand. Either way, I refuse to start off with "Dear journal" and this sure as hell isn't a diary, so whatever. Anyway, I'm writing because there's this girl named Hal, and I think I'm in love with her, and I need to tell someone, and I'm living a lie. Even now. Especially now. But it's the only way I can bring myself to do this. I have to believe there's somebody out there who will understand. I am filled with so much love, and so much hate, and it's difficult to draw a line between the two because they blur into each other. And at the center of it all is a time bomb, embedded in the shadow of my soul, ticking down the seconds until I die.

TWENTY-THREE

It took me a while to absorb that first paragraph. I read it over and over again, trying to make sense of it, but my heart was beating too hard, too fast, too loud, for me to think. I could feel the blood throbbing in my ears. I did, however, manage to make a simple list in my defragmenting state of mind:

1. Shane was in love with a girl named Hal.
2. The notorious computer hacker of HVHS was called HAL.
3. Aaron's List told us to "find and stop HAL."
4. Shane had extremely conflicted feelings about Hal.
5. Shane was dead.

There wasn't a "holy shit" in the world that was holy enough for this shit.

I kept reading.

Her name is actually Haley, but I call her Hal. It doesn't matter where I met her, or how, or what she looks like, or who she is, really.

The first thing you need to know about me is that I don't fall in love. Ever.

Before Hal, I had sex thirteen times, with thirteen different girls. I think. I only remember four of their names. Don't even ask me how many girls I've made out with. There might not be a number that big in the English language. I love sex. If we make out and it doesn't lead to sex, I love masturbating. I don't even care how socially frowned upon that is. It's just so damn convenient! A hand that knows exactly how you want it? Sign me up!

And I don't ever ever ever ever ever fall in love.

At least, I didn't until I met Hal.

One of the first things I learned about Hal is that she knows computers better than I know juvenile delinquency. I discovered this when she hacked into Zoo Entertainment and leaked music from Tool's new album. I mean, the music was shitty, but still! TOOL'S NEW ALBUM! That's like hacking into Area 51 and discovering the existence of real-life shitty aliens!

And that's how we became friends.

If you go to Happy Valley High School, then you probably have heard of the infamous computer hacker who goes by the cryptonym HAL. That's us. I came up with the ideas, and Hal did the hacking. I mean, replacing everyone's faces in the yearbook with Nicolas Cage? That has to be the greatest hack of all time!

So we did this for a while. And then I started liking Hal, but I didn't fess up to it, because Hal REALLY wasn't my "type." Not that I had a type. But she wasn't it. I actually fought it for a long time. I always kind of suspected that Hal had a thing for me, but she never said it, and I didn't say it, and we had fun, so what did it matter?

But then everything changed.

I don't even know how it happened. I took Hal to this old, abandoned building we call the Monolith. I guess I was acting kind of flirty, and she was too, and our hands touched on the stairway railing, and then we got really close, and I told her how not into her I was, but I said it really soft, and she said she didn't know what I was talking about, and she said it even softer. And then we kissed.

And that's when I felt it. Everyone calls them fireworks, but this felt more like a nuclear explosion, but with less death and destruction and more amazingness.

So that's how it started. Things have gotten a little more serious since then. We haven't had sex yet, and frankly, having sex with her kind of scares me, which probably sounds weird, but if you knew her, you'd understand. At the same time, I want it so bad. But not now. I want it when the time is right, which totally doesn't sound like something I would say, but it's true, and I mean it. Being with Hal is like seeing and feeling sunlight for the first time, after living underground all my life, only seeing pictures of the sun.

You can't experience the sun through pictures. Love is the same way.

I blinked as my eyes moved past the words, past the last line, and into the whiteness of the page.

Shane was in love?

Shane and this girl, Haley, were HAL?

And he never told me any of this?

I wasn't going to lie—that kind of hurt. I thought Shane told me everything, and almost a year later, I was learning that he told me nothing.

And why would having sex with her scare Shane? That didn't make any sense to me at all.

I turned back the pages to the beginning of the journal entry. There was no date. I turned the pages again, returning to where I left off, and continued on to the next entry.

Dear friend,

It seems like I've told you a lot, but I really haven't told you anything.

I am a liar. The truth is that I don't know how to tell the truth, to you or to anyone.

I've been freaking out a lot lately, and I've been taking it out on Hal. Which isn't fair. It's not her fault I'm in love with her. At first I was asking myself how I could love someone so much and hate them at the same time. But now I realize that she's not the person I hate.

I hate myself.

I started saying some stuff that really scared her. We thought maybe getting high would make things better, so we started buying marijuana. But being high doesn't stop you from hating yourself. It only makes you forget for a little while. Maybe I needed something stronger? I did a favor for this local dealer, and in exchange, he hooked me up with some cocaine.

That was right about the time I heard about this cokehead,

Birdy, who will do anything for her next hit. She works at Guns n' More.

   I told her that maybe I'd be able to get her some for the right price.

That was the end of the entry.

I frantically turned the page. This was the most important book I had ever read in my entire life, and the answers—from the very mouth of Shane—were here.

The next page was ripped out.

Actually, several pages were ripped out.

Beyond those ripped pages, the book was empty. I flipped through it once. Twice. On the third go-round, I turned each page individually, looking for anything. For the slightest trace of a clue. All I needed was to know who Haley was.

If I could find her, then I could find the answers.

TWENTY-FOUR

I walked through the front door in a cognitive daze—so deep inside myself, I was barely aware of my surroundings. In some far-off place called reality, I noticed my dad was watching football. Although I say *watching* in the loosest definition of the term. Really, he was so drunk, I don't think he even *comprehended* what was going on. He stared through the television screen like it was a window into outer space. When my dad got *this* sloshed, he was relatively harmless.

I'd almost disappeared into my room—to rack myself over the contents of Shane's journal, to study the broken fragments of a mystery—when I noticed my mom. Today was one of those rare cosmic anomalies in which she had the day off work. So naturally, she was in the kitchen, filling the left sink with hot water and dish soap. Yep, my mom was commencing her rare day off by washing the dishes. A rather impressive stack had accumulated since the last time she had a spare moment to do them, almost a week ago.

Something melted inside of me.

I veered into the kitchen and joined my mom—commandeering the right sink, rinsing and racking the few dishes she'd already washed.

My mom looked at me like I was on drugs again.

"Thanks . . . Cliff," she said, finally. Awkwardly.

I rinsed dishes silently. Stacked them in the dish rack to dry.

Thought of Shane's journal.

Who was Haley?

Suddenly, whether out of maddening curiosity or mental short-circuiting, I asked the question that was running its zillionth lap around my brain:

"Did Shane ever date anyone?"

My mom blinked—clearly surprised. "Um . . . I'd *seen* him with a few girls before. No one I knew. But . . ."

"But . . . ?"

"But I don't think I ever saw him with the same girl twice. I always figured he was . . . you know . . . a player."

I couldn't blame my mom for thinking that. Until moments ago, I had always thought the exact same thing.

"Is there a reason you're so damn curious 'bout Shane's side hos, Cliff?"

This came from my dad, tilting his head on the recliner.

My mom pursed her lips shut. Lowered her head, suddenly very interested in the dishes. This was my mom in classic form. In times of peace, she was Mother of the Year. In times of war, she was a mannequin.

"He's my brother," I said calmly. "Is there a reason I shouldn't be interested?"

"Well, I just think it's funny since you're obviously a Mary Poppins little queer."

"Excuse me?" I said.

My mom tensed.

"Oh, you're excused," he said. "I've gotten used to it. You're never gonna join the football team. Fairies come in all shapes and sizes, I get it. But so help me, if you join the theater, I'll kick you out faster than you can sew sequins on a leotard."

"You know, I have a friend who's gay—" I said.

"Oh boy, here it comes."

"—and he's one of the best people I know. And you trying to use that as an insult is really kind of pathetic."

"Excuse me?" My dad's body went rigid. His fingers drilled into the arms of the recliner.

"I'd say it's beneath your intelligence," I said. "But maybe not."

I clearly had a death wish. At this rate, I'd be able to ask Shane who Haley was firsthand.

My mom had been washing the same plate for several minutes now. At this point, she was just holding it, lathered in soap suds.

"Your shithead brother sure has rubbed off on you, hasn't he?" My dad stood up, every muscle knotted fiercely and pulled tight. "He knew how to run his mouth. Didn't give a shit about the consequences. And boy, were there consequences."

My dad strode right up to me and grabbed me by the collar.

"I kinda miss that," he said. His warm breath splashed over me. "Guess that's the one downside to him eating a bullet."

There was a swift crack—and then the clatter of broken pieces hitting the floor. My dad and I both jumped, our heads practically spinning.

My mom gripped shards of the plate she'd smashed against the counter.

"Hank," she said. Her voice was quivering but dangerous. "Don't."

My dad stared at her. She stared right on back. It was like a good, old-fashioned staring contest, and whoever blinked lost. Except the stakes were life and death.

I swear, neither of them blinked for a solid minute.

Finally, my dad caved. He blinked, and he chuckled, and he let go of my collar. Reaching up, he messed up my hair like this was all just a game. Like he wasn't just seconds away from kicking my ass up my skull.

"Kids say the damnedest things," he said, still chuckling.

He returned to the game and his Bud Light, slumping into his chair.

I think my mom and I had been holding our breaths the entire time because, when the coast was clear, our combined sighs of relief were like a rogue wind. Slowly, we drifted back to the kitchen sink, channeling our pent-up energies into the dishes.

Together, we finished in ten minutes.

TWENTY-FIVE

A rumor was worming its way through the halls of HVHS. A two-parter actually, and it was rather sweeping.

1. Aaron was coming back to school today.
2. He was officially cut from the football team.

No longer quarterback. No longer the star player. No longer a part of the team. (Unless he tried out for waterboy.) Aaron had been promoted to spectator. The justification was obvious: You don't let a kid with a traumatic brain injury play football. Ever. The end.

But still, that had to suck.

Of course, that was only the surface level. Over lunch, I eavesdropped on a conversation between Kyle, Lacey, Heather, and Desmond. According to Desmond—who heard it from his mom, who was friends with Mrs. Zimmerman—the physical restrictions placed upon Aaron by the doctors, postseizure, were much more draconian than before. Not only could he not play football, he couldn't do *anything* physically risky—play any other demanding sport, horse around, or do any of the normal reckless things teenage boys take for granted.

The timeline on these restrictions was indefinite. Possibly infinite.

Aaron arrived at school five hours late. I knew this because he walked into fifth period English—being semipermanently substitute-taught by some Stephen King look-alike, Mr. Garfunkel—halfway through a highlight reel of random Hemingway facts. Of particular interest was Hemingway's odd friendship with F. Scott Fitzgerald, author of *The Great Gatsby*. For example, one time Fitzgerald proofread an early manuscript of Hemingway's *A Farewell to Arms* and responded with a ten-page letter of edits, including an entirely different ending that Fitzgerald wrote himself. Hemingway responded to the letter with only three words: "Kiss my ass." On another occasion, Fitzgerald expressed anxiety over the size of his dick. Hemingway escorted him to the men's room, observed it thoroughly, and assured him it was normal.

Unfortunately, learning about friendships of any sort only reminded me that my friendship with Aaron was the product of a coma and hallucinatory delusions of grandeur.

Aaron walked into class, handed Garfunkel a doctor's note, and sat down. To say that Aaron looked depressed would have been an injustice. He looked numb. Hollow. Emotionally and psychologically dead. Like the switch in his brain that dealt with "feelings" and "coping" was turned off. It was kind of scary.

I noticed Lacey trying *not* to notice him. She wasn't doing a very good job of it.

———

I'll be honest—I completely and utterly dreaded talking to Aaron. He was a lot of things, but he wasn't dumb. He *had* to know what his brain hemorrhage meant in regards to the List. To his near-death experience. To everything we were striving for.

To our friendship.

I wasn't ready for that conversation.

But Aaron *didn't* know about Shane's journal. What *that* meant.

I dreaded talking to Aaron, but just looking at him—seeing his brokenness—was a torture all its own. If knowing about the journal could fix something inside of him, then by God, I guess I had to tell him about it. It was hardly proof of anything, but it was something.

Sometimes, "something" was all you could hope for.

I followed Aaron to his locker—stealthily, at least twenty feet away, wishing that I *wasn't* the size of the Lincoln Memorial.

He never saw me. Actually, he didn't seem to be seeing anyone or anything. His gaze was numb—a straight line into his locker, piercing out the back side, stretching indefinitely into a parallel dimension where he was still quarterback, he wasn't insane, and that awful fight with Lacey never happened.

I scraped for an icebreaker, but nothing was coming. So I just went for the first thing that came naturally.

"YOU'RE ALIVE," I sort of screamed.

Aaron turned (actually, he sort of jumped) and looked at me. His eyes narrowed.

"Go away, Cliff."

Well, this was going as expected.

Just like that, Aaron returned to his locker. He was much more focused now—grabbing the books he needed and shoving the locker door shut. And then he walked off.

"Hey!" I said. "Where are you going?"

"To class," he said.

I chased after him. He kept walking—maybe a little faster than before. You could smell the irritation emanating from every pore of his body.

"Look," I said. "I know you're going through a hard time right now. I get you not wanting to talk to anyone. But there's something I need to tell you. Something important."

Aaron ignored me. His face was cold and hard, eyes fixed straight ahead. His quick pace was scraping me to the very edge of my powerwalking abilities.

"Jesus, Aaron...can you slow down...for one second?" I said, wheezing. "Your fat friend...can't keep up."

Aaron was a Rottweiler, and I had just waved a hunk of meat in front of his face. He snapped at it.

"Friend?" said Aaron. "That's funny, Cliff. Because the entire foundation of our *friendship* is based on an elaborate *delusion* I imagined in my bleeding fucking *skull* because apparently I have *brain damage*!"

Okay. That hurt. I had to physically shake my head—as if I were literally shaking the pain away—to remind myself that I had something important to tell Aaron.

"No," I said. "The List isn't a delusion."

Aaron stared at me. The sort of stare that had volume. That made the air feel thick.

"Cliff..." he said, finally. "I had a brain hemorrhage. I imagined the List. I imagined everything."

"Okay, look," I said. "That's what I thought at first, but I found something. Something huge. It *proves* the List is real."

"Does it prove that I didn't have a brain hemorrhage?"

"Wha—? Well, no, but—"

"Then it doesn't prove anything."

"No, you don't understand. Just listen to me. I found this journal that belonged to Shane. It just appeared out of nowhere, and—"

"Oh my God, Cliff. It always comes back to Shane, doesn't it?"

"What? No! Aaron, you're not listening to me!"

"You can't prove that the List is real because it's not. You can't prove that I saw God because he doesn't exist. I mean . . . Jesus, Cliff! The only reason you believe in God is because you have to! Because if God doesn't exist, then Shane doesn't exist anymore. And you just can't handle that possibility, can you?"

You know that scene in *Temple of Doom* when the evil priest shoves his hand in that dude's chest and pulls out his beating heart?

Yeah.

"I'm sorry, Cliff," said Aaron. "But Shane's gone. The List isn't going to bring him back."

In some far-off cubicle of reality, I saw Aaron turn and walk away. I was left in the storm of his tumultuous wake—shattered, and broken, and alone. I was only abstractly aware of the students around me— laughing, slamming locker doors, rushing off to their sixth-period classes before the bell rang.

But it was all background noise.

TWENTY-SIX

By lunchtime the next day, I decided that Aaron didn't exist. I just didn't care anymore.

I mean, obviously he *did* exist. And I cared so much, it was killing me. But what else could I do? When life gives you lemons:

1. Add Mr. Spinelli's half gallon of Smirnoff vodka.
2. Drink vodka-ade.
3. Don't stop until you have amnesia.

It amazed me how much I hated my drunk dad, and how much he inspired me to want to drink all of my problems away.

Maybe, deep down, I was just like him.

That's what I thought in the cafeteria, sitting alone at my table, while Aaron abided the interstellar laws of my invisible quarantine force field. Then again, he wasn't sitting at his old table, either. That involved sitting with Lacey, which was so far out of the question, it was a nonquestion.

Aaron was just gone. Nowhere in sight.

I don't know what my face looked like, but I'm sure it wasn't good. The moment Tegan saw me, her smile inverted.

"Oh no," said Tegan. "What's wrong?"

"What's *not* wrong?" I said.

"Ah hell no. You tell me what's wrong, or Mama will bring out the whip and handcuffs. Don't you test Mama."

You had to appreciate that, with Tegan, a threat and an innuendo were basically the same thing. If I wasn't so depressed, I might have challenged her.

But I was *sooooooo* depressed. So I told Tegan everything.

Tegan listened—completely deadpan. No reaction to Shane's journal. No reaction to any of Aaron's hurtful words. Which was a good thing, because if *she* reacted, *I* might've reacted—be it sobbing or swearing or sobbing AND swearing. It was like I had two default emotions—*Sadness that Knows No Depths* and *Fuck Fuck Fucking Fuckers Fuck!*

Regardless, Tegan was a really good listener. It was one of those stellar human qualities that I'd never even recognized in her until now.

I finished my story. Tegan responded with a fierce, turbulent silence. Finally, she said, "Do you really want to know what I think?"

"Uh . . ." I said—filled with a sudden dread of inconvenient truths. "I dunno. Do I?"

"First off, I think it's rad that you found Shane's journal." Her tone was uncharacteristically soft, and she chose each word carefully. "Secondly . . . I don't think that it necessarily *proves* that the List is real."

"What?" I said. My tone was low-key devastation.

"It's just, I think you *want* the List to be real so bad, your brain is latching on to any evidence it can get."

"But it just showed up on my doorstep! How else did it get there?"

"What? You think *God* dropped it off on your porch?"

I knew Tegan wasn't trying to make me feel stupid. With that said...I felt pretty stupid.

"It's almost the year anniversary of Shane's death, right?" said Tegan. "That Haley chick prolly dropped it off on your porch. Prolly feels like a bitch for making Shane wanna kill himself. Or *whatever* that shit's all about. Shane was a little cryptic on the details."

"Well..." I said. I was running out of arguments. It kind of felt like running out of oxygen. "What about Aaron?"

"What *about* Aaron?"

"Do I just *not* be friends with him anymore?"

Tegan rolled her eyes. "Aaron has some emotional baggage. He did a really douchey thing to Lacey, he got cut from the football team, and he has a brain injury or whatever, and now he doesn't know what to believe in. Baggage like that don't resolve itself."

"But that doesn't mean we can't—"

"Does Aaron want to talk to you?"

"Um..."

"Does Aaron want anything to do with you?"

"Uh..."

"Then you can't."

I pursed my lips into a perfectly straight line. Arguing with Tegan was like arguing with an evolved, highly intellectual honey badger. Not only did she appear to be right in the most infuriating ways possible, but she wasn't even nice about it.

"I mean, if you *want* to keep getting your feelings stomped on, be my guest," said Tegan.

You know, maybe honey badgers were *nicer* than Tegan.

"*Ugghhh,*" I said, grabbing great clumps of my hair—as one does in times of suck. "What am I supposed to *do* with my life?"

"I dunno," said Tegan, shrugging. "I mean, you have a girlfriend. You can always do the things boyfriends *usually* do with their girlfriends. But, you know, whatever."

On the outside, Tegan was being her usual smart-ass self. But deep down—beneath the hostility and the badassery—I could see it.

She was hurt.

"Hey," I said. "I'm sorry."

Somehow, "sorry" didn't feel like enough, so I attempted to give her an awkward remedial hug—like I was eleven years old or something.

Tegan shoved my awkward hug away. "Man, keep your stupid hugs to yourself. What am I, a Care Bear? Fuck!"

I shoved my hands into my lap and blushed.

"Just—!" said Tegan, suddenly, intensely. "I *get* that the List is important to you. I don't want to be the one who tells you it's crazy. Maybe it is…but maybe it isn't. That's for you to figure out. I just want you to know that I support you. And if you *do* find out that the List is crack-ass crazy, just know that I won't think any less of you. You'll still be my bitch."

"Thanks?"

"My question is: Do you really need Aaron to do it?"

"Do what?"

"*It.* The List. Do you need Aaron to do it?"

I wanted to point out the sheer stupidity of this thought, but the words weren't cooperating with my brain. All I could come up with was: "It's Aaron's List."

"Is it?" said Tegan. "'Cause last I heard, it was God's List."

TWENTY-SEVEN

Tegan invited me to her place after school. I was all in favor. If I didn't distract myself from my current downward spiral, I was going to lose my mind.

What I failed to realize was that Tegan didn't have a car. Due to the fact that she didn't have a license. Due to the fact that she couldn't drive.

"I drive just fine on *Need for Speed*," said Tegan, disclaimerishly. "But you can drive into walls and shit there, and apparently that's frowned upon in real life."

"Ah," I said. "So... do you ride the bus?"

"The bus? Nah, man. School buses are for wieners. I ride home with Frankie."

Had I known that earlier, I might have developed a sudden case of pneumonia. But seeing as the bell had rung, and school was out, I figured my window of opportunity was gone.

"I don't think Frankie's gonna wanna gimme a ride," I mumbled nervously.

"Of course he will," said Tegan. "Frankie loves giving people rides."

Frankie drove an ancient two-door Chevy 4 × 4 that, as far as paint goes, hadn't made it past the primer stage. But it *was* equipped with a subwoofer, an honest-to-god gun rack, and mud tires that were about seven sizes too big. Seriously, these puppies belonged in a monster truck rally.

Frankie was just climbing into his truck when he saw us. *Both* of us. He read the situation with his eyes, and then he shook his head.

"Nope," said Frankie. "Hell no. I ain't givin' Neanderthal a ride home."

"You don't have to," said Tegan. "He's coming to our house."

"*Hell. NO.* Have you seen my cab? It's a two-seater."

"It's a three-seater."

"Nuh-uh, it only has two seat belts."

"Have you ever worn a seat belt in your life?"

"Your boyfriend is the size of that big hairy dude in Harry Potter."

"His name's Hagrid, dumb-ass! And if you don't let Cliff in the truck, I'm gonna drop your ass, right here in the parking lot."

"Are you on your period?"

"Do you wanna get stabbed to death with a tampon, fucker?!"

"Whatever," Frankie said in surrender. He climbed into the cab of the truck. "Get in, losers."

Tegan turned to me and offered an uncharacteristically girlish smile. "See! I told you he'd be cool with it."

———

When we arrived at Château de Robertson, Tegan grabbed my hand and pulled me inside—rather forcefully, I might add.

"It'll be another hour before my dad gets off work," she said—suddenly all business. "And it's a twenty-minute drive home. Thirty if he stops at the Junction and grabs a beer. Ricky always talks his ear off. That gives us a small time frame to work with, but really, it's all the time we need if we cut the foreplay and get down to *biz-naaaaas*, if you know what I mean."

Tegan tilted her head and winked at me.

Whoa.

Wait.

What?

Tegan's head whipped forward, and she towed me across the entry, up the stairs, down the balcony hallway, and into her bedroom.

Hoooooooly shit.

Okay, so I probably spent about eighty-nine percent of an average day thinking about sex. But now that it was possibly *actually* happening, I didn't know if I could go through with it. Hell, I didn't even know if I could do it right! I mean, I get that you stick the thing in the other thing, but I had a feeling it was a little more complicated than Tinkertoys.

The moment Tegan shut the door behind us, she went straight to the window—which she opened. You know, instead of closing the blinds, which I always assumed was a thing you do when you do the thing. Then she rushed to her dresser, pulled the top drawer open, and dug through her panties. Seemed like a reasonable place to hide condoms.

She pulled out a Ziploc bag of pot.

Oh.

Oh!

Tegan raised it high over her head and grinned. "Who's ready to get roasted?"

Part of me was relieved that we were merely breaking the law (rather than breaking my man-cherry). The other part of me was *so hard*, I could've sunk the *Titanic* just by turning sideways.

I spent the next five minutes trying to turn myself off by conjuring the most unprovocative images imaginable—dirty public toilets, tuna fish casserole, Mr. Spinelli in his underwear—while Tegan rolled a single joint for us to share. We both sat on her bed while she leaned over her nightstand, all the tools and ingredients strewn across the surface.

She was an origami master with that rolling paper.

It was then that the thought occurred to me: I didn't *want* to smoke pot. It mostly had to do with the fact that it was illegal—recreationally speaking. It didn't help that I kind of hated the shit. The last incident left a bad taste in my brain.

"Isn't there something else we can do?" I said.

Tegan tacked the bottom of the joint and licked the length of it.

"Yeah, man," she said. "We can do whatever you want." And then she grabbed a pen off the nightstand and packed the pot in.

Apparently she meant *whatever you want* after we were ripped to the tits.

"I mean, aside from smoking pot."

Tegan blinked as "smoking pot" registered as the activity for which I was seeking an alternative. Her face was like a loading screen. Loading...loading...*ding!*

"Oh!" said Tegan. She hastily discarded the joint on the nightstand. "Yeah, of course. Sorry, I just assumed...Do you not like weed?"

"I've only smoked it twice," I confessed. "I was having a bad day when I asked Frankie for that free sample. And honestly, it only made things worse."

"Yeah, yeah, sure." Tegan seemed more embarrassed than me. "No need to explain. It's cool. Peer pressure is for wieners."

I nodded. Apparently, I had a misconstrued understanding of what makes one a wiener. No school buses, no peer pressure. Got it.

"So . . . whaddaya wanna do?" said Tegan.

A valid question. I still had the Leaning Tower of Pisa in my pants, so anything involving standing up was out of the question. I shifted forward in an effort to hide the incriminating evidence.

"I dunno," I said. "We could just . . . talk."

Tegan leaned back and chuckled. "I always do the talking thing better when I'm *not* stone-cold sober."

"Sorry."

"No," Tegan snapped. "Don't be sorry. Believe it or not, I actually respect people who don't wanna get fucked up."

"You do?"

"'Course I do! Andre 3000 doesn't do drugs anymore. He devotes his body to his art. To his music. Christ, he's a vegan now! I respect the fuck outta that."

"Oh. That's cool."

"It's just . . ." said Tegan, "I guess I'm like you. I tend to smoke when I'm having a bad day."

"*You're* having a bad day?"

Tegan tensed up—like the question itself had somehow backed her into a corner. I saw her eye the freshly rolled joint, lying indiscriminately on the nightstand. She shoved her hands into her lap.

"It's my mom," she said.

"Your mom?"

"I guess you don't know anything about her. I'll give you the Bernadette Robertson starter pack: she's a hard-core heroin junkie.

Has been since the invention of the needle. She walked out on us the week after I was born."

"She just left? Why?"

You know that moment when you ask a question, and exactly one second later, you realize that was the absolute *dumbest* thing you could possibly ask? Yeah. That. Fortunately, Tegan didn't take offense.

"That's the million-dollar question, ain't it?" she said. "It's not exactly rocket science. Two possibilities: either she left 'cause she's an addict, and that's what addicts do—they walk out—or she left because I was the kid that she didn't wanna have. Obviously, I try to pretend that the first option is the reason why. Makes me feel less shitty about myself."

I frowned.

"She called me today," said Tegan. Her lips pinched shut, like this was the worst sort of bad news.

"And . . . that's a bad thing?"

"She asked if Frankie has any heroin."

"Oh."

"Like, that was literally her icebreaker. Not *Hey, how've you been?* or *Sorry I haven't talked in so long.* Just straight to the heroin."

I just stared at her, sort of speechless.

Note to self: Never complain about my mom ever again.

"Which Frankie does," Tegan continued, when I failed to have a response. "Have heroin, I mean. He's got this rich-ass customer in Helena Valley West Central. Makes a run every couple of weeks. But that's more of a side thing. He doesn't advertise it—"

"What'd you say?" I blurted out.

"What'd I say?" Tegan looked confused.

"To your mom. What'd you say to her?"

"I told her to fuck off. What do you think I said? Of course, she immediately backtracked. Told me how much she missed me, that she wanted to 'rebuild our relationship,'" Tegan air-quoted. "She tried to make it seem like this could be our thing: me hooking her up with Frankie's heroin. Said we could shoot up together. That's her idea of mother-daughter bonding."

"Wow," I said. "That's awful."

"Is it bad that I actually considered it?"

"WHAT?"

Tegan shrugged. A single tear budded at the corner of her eye, then trickled down the contour of her cheek.

"I *want* to hate her," she said. "I want to, but I can't. Instead, she's just a reminder of everything I hate about myself. She didn't walk out when she had Frankie. Apparently, she was a halfway decent mom when she had him. She cleaned up her act and everything. I was the baby she didn't want to have. She left us—she left *all* of us—because of me."

The dam broke, and the tears came flooding in. Her body went limp, and I caught her, held her close. Her frame trembled and dissolved into me.

"I was a mistake," she said, sobbing. "I wasn't supposed to happen."

"Hey!" I said. I grabbed Tegan's shoulders. Held her back so she could look me in the eyes. "Don't say that. If there's anything in this world that was *supposed* to happen, it's you. If the universe tried to give me a world without Tegan fucking Robertson, I'd ask for a refund, because that's bullshit."

Tegan simultaneously laughed and cried even harder. I wasn't quite sure what to do with her in this splintering state of emotions, so I just hugged her. Squeezed her until the trembling stopped. Which it did.

"Cliff," said Tegan, "you have questionable taste in girls. Sorry you got stuck with me."

"Shut your face hole," I said. "We both know that I have superior taste in everything."

"Superior? Ha! Prove it."

"You want me to prove it? Okay. I'll prove it." I pulled away from her, just enough to point to the mirror on her dresser. It was low enough that you could see both of us, intertwined in each other. Even though she'd been crying, and her eyes were rimmed in red, she was beautiful. It was kind of breathtaking just stepping back and looking at her. Her hair was dark and wild with a rocker's edge, rounded pouty lips pressed into a cutting smirk, and her face like a diamond—an exotic cut of perfect symmetry.

"There," I said, pointing at the mirror. "She's your proof, right there."

"Her?" said Tegan. "I dunno, man. Looks like a hot mess on the edge of a walking disaster."

I shrugged. "Shows how much you know."

TWENTY-EIGHT

Twenty-four hours passed like a dream. School came and went like foggy memory. All the while, Tegan's words from lunch the other day were ringing in my head.

Do you really need Aaron to do it?

It. *The List. Do you need Aaron to do it?*

'Cause last I heard, it was God's List.

I started walking home from school but I didn't get far. Tegan's words gripped the helm of my mind, veering me in a direction that I did not plan to go.

Technically, it was about the List—but on a much deeper level. It was about the *meaning* behind the List. Why it mattered so damn much to me.

Sometimes we get so caught up in the things *we've got to do . . .*

. . . that we forget about the people.

I found myself on Spinelli's doorstep. The lawn was crisp and sharp, and the HOA letters had been removed. In addition, the shrubs surrounding the house appeared to have been trimmed into a neat, boxy perimeter. All in all, the place looked civilized. Maybe even nice.

I knocked.

I noticed the peephole go dark. Not a good sign. However, before I even had a chance to lose hope, the door opened. Spinelli—against all the lack of motivation in the universe—was wearing pants. So thank God for that. They were pulled up to an indefinite waistline and belted into place, with a blue polo tucked in.

"I trimmed the boxwood," he said in a completely flat tone. "So if that's what you're here for, you're out of luck."

I didn't know Spinelli well. I certainly didn't know anything about his alleged "good side." But I swear, somewhere—deep beneath his resting grump face—he was smiling.

I laughed. "That's actually not what I came here for."

"Oh. Well do you wanna weed the shrub bed?"

"Uh, I mean—"

"I'm just messing with you. I weeded that, too. There literally isn't a thing for you to do on this property."

"I'm sorry Shane was such a dick to you."

I just sort of blurted that out. I mean, it was something I *meant* to say. I'd just hoped to preface it with an icebreaker. Maybe some friendly banter.

Spinelli looked at me. Due to the "resting grump face" situation, it was difficult to tell just what sort of look that was. But whatever it was, he looked it hard.

"He never meant to be," I continued. "Shane wasn't like that. He just liked the attention. But sometimes he took things overboard, and I'm sorry if that made things hard for you. I know we all have our own struggles, and all it takes is the last straw to break the camel's back or whatever. Shane had struggles I never even knew about—struggles I *still* don't know about completely—and I just . . . I'm sorry. Please don't hate him. He was my best friend."

I took a deep breath. That was all that I had to say to Spinelli. I was done.

"Are you hungry?" he asked.

"Uh . . ."

"Who am I kidding? Look at you. Of course you are."

Apparently Spinelli's good side and smart-ass side had a broad overlap.

"Come in," he said. He opened the door wider and moved aside, motioning for me to enter. "We're having pizza."

I bit my lip. Hesitated. Then stepped inside.

The interior was the sort of quaint, overcluttered, underappreciated décor you'd expect from someone inching close to the doors of senior citizenship. This was due mostly to the pictures of him and his wife and their children (clearly adults now) and grandchildren. But mostly his wife. They were everywhere—hanging from the walls, on side tables, console tables, the coffee table, and bookshelves—and the images they portrayed and the stories they told were intertwined in every imaginable scenario and phase of life: campouts, vacations, birthdays, weddings, and all of the small, intimate moments in between.

Mrs. Spinelli had soft sandy hair and a softer smile. Spinelli looked so happy with her—with his family—it was almost difficult to look at.

Spinelli noticed me noticing his wife. His mouth flattened into a grim line.

"Helen, meet Cliff. Cliff, meet Helen. She's dead, too."

I followed Spinelli into the kitchen. Spinelli removed a large piping-hot pepperoni from the oven, then proceeded to pull out plates, cups, and a two-liter of Dr Pepper from the fridge.

"Help yourself," he said. "We're kickin' it buffet-style."

I did as I was told. I wasn't really hungry before, but now—with the hot aroma of pepperoni, cheese, and trans fat overwhelming my better judgment—I became ravenous. I helped myself to four heaping slices, stacking them into a greasy pile. We took our pizza and soda to the dining room, sat down, and dove in.

"I'm sorry about Shane," said Spinelli.

I glanced up from my pizza.

"That's something they never teach you," he said. "Not in high school, not in college. How do you *deal* with something like that? How do you cope with the loss of someone you love?"

My hunger disintegrated.

"You know," he said, "Helen was like Shane in a lot of ways. She was an insufferable prankster. Smart as a whip, too. Got me every April Fool's Day. Mayonnaise in the toothpaste bottle, cupcakes frosted in mustard... One time, she froze Mentos in ice cubes and put them in my Coke. I was halfway through drinking it when the thing went Pompeii on me. Scared the shit out of me. I think that was her goal: to make her husband shit his literal pants."

I laughed—mostly to defuse the immense pressure building in my tear ducts.

"It's too bad I met Shane after she died," he said. "I think my sense of humor passed away with her."

Spinelli glanced up at me from his pizza, and there it was—a single tear—trickling down the creases of his cheek.

"I guess what I'm trying to say is... you're not alone."

Something in me broke. Suddenly, I was sobbing—so hard, I felt like my chest was folding inside out. I was a rainstorm. My body was shaking, and my face was crumbling, and I hurt so much because of a hole that could never be filled.

"Hey, hey, hey," said Spinelli. "Stop that. Come here."

Spinelli didn't even wait for me to come. He met me instead—moving around the table, reaching out, pulling me into a hug. I hugged him back.

"It's going to be okay, Cliff," said Spinelli. "You hear? Everything's going to be okay."

I didn't know if it would be or not. I didn't even know what that meant, really. Okay? What exactly qualified as okay? Who was the asshole that invented such an ambiguous word of reassurance?

And yet, something in Mr. Spinelli's presence told me that it would be.

TWENTY-NINE

I made a decision: I was going to move forward with the List—with or without Aaron.

The sunset bled through the clouds. It was a rust stain on the cold metal horizon. A playful storm was flitting past the mountains—swollen and bloated as it collected along the ridge. It hadn't reached town yet, but you could already smell the rain—like lilies and memories and rebirth.

Spinelli offered to drive me home, but I told him I needed some fresh air. Truth was, I wasn't ready to go home. Not yet.

If I was tackling the List solo, I needed to remind myself of something. I needed to recharge my zen.

I called Tegan. She answered on the first ring.

"Hey," she said. "You okay?"

"I want to take you somewhere special."

"Special?" She sounded more surprised than flattered—not completely unwarranted. I was hardly in a state to pretend I was Romeo McSuavepants.

"Disclaimer: it's not romantic," I said. "But it's special. Believe me. Meet me at Hideo's Video."

———

In broad daylight, Hideo's was a shabby white building trimmed in red. The neon lights were turned off, diminishing the flashiness factor astronomically. Honestly, the place looked like more of a shithole than I remembered. But maybe that was just my state of mind?

I walked in, and a bell chimed. This garnered the attention of a single person in the entire store. And he wasn't my mom.

"Oh, great," said Hideo. He leaned forward on the checkout counter and shook his head. "You here to rent more shitty American robot movies? I recommend *Transformers 5*. It sucks ass."

"Where's my mom?" I asked.

"You just missed her. She's on her lunch break."

"Oh. Well do you have *2001: A Space Odyssey*?"

Hideo leaned back and scratched his chin, as if to reevaluate the situation. "Wow. *2001*, eh?"

"If you have it."

"Maybe your shitty taste not so bad after all. *2001* is greatest robot movie of all time."

"It was Shane's favorite."

"Yeah." Hideo nodded thoughtfully. "Yeah, Shane did like it, huh. Hold on."

Hideo weaved around the counter and strode into the sci-fi section with determined force. "Let's see, *2001* . . . *2001* . . . *1984* . . . *12 Monkeys* . . . ah, here we go."

He raised it above the shelves for me to see.

"You know," he said, carrying it back to the register, "I say it's greatest robot movie, but it's not actually about the robot."

"Oh yeah? What's it about?"

"It's about evolution. It's about what's next for mankind. It's about transcendence."

"Transcendence?"

"Becoming God."

"God?" This had become an unfortunate trigger word for me.

"Or, at least, becoming more than man."

"I don't get it."

Hideo chuckled. "Most people don't. That's why Michael Bay makes *Transformers 5*." He scanned the movie, printed the receipt, and handed it to me. "Here. It's yours to keep."

I started to take the movie, but my brain stalled at the *to keep* part.

"Huh?" I said. "You're giving it to me?"

"Store has two copies," said Hideo. "I'm giving you the shittier copy. I was gonna give it to Shane, but I guess you'll have to do."

I didn't even have the words to express how grateful I was. So I just nodded. Hideo nodded back. He seemed to understand.

I glanced past the counter at a small stack of portable DVD players available for rent. I pulled out my wallet and opened it—still filled with the two twenties Aaron gave me to ask Tegan on a date.

"How much for one of those?" I asked.

———

Frankie's redneck-mobile rolled up to the corner of Gleason and Randall, delivered Tegan, and rolled out, sending plumes of dirt clouds in its wake.

"So," said Tegan, clapping her hands at her side. "Where's this nonromantic place?"

I slung my backpack onto my shoulders—slightly heavier than before—took Tegan's hand, squeezed it, and forced a smile. "Follow me."

I led her down Gleason Avenue, all the way to Gosling. To say that I knew what I was doing would be giving me undue credit. I only knew certain actions—certain steps—needed to be taken. Where those steps led was wildly out of my control.

At last, we reached the Monolith.

It used to remind me of a silhouetted middle finger, flipping off the world for allowing horrible, tragic, shitty things to happen. It was a reminder of the shittiest day ever shat out of the rectal sphincter of existence. It was a seven-story tombstone.

The sun was slipping beneath the mountains, growing orange with distance. At this time of day, the sun was probably a spark on the horizon of the Kerguelen Islands—also known as the Desolation Islands—one of the most isolated places on Earth. I knew this because I googled it. And I googled it because I wanted to know where the exact opposite place on Earth was from Happy Valley, Montana. The Kerguelen Islands were it. I sometimes daydreamed of escaping there—to this place that I knew literally nothing about—just because it was the farthest point from Happy Valley and yet was connected. If only in a spiritual sense. Because who can really run away from their home and never look back? I, for one, was way too stuck in the past. I would always look back. I would always wonder.

"Here it is," I said.

"Behind the old abandoned building?" said Tegan.

"It *is* the old abandoned building."

"Wow," she said. "You weren't kidding when you said it wasn't romantic."

"It's where my brother killed himself."

Tegan just looked at me. "Oh. You *really* weren't kidding."

The Monolith was a labyrinth in ruin. I had its mazelike corridors mapped out in the scars of my soul. It only felt right. Tegan and I navigated past peeling, graffitied walls, stepped over broken boards, through trash and debris and caked layers of dust, and ascended a long, square spiral of stairs. The flimsy metal railing was bent and broken in sections, so Tegan chose to hold on to me instead.

Each step I took was like an ice-cream scoop out of my insides. Maybe it was because the Monolith felt like a gateway. It was my own personal door to the other side.

What was on that side? I had no idea.

At last we reached the open mouth of the Monolith. It was almost *obscenely* picturesque—this watercolor mural of oranges and pinks radiating across the town—as if the universe felt this morbid need to beautify the moment.

My gaze drifted from the opening to the dark, abysmal corner. A corner that sucked life and light like a tangible black hole.

Tegan eyed me, visibly confused as I approached the corner. Then she followed my lowered gaze and her jaw detached.

"Oh my God," she said. "Is that blood?"

It was, indeed, blood. Blackened. Decomposed. Forever etched in the concrete. There were two splotches: (1) on the wall where Shane stuck a gun in his mouth and blew his brains out of his skull, and (2) on the floor where his cerebral leftovers formed a pool—a red halo around his head. Two black holes unspooled on adjacent planes. Like an interstellar passage between dimensions.

I was the one who found Shane's body.

For better or worse, the entrance and exit wounds of the bullet didn't damage his face. I *still* remembered his lifeless expression, frozen in a moment of fear. Pure and raw and unadulterated. It was fear that choked, blinded, and stabbed in every vulnerable place. In that final moment, Shane was the most vulnerable thing that ever lived.

"Cliff?" said Tegan.

It wasn't until she said my name that I realized I was crying.

It reminded me of a year ago when I thought I would never stop crying. For weeks, it was my perpetual state of existence. I was *so tired* of crying. It was exhausting. I just wanted to glue my eyelids shut and let the tears fill me up and drown me from the inside. Surely *that* would be better than all this goddamn crying.

"My greatest fear is that I'll actually complete the List," I said, "and when everything's said and done, I'll realize that it never made a difference. Not for Shane."

"Cliff…"

Tegan didn't try to dissuade me. Perhaps she knew I was right.

"I just want it to be enough," I said. "But it's too late."

"Cliff, stop it. You're fighting, and that's what's important."

"Fighting *what*? He's gone, Tegan. He's gone forever. It's like he doesn't exist anymore. You can't *fight* something like that."

My insides were collapsing. I couldn't breathe, so I gasped harder and faster, scraping for something that would keep my lungs from imploding.

"And it's not just him," I said. "It's all of us. We're *all* dying. We pretend we're living, but really, we're just dying slowly. All it takes is just one moment, and then bam! We don't exist either—"

Tegan slapped me.

"Shut your fucking mouth, Cliff. You think you're the only one hurting? You think you have a monopoly on pain and suffering? Well guess what? Everyone's hurting. That's life. And the more you hurt yourself, the more you hurt me, so just shut the fuck up, because I don't want us to hurt anymore, I don't want us to give up on living, I don't want us to die, dammit!"

Tegan sniffed. Her rage storm melted into a gentle rain, trickling down her tender cheek.

"I don't want us to die," she said.

I couldn't take it anymore. I crumbled to pieces. Tegan took me into her arms, and together, we fell against the wall. My face became wedged between Tegan's shoulder and the black-hole bloodstain on the wall. I painted the wall with my tears, trying so hard to absorb the little bit of Shane that hadn't been buried. His death felt so real again, like I was experiencing it again for the first time, and I just couldn't take it anymore.

"I miss him," I said, sobbing, choking on the infinite void that might never be filled. "I miss him so much."

"I know, Cliff," said Tegan. She pressed her teary cheek against mine. "I know."

We stayed that way for a moment—holding each other, neither one daring to let go. I needed her, and she needed me, and that was enough for both of us.

The sadness ended like one season bleeding into the next. Slowly, we let go of each other and breathed. We breathed like it was an important task. Sat down, pressed our backs against the wall, basked in the shadow and moonlight, and breathed.

"What am I fighting for?" I said.

"The same thing we're all fighting for," said Tegan. "Hope."

Maybe that's what the List was—among a slew of other things. Maybe it was far-fetched. Maybe it was crazy. Maybe it was even impossible.

"What do you hope for?" I asked.

"Me?" said Tegan. "I hope for lots of things."

"Such as?"

"Well, for starters, I want to be a spoken-word poet."

"A spoken-word . . . poet?"

"Yeah."

"That's a thing?"

Tegan rolled her eyes. "Of course it's a *thing*. I love poetry. But the rhythm of poetry rolling off the human tongue? Man, that carries power. All the greatest rappers are—first and foremost—spoken-word poets. The music is just an aesthetic."

"Can you recite one for me?"

"No."

"C'mon, please?"

"No way."

"Why not?"

"Because it's *embarrassing*," said Tegan. She was actually blushing. "Besides, I'm not that good."

I bit my lip, and poured all of my energy into having the biggest, most pleading puppy dog eyes ever.

"Put those puppy dog eyes away. Save 'em for someone who cares."

I channeled all my chakras into those puppy dog eyes and amped the voltage up to eleven.

"For Christ's sake," said Tegan. "Fine."

She relaxed her muscles, leaned her head back, and closed her eyes. The words poured out of her.

"I hope it was worth it. I hope that needle was the child you wanted.

I hope it fills that thing inside of you. That empty place. You have one of those? I do. You should know. You made it. You shoveled it out with your own bare hands. You filled it with poison so nothing could ever grow there. So I hope that needle was the child you wanted. I hope it fills that thing inside of you. Take it, and shove it up your ass."

Tegan opened her eyes.

"I call that one, 'Fuck You, Bitch,'" she said.

"Oh," I said. "I like it."

"Don't lie to me."

"No, it was really good. It has personality."

"*It has personality,*" said Tegan, attempting to mimic my voice, but making it approximately one hundred percent stupider. Perhaps this was an excerpt from *Cliff: The Movie*, in which the titular role is played by *Sesame Street*'s very own Mr. Snuffleupagus. (He was the only candidate big enough and hairy enough to fit the role.) "Man, that's just a nice way of saying it sucks."

Tegan lowered her head, crossed her legs, and shoved her hands in her lap.

"Wanna see a picture of her?" she asked.

"Who?"

"The Queen of England," she said. "My mom, dumb-ass!"

"Oh. Yeah, sure."

Tegan pulled out her phone, navigating the menu with her finger. She didn't have to scroll far. She scooted her butt right up next to mine, leaned into me, and angled the phone screen for me to see—a young woman with cat eyeliner and sharp ebony hair done in a beehive. She was either going for the '60s or Amy Winehouse. A sleeveless dress exposed slender, tattooed arms and a pink bundle in her arms.

A baby.

Tegan.

"She looks happy, doesn't she?" said Tegan.

She *did* look happy. She wasn't smiling per se, but there was something serene—almost spiritual—in her gaze.

"This is what I hope for," said Tegan. "This woman right here. I don't know who she is, but she's definitely not the junkie who up and leaves her own child. I want this woman back in my life—whoever she is."

I nodded, but it was a ghost of a response. Because as I stared at this woman, this mother, cradling newborn Tegan in her arms, I realized something.

I had seen her before.

It was at Guns n' More. I tagged along with Shane on one of his random excursions. He had a mild obsession with firearms, so this wasn't a particularly unusual visit for him. Tegan's mom was working the register. They seemed to know each other, complete with inside jokes that I didn't get. Except Shane didn't call her Bernadette.

What did he call her?

The last lines of Shane's journal flashed across the retinas of my mind:

That was right about the time I heard about this cokehead, Birdy, who will do anything for her next hit. She works at Guns n' More.

I told her that maybe I'd be able to get her some for the right price.

Holy shit. Tegan's *mom* gave Shane the gun that he used to kill himself! How was I just now making this connection?

I looked at Tegan. At the pain she was feeling. There was no way I could tell her this. Not now, at least.

I decided it was time to take this thing to Phase 2.

"Wanna watch a movie?" I blurted out.

Tegan blinked and looked at me. "What?"

I responded by grabbing my backpack, unzipping it, and removing the portable DVD player and *2001: A Space Odyssey* for her to see.

"It was Shane's favorite movie," I explained. When Tegan didn't respond right away, I immediately felt kind of stupid and backtracked. "But it's an old movie, and this is a gross, old building, so I totally understand if you don't want to—"

"I would love to," said Tegan.

I met her gaze. Everything in there said that she meant it.

We set up camp on the concrete lip—"camp" being the portable DVD player, and the DVD itself. What better place to watch *2001: A Space Odyssey* than under the stars? They weren't visible yet, but the sun had completely receded, shedding afterglow like a fluorescent shadow. Resting our backs against the wall, we leaned into each other with the DVD player propped on my lap.

I inserted the movie in the disk tray, pushed it in, and pressed Play.

———

On the surface, *2001: A Space Odyssey* is an allegory of evolution and technology. And the message it conveys about both is slightly troubling.

The film is broken into three deliberately labeled parts.

THE DAWN OF MAN

This first part, beginning in the African desert, 4,000,000 BC, chronicles a tribe of ape-men as they encounter a towering black rectangle that has mysteriously appeared in their midst—the Monolith. This encounter marks an evolutionary stepping-stone. One of the ape-men discovers the first tool—the first *weapon*—when he happens upon the femur bone of a dead animal.

He bludgeons another ape-man to death.

In victory, he tosses the bone in the air, and suddenly, that bone becomes a spaceship and we are millions of years in the future in space. A group of scientists has discovered a Monolith on the moon, identical to the one the ape-men encountered.

Only this one is sending a signal somewhere.

JUPITER MISSION

Five astronauts—three in hypersleep—are on a top secret mission to Jupiter. It's so secret, in fact, that no one *really* knows the purpose of their mission. No one except for the ship's artificially intelligent supercomputer, HAL 9000. Unfortunately, HAL is faulty. First, he errs in predicting ship malfunctions. Then, when he senses mutiny from the crew, he becomes lethal. What follows is essentially a slasher movie in space. HAL succeeds in killing four of the five crew members. The fifth and final member—Dr. David Bowman—deactivates HAL's core processor.

JUPITER AND BEYOND THE INFINITE

This is when things get weird. Bowman discovers the purpose of the mission. That signal the Monolith on the moon was sending? It was directed at Jupiter where yet *another* Monolith is detected, orbiting the planet.

Bowman takes a space pod and goes in for a closer look.

What happens next could best be described as an acid trip. It appears that Bowman has been pulled into some sort of psychedelic wormhole—lights and colors, shapes and symbols, ejaculating from the Prism of the Universe in an electric neon glow. We witness the birth of worlds, stars, and galaxies. Drift across alien landscapes.

Suddenly, Bowman finds himself in a neoclassic-style bedroom. Time becomes a shadow as Bowman sees—and then becomes—older versions of himself.

Middle-aged.

An old man.

Lying on his deathbed.

And then he becomes something else.

"A space baby?!" said Tegan. She stared at the miniature screen, slack-jawed, as the end credits scrolled. Then she looked at me. "He turned into a giant, floating SPACE BABY?"

That was, in a sense, what Bowman had become—a glowing fetus of questionable size, encased in a transparent orb, drifting alongside planet Earth, as if observing it.

According to Shane and the vast *2001* mythos, this "giant floating space baby" had a name: the Star Child. But I felt stupid to point this out to Tegan. So instead, I shrugged.

"Or something," I said.

"I dunno, man. I can handle some weird shit. But I can't handle no effin' space baby."

"Why not?"

"Why *not*? He's a space baby! What's that even supposed to mean?"

I bit my lip contemplatively. Again, the surface-level interpretation seemed to be a cautionary tale about evolution and technology. That whether it was a bone or a sentient supercomputer, technology in desperate hands resulted in violence and death. The truly disturbing thing was that both the ape-man and HAL 9000 became *capable* of killing because they had evolved into something *more human* than what they previously were.

But then there was Bowman—a human—who became something else. He overcame death, yes. But had he overcome something far greater?

I thought of what Hideo said. His crazy words were Plinko chips bouncing down the pegs of my mind to the center of my consciousness—*plink, plink, plink!*

It's about evolution.

It's about what's next for mankind.

It's about transcendence.

Becoming God.

Or, at least, becoming more than man.

"We're meant to become more than what we are," I said.

"More than what we are?" Tegan seemed to test the words on her tongue. Then her face scrunched, rejecting the taste. "What does *that* mean?"

What *did* that mean? Even I didn't know.

THIRTY

I walked Tegan home after the movie. Made the trek home, alone and on foot, in the breathlessness of night. By the time I reached Arcadia Park, most of the trailers had their lights out. Only a select few were still lit, the insomniacs and the jobless, serving to light my shadowy path.

And then I froze—a solid twenty feet from my house—because there was something on my doorstep. Again.

It wasn't a journal though. Not even close. It was big, and human shaped, and alive.

"Hey," said Aaron.

He was just sitting there, hands on his knees, chilling.

I let out the longest breath of my life. My hand was on my chest like I was going to give the Pledge of Allegiance of the century.

"Jesus Harvey Christ!" I said. "What are you doing?"

"Sorry." Aaron bumbled to his feet. His awkwardness was on point. "I should have called first. I just didn't know what to say."

Didn't know what to *say*? After my last encounter with Aaron, there wasn't a thing he left *unsaid*.

"Are you okay?" he asked.

The sad look on my face probably said way too much.

Aaron sighed. "Look. I said a lot of things the other day that I shouldn't have said. Shitty, horrible things. I wish I could take it all back. It's just...I was in a bad place. The fight with Lacey was bad. Being cut from the football team was bad. Being told I can't do anything physically risky again—possibly ever—was bad. *Is* bad. I'm still trying to wrap my brain around that one. But still—none of that compared to realizing the List might be bullshit. It made me realize that the List—of all things!—is the closest I've ever come to having a purpose. And suddenly, that purpose was taken from me, and I didn't even know what was real anymore, and I...Anyway. I'm sorry. I was a dick."

"You *were* a dick," I said.

Aaron's pursed his lips solemnly.

"A rock-hard dick," I said.

The corners of his mouth formed a smile.

"Ejaculating with all sorts of dick moves," I said.

Aaron laughed. "I've missed your jokes, man."

"I missed you," I said—probably a little too intensely. But I meant it.

"I missed you too, Cliff."

We were silent for a moment. In that moment, I felt an itch on the back of my tongue. It wormed its way out of my mouth.

"I need to show you something."

"Show me something?" said Aaron. "What?"

"I could tell you," I said, "but I think it'd be better if you saw it for yourself."

I pulled off my backpack, unzipped it, and shuffled through the contents. Beneath the textbooks and notebooks, the portable DVD player and *2001: A Space Odyssey*, I unearthed a small black journal. I handed it to Aaron.

"Read this," I said.

"What is it?"

"Just read it."

It wasn't until seconds later that I realized I had tasked Aaron to read a handwritten journal in a barely lit trailer park in the middle of the goddamn night. But Aaron didn't take my request lightly. He pulled his phone out, held the lit screen over the first page of the journal, and read. His eyes widened at *Property of Shane Hubbard*. From there, his eyes were like the phases of the moon, growing wider and wider until they were complete circles.

"What is this?" said Aaron.

"Did you finish reading?" I asked.

"No, but—"

"Keep reading."

Aaron took a large bite of his bottom lip and kept reading. Turned the page. I watched his eyes, bouncing from side to side like synchronized Ping-Pong balls. At last, he blinked.

"Did you read it?" I asked.

Aaron looked at me with a cloudy gaze, like someone in the fluttery moments of waking, struggling to separate dream from reality. "Where did this come from? Have you had this all along?"

"What? No. Are you kidding me, Aaron? I *told* you about this."

"Mmmmmmmhhh, no." Aaron shook his head, lips compressed. "You definitely never told me this. I would remember that conversation: *Hey, Aaron, did you know that HAL was actually my brother and his secret girlfriend?*"

"I *tried* to tell you, dick-skin. But you went all *It always comes back to Shane, doesn't it?* on me." My Aaron impersonation was spot-on.

Aaron's eyes swelled as the pieces clicked together. "Shit. *That's* what you were saying?"

My mouth flattened into the straightest line ever formed. "Yes, Aaron. *That* is what I was saying."

"So . . . where did it come from?"

"That's a great question. I have no idea."

"You don't?"

"It just showed up on my doorstep."

Aaron blinked incredulously. "It just showed up."

"Yes."

"On your doorstep."

"Yes."

"Meaning that Hal needs to be found . . . and possibly stopped."

"Reminds you of something, doesn't it?"

"Holy shit," said Aaron. His already big eyes got even bigger. "The List isn't bullshit!"

"Hells yeah, it isn't!"

"I'm not crazy!"

"Well, that's debatable."

Aaron punched me in the shoulder, but he was smiling—so much, so hard, so *intensely*, it was contagious. Had more people been in the immediate vicinity, it would have been a pandemic. But as it was, only I was infected.

I was practically smiling myself to death.

The first thing you realize when you hit rock bottom is that there's actually no such thing as rock bottom. *Rock bottom* indicates that there is a limit to the shit that can happen to a person, and once you hit that limit, then the Magic Shit Gnomes who are employed by the Shit Distribution Factory of Life have to push a button that ceases shit production.

But that's just silly.

What Aaron and I had experienced was merely a synchronized low. We shared the same destiny, after all. The beautiful thing was how much room there was to go up!

One thing, however, was abundantly clear. In order to move forward with the List, we had to have our shit together.

Aaron had to have *his* shit together.

Just to be clear, Aaron came to this conclusion of his own volition. That's why, directly after school, we drove to Lacey's house.

I was there for emotional support. And to make sure that Aaron didn't wuss out.

When Aaron shut the engine off, the silence was vast and heavy— like the entire Pacific Ocean, perceived from the bottom of the Marianas Trench. Seriously, the pressure should have killed us. Aaron appeared to be dying, at least. His jaw was tense, his throat was constricted, and his complexion was cadaverous. He looked anemic at best.

"We don't have to do this," I said.

"*We* don't," said Aaron. "*I* do."

Aaron exited the car, walked stiffly up to the door, and knocked.

Lacey answered.

Now I had fully intended to give Aaron his privacy while he made impossible amends with his past. But now that he was face-to-face with his greatest fear, and Lacey looked like she had opened the door to Satan, I was just too damn curious.

I manually rolled down my window—just a crack.

I couldn't hear everything Aaron said, but I caught enough of the highlights to compose an informative bullet-point list:

- I'm sorry.
- I've been the absolute worst to you.
- I don't know how to undo all the hurt I've caused you—I probably can't—but I want you to know that I hate myself for what I did.
- I don't expect you to forgive me, but I hope you—

That was as far as Aaron got on the fourth bullet point before Lacey assaulted him in a fierce hug.

It was in that moment that I realized something about human beings: We always care. Even when we don't care, or we don't want to care, or we've been broken beyond the capability of caring...

We always do. It's our ultimate infallibility.

———

Aaron got permission from Mr. and Mrs. Zimmerman for me to stay the night again. We were going to figure the shit out of this List.

So naturally, we kicked things off with the continuation of our Tarantino marathon.

Aaron and I breezed through *Jackie Brown*. And because the night was young, and we were unstoppable, and Quentin Tarantino was life, we popped in *Kill Bill Vol. 1*.

The film opened to a black frame and labored breathing. And then a man's voice:

"Do you find me sadistic?"

The camera panned to Uma Thurman—aka the Bride—lying

bloody on the floor after receiving a severe spaghetti-western-style ass-kicking. A powerful hand with a handkerchief entered the scene, wiping her face. An Old Testament god, merciful and vengeful. A name was sewn on the corner of the handkerchief—the titular *Bill*.

"Best. Revenge film. Ever," I said.

"Tru dat, broseph," said Aaron.

"I bet I could fry an egg on your head about now, if I wanted to," said Bill.

"You know, the Bride has a List too," I said, observationally. "Or she will. Shortly. After this bastard tries to kill her and fails catastrophically."

Aaron rolled his eyes. "Yeah, okay, man."

"A List of five things. Just like us. Just sayin'."

"It's a List of five *people*, actually. But kudos for trying to find real-life application in Tarantino."

"Our List is about five people, too."

Aaron gave me a look.

"I interpret 'JTs' as 'Esther Poulson,'" I clarified.

Aaron rolled his eyes. "It's a *hit* list, Cliff. This is a *revenge* film. It bears no resemblance whatsoever to our List."

"I'd like to believe, even now, you're aware enough to know there isn't a trace of sadism in my actions," said Bill.

"Revenge is just vigilante justice," I said. "It's taking the law into your own hands."

"Oh, okay, Batman."

"Question: Is it possible to exact revenge against *concepts*? You know, instead of people?"

"Uh…"

"I mean, could the List be a form of revenge? But against social norms and complacency and hate?"

"I don't think that's 'revenge' anymore. I think the word you're searching for is *activism*."

"Well, yeah, I guess," I said, deeply unsatisfied. "But revenge is so much *cooler*. There's so much more *passion* in revenge. Like, the Bride? She just *really* wants to kill Bill. What if we had that kind of passion with the List? This passion that was at the very root of our existence, and the injustice of it made our blood boil, and if we didn't complete the fuck out of this List, we would at least die trying."

Aaron finally pulled his gaze away from the screen. "Does this have anything to do with that mystery girl, Haley?"

I didn't have a response for that.

I was actually trying really hard not to think about it at all. Because when I did, I felt something dark and dangerous inside of me—a large shadow moving beneath the surface of a calm lake. I felt solemn and furious and scared.

I guess there was a small part of me that wanted revenge—the real thing.

THIRTY-ONE

The List was back on track and more serious than ever.

Aaron picked me up for school on Monday. But even as his eyes were sniper scopes trained fiercely on the road ahead, his mind was unraveling with questions that cascaded out of his mouth like a verbal waterfall.

"Who is Haley?" he said.

"No idea," I said.

"What girls did Shane hang out with?"

"I don't even have a fraction of a clue."

"You don't know a single girl he hung out with?"

"Not really."

Aaron snorted, which could be loosely translated as: *Cliff, you are useless*. And frankly, I couldn't disagree.

"I mean, the girls I *did* see him with were sort of . . . one-night-stand-ish," I said, as awkward as humanly possible. "One and done—that was his dating style. C'mon, you read his journal. He didn't *do* relationships."

"But obviously he *did*," said Aaron. "At least *once*."

"Obviously. But whoever she was, Shane hid her from the world like she was the buried treasure of Montezuma."

"Treasure? Dude. He hid her like Frollo hid Quasimodo."

I responded with my expressionless, straight-mouthed *No comment* face.

"No disrespect to your brother," said Aaron, "but he seemed ashamed of her. Don't you think?"

Aaron was right. Shane *was* ashamed of her.

So why was he so simultaneously *obsessed* with her? It didn't make any sense.

"So which freaky weirdo girls at school do we know who fit the profile?" said Aaron.

"Freaky weirdo girls?" I said. "How many Haleys or Hals do we know?"

"Um. Zero?"

"Big fat zero."

We brooded in a moment of stilted silence.

And then the lightbulbs of Aaron's eyes flickered—an idea. "But I *do* know a couple of nerds who have access to the names of every girl at HVHS."

Oh.

Oh!

"A couple of nerds who already promised to deliver HAL's identity on a silver platter!" I said.

I looked at Aaron, and Aaron looked at me, and the inspiration jolted through us like an electric current.

We had a lead.

Jack and Julian barely noticed us as we entered Mr. Gibson's computer lab. They were at side-by-side computers, playing something *World of Warcraft*–ish. Their faces were so intense, they might as well have been in the honest-to-god Hunger Games.

"Heal me, heal me, heal me!" Julian squealed.

"I'll heal you if you sit your Paladin ass *still* for half a goddamn second," said Jack.

"Aw, yeah! Full health, baby! Eat my broadsword, wankers!"

"The harpy! Get the harpy!"

"*Unh! Unh! Unh!* Suck it, bitch! *Unh!* Oh yeah! OH YEAH!"

"Whoa, calm your loins, man. Can you fight *without* sounding like you're getting a BJ?"

Aaron put his fist to his mouth and coughed gracelessly. "Hey . . . guys. Any luck finding HAL?"

Jack and Julian looked up, surprised.

"You still want us to do that?" said Jack.

Aaron's eye twitched.

"We just assumed . . ." said Julian. "You know . . . since Aaron . . ."

Jack and Julian looked at Aaron. Aaron just dropped his head in his hand and rubbed his spazzing eye.

"Just do it," I said. "Also, can you look up Haley in the student directory?"

Jack shot me a well-deserved weird look. Julian managed to put Jack's weird look into words.

"Did you just pull that name out of your ass because it starts with 'HAL'?"

"GOD, JUST LOOK IT UP FOR US, OKAY?" I said.

"Okay, okay!" said Jack. He opened up a new window on his computer, and his fingers danced across the keyboard. "Searching . . . searching . . . searching . . . aaaaaaand . . . no results found."

He glanced back up at me, anticlimactically.

"Okay," I said. It came out more as a mumble.

"Sorry about the HAL thing, though," he said. "We'll get on it. A deal's a deal. Right, Julian?"

"Hells yeah, it is," said Julian. "I'm a karate brown belt, and the first rule of karate is honor."

———

It wasn't until then that I remembered that I had a girlfriend. It had been days, and I still hadn't told Tegan that Aaron was back on board with the List.

Now that I thought about it, I hadn't noticed her at school on Friday.

I texted her during first period—nothing. Second period—still nothing. By third period, I assumed she was sick, and practically begged her for confirmation. By fourth period, I had received so much nothingness in response, I was going a little bit insane. I practically charged into the cafeteria, then I veered outside to Frankie's corner with every worst-case scenario in mind.

As I drew near, I could tell from a distance that Tegan wasn't there. No one was—except for Carlos. I couldn't help but decipher this as a red flag.

I walked faster until I reached Carlos, and then broadsided him in an artillery fire of questions.

"Where's Tegan? Is she sick? Where is everybody?"

Carlos rolled his eyes, and shook his head, and chuckled in a way that meant the opposite of funny.

"Sick?" he said. "Bro, do you even *talk* to your girlfriend?"

I was trying really hard not to look stupid. However, my efforts were overwhelmed by the fact that I was, in fact, the King of Stupid. I sat on a throne of idiocy, and my scepter was a raspberry-flavored Dum-Dum.

Carlos sighed. "Tegan stole Frankie's heroin and took off."

"WHAT?"

"She took all of it."

"How much did he have?"

"I'd say somewhere between *Trainspotting* and *Requiem for a Dream.*"

Jesus Humphrey Christ.

"Where is she?" I asked.

"Bro," said Carlos. "If we knew that, Frankie'd already have his shit back. And Tegan'd be six feet underground, for that matter."

"Where's Frankie?"

"Where you think? Out in his truck scouring town for Tegan. And probably a nice plot o' land to bury her ass."

"Shit."

"If it's any consolation, Jed's with Frankie, tryna cool him down. Helping him weigh the pros and cons of murdering his little sister."

"Shit, shit, shit." I turned back around and started walking.

"Bro! Where you going?"

"Where do you *think* I'm going?"

Really, I wasn't going anywhere—not on foot, at least. I pulled my phone out of my pocket and dialed the first number ever programmed in its retrotastic memory databanks.

Aaron picked up on the first ring.

"Dude, where are you? It's pizza day!"

"I need a ride."

"A *ride*? On *pizza* day?"

"I'll explain on the way," I said, hoping he would hurry his ass.

"Um..." said Aaron, in a way that indicated the opposite of ass hurrying. "What if I told you that I promised Lacey I'd sit by her in English...?"

"What? No."

"And that I was actually looking forward to it."

"NO. Bro code, man! God, you're choosing *now* to fall in love with Lacey?"

"Whoa, whoa, whoa. In love? You're like four bases ahead of me, man. We're just sitting next to each other—in completely *segregated* desks, I might add."

"Tegan stole a shit-ton of Frankie's heroin. She's giving it all to her junkie mom. There's also a pretty solid possibility they'll get high together—mother-daughter bonding and such."

"GAHH!" yelled Aaron. "Where are you?"

"Outside, past the fence. By Frankie's corner."

"Meet me at the front doors. I'm giving you the keys."

"The... *car* keys?"

"No, Tony Robbins's keys to massive success. *Yes*, my car keys!"

Aaron hung up. I took that as my cue to run. And as I ran, I struggled to process the life-altering event that was in the throes of transpiring.

I was about to drive Aaron's car.

Aaron drove a Camaro.

But *Camaro* was just a word. What Aaron *really* drove was the Fifth Horseman of the Apocalypse. A 1969 Chevrolet Camaro Z28 RS, painted a sleek, devastating black—the same impenetrable shade as Steve McQueen's soul. It was basically an orgasm with a steering wheel.

I was so lost in excitement, I almost collided with Aaron inside the front doors.

Aaron grabbed me by the wrist, placed the keys into my sweaty palm, and closed my fingers around them. It felt like a mantle of power being passed down from the hero of a lost era—seeping through the pores of my skin, sparking my nerves, and igniting the fire in my soul.

"Wreck my car, and I'll wreck your dick," said Aaron.

Fine by me. I was so sexually aroused by Aaron's car, my dick was probably indestructible.

Like Tegan, I didn't have a driver's license. But I did know how to drive. Shane taught me in one of his buddies' cars, educating me in all of the driver's ed essentials—doughnuts, burnouts, J-turns—aka, How to Survive a Jason Statham Film 101.

I ran to Aaron's car, turned the key in the ignition, and basically re-created the car chase in *Bullitt*—McQueening around corners, flooring it on every stretch, cremating rubber all the way to Guns n' More.

It was just a hunch. But it was better than what Frankie and Jed had.

A bell chimed as I walked inside. This drew the attention of a burly forty-something-year-old dude behind the counter. He had a black beard and long, ratty hair hanging beneath a backward base-ball cap. To top it all off, he was wearing a Mother Love Bone T-shirt beneath an actual trench coat. Indoors. He was like a forgotten relic of the '90s grunge scene.

He squinted as I walked in. "You don't look eighteen."

"I'm not looking for a gun," I said. "I'm looking for a woman named Birdy? Or Bernadette? Or something?"

"Birdy?" Grunge chuckled to himself. "Man, you're about a year late. She got fired a long time ago."

"Do you know where I can find her?"

"Do you know where to find some heroin? 'Cause if you can, that's probably where she's at."

"Dammit." I grabbed tufts of my hair and started walking in circles.

This was it. This was my one lead. If Birdy wasn't here, then she could literally be anywhere. *Tegan* could be anywhere.

"I know it's none of my business," said Grunge, "but can I ask what you want with Birdy?"

"It's nothing," I lied.

"Don't look like nothing."

I sighed. "I'm friends with Birdy's daughter. I think she's about to do something really stupid."

"Daughter?" said Grunge. "You mean Tegan?"

I stopped pacing. My whole body locked up. "You know Tegan?"

"Well, I don't *know* her. But Birdy talked about her all the time. Said she screwed up bad. Wanted to fix things with her *and* her son . . . oh, what was his name?"

"Frankie?"

"Yeah, yeah, Frankie! For a couple of kids she abandoned, Birdy was totally obsessed with them. Just got out of rehab when she started working here. She was so determined to fix things with her kids, I thought for sure she was gonna clean up her act. Nope. Fell right back into the same shit."

Grunge shook his head, lips pinched shut. "You say Tegan's gonna do something stupid?"

"I think so."

"With Birdy?"

I nodded hopelessly.

Grunge bit his lip. Tapped his fingers on the glass counter.

"Hold on a sec," he said.

He turned and disappeared into a back room. I only had a sliver of a view from a half-open doorway—some sort of makeshift office space with an archaic computer, file cabinets, and shelves upon shelves of back stock. Grunge pulled open one particular file cabinet and thumbed through its contents until, finally, he removed a single sheet of paper. He laid it flat on the desk and copied something down on a sticky note.

He came back out, sticky note in hand, and gave it to me. It was an address: 89 Lazy Creek Way.

"This was where Birdy lived when she applied for the job," said Grunge. "I don't know if she's still there, but if she is, well . . . I hope you find your friend."

I stared at the address. I was vaguely familiar with Lazy Creek Way. It actually wasn't that far from Arcadia Park.

"Oh, and one more thing," said Grunge.

I glanced up.

"Don't tell Birdy where you got that address."

I rolled down Lazy Creek Way in Aaron's Camaro, scanning the house numbers. If you could even call these things houses. Arcadia Park was bad, but this neighborhood was like the cold gray hills of *Winter's Bone*—this cemetery of a town built on the blood of a pervasive meth-amphetamine underworld—minus the hopeful presence of Jennifer Lawrence to alleviate the existential dread.

Eighty-nine Lazy Creek Way was this decrepit little white box with a roof and windows. Except it wasn't so much white anymore. If Home Depot carried the color, it would probably be called "Two-Hundred-Year-Old Rotting Skeleton." With its freelance patchwork, the roof vaguely resembled a quilt. Also, two of the windows had been replaced by plywood. Over one of the plywood squares someone had spray-painted KEEP OUT.

I parked the car and took a deep breath—allowing myself a brief moment to reevaluate my place in the universe. And then I walked up to the front door. Greeted it with three heavy knocks.

The peephole went black almost instantly. Like whoever was on the other side had been waiting on their toes. It stayed black for a long, uncomfortable moment. Finally, the door opened.

The woman on the other side was a skeleton of the Birdy I remembered. Her skin was sallow, hanging on a gaunt frame, with clothes that fit like curtains. Even her hair seemed to be physically suffering—thinning, with premature strands of gray. Her makeup looked like it had been left over from last Wednesday.

"You friends with Tegan?" she asked.

"Uh," I said. "Yeah?"

"You got the junk?"

"The . . . junk?"

"The smack, the H, you got it?"

Her fingernails clicked impatiently on the door frame.

"Uh. No. Sorry."

"Fuck," she said.

She reached into her back pocket and pulled out a pack of menthols. She removed a cigarette, inserted it in her mouth, and pulled out a pink Zippo lighter. Lighting the cigarette, she took what might have been the longest drag of her life. Let it out like a corpse releasing its last breath.

"Do you know when she'll be here?" she asked.

I shook my head—slowly—processing the information as it came into my possession.

She wasn't here yet.

Why wasn't she here yet?

Surely, if she was coming here, she would *be* here already.

Wouldn't she?

"Who are you?" she asked. She removed the menthol from her lips. "What are you doing here?"

"Um..." I said.

And then I turned and walked off her porch. That set Birdy on fire.

"Is this some kind of joke?" she said. "You tell that little bitch if she doesn't get here soon, we're through. I'm *done* being her mother."

I wondered if this woman registered a word coming out of her mouth. How could she *possibly* be the same Birdy that Grunge was talking about? The same one who was so anxious to rekindle a relationship with the children she abandoned. Whoever this woman was, she was a shell of that person.

"You tell her!" Birdy screamed. "You tell that little bitch!"

I climbed into Aaron's car, turned the key in the ignition, and drove off.

I pulled out my phone, scrolled through the contacts, and took another stab at calling. As the phone dialed, I stared at the road ahead of me, and the endless places it led.

"Where are you, Tegan?" My voice was a breath in my throat.

Somewhere in the universe, my question was heard. Maybe it was even answered. I didn't drive ten seconds before I turned onto a small creek bridge leading out of the neighborhood. There was Tegan, sitting on the dirty creek bed, arms folded around her knees, brooding. Beside her was a backpack—chock-full of illegal substances, no doubt.

In all my excitement, I overestimated the proficiency of Aaron's brake. When I hit them, my entire body jackhammered into the steering wheel. I even managed to inadvertently honk the horn.

Tegan's head snapped up. She climbed to her feet—jaw tense, fists ready—fully prepared to deliver a piece of her mind to the Camaro-driving asshole who thought it was a good idea to stop and honk.

"Hey, you got a problem, fuckface?" said Tegan.

I fumbled to put the car in Park, then waged a mighty battle with my own seat belt. Finally, I managed to stumble out of the driver's-side door.

"Cliff?" said Tegan. Her gaze shifted past me. "Whose car is that?"

"What, you don't think this is my car?" I said.

Tegan tilted her head forward, dangerously skeptical.

"It's Aaron's," I confessed.

"Good. I hate Camaros."

I opened my mouth, appalled.

"It's all about the Mustang," she added.

I shook my head. "You're walking on a slippery slope."

"Am I now?"

"Did you know that in Aldous Huxley's *Brave New World*, the World State is based on the Ford Motor Company?"

"The hell is *Brave New World*?"

"It's like George Orwell's *1984*."

Tegan continued to stare at me, clueless.

"*Fahrenheit 451*?"

"Are you just saying random words and numbers?"

I continued to shake my head, tragically.

"Man, what do you want anyway?" said Tegan.

"Can I sit with you?"

Tegan took an overdramatic moment, looking up and down the creek bed—a long stretch of nothingness, except for the beer bottles, McDonald's wrappers, and condoms littering the premises. It was actually quite disgusting.

"You can sit wherever you want," she said. "Ain't no one stopping you."

I walked off the road into the grassy bank, navigating my way through the trash. Tegan sat back down and continued to hug her legs to her chest. I sat down beside her.

"How are you doing?" I asked.

"Just cut to the chase. You're here because I stole Frankie's heroin, because I was gonna give it all to my mom, and—who knows—maybe I was gonna shoot up with her, too."

"But you didn't."

Tegan didn't respond. Instead, she seemed to physically retract—pulling her legs closer, burying her chin into her knees.

"Why didn't you?" I asked.

"I dunno. It's . . . fake. It's all fake."

"What's fake?"

"My mom," said Tegan. "I mean, obviously she's a real human being. But this person who's pretending to reach out to me? Who wants a 'relationship'"—she air-quoted—"with her 'daughter'? She doesn't exist. I'm just an obstacle in the way of her next hit. Every text she sends, every voice mail she leaves . . . it's all so fake. You'd have to be the most desperate, pathetic loser in the world to not see it."

Suddenly, ferociously, she grabbed the closest breakable object she could find—an empty liquor bottle—and chucked it at the biggest rock in the middle of the creek. It spun, then shattered like the birth of a macrocosm, sparking life across all corners of space.

"Gah!" said Tegan, grabbing her hair. "I'm such an idiot! What was I thinking?"

I shrugged. "I don't think it's about what you were *thinking*. It's about what you were *feeling*."

"Oh my God, Cliff. Please don't talk to me about my feelings."

"Why not?"

"Because they're just fucking *feelings*! Fuck my feelings! My feelings don't matter."

I frowned.

"Please. Stop with the sad puppy dog thing."

"You know what the most dystopian idea in the world is to me?" I asked. "The idea that our feelings don't matter. We might as well be robots."

Tegan bit her lip. Her gaze was like a sniper scope, fixed with deadly precision on the biggest rock in the creek. Bits of shattered glass glinted on its surface.

"Cliff?"

"Yeah?"

"I need you to do something for me."

"What's that?"

"I need you to take me to Frankie. I need to tell him something."

Her gaze rotated until the scopes of her pupils were trained on me.

"I need to tell him something about my *feelings*," she said.

———

Tegan called Frankie. It was bound to be an unpleasant call, but we still had no idea where he or Jed were. What could we do?

Frankie answered on the first ring.

"Hey, Frankie—" said Tegan.

Those were the last words uttered before the Frankpocalypse broke loose. Since he wasn't on speaker phone, his words were indiscernible to me. His rage, however, was loud and clear. He ranted and screamed for a solid thirty seconds. Tegan let it happen. Remarkably, she was calm, cool, collected. But there was something stirring beneath the surface of Lake Tegan.

"Yep. Yeah. Uh-huh," said Tegan. "Look, I'd love to hear the rest of your temper tantrum, but maybe we could meet up so I can give you your shit back? Hey, I'm just saying. Uh-huh. Uh-huh. Home? Okay, got it." And she hung up.

She looked at me.

"We're meeting at my house."

We drove—mostly silent—all the way there. I was tempted to ask what *exactly* she had planned. But I refrained. She wasn't volunteering the information, and the look on her face was a steel vault of nonemotions.

When we pulled into the Robertsons' long, wide driveway, Frankie and Jed were already there, chilling in the back of Frankie's truck. Although I say *chilling* loosely because, really, Frankie was a sack of nerves. The moment he spotted us, he hopped off the tailgate. His fists were so tight, it seemed they might implode on themselves.

Tegan's implosion, however, had been incubating for the past several hours.

And now, a science lesson:

It is a little-known fact that many nuclear weapons employ the concept of implosion in their detonating process. The way this works is that an outer layer of explosives are arranged so that their detonation waves move inward on a fissionable core (plutonium, uranium, etc.), compressing it, and in turn, increasing the density to the point of supercriticality. To do the math in stupid:

Implosion + Fissionable Core = Big Boom Boom.

Tegan hopped out of the car, backpack in hand, before I could even turn off the engine. Frankie stormed up to meet her, clearly intending to be the force of reckoning here. What happened next was a two-part lightning strike.

1. Tegan tossed the backpack into his chest—hard—like a basketball. This caught him off guard. It also occupied both of his hands.
2. She decked him in the face.

Unfortunately, the lightning was far from done. Frankie hit the floor, and Tegan was on top of him, demolishing his face with the ole one-two on repeat.

"You know why Mom left us?" Tegan screamed. "She left because of that fucking poison you're selling. *That fucking poison!*"

Jed and I reacted with equal amounts of holy fuckness. By the time our brains caught up to the shit going down, we dared to pull Tegan and Frankie apart. This mostly involved prying Tegan off of Frankie's soon-to-be corpse. I wrapped my arms under Tegan's armpits, practically lifting her kicking-and-screaming body off the ground. Jed attempted to drag Frankie out from under her. Frankie's initial contribution was to flail awkwardly, completely disconnected from his own motor function. But eventually, the wires found their correct sockets. Frankie staggered upright.

Tegan squirmed and broke free of my grasp. Once again, she lunged at him—shoving, hitting, slapping, kicking—a bombardment of everything she could throw at him.

"She left because some asshole like you decided he could make bank on her fucking life!" said Tegan. "How does that make you feel, Frankie? Huh? *How does that make you feel?*"

I wrapped my arms around Tegan, squeezing her arms to her sides. Tegan thrashed harder than ever.

"Let go of me, Cliff! Let go! Let *go* of me!"

And then, like the aftermath of every explosion, a calm fell. Not a peaceful calm. This calm was filled with death and destruction and sadness. She collapsed in my arms.

"Let go," Tegan cried. "Let go, let go of me, let go, let go . . ."

It was at this point that I glanced up at Frankie. He stared at his sister, completely shell-shocked.

"Tegan . . ." he said. He reached out to touch her shoulder.

She exploded. "Don't touch me! Don't you dare touch me!"

Frankie retracted—clearly hurt.

Eventually, Jed led Frankie inside. Jed seemed to understand that the only way to defuse the situation was to get Frankie as far away from Tegan as possible. Tegan and I stayed on that driveway for a small eternity. Seconds passed like years, minutes like decades or even centuries.

Her tears dried, and her brokenness settled.

"I feel better," Tegan said finally. She tilted her head. Looked at me through clear eyes. "I feel better now."

THIRTY-TWO

I had gotten so used to having a cell phone over the past few weeks, I didn't process that maybe my dad would have a problem with that.

Spoiler alert: He did.

As I walked in the front door, I pulled out the phone to text Tegan, making sure that she was all right.

"What in the hell is that?" he said.

I stopped—walking, texting, breathing, everything.

My dad was perched like a gargoyle in his recliner—cold, ominous, ever-watching. God, somebody put this guy on a castle wall.

"Uh," I said. "A cell phone?"

"I know what it is, Copernicus. What the hell is it doing in your hand?"

I had encountered about every sort of confrontational scenario with my dad, but this was new ground. I decided to take a stab at honesty.

"My friend gave it to me?" I said.

"Okay, stop bullshitting me, Cliff. I know you ain't got no friends."

Okay, now for a well-timed, self-deprecating joke.

"You're right," I said. "I forgot. Aaron Zimmerman gave it to me—but he's definitely *not* my friend."

"Aaron Zimmerman?"

Shit.

"The same Aaron Zimmerman who got you suspended because he kicked your bitch ass?"

My dad stood up from his recliner. The gargoyle had awakened.

"The same Aaron Zimmerman who's quarterback of the football team? What, he's your *friend* now? He *gave* you that cell phone?"

I didn't even know what to say. So much had happened since *that* fight, trying to explain it would be like trying to explain quantum physics to someone who didn't believe in science.

"Aaron's not on the football team anymore," I said.

My dad's eyeballs practically did backflips in their sockets. "Ah, well there it is. What, did they cut him 'cause he's a queer? And no, I don't mean that as an insult. I mean an actual, literal homo."

He was goading me. This was leftovers from our most recent argument—where my mom intervened. My dad *wanted* to kick my ass. He was just looking for a reason.

I clamped my mouth shut.

"What, you got something you wanna share with the class?" he asked. "Don't be a pussy. Spit it out."

I inhaled and exhaled deeply through my nose. I didn't dare open my mouth to breathe.

"No sir," I said, with master-class self-control. I straightened my back, standing tall. Erect. Unyielding. "I do *not* have anything to share with the class."

My dad had probably expected any variety of sarcastic or submissive responses. He probably did not expect me to deflect it with such stoicism. He glared for a solid thirty seconds. Peeled me apart with his flaying gaze.

"Don't think I forgot about you talking back to me," he said.

He leaned in. Close enough that his beer breath stung my eyes. "I've got half a mind to kick your ass, right here, right now."

"Then do it already," I said. "Cut the alpha-dog bullshit."

My dad's face flinched. For a split second, he smiled. Then his left arm swung like it always did, on a direct course to my face.

I caught his fist in my right hand.

Now don't get me wrong—it hurt like hell. Like I was catching a professionally pitched baseball without a glove. Or possibly a small cannonball launched from an actual cannon. I felt like I should have had a hole in the palm of my hand—like a ring of skin with fingers dangling from it like keys on a keychain. But as it was, his fist stopped, wrapped in my grasp. The ball of our hands trembled in between our faces.

I had just declared all-out war.

Which apparently meant my dad could fight dirty.

His knee launched upward, rocketing into my ball sack, sending my testicles clear up into my brain. The pain I felt was on a whole new level. Practically spiritual—the sort that could have been accompanied by angelic trumpets, marking a watershed in the traditional human understanding of physical pain. It also added a certain uncertainty to the future posterity of Clifford Hubbard.

I crumpled to the floor, hands cradling my balls, curled in the fetal position.

Maybe there was something mystical in the works here. Because even though I didn't hear it—"it" being the sound of a car pulling up on the gravel in front of our house, the footsteps marching up our front steps—I sure as hell saw the door fly open, and the look in my mom's eyes as they shifted between her giant, broken child on the floor and the monster who she deliberately married.

"Get out," said my mom.

"Oh, c'mon," he said. "We were just messing around."

"GET OUT!" she screamed. "GET OUT OF HERE, GET THE FUCK OUT!"

My dad didn't move, but he certainly seemed spooked. But "spooked" wasn't gonna cut it, because he needed to get the fuck out, right now.

She marched into the kitchen and opened the refrigerator. Grabbed a bottle of Bud Light by the neck.

Smashed it on the counter.

Glass sprayed and beer sloshed everywhere.

"What are you doing?" he shrieked.

Instead of responding, she dropped the neck of the broken bottle. Grabbed another Bud Light out of the fridge.

Smashed it on the counter.

Glass shrapnel jettisoned to all corners of the kitchen, and beer discharged like a liquid bomb. My mom's work uniform was soaked.

"Stop it!" he said. "Just stop it, you—"

He stepped into the kitchen, arms raised with every intent to restrain her.

That was a bad idea.

My mom raised the broken bottle like a weapon. "Stay away. You stay away from me and my son."

"Whoa, hey," he said. His hands veered upward, palms open, defensively. "Just take a deep breath..."

Deep breath? Ha! My mom took a *deep* fucking breath. Then she marched around my dad, makeshift shank bottle extended, and set a direct course to the TV set.

She grabbed it by the edges and heaved it to the edge of the stand. It tilted slightly over the edge—supported only by my mom's fierce grasp.

"Whoa, whoa, whoa, whoa, whoa!" said my dad. "Wait! Just wait!"

"GET OUT!" she screamed.

"I'm going!" he said, hands still raised. "I'm going to the bedroom."

And he was. He scurried to the bedroom as fast as he could—all but tucking a literal tail between his legs. Maybe it wasn't what my mom meant by *get out,* but it seemed good enough for the time being. He stepped inside the bedroom, and grabbed the doorknob, motioning that he was closing it.

"See?" he said. "Going."

My mom did not budge from her position with the TV.

My dad backed further into the bedroom, ever so slightly, and inched the door closed.

My mom did not budge.

He closed the door.

All of this I viewed from the living room floor, curled in the fetal position.

There was a moment of deliberation in which my mom seemed to consider whether or not she was satisfied with how the scenario had played out. Finally, she let out an exasperated breath and heaved the TV back onto its stand.

Her eyes met mine. Only then did they soften.

"Let's get you some ice," she said.

THIRTY-THREE

A girl came to school who looked, sounded, and behaved exactly like Tegan—but something was different. I couldn't even put my finger on it. It manifested itself in little things. Like the way she would occasionally smile for no reason. Or the random whistling of a peppy tune that seemed *very* non-rap-oriented. And I hate it when people use the word *twinkle* to describe the look in someone's eyes, but I swear, there was a twinkle.

I was no fool. I'd seen *Invasion of the Body Snatchers.* I knew what was up.

"Who are you?" I asked Tegan at lunch. "And what did you do with my girlfriend?"

"I'm Tegan Azalea Robertson, bitch. And I'm gonna do something with my life."

"Your middle name is Azalea?"

"Yeah, why? You gotta problem with that?"

"That is so hot."

Tegan's lips curled into that sexy smirk of hers. She wrapped her finger around my collar and pulled me close. "I'll show you hot, princess."

"Oh my God," said Aaron with a full mouth and a gaggy look on his face. He reluctantly swallowed. "People are eating at this table."

"People *were* eating at this table," said Tegan. "But now I'm'a throw my princess on the table and make unsanitary love."

For the first time in the history of ever, Lacey Hildebrandt was sitting within the now nonexistent confines of the invisible quarantine cafeteria force field. She also had this look of mild alarm.

"The List!" said Aaron. "We're here to talk about the List! Cliff, back me up here."

I *would* have backed Aaron up—except that I was so sexually overwhelmed, it was incapacitating. With a lot of concentration, I managed a nod.

Aaron reached into his pocket and removed a folded sheet of paper—the *original* hard copy of the List, scribbled in his shitty handwriting. It was severely crinkled, however, as if it had been crumpled and chucked in the trash. He laid it flat on the table and attempted—without success—to smooth out the wrinkles.

After a long, dramatic moment—the four of us hovering over this sad sheet of paper—Tegan broke the silence.

"Dude. You have worse handwriting than Frankie."

"Really?" said Aaron. "A list from God, and *that's* your first observation?"

"I know, right?" said Lacey. "It's worse than my little brother's handwriting. He's eight years old."

"Lacey!"

Lacey shrugged. "It's true."

"Dude!" Tegan exclaimed. "*Frankie's* on the List?"

Aaron seemed to get over himself quickly. "Cliff didn't tell you that?"

He looked at me. I pretended to become invisible.

"Wait—Frankie's *gang*?" said Tegan. "Holy shitballs. *I'm* on the List!"

"Cliff!" said Aaron.

"Hey, I was going to mention it!" I said. "You know . . . sometime."

"That's awesome!" said Tegan, ignoring both of us.

My and Aaron's heads turned to her like a pair of double doors.

"It is?" said Aaron.

"I'm on a List that *God* made!" said Tegan. "That's badass!"

"Yeah . . ." I said. "Yeah! That *is* badass."

"That's one item we can check off the List."

"Yea—wait, what?"

"*Show Frankie's gang a better way*," said Tegan. "We can check that off the List."

Aaron and I exchanged looks of profound confusion.

"What do you mean?" I said.

"Well, after you told me to express my feelings, and I beat the shit out of Frankie—"

"WHAT?" said Aaron.

Tegan gave me the exact same look Aaron had given me. "You didn't tell him?"

"Uh . . ." I said. "Was I supposed to do that?"

Tegan's eyeballs did a three-sixty. "Long story short: I stole Frankie's heroin, I was gonna give it to my junkie mom, and maybe I was even gonna shoot up with her. Then I changed my mind. Cliff found me on the side of the road and told me to embrace my feelings. That's when I realized I fucking hate heroin, 'cause it stole my mom from me. So I told Frankie that, punched him in the face, and now he doesn't wanna deal heroin no more."

"Holy crap," said Lacey.

"Shit on a biscuit," said Aaron.

"Anyway, I'm out," said Tegan. "I'm done dealing. I'm cleaning up. Now, I don't know what the marijuana situation is—Frankie, Jed, and Carlos will prolly keep dealing that shit until recreational use is legalized, they get a seller's permit for medical, or they're busted—but at least they're done with the dangerous stuff." She paused before adding, "It's not the *best* way ... but it is a *better* way."

My and Aaron's jaws dropped like an EDM bassline.

"So we can check that one off," said Tegan. "Right?"

"Hell yeah!" said Aaron, fist-pumping. "And Niko's not bullying anymore. That makes *two* items checked off the List."

"*And* Spinelli doesn't hate us anymore," I offered. "That's like half the battle."

"Right! I'm going to give us the benefit of the doubt and say we've accomplished two-point-five items on the List. That's exactly halfway, team!"

Yes, we were being awful generous in regards to our supposed progress on the List. But I liked to think of it as positive reinforcement.

"Not to poop on your party," said Lacey, "but you two still need to figure out what you're doing for the Sermon Showdown. It's in three days."

So much for positive reinforcement.

"Three days?" I said.

"*Three days?*" said Aaron, channeling the volume of the voice that was currently screaming inside my head.

"Um, yeah," said Lacey. "Did you guys seriously forget? Don't you have a calendar or something?"

"Hey, it's okay," I said consolingly (although I didn't know who I was consoling—Aaron or myself). "We'll just talk to Esther and tell her we need to reschedule. It's that simple."

"Yeah..." said Aaron, nodding slowly as he processed the notion. "Yeah, okay."

"Actually, it's *not* that simple," said Lacey. "Everyone knows this thing is happening in three days. The JTs put up posters and everything. And—as a champion of the Happy Valley High gossip channels—I can tell you without a *doubt* the whole school is going to be there. Trust me."

Now that she mentioned it, I *had* noticed some extra posters cluttering the walls. Unfortunately, I tended to walk the halls with my blinders on. Life was too short to stop and read about the Rubik's Cube Club or whatever.

"She's right, man," said Tegan. "This Sermon Showdown's gonna be the biggest thing since Ronda Rousey versus Holly Holm. If you try to postpone it now, it'll look like you're wussing out. Do y'all wanna look like wussies?"

I, for one, was in favor of *not* looking like a wussy. Aaron and I exchanged looks that reciprocated the feeling.

"Tell me you at *least* talked to Esther about having the entire audience judge," said Tegan.

"Uh..." I said.

"Ah..." said Aaron.

By some cosmic force of nature, my and Aaron's vacant, horror-stricken gazes homed in on a single point. A cluster of tables in the corner of the cafeteria—JT feeding grounds. At the center of it all—like a gravitational singularity—was Esther.

Aaron stood up. He dragged me up with him by my meaty elbow.

"Excuse us, ladies," said Aaron. "Cliff and I need to have a word with Esther."

———

The good news was that Esther consented to our first proposition—that the Sermon Showdown should be judged by the entire audience. We clarified that this would be gauged by audience reaction—clapping, cheering, stomping, etc. If the audience reaction was too close to call, then we'd resort to a paper vote and bring in the assistance of an unbiased teacher or faculty member to tally the numbers.

The bad news was that in regards to our second proposition—that we postpone the Sermon Showdown—Esther laughed in our faces. This resulted in the entire JT corner of the cafeteria erupting in a shock wave of laughter.

"Oh, boys," said Esther, suddenly humorless. "What are you so scared of? You have *God* on your side, don't you? How could I deprive you of the opportunity for Him to work His wonders? You're Daniel in the lion's den! Shadrach, Meshach, and Abednego, about to be cast into the fiery furnace! This is the moment when God intervenes with his mighty hand, saving his servants from complete and utter destruction—not to mention horribly embarrassing public humiliation. Provided you aren't a couple of frauds, of course. Then he'll probably let you burn."

"But—" said Aaron.

"Butts are full of crap," said Esther. "Are *you* full of crap, Aaron?"

"What?"

"Burn," said Zeke, offering Esther a fist bump.

Esther bumped his fist without even looking at it. "No, Aaron. No postponing. We're going to let this play out in a natural-selection sort of way—pardon the Darwinism. Now if that's quite all . . ."

She shooed us with a dismissive wave of her hand.

I had known all along that the Sermon Showdown was an exponentially bad idea. But apparently, it hadn't sunk into Aaron's skull until now. Between the two of us, we didn't know shit about public speaking—let alone conveying some profound message of spiritual significance.

"Maybe we can rip off Bill Pullman's speech in *Independence Day*," I suggested in the hallway.

"Who's Bill Pullman?" said Aaron.

"Wha—? He's the president of the United States!"

"What?"

"Well, in the movie, he is."

Aaron rolled his eyes.

"*Who's Bill Pullman?*" I said, mimicking Aaron's voice but with an unsubtle dose of Bullwinkle. "Jesus. Kids these days."

"Whatever, assclown. You're the one who wants to rip off the speech in a sci-fi movie."

"Just the applicable parts. *We will not go quietly into the night! We will not vanish without a fight!*"

"It's about fighting aliens."

"Well, yeah, but . . . it gets you pumped, doesn't it?"

Aaron shook his head. "I worry about you sometimes."

THIRTY-FOUR

According to Newton's third law of motion, for every action there is an equal and opposite reaction. This rule is typically applied to physics. However, in tumultuous times, it can also apply to social change.

Noah got approval to create a Gay-Straight Alliance.

After all his efforts on the school level had failed, Noah took it to the district level. He wrote a moving letter to the superintendent, pleading his case. Not that much pleading was necessary. When the superintendent learned of HVHS's ban of all extracurricular clubs—and yet allowing dozens upon dozens of questionable curriculum-related clubs to exist—the ban was overturned. It was an executive order, more or less. To emphasize the executiveness of the situation, the superintendent sent a scathing e-mail to every principal in the district, making sure no one else was instituting fringy rules that might be overstepping silly things like the Free Speech clause or the Equal Access Act.

The whole school was talking about it. The icebreaker was plastered all over the walls. Noah didn't waste a moment; he set up flyers everywhere—the cafeteria, the library, every square inch of the hallways. Even the bathrooms fell victim to Noah's rabid flyerization. It read:

WE HAVE A GAY-STRAIGHT ALLIANCE!

WHEN: DIRECTLY AFTER SCHOOL.

WHERE: ROOM 206

WHY: BECAUSE WE CAN!

This first meeting is more of an impromptu get-to-know-you. We can figure out what day/time works best for a regular meeting, and we can address what we want to accomplish. And this probably goes without saying, but this is a Gay-STRAIGHT Alliance, so even if you don't identify with the LGBTQ+ crowd, please come to show your support, to increase your understanding, and to stand up for love and tolerance. This is a judgment-free zone, so leave that crap in your locker.

This was obviously a big deal—a spark in the fires of revolution. So naturally, the fire spread. For the first time since Noah set foot in HVHS—almost three years ago now—someone new came out. A freshman girl named Robin Dunston.

Kyle Dunston's little sister.

More on that later.

So you're probably asking yourself: What does this have to do with Newton's third law of motion? Well now that you know about the "action," let me tell you about the "reaction."

The JTs weren't happy. What ensued was protesting at best. At worst, it was a full-scale riot.

Room 206—where the first GSA meeting was set to take place—was Ms. Carmen's art class. Ms. Carmen was apparently one of the few outspoken LGBT advocates on the HVHS payroll. She was more than happy to volunteer her classroom to host a Gay-Straight Alliance.

The JTs skipped first period to raid her classroom. They completely pillaged it. There was an ulterior motive—they needed poster board and markers for their own revolution. So they pilfered what they needed and ransacked the rest. Scattered supplies across the floor. Turned over desks. One particular JT felt the need to open up a tube of purple acrylic paint and finger-paint on the outside of the door: *Leviticus 20:13.*

And that was only the start. Because the JTs proceeded to march the halls, waving homemade signs that said things like HOMOSEXUALITY IS A MENTAL ILLNESS and NO TOLERANCE FOR EVIL.

This went on for hours.

Once it became abundantly clear that this was out of the school's control, Principal McCaffrey called the police. The police came. Well, a single officer came—Sheriff Barton. He was a roly-poly dude with a gut that spilled over his belt, forearms like whole otters, and a salt-and-pepper mustache that hid the mouth-cleavage of his great, quivering jowls. The bell rang, dismissing third period, when I saw him. He waddled into HVHS with one hand on his belt, the other swinging like a pendulum made of bratwurst. The picketing came to a staggered halt. Esther, however, pushed her way through the crowds and met him like a crashing wave.

There was a nearby water fountain. I decided that I was suddenly very dehydrated.

"Now, Esther—" said Barton.

"Sheriff Barton, we are completely within our rights," said Esther. "This is our freedom of assembly. Our freedom of association. Our freedom of speech! And that's to say nothing of our religious freedom, which nobody gives a *shit* about."

"I'm afraid it doesn't work like that," said Barton. "I heard you guys trashed a classroom?"

"Trashed?" said Esther. "That's debatable. Personally, I think we made an improvement. Besides, Ms. Carmen is a socialist."

"Socialist or not, you can't go defacing people's classrooms. That's called vandalism. It's against the law."

"So what? Are you going to arrest us?" Esther placed her hands defiantly on her hips. "There are fifty-three of us, so I sure hope you have enough room in your car."

"Look, don't worry about the classroom. I'll take care of it. But I already called your father. Told him about the situation on the drive over. He said this needs to stop."

Esther's mouth compacted, her eyes swelling with indignation.

"I get where you're coming from, Esther. But there are other ways to fight this."

"Such as...?"

"I don't know. Like, attending school board meetings. Signing petitions. Making shirts that state your stance. Literally anything that's not *against* the law is within your God-given rights to protest. But right now, the law says you need to go to school and attend your classes. Otherwise, that's called truancy."

I glanced up from the fountain. Esther seemed thoroughly unimpressed with Sheriff Barton's suggestions, so he leaned forward and covered his mouth.

"Look," he said in a low voice, "They have their little club. But what if people are too...*nervous* to go to the meetings? That would be a shame, but it wouldn't be your fault."

Esther smiled. Sheriff Barton winked. With that, they parted ways.

———

Robin Dunston was a quiet, mousy bookworm who did everything in her power to not draw attention to herself. She wore glasses and cardigans, and she looked like she had the equivalent body mass of my left butt cheek. She was mostly invisible, but I sometimes saw her in the hall or the cafeteria, lost in the pages of a light read—Stephen King, or Haruki Murakami, or Fyodor Dostoyevsky. No kidding. She was like a miniature philosopher. Her blood relation to Kyle was baffling.

By the end of sixth period, Robin's locker was plastered in female porn.

She took one look at her locker—and the laughing crowd it had accumulated—and took off.

I found her around the corner, curled in a ball, sobbing.

I wanted to say something. But what? My only connection to her was Kyle, and my connection to him was that I hated his guts and got suspended for punching his smug face out the back of his skull.

I started to walk past her because this was what I was—a coward—but for some reason the image of the Star Child flashed in my brain.

We are meant to become more than what we are.

I stopped. Looked at her.

"Hey," I said. "You okay?"

Robin jolted with a start—unfurling from her ball, limbs flailing. Her frantic gaze did a wide horizontal sweep. Locked onto my legs. From there, she vertically scanned the giant, concerned Neanderthal, hovering over her like a monument. When she realized I was a non-threat, she sniffed, wiped her eyes with her sleeve, and attempted to nod. However, the gravitational axis of her head seemed to rotate sideways. Her head bobbled for a moment, and then she shook it fiercely. She bit her lip, and a second wave of tears welled in her eyes.

"Is it okay if I sit?" I said.

Robin could barely control the movement of her head anymore, let alone speak. So instead, she pulled her knees in, stuffed her face in the crook of her arm, and gave me a thumbs-up.

I sat down.

"We're going to stop this," I said.

Robin pulled her face out of her arm. Looked at me with red, swollen eyes.

"Don't take this the wrong way," she said, "but I don't believe in God."

"You don't need to," I said. "We don't care what anyone believes in. That's not why we're doing this."

"Why *are* you doing this?"

"Because Happy Valley High School sucks. It has to get better than this."

———

After school, Tegan and I found each other. In light of recent events, my mind was on a single track. I immediately proceeded to blurt out the contents of my brain.

"Can I ask you a weird question?" I said.

"Uh-oh," said Tegan, in a state of low-key panic. "Sure?"

"Are you bisexual?"

Tegan laughed. "Oh god. Okay. Fair enough."

"Are you?"

"I assume you're talking about that thing with Crissy Cranston?"

I mean, I wasn't *not* talking about that thing with Crissy Cranston.

"I guess I am," said Tegan. "Although when I told you about that, I was totally just trying to get your attention."

"What? Seriously?"

Tegan laughed again—even louder this time—rolling her head

back and pressing her palms to her eyes. "Oh god! I'm not sure what's at fault here: my flirting, or your inability to pick up on flirting. Or both. Prolly both, right?"

"Wait. You were *flirting* with me?"

"Oh my God, Cliff! Seriously? Of course I was flirting with you! I invited you to a hypothetical three-way with me and Crissy!"

"Oh."

Tegan seemed to laugh and moan simultaneously. Her hands slid down her face, pulling her cheeks and bottom lip down. "Bluhhhhhhh."

"Are you okay?"

"Yes, Cliff, I'm fine. Look, I'm'a just come out and say it: I've had a crush on you for the past three years."

"Three years?"

"Maybe longer. I think I liked you in middle school, too—although it's kind of an obsessive blur."

I stared at Tegan, completely open-mouthed. It was a miracle my tongue wasn't lolling out like a banana slug.

"What I'm trying to say is: Yes, I'm bisexual. But I'm also *soooooooo* overwhelmingly Cliffsexual, it kind of overrides everything else." Tegan paused before adding, "I guess you're asking this to see if I want to go to the GSA meeting with you?"

With that, Tegan and I had a destination.

"Can I ask *you* a weird question?" said Tegan.

I looked at Tegan.

"Back when I"—she rolled her eyes—*"flirted* with you . . . I didn't make you feel uncomfortable, did I?"

"Uncomfortable?"

"It's just . . . my cousin, Madeliene, is always on Facebook, talking about how men either treat women like sex objects or they body-shame them, and it made me think of how I catcalled you, and how it mighta made you feel like an object or like I was making fun of your body, but honestly, I was just a dummy who didn't know how to express my feelings for you, so I did what I always saw Frankie doing to girls, which is stupid. Anyway, if I ever made you feel uncomfortable, I'm really sorry."

"Tegan?"

"Yeah?"

"Thanks. I appreciate it."

Tegan smiled bashfully—blushed, even—although she attempted to hide the evidence by popping her jacket collar and sinking her head into her shoulders.

"Don't look at me," she said.

"Are you blushing?"

"Dammit, I said don't look at me!"

I laughed, Tegan blushed even harder, and she shoved me—which only seemed to feed the cycle of laughing and blushing. Although both of our reactions faded in the wake of room 206. I heard voices coming from the open doorway.

"You need to get out," said a voice that was definitely Noah.

"But I thought *anyone* was invited," said a voice that was definitely Esther. "We just want to hear what you have to say. Isn't that right, everyone?"

There was a roar of a response—cheers and laughter and one very distinguished homophobic slur. This only fed the laughter.

Tegan and I rounded the corner and stepped inside. There was Noah. And Esther. And all fifty-something members of the JTs, occupying the space like it was Wall Street.

My jaw disconnected.

"The fuck is this?" said Tegan.

Esther looked at her and shrugged innocently. "Well, it's *supposed* to be a Gay-Straight Alliance. Personally, I came to educate myself on the ways in which straights and gays can maintain peaceful relations. But I'll tell ya, I've felt nothing but discrimination!"

Noah was standing rigid at the head of the classroom. His arms were straight metal rods, clear to his iron-knob fists.

"I mean, was there a dress code that I missed?" said Esther. "Let me guess: leather chaps and those cute little Chippendale cuffs?"

"If you don't get out..." said Noah, his voice a warning.

Esther widened her eyes at me, faux-appalled, and gestured at Noah. "Are you hearing this, Cliff? You know, it's a wonder *he's* not on the List. You and Aaron should look into that. Make sure you guys didn't miss something." Her gaze shifted past me to the doorway. "Oh, hey, company!"

Tegan and I turned around. There was Robin Dunston—standing small in the doorway, clutching her purse tight in front of her. Her entire frame seemed to shrink, as if she were trying to take up as little space as possible. Frankly, I was surprised to see her, after what the JTs did.

But not nearly as surprised as I was to see her big brother, Kyle Dunston, behind her.

He did not look happy.

"No way!" said Zeke. His lanky frame was wedged awkwardly in a tablet arm desk, his legs kicked up on the surface. He was practically folded in half. "Kyle, are you into dudes? I should let you know, I don't give it on the first date."

Kyle marched right up to Zeke's desk. Zeke seemed to realize his mistake. Unfortunately, he was also folded like a lawn chair. Kyle shoved the entire desk-chair combo over, with Zeke still in it. Naturally, Zeke screamed like the backup singer of a bad emo song. The surrounding JTs scattered like ants in a disturbed anthill.

"Mess with my sister again, and I'll kill you," said Kyle. With that, he started for the door. "We're going, Robin."

Robin—still standing silently in the doorway—nodded. Together, they disappeared out the door.

That was the last brick in Noah's crumbling resolve. He didn't last ten seconds before he exited after them.

Tegan and I reluctantly followed.

Behind us, cheers erupted in unsettling victory.

THIRTY-FIVE

The next day, I discovered a small gift in my locker—an unlabeled DVD, accompanied by a most peculiar note:

Use this against Esther at the Sermon Showdown.
—HAL

If there was any doubt that Shane's secret girlfriend—the mysterious Haley—dropped the journal off at my house, it was gone now. For whatever reason, she was reaching out to me.

But that was a rather trivial observation compared to how badly I needed to watch this DVD right now.

"Aaron! Aaron! Aaron!"

I ran and screamed all the way over to Aaron's locker—which was only eleven units away on the opposite wall. He eyed me with savage skepticism.

"If Tegan bank-robbed your virginity last night," said Aaron, "you really don't need to lather me in the details."

I took the DVD with the note Scotch-taped to its blank surface and shoved it in Aaron's face. "Read this."

Aaron reared his head back defensively. He grabbed the DVD and read. "Holy shitballs."

We didn't even need to say anything to each other. We turned and sprinted in the direction of Mr. Gibson's computer lab.

———

I always just figured Jack and Julian lived in the computer lab—like the Boxcar Children, but nerdier. No home, no normal school classes—they were just these computer-nerd orphans who were capable of skipping so many grades, the school district tossed up their hands in exasperation, and threw them in the computer lab, and said, "Okay, nerd-orphans, teach yourselves."

Much to my disbelief, as Aaron and I entered the computer lab, Jack and Julian were nowhere to be seen.

But the lab wasn't empty. Mr. Gibson's computer lab was occupied by none other than Mr. Gibson.

If I were to describe Mr. Gibson in three words, those three words would be *frazzled* and *awkward* and *mustached*. Of those three adjectives, *mustached* would be his primary personality trait. He groomed that thing like it was a Kentucky Derby racehorse. It was the source of all his confidence—which was a tragedy, really, because the thing looked ridiculous.

The tardy bell rang.

"Can I help you boys?" said Mr. Gibson.

"We just wanted to watch a movie," I said.

Aaron elbowed me. "An *educational* movie," he said.

"Y-y-y-yeah," I stammered. "For school."

"Our teacher is giving us the period to research."

"Huh," said Mr. Gibson. "Well, knock yourselves out. Username and password is the same as your student e-mail."

We complied—sitting together at the computer farthest from Mr. Gibson.

Aaron inserted the mystery DVD in the disk drive. It opened in the default media player, and I pressed Play.

The video opened to the setup of a porno.

Okay, *technically* it was a desktop webcam view of Esther Poulson's bedroom. Zeke Gallagher was guest-starring, wearing nothing but gym shorts—spread-eagled, back exposed, wrists tied to the sturdy curtain rod of Esther's bedroom window. Esther, meanwhile, was holding an honest-to-god tasseled whip.

"Why are you being punished?" said Esther.

"I . . . I keep having impure thoughts," said Zeke.

Esther whipped Zeke's back. He yelped—although there seemed to be a fine line between pain and excitement.

"No. Way," said Aaron.

Esther lifted the tasseled whip to her nose and smelled it like a bouquet. "Mmm. *Just* impure thoughts?"

"No," said Zeke. "I masturbated to your family vacation pictures. You were wearing a red swimsuit with white polka dots."

"How many *times* did you masturbate to those pictures?"

"Nineteen. Nineteen times."

"Christ on a Triscuit!" I said.

"Nineteen times." Esther shook her head, *tsk-tsk*ing. She whipped him again.

"Ohhhhh," said Zeke. "Ohhhhhhhhhhh."

There wasn't an inch of his body that wasn't totally enjoying this.

"Tell me what you want," said Esther.

"I want your body," said Zeke.

Esther whipped him again. Zeke howled so loud, I felt embarrassed for everyone in the neighborhood.

"Well, you can't have it," she said. "My body is a temple."

Again with the whip.

"AHHHHHHHHHH."

"Judas Priest!" said Mr. Gibson from his far corner of the computer lab. "What the heck are you boys watching?"

"Uh . . ." I said.

"Um . . ." said Aaron.

"Er . . ." I said.

We ejected the disk and ran like hell.

———

So, just to recap, HAL gave us a Puritan-style dominatrix-BDSM pseudo-porno starring Esther Poulson and Zeke Gallagher. The only thing missing was gift wrap and a literal silver platter.

At first, I thought it was homemade. But considering this was HAL we were dealing with, I wondered if maybe she'd hacked Esther's computer webcam. It was, after all, slightly off center, and neither Esther nor Zeke paid the camera any heed—highly unusual for their level of narcissism.

After school, we drove to Aaron's house where we rewatched the video in its kinky entirety—this time within the privacy of his bikini-clad bedroom. It lasted a grueling twenty-three minutes, and Esther never gave Zeke any. Unless "any" was a raging boner.

The video ended on its own, rather than being turned off by Esther—solid evidence that HAL hacked the *shit* out of Esther's webcam.

Aaron and I leaned back in our chairs and processed exactly what it was we had in our possession.

"This would destroy Esther," said Aaron.

"Yes," I said, nodding definitively. "Yes, it would."

"What do you think? Can we use this?"

"Can we? Or *should* we?"

"Um . . . either?"

I sighed. "Would it sound stupid if I said I felt wrong about using this?"

The words already sounded stupid coming out of my mouth. Esther and Zeke totally deserved this. After the stunt they pulled with Robin and the GSA meeting, this was karma at its best.

"No, I agree," said Aaron.

"What? You *do*?"

"Well, number five on the List is 'Find and stop HAL.' So if we're firing the ammunition that HAL gives us, we're kind of doing the exact opposite of that."

Yes. There was also that.

"So I guess that means we're back to square one with the Sermon Showdown?" I said.

"Bro," said Aaron. "We're at square zero. Maybe in the square negatives."

———

There was something of a paradigmal shift in the Hubbard household. It mostly involved my mom not putting up with my dad's shit anymore, and my dad not knowing what to do about it. He was acting more and more like the paranoid weasel captain of a mutinying ship. She stopped buying his beer when she went grocery shopping, she stopped making him dinner, she even stopped doing his laundry. She would actually physically separate his laundry from hers in their shared hamper, do her laundry (and mine), and leave his dirty clothes in a pile on the floor.

At first there was yelling. But then it was discovered that my mom could scream even louder than my dad—hitting ungodly vocal frequencies—with the added bonus of portraying a certain Helena Bonham Carter level of psychoticism.

Basically, I was eyeballs deep in tension. Eight hundred square feet of Marital Battlezone.

I had been waiting my whole life for this insurrection. But now that it was happening, I didn't know what to do with myself. So I pulled a notebook and a freshly sharpened pencil out of my backpack, opened to a blank sheet of paper, and wrote *Sermon Showdown*. I underlined it.

I stared at the stretch of infinite white beneath that line. It was a blizzard—vast and impenetrable. My pencil hovered over the storm. Trembled in the wake of its pale fury.

My resolve crumbled within five minutes. I retreated to my bookshelf of movies, grabbed a Lord of the Rings DVD—I didn't even pay attention to which one—and inserted it in the DVD player.

Orcs and Dark Lords aside, Middle-Earth just seemed a lot friendlier place than real life.

I hate the phrase *life goes on*.

I mean, sure it does, technically speaking—but it doesn't always go on the way that it's supposed to. Like, if a nuclear reactor melts down, and Earth is showered in fallout, yeah, life will go on—with

Siamese vegetables, two-headed super-rats, and the mutant cast of *The Hills Have Eyes*.

After the JTs' initial victory over the GSA, school went on, so to speak. Everyone was rushing to their lockers, rushing to their friends, rushing to their classes. Noah, however, was an effigy—a stationary monument representing the pinnacle of suck. He was partially hidden at the end of a row of lockers, leaning into the nook, staring at his phone. It looked like he was texting—or trying to, at least. The words in his head seemed to experience difficulty traveling to his thumbs.

"Hey there, lover boy," said Roy Porter—not only a JT, but also a VIP member of the football douchebag clique. I assumed he was a lineman, based on his physique, which resembled a two-hundred-pound bipedal frog. "Who ya textin'?"

Noah glanced up, deadpan, and said, "Your mom."

Apparently, Roy didn't expect the tables to turn so quickly, because he immediately took the defensive. "Hey, don't you dare talk about my mama."

"I'm not talking about her. We're just having sex."

Hooooooo boy. Noah was definitely having a bad day, because he never shit-talked like this.

"You goddamn queer!"

"Hey, it's cool," said Noah. "If I become your stepdad, you don't have to call me Dad. 'Sir' will suffice."

Either Noah had overestimated his luck, or he didn't give a shit. (Most likely the latter.) Roy lunged at Noah, fists tight.

I intervened like a freight train.

I didn't attack Roy, per se. I just sort of speed-walked into him. He bounced off my gut and into the nearest locker.

"What the HEY-ell?" he said, unleashing the Gift of Tongues in true redneck form. "Why you lousy piece o—!"

Roy regained his balance, pulled his fists into orbit, took one step toward me, and then his spine bent backward as he absorbed me in my tsunamic entirety.

"—Hoooooooly shit," he concluded. He took a step backward and sized me up, from my head to my size-fourteen sneakers. "Damn, you're big. Why ain't you on the football team?"

"I don't like football," I said.

"Huh," said Roy. "Well that's a damn shame." He slowly backed away, but not before pointing a threatening finger at Noah. "I'm not through with you, Poulson."

"Yes, you are," I said.

Roy looked at me, mouth ajar. His pointed finger hung awkwardly in the air. He moved his finger uncertainly, like a drunk magician.

And then he shuffled away.

I glanced at Noah. His mouth was small and tight, and his eyes were hard. He looked anything but grateful. "I don't need you to protect me, Cliff."

"Oh, don't worry, I walked into him by accident. Nothing personal."

Noah's mouth flinched—almost a smile.

"Hey," I said. "Sorry about the other day."

"It's okay, Cliff," he said. Even though it very clearly wasn't.

"So what's the plan?"

"The plan?"

"You know. For the GSA."

Noah shrugged. "There is no plan."

"You mean, you don't know where to move it?"

"I mean, I don't know what would be the point of moving it."

I stared at Noah. Waited for the smirk that indicated he was just messing with me. Of course there was a point! Noah had only spent his entire high school career working for this.

The smirk never came.

"Suppose I move it," said Noah. "What then? The JTs will just crash the new location. Suppose there are others like Robin? The JTs will just harass them, too—make their lives a living hell—and they'll have nowhere to go."

"So you're giving up?" I said. "Everything you've worked for—you're just gonna throw that out the window?"

"I don't *know*, Cliff!" Noah's voice was a crack of thunder. "I just . . . I need time to think."

Noah pushed past me and walked away, plunging himself into the crowd.

A blur in the chaos.

Gone.

THIRTY-SIX

I found Tegan in the Quad, nonchalantly spying on the JTs. She was leaning, James Dean–style, against the wall, thumbs in her belt loops, aggressively chewing a piece of bubble gum.

Okay, so *spying* was a loose term. It indicated she was trying not to be seen when, in reality, Tegan was the most visible thing in a hundred-foot radius. Even *with* Esther spewing her usual fire and brimstone.

Tegan blew a bubble half the size of her head. It popped loudly, and somehow managed to get back in her mouth without swallowing her face.

"Bubble gum?" I said.

"When I don't smoke pot, I smoke cigarettes," said Tegan. "Except I quit smoking when I was fourteen. Saw this documentary in Health about lung cancer. Scared the livin' fuck outta me. But I need to keep my mouth busy. Therefore, bubble gum."

"Ah."

"Want some? It's Bubble Yum. Cotton candy flavor."

"No thanks."

"Suit yourself. Cotton candy's the shit."

Normally, Esther had no problem condescending to anyone who dared to crash JT gatherings. She was, after all, the very definition of alpha. But Tegan was in a category all her own. She was more like a lone wolf. A Gigantor-size, Mordor-bred wolfasaurus rex from Middle-Earth. With rabies. She would tear the esophaguses (esophagi?) out of any pack that dared to challenge her.

I think Esther was a little intimidated by Tegan.

"Satan is disguised beneath a cloak of so-called tolerance!" said Esther—louder and more maniacal than usual. "He takes sin and sugarcoats it in political correctness. But this idea of 'tolerance' simply means tolerating sin. And I, for one, won't tolerate it."

"This bitch makes me wanna punch a brick wall," said Tegan loudly. "How can people even listen to this bullshit?"

I shrugged. "She's a good public speaker, I guess."

"She's a good public menace."

"Yeah, but she knows how to articulate things."

"*You* know how to articulate things."

"Not in front of a crowd of people."

"Do you and Aaron know what you're gonna say?"

"Do you mind?"

That came from Esther, who was clearly done with our loud side conversation.

I was suddenly staring down a scowling army of upper-class white kids with a Sunday School complex.

"We're *trying* to have a spiritual moment here," Esther continued.

Tegan stopped chewing. She spit out her gum like a viscid pink bullet, halfway across the Quad.

And then she marched straight toward Esther.

Esther, realizing her spiritual bubble was being encroached upon, panicked and took several steps back.

"Hey," said Zeke, stepping between them. "What do you think you're— Ow, ow, ow, ow, ow!"

Tegan grabbed Zeke's skinny arm and twisted it behind his back. She held it for only a few seconds before shoving him aside.

She closed the gap between her and Esther, who had unwittingly cornered herself against the fountain, calves pressed against the Aztec-tiled surface.

"Lemme tell you," said Tegan. "I'd love nothing more than to kick your self-righteous ass to the Vatican and back."

Esther swallowed hard.

"But I don't have to," Tegan continued, "because Cliff and Aaron are gonna do that for me. When this Sermon Showdown goes down, they're gonna blow you out of your holier-than-thou stratosphere and power-slam you down to Planet fucking Earth where you belong, you hoity-toity psycho bitch."

With that, Tegan turned and left Esther and the JTs in the meta-phorical dust of her badassery. She made a drive-by grab at my hand and towed my shell-shocked ass behind her.

"Hey, Tegan," said Esther. "Just curious—who's the man in this relationship?"

This earned more than a few laughs from the JTs.

"I'm sorry," said Tegan. "Tegan's out of the office right now. If you have any questions, comments, or concerns, you can take them up with her secretary." Tegan flipped her middle finger, and then brought it to life with a cartoonish, falsetto voice: *"Hello, how may I fuck you?"*

And on that note, we left Esther and the JTs.

"So . . ." I said, finally—when I was sufficiently convinced that the JTs wouldn't mob us and subject our pagan asses to death by pressing,

Salem witch–style. "You know there's no way in *hell* Aaron and I can out-preach Esther, right?"

"I know."

"Oh," I said, mildly wounded. "Well...thanks for the vote of confidence."

"I'll tell you what your problem is," said Tegan. "You need to stop worrying about out-*preaching* her. Preaching is the *problem*. Show her what it means to be a human being. I'm pretty sure the whole damn school knows how to do that better than her."

That's when it happened. My brain was the Death Star, and Tegan had just fired a couple of proton torpedoes into the thermal exhaust port, and *BOOM!*

"Holy shit," I said.

"What?"

"I have an idea."

———

I told Aaron my brilliant idea. At least, I *hoped* it was brilliant. Aaron was sort of the determining factor. Tegan told me the idea was "dope"; however,

1. she was a biased entity interested in boosting my fragile self-esteem, and
2. I also recalled Tegan calling *Sharknado*—an objectively terrible movie—dope, and now I had all sorts of mixed feelings regarding its connotation.

I told Aaron the idea. He basically had a conniption of raging excitement.

"AHHHHHHHHHHHHHHHHH," said Aaron.

I nodded, cluelessly. "So . . . is that a good *ah* or a bad *ah*?"

"Good *ah*! Definitely good *ah*!"

Oh phew. I let out an intense sigh of relief.

"It's brilliant!" said Aaron. "This is it. This is the sermon that's gonna kick Esther's ass."

"Technically, it's not a sermon."

"No, it's *better* than a sermon! Shit, we need to talk to Jack and Julian ASAP."

———

Jack and Julian were essential to the plan in one crucial aspect. And because Aaron was experiencing a nuclear-powered adrenaline rush, we found them rather quickly. It helped that it was lunchtime, and they were sitting at the nerdiest table this side of Comic Con.

Jack and Julian were merely the tip of the geeky iceberg. When you dared descend to the shady underbelly of HVHS's fandom subculture, there was no unseeing and unhearing what you saw and heard. The major players in this pit of nerdophilia included:

1. Seth Glover—chubby, with a mushroom cloud of curly hair, and visibly sexually frustrated. It was also rumored that he could quote the entire first season of *Battlestar Galactica*.
2. Diego Martinez, whose life was cosplaying. Even now—at school—he was half-cosplaying. Today, he was wearing an official *Assassin's Creed* jacket, gothy fingerless gloves, and combat boots that reeked of Hot Topic.
3. Becky Winston, who kind of resembled an anthropomorphic aardvark from the PBS cartoon *Arthur*. She was also deeply,

romantically, sexually in love with the Doctor. The character from *Doctor Who*. All thirteen incarnations.

Naturally, they were taking part in the archetypal nerd debate:

SETH: Star Wars and Star Trek are two entirely different things. You can't just say one is better than the other.

JULIAN: But I did. Star Wars is rad, and William Shatner has the past tense of *shit* in his name.

BECKY: Dude. Shatner is so hot.

DIEGO: (*melodramatically*) Shatner's idea of . . . acting resembles a teenage . . . girl trying to drive a . . . stick.

BECKY: Dude. *I* drive a stick. *You* drive a Prius.

SETH: Okay, Shatner is bad. But both series have had highs and lows. I mean, what about *Attack of the Clones*?

BECKY: Dude . . . Hayden Chris . . . tensen is so . . . hot.

DIEGO: Nice use of the Shatner pause!

JULIAN: *Clones* only sucked because Jar Jar Binks got so much hate, George Lucas decided against revealing him as a Sith Lord.

JACK: Oh boy, here we go.

SETH: That's just a fan theory. Jar Jar Binks is *not* a Sith Lord.

JULIAN: That's what Lord Jar Jar *wants* you to think.

SETH: He's also not a real person.

JULIAN: Why do you think Count Dooku was such a lame villain?

JACK: Because George Lucas is a shitty writer?

JULIAN: Because he's a filler villain! Because it was meant to be Jar Jar all along!

Enter AARON, Savior of Happy Valley High School; and CLIFF, his ginormous-ass sidekick.

"Trek and Wars are great and all," I said, nonchalantly strolling onto the nerd scene, "but have you seen *Firefly*?"

"OH MY GOD, YES," said Diego.

"THANK YOU," said Jack.

"MAL REYNOLDS IS SO HOT," said Becky.

"Wow," said Aaron. "Nice icebreaker. So you guys like bugs?"

"Not that firefly," I whispered.

"Right." Aaron cleared his throat into his fist. "Hey, guys. And girl. Not to interrupt, but Cliff and I are working on a...*film* project...of sorts. And we were wondering if any of you nerds knew anything about filming. And video editing. Bonus points if you have equipment."

"Um, do you have a smartphone?" said Diego.

"Disregard this Hot Topic–clad, wannabe-assassin imbecile," said Julian.

"Hey!"

"What you want is a Galaxy S7 Edge. It's a twelve megapixel f/one-point-seven shooter. Best dynamic range, widest aperture, best texture and contrast, best low-light shooting, and fastest autofocus. You can even shoot it underwater! Sort of. Also, I have one."

"Or you can use an iPhone," said Jack.

"Or you can use an iPhone if you want to Snapchat nudes to your hipster baby mama while using a filter to turn your face into a piece of toast BECAUSE YOU'RE A MORON."

"Star Wars sucks."

"Okay. That's it." Julian pushed his chair back and stood up from the table. "I'm gonna karate-brown-belt your ass."

"Is a 'brown' belt what they give people who are full of shit?"

"AHHHHHHHHHHHH!" said Julian, hands in karate-chopping position.

"Whoa, hey hey hey!" said Becky. "Chill, boys. You're both pretty."

"Look, we're just trying to film something for the Sermon Showdown," said Aaron.

That shut everyone up. It also stopped what might have been the funniest martial arts battle of all time. But it was a loss I was willing to take because we had shit to do.

"Wait," said Jack. "You want us to *film* your sermon for the Sermon Showdown?"

"Well, it's not really a *sermon* per se," I said. "But yeah, basically."

"I'm filming," said Julian.

"No, *I'm* filming," said Jack.

"I've got some video-editing software," said Seth.

"Do you need music?" said Diego. "I can mix music."

"Hey, I wanna help!" said Becky.

And just like that, we had an entire crew of techie geniuses at our disposal. It was time to get started.

———

Aaron and I were pumped. We were actively discussing the details of our highly experimental film project—set to begin ASAP—when we walked into fifth-period English.

There, sitting behind Mr. Spinelli's desk . . .

. . . was Mr. Spinelli.

I made it about three steps through the door before I stumbled to a halt and said, "Holy shit."

"Language, Mr. Hubbard," said Spinelli. He sent me a stern, Grinchy glance.

And then he smiled.

The tardy bell rang. Aaron and I hurried to our seats, but our mouths were hanging permanently open.

Spinelli stood up, grabbed his mangled copy of *The Old Man and the Sea*, and began pacing. "Some of you," he said, "might be wondering why Mr. Spinelli cares so much about this godforsaken book. Maybe you're saying, *Well, this doesn't apply to me. I don't even like fishing.*"

This earned him several laughs. I wasn't one of them because I still couldn't figure out how to move my mouth—a necessary function for laughter.

"From the very first page," said Spinelli, "the old man, Santiago, is characterized as a person struggling to overcome defeat. He's gone eighty-four days without catching a fish—almost reaching his eighty-seven-day record. Everything about Santiago is downtrodden and defeated. He is a mere speck in a vast ocean that is so much bigger and more powerful than he is. And yet, despite the complete and utter hopelessness of his situation, he resolves to sail beyond the other fishermen, to the deepest, darkest, uncharted reaches of the ocean where the greatest fish are rumored to reside."

Spinelli ceased pacing, and turned to face us. His eyes were deep and strange.

"Why?" said Spinelli. "Why does he do this?"

Lacey raised her hand timidly.

"Yes, Lacey."

"Because he has hope?"

"Hope is certainly a part of it. But hope in what? Does he hope that the universe will just cut him a break and give him a fish already?"

I thought of Aaron and the List. I thought of who I was before I met him, and all of the horrible, horrible shit that had happened. And I thought of who I was now.

I raised my hand.

Spinelli's eyes narrowed on me. "Yes, Mr. Hubbard."

"He has hope that the ocean will make him into something stronger," I said. "Maybe even strong enough to *defeat* the ocean."

Spinelli smiled.

"We are all in an ocean," he said. "Every one of us. Some of us are barely swimming, some of us are drowning, and there are some of us still who are being tossed in waves and dashed upon the rocks. And often we feel that we won't survive. Maybe that ocean is school, and we're struggling to get decent grades, or to fit in, or maybe we're just trying to survive the hurtful words and actions of people who don't understand their own cruelty. But one thing is certain—something that Hemingway is trying to teach us through Santiago—we, as human beings, are made to transcend. I believe that there is something deep down inside of us that resonates with the universe. A purpose. And once we learn what that purpose is"—Spinelli looked directly at me—"even the whole ocean cannot stop us."

THIRTY-SEVEN

Aaron and I split up to cover more ground. Jack followed me, and Julian followed Aaron.

What we were filming was basically an interview/montage/documentary/poem.

This involved talking to lots of people—although we didn't really have set questions. It was mostly just explaining the nature of the project and letting people say what they *wanted* to say.

The results were rather astounding.

We started with the easy targets—those who were morally obligated to talk to us (aka Tegan and Lacey), and branched out from there. Heather Goodman, Jed, Carlos...even faculty like Spinelli.

Even Robin, who seemed like she was doing okay.

Even Noah, who clearly wasn't.

Even Niko!

It helped that our cause had already become the stuff of bizzaro legend. Everyone knew about Aaron's alleged God experience, that Neanderthal was his "divinely appointed" sidekick, and that the Sermon Showdown was essentially another bullet on the List. And whether people thought we were insane or awesome or—most likely—both, *everyone* was fascinated. Our cause was so weird, it was impossible to feel indifferent about it. So when word spread that we were making a film and "interviewing" people as our response to the Sermon Showdown, we didn't even need to find people. They started coming to us.

Some more awkwardly than others.

"Neanderthal!" said Frankie. "'Sup, *dawg*."

He swooped up from behind and gave me a sideways hug/fist-bump thingy. Actually, it all happened so fast, I wasn't sure *what* it was, but it seemed assuredly masculine.

Jack went rigid, like he was witnessing a mugging.

"Heard y'all were making a movie," said Frankie. "Interviewing people for this Sermon Showdown shit. Thought you'd like to talk to the most spiritual-ass person here."

I wasn't quite sure how to respond to that.

"Uhrrrm…" I said. "Yeah. Sure. Of course."

"Great. So. Um…" For whatever reason, his volume dropped to a whisper. "Do you think Tegan will see this?"

Again, an appropriate response seemed to elude me.

"Probably…?" I said with infinite indefiniteness.

"Okay," said Frankie, nodding with increasing enthusiasm. "Okay, cool. Yeah. Great."

We filmed Frankie. And what he said was kind of mind-blowing.

Frankie wasn't an anomaly. Everywhere, people were opening up.

Jack was kind of amazing, too. Whenever I wasn't interviewing people, he was filming everyone and everything—capturing the world in its every waking moment. The sun had reached that perfect spot in the sky when it was bright but not glaring, warm but not uncomfortable, breathing light and life across the small-town horizon. I heard thrushes singing their whirling, reedy love songs, and the cicadas had composed a symphony in the western yellow pines—a sound track to a simpler form of life. You could feel the human connection. It was an existential string connecting soul to soul in a web with a perfect center.

There was a togetherness to the world. A fullness. Everything was in its right place.

Everything just felt . . . *more*.

That night, the Nerd Herd (Jack, Julian, Seth, Diego, and Becky) pulled a video-editing, all-nighter pizza party—funded by Aaron's college tuition. This involved four larges from Pizza Hut, every caffeinated product known to man, and several hours of raw footage that needed to be chopped down to five minutes tops—preferably three, according to Jack and his "YouTube statistics."

"You go longer than five, and you'll lose everybody's five-minute attention span," said Jack. "Four is better. Three is ideal."

Fortunately for us, pumping five teenage techie geniuses full of caffeine was the equivalent of building a sentient supercomputer.

THIRTY-EIGHT

The day of the Sermon Showdown had arrived.

The school was buzzing—a beehive of throbbing, pulsating antici-pation. The halls were so filled with excited chatter, all the words and squeals and laughter blended together into a whirring drone. It was giving me a headache. Aaron too. Except his headache looked like he was being crushed in a trash compactor of sound claustrophobia.

"Are you okay?" I asked.

I spotted Aaron hovering in front of his locker, index and middle fingers pressed to his temples, attempting to locate his cerebral Make It Stop button.

"Yeah," said Aaron, kind of blankly.

"Oh," I said. "Okay. If you're sure..."

And that's when Aaron collapsed. His body went limp, and he dropped like a noodle.

The good news was that Aaron regained consciousness within fifteen seconds. The bad news was that I had no way of knowing if his brain was bleeding again or not. So consciousness notwithstanding, I cradled Aaron in my arms like the world's buffest baby and ran him to the nurse's office, screaming "Nine-one-one! Somebody call nine-one-one!"

"I'm fine, Cliff!" said Aaron. "Oh my God, put me down!"

"Don't move, Aaron. You might be dying. CALL NINE-ONE-ONE."

So naturally, about one hundred teenagers frantically dialed 911, informing about one hundred different 911 operators of a very horrible and ambiguous medical emergency.

It was enough to get an ambulance to HVHS in ten minutes flat.

"I'm *fine*!" Aaron explained to the two EMTs—one who was built like an *actual* bodybuilder, with muscles on top of his muscles, and the other who bore a remarkable resemblance to a weasel (in both stature and facial construct)—both of whom were preoccupied taking his vitals. "I was out for, like, ten seconds."

"It was more like fifteen seconds," I said.

"Go away, Cliff!"

"I told you, you need to leave," said Weasel.

"It's okay, I'm his brother," I lied.

The muscular EMT glanced between the two of us, probably noticing that Aaron looked like a Calvin Klein underwear model, and I looked like the missing link of human evolution.

"He is *not* my brother," said Aaron.

"He doesn't know what he's saying," I assured them.

"You need to go," said Muscle.

"Did I mention he's had a seizure before? He had a traumatic brain injury. His brain was hemorrhaging inside his skull. He needs a CAT scan."

"Cliff, I swear to God—" said Aaron.

"Do you want to swear to God in person, Aaron? WHEN YOU *DIE*?"

"You. Out," said Weasel. He placed his palm in the middle of my back and forcefully guided me out of the nurse's office. Except, when he opened the door, we were greeted by a wall of teenagers—Esther and her army of zealots.

"Don't you hate it," said Esther, "when you're about to give a spiritual discourse in front of the whole school, but you realize you're a fraud with nothing important to say, and you have a sudden, inexplicable nine-one-one emergency. Gets me every time! Am I right?"

"Oh my God, shut your Communion hole," I said.

"Is that Esther?" said Aaron. He attempted to sit up on the vinyl recovery couch—much to the disgruntlement of the EMTs.

"Do *not* sit up," said Muscle, gently grabbing Aaron's shoulders and guiding him back down.

"But seriously, Aaron's health is the important thing here," said Esther. She shook her head in a *tsk-tsk*ing manner. "I sure do hate for it to come to this, but if you have to forfeit the Sermon Showdown so that Aaron doesn't die, I guess I understand."

"Huh?" I said.

"Fine!" said Esther, throwing her hands up in faux-surrender. "It is with a heavy heart that I *accept* your forfeit."

"What the hell is going on here?" said Weasel.

"Like *hell* we forfeit!" I said. "Who died and made you boss?"

"Well, Jesus died so that good may triumph over evil, *sooooo*..." Esther gave an emphatic shrug.

"Oh my God, why are you so annoying?" I kind of screamed.

"Look, not to be rude, but I have a busy schedule," said Esther. "I don't have time for injury-faking athlete babies."

"Oh no, she didn't," said Aaron, sitting up.

"Oh no, *you* don't," said Muscle, laying Aaron back down.

"If Aaron goes to the hospital," said Esther, "I'm telling the whole school that you two chickened out."

"I hate you," I said.

"Hey, there's no shame in crumbling beneath the fear of God," said Esther. "I mean, there *is*, but . . . you know what I mean."

"Well, you can take the fear of God and blow it up your ass," said Aaron, "because I am *not* going to the hospital."

"*What?*" I said.

"Oh yes, you are," said Weasel. "The big guy's right."

"THANK YOU."

"What you experienced was probably a mild seizure. And if you've already had one in the past due to a traumatic brain injury, then it's possible that you've developed epilepsy."

"What?" said Aaron.

"It's not as serious as it sounds," Weasel clarified. "*Epilepsy* is kind of a blanket term for people who experience seizures—varying from extremely mild to severe. Yours was obviously mild. Typically, in epilepsy, these seizures recur and have no underlying cause. But there are several cases that occur as a result of brain injury. Due to your medical history, you at *least* need a CT scan before we just let you go. And we gotta take you to the ER for that."

"And if I refuse?" said Aaron.

I swear, if Aaron wasn't being diagnosed as a possible epileptic, I would punch him in his seizure-having face.

"Seeing as you're under eighteen, you don't really have a choice." Weasel patted Aaron on the shoulder. "It's the law, pal."

"That's it then," said Esther. "You forfeit. I win."

"Not so fast," I said. "*Aaron's* leaving. Not me."

Esther looked at me like I had attempted to tell a joke but delivered the punchline wrong.

"Yeah, so?" she said.

"So," I said, "*I'll* give our sermon."

Esther's look evolved into that of finally getting the punchline, and realizing it was about dead babies.

"Fine," she said. "You want to play with fire? Then prepare to be toast."

Esther marched off—chin up, arms straight, fists clenched into tiny balls of fury.

Finally, after a sprawling silence, Aaron said, "Dude."

Dude, indeed.

I nodded, slightly breathless. "I'm so glad we made that video."

Needless to say, school may or may not have been thrown entirely off its tracks. Several kids had failed to make it to class, and now Vice Principal Swagley was galavanting about the halls, rounding up kids like the Child Catcher from *Chitty Chitty Bang Bang*. Seriously, all he needed was a top hat and a handful of lollipops.

Given my fondness over the idea of *not* being caught by the Swagster, I made another quick stop by my locker (I had missed the previous period entirely) and made a straight line to my next class.

"Hey! Cliff!"

It was Lacey—clear at the opposite end of the hall. She rushed to catch up with me, a strange black bundle clutched in her hands.

When she finally caught up to me—duly out of breath—she extended the bundle.

"Heard you were doing...the Sermon Showdown...by yourself," said Lacey, in between gasping breaths. "Thought you'd want your lucky hoodie back."

"Thanks...?" I said. "You do remember the part where I said my lucky hoodie was actually *unlucky*, right?"

"Well, yeah, but...you don't actually believe that, do you?"

I gave Lacey a look of supreme disbelief.

"Your brother gave it to you," said Lacey. "For your *birthday*."

"That's debatable. He was *going* to give it to me for my birthday. But then he died. Pretty sure it's cursed."

"So you don't want your hoodie back?"

"Well...I *do*," I said, thoroughly divided. "Just not now. Not right before the biggest, most terrifying event of my life."

"You're playing a video. I mean, all you have to do is sit there. Jack and Julian are operating the projector. What could possibly go wrong?"

"Bird shit *and* dog shit," I said. "In a three-second time frame. Fate always finds a way."

Lacey took my lucky hoodie and pressed it into my chest.

"Take it," she said. "Also, I went a little crazy with that thumb-in-the-hole thing. The hole is about the size of my fist now. Sorry about that."

"How in the hell did you—?"

"I didn't want Aaron to die! OKAY?"

Fair enough.

I took the lucky hoodie and pulled it over my head, slinking my arms in a sleeve at a time. As I did, I felt something—a trace of Shane, lingering in the fabric. A vestige of his spirit.

Lucky or unlucky, fate had decided for me.

I was wearing this sentimental time bomb to the Sermon Showdown.

THIRTY-NINE

It was one of those iconic '70s Alice Cooper/"School's Out" moments. The bell rang, and everyone jumped out of their seats and funneled madly out of the classroom door, flooding the halls in violent droves. Most passed their own lockers and—in a Black Friday–level panic—made a straight shot for the Quad.

Thanks to Lacey, I was now wearing my lucky hoodie. So it should have come as no surprise when shit hit the fan.

"WHAT IS GOING ON HERE?" Principal McCaffrey roared.

She asked this in regard to the four hundred students—basically the entire HVHS student population—trying to sardine themselves into the Quad.

Esther and I had to battle our way through the masses.

"It's a Sermon Showdown," said Esther. She went on to explain just what the hell a Sermon Showdown was. The more she talked, the more McCaffrey's face twisted into a pretzel of knotted skepticism. Extra salt, no butter.

I stood on the sidelines, speechless. Things were not looking optimistic for the Sermon Showdown. I *should* have been relieved. Instead, all I could process was how much time and effort we'd put into this, and how it was all going to be for naught.

"And *that*," Esther concluded, "is why we need to have this Sermon Showdown."

"That sounds wonderful and all," said McCaffrey, with an appropriate level of teacherly sarcasm, "but I doubt everyone's parents will be okay with us holding a school-sponsored religious event. I'm sorry, but I have to shut this down."

"It's *not* school-sponsored, though," said the Grinchiest voice at HVHS.

Spinelli entered the two-and-a-half-person conversation, placing a gnarled hand on my shoulder. Which, considering the height difference, he kind of had to reach for.

"The school didn't organize this event," said Spinelli. "These kids did. To simply shut it down would be to disregard their ingenuity and their ability to debate controversial topics. Not to mention their First Amendment rights. Are we the sort of institution that snuffs a teenager's freedom of speech?"

"Roger," said McCaffrey, "I'm sure you're well aware the Establishment Clause imposes *limitations* on religious speech. It all comes down to government *endorsement* of religion. To simply host an event of this sort on school grounds would be to endorse it."

Spinelli waved a dismissive hand. "Oh, baloney. It's called *debate*. I used to run the debate team at this very school, and the district hosted all *sorts* of religion-oriented debates. *Should public prayer be allowed in schools? Should intelligent design be taught in science classes?* As long as you have two parties arguing opposite ends of a topic, it's fair game."

McCaffrey glanced at Esther, who was the apparent spokesperson for teenagekind. "Do you have a specific topic that you're arguing?"

Esther puffed herself up sumptuously. "*I* am arguing that the List Aaron *claims* he received from God is fake."

McCaffrey turned to me. "And you?"

I didn't even need to think about it. "I'm arguing that it's not," I said.

"These kids are totally in their rights," said Spinelli. "If you need an adult to officiate, I volunteer myself."

"*Really,*" said McCaffrey.

"Also, can we move this thing to the gymnasium? I think we could use a little more room."

McCaffrey nodded slowly—not entirely convinced that this wasn't a trick. "Yeah. Okay."

"Thank you, Joan." Spinelli turned back around and cupped his hands over his mouth. "All right, you little cretins! We're moving this party to the gym!"

This caused an optimistic uproar—a supernova of cheers and whooping and overall teenage cretinism. The crowd funneled in every direction they could, just to get out of the Quad—slowly stampeding to the gymnasium.

Spinelli was at the head of the pack—neck and neck with Esther, who clearly didn't want there to be confusion as to who was *really* in charge.

"What *happened* to that man?" said McCaffrey.

I shrugged, feigning cluelessness. "I guess he remembered why he chose to teach?"

McCaffrey's eyelids became narrow slits of skepticism. "Uh...huh."

She slowly wandered off. Probably to spy on Spinelli.

———

"Hello, Happy Valley High School," said Spinelli. "And welcome to the...uh, what's it called again? Sermon *Showdown*? Who the heck came up with that?"

I had whispered the title into Spinelli's ear. At this question, however, I shrugged awkwardly and sat back down in my seat.

"Welcome to the Sermon Showdown!" said Spinelli. Under his breath, he muttered, "I guess."

Esther glared.

The crowd, however, thundered their approval. For a crotchety old fart, Spinelli made quite the MC.

Spinelli stood at a portable podium in the middle of the gym—the nucleus of wall-to-wall bleachers, just as packed as any basketball game. On either side of the podium was a chair. To Spinelli's left sat Esther. To his right—me.

Nearby, Jack and the gang (*minus* Jack, notably) were setting up the projector, positioned to display the film against the sprawling pull-down screen on the north wall.

I thought Esther might be upset about this—that we were essentially replacing our "sermon" with a homemade movie. Not that it was a secret. We basically filmed the entire school. *Everyone* knew about it.

But she wasn't upset. In fact, she seemed rather pleased with the situation. And more than once, I noticed her cast a conspiratorial glance at the Geek Squad, then smile underhandedly.

Now that I thought about it, Julian, Seth, Diego, and Becky *all* seemed rather stressed about something. But that was normal, right? They were just stressed because this was a big event, right? Everything was fine.

Everything

was

fine.

Remember what I said about public speaking being one of my greatest fears, second only to little people? Well, let me clarify. Just sitting here—not even *doing* anything yet—I was somehow paradoxically sweating *and* shivering. It was hardly a stretch to call my symptoms flu-like. Also, my throat felt like the setting of a Mad Max film.

"Now, for the sake of school ethics, we're gonna do things a little differently," said Spinelli. "Despite what the . . . erhrm . . . *title* of this event may suggest—this is a debate. An unconventional debate, yes, but a debate regardless. Meaning our two debaters here are arguing a topic. And boy, do we have one for you. Recently, one of our students has claimed something rather spectacular. Aaron Zimmerman claims he has received a List from God. A List—he claims—that will make Happy Valley High School a better place."

This elicited quite the response—laughter and booing and cheering—all on a rather equal scale.

"On the affirmative side, we have Clifford Hubbard, defending Aaron's claim—namely the validity of the List. On the negative side: Esther Poulson, who thinks it's a load of hogswallop. Now the way this goes, we have two speeches from both parties. To kick things off, we'll receive a constructive presentation on the affirmative side—aka, Cliff—introducing his side of the argument and any evidence he sees fit to present. Then the negative side—Esther—will refute his claims and present her side of the argument in a constructive speech of her own. This will be followed by one rebuttal presentation from each party, in turn. Any questions?"

I didn't know who Spinelli was asking, but I, for one, wanted to know if there was any way I could move to Canada. Immediately. Our video would only cover *one* of the two speeches I was required to give. Which meant that, eventually, I had to do *real* public speaking.

Like, the kind that comes out of one's mouth. And I just didn't know if I could handle that.

"No? Then let's begin." Spinelli turned and gave me an encouraging grin. "Cliff, the floor is yours."

Spinelli stepped aside and gestured me to the podium.

I took a deep breath.

I stood up.

I walked to the portable podium—a whopping five feet away. Somehow, I managed to turn this into a three-minute commute. When I finally reached it, I lifted the microphone to my mouth, which apparently was a terrible mistake because I proceeded to breathe loudly into it.

I glanced at the large pull-down screen. It was still blank.

"So . . ." I said, somewhat out of breath. "Aaron and I made a movie . . ."

Aaaaaaaand that was about all I had. I turned around to give Julian and the gang a desperate *Please start the movie now* look.

Except Julian was already jogging toward me. To say that he looked distressed was an understatement.

When Julian reached me, he whispered, "We're experiencing a little bit of a, um, technical difficulty? But it's cool."

I stared. "How *exactly* is it cool?"

"Jack's taking care of it."

"Taking care of *what*?"

"So, the drive that the video is saved on . . . ?"

"No," I said, pointing a finger. "Don't you even."

"We may or may not have somehow . . . lost it."

"Oh my God."

"But it's *cool*," said Julian. (For the *second* time. Did he even know what *cool* meant?) "Jack ran home half an hour ago to find it. And just so you know, according to Pottermore, he's a Hufflepuff. And Hufflepuffs are *excellent* finders."

"I'm supposed to be speaking now!" I whisper-screamed.

"It's cool. He lives just down the street. We'll have the video ready by your rebuttal speech—promise." Julian snapped his fingers, pointed at me, and gave me a *Go get 'em, Tiger* wink. "You got this."

And then he hastily retreated to the projector.

I rotated—slowly—like the second hand of a clock. I made vague eye contact with roughly four hundred faces, waiting for me to say something. Anything.

I turned back around and—like Julian—retreated.

But I didn't get far. I stopped and stooped in front of Spinelli, trying to make my body as small as possible. "So, um, something happened—technical difficulties and such—can I forfeit my first speech, please?"

"Uhhh..." said Spinelli. "You *can*. I wouldn't recommend it, though. It doesn't exactly make your side of the debate look good."

But I was already nodding vehemently at the *can* part. All the words that followed didn't matter, because if I even *tried* to speak into that microphone, I was going to be sick.

"Yes," I said, still nodding. "Okay. Let's do that."

Spinelli gave a frustrated snort. He turned to Esther, who was clearly in hearing range and eavesdropping like it was one of the Ten Commandments. "You hear that, Poulson? You ready?"

Esther smiled. "Of course, Mr. Spinelli."

She rose from her seat like a flower blossoming in fast-motion time lapse. Approached the podium with elegance and grace. Cleared her throat into the microphone—even *that* sounded angelic.

The whole display was rather disgusting.

"So apparently Aaron thinks he received a List from...God?"

said Esther, impressively deadpan. "And it's my job to convince you that he's . . . crazy?"

The bleachers erupted with laughter.

I mean, it *was* funny. I might've laughed, too—if I wasn't in the process of realizing how extraordinarily fucked we were. Myself *and* Aaron *and* the List.

"There are just so many places I could start," Esther continued. "Logic, perhaps? Maybe we could get crazy with some *common sense?*"

The laughs kept coming.

"But I think there's a really easy place to start. I'm sure you all know about Aaron and Clifford's little home movie. I mean, they basically filmed all of you. But hey, congratulations on becoming movie stars!"

Esther was killing it. Her audience—and it was definitely all *hers*—was dying from a terminal fit of laughter.

"Well, my friends and I made a film, too. Except we didn't actually *film* anything. Rather, we compiled some footage that's existed for quite some time now. I like to call it W.W.A.D., or What Would Aaron Do? Zeke?"

But Zeke was already on it—wiggling out of the bleachers, down the stairs, across the gym to the projector, flash drive in hand. Julian, Seth, Diego, and Becky parted awkwardly as he inserted himself, seized control of the projector and its adjoining laptop.

The lights turned off—another JT.

The projector screen lit up, displaying the title—just as Esther had introduced it:

W.W.A.D.
(What Would Aaron Do?)

The opening scene is a close-up of Aaron's face, shot from his own phone. But this is a different Aaron—flashing his trademark pre-List douchebag smirk.

AARON: Let's go f[*bleep*]k with some people.

The sound track opens to "Sabotage," by the Beastie Boys, and we are treated to a glorious montage of Aaron "f[*bleep*]k"-ing with a wide variety of people. Pantsing guys on the football team. Pantsing guys *not* on the football team. Ripping guys' towels off in the locker room, only to whip their bare, black-bar-censored asses with it.

AARON: What can I say? I just really like butts.

Another montage—this time Aaron is smacking the ass of every girl he passes in the hallway.

AARON: I feel like consent only applies to people who *aren't* irresistible.

Aaron is seen making out with just as many girls, and in every location fathomable—the boys' locker room, the girls' bathroom, the school kitchen, *and* the copy room in the main offices—to name a few.
Several clips of Aaron's inspiring feminist commentary are sewn together.

AARON: Emma is such a slut.
AARON: Olivia is a virgin bitch.
AARON: Jennifer would totally be hot . . . if she laid off the pizza.

(*Cups hands over his mouth like a megaphone.*)

AARON: (*cont'd*) SOMEBODY CALL SEA WORLD. I'VE FOUND THEIR MISSING WHALE.

AARON: There are anorexics. Then there are bulimics. And *then* there are Holocaust victims.

(*Meaningful pause.*)

AARON: (*cont'd*) I think Lacey Hildebrandt falls into the third category.

Aaron decks some random dude in the jaw. Dude one-eighties and collapses on the floor.

We're thrown balls-deep in the epic fistfight between Aaron and myself—in all its locker-smashing, neck-strangling, titty-twisting glory.

AARON: Wow . . . the Neanderthal knows . . . words and shit.

And then, a new scene—Aaron and I, walking dramatically side by side. In slow motion, no less. This drastic change is complemented by Clint Mansell's "Lux Aeterna"—aka, the Most Dramatic Piece of Music Ever Composed.

Words fill a black screen, like some intense movie trailer:

THEY HAVE A MISSION

And then:

A LIST FROM GOD

And then a list:

1. PUT AN END TO NIKO'S BULLYING

Flash-forward to Aaron and I beating the ever-living shit outta Niko's face. Naturally, this includes the part where I drag an aluminum baseball bat to finish the job. It was kind of terrifying.

2. CALL THE JTS TO REPENTANCE

Aaron is clearly drunk at somebody's pool party, standing on top of a small rock waterfall, wearing a Sexy Nun costume. (Seriously, it was mostly a headdress, a bling-ish cross necklace, and lingerie.) It was censored around his crotch—probably because it was too little fabric and too much nether region.

3. REMIND MR. SPINELLI WHY HE CHOSE TO TEACH

A stealthy camera phone peeks around the entrance of the main offices. At first, all we hear is yelling. Then, we see Spinelli in front of McCaffrey's open office door. Fuming. Screaming. *Demanding* that Aaron and I be expelled.

Aaron and I stand off to the side, looking thoroughly defeated.

4. SHOW FRANKIE'S GANG A BETTER WAY

Again, some random party I've never been to. Aaron and a group of friends (including Kyle) are in someone's suspiciously cloudy basement. Aaron takes a long drag of something that definitely isn't tobacco.

KYLE: Dude.
AARON: (*in agreement*) *Dude.*

Aaron stares cluelessly at us, via his own phone camera. He glances at the walls. He glances at the ceiling.

AARON: Uhhhhhhhhhh...

And on that note, Esther's video ended.

FORTY

Okay, so a few things:

1. Aaron was so popular, he apparently had his own paparazzi. I mean, how else could you explain all this footage? It was like Aaron's entire life was one big scandal waiting to be immortalized on film.

2. Being a video-editing wizard and loving Jesus were evidently not mutually exclusive things. Either that, or the JTs hired a professional because *hooooooooly* shit.

3. I mean, "Sabotage"? Classic! Now the real question was: Had Esther even listened to Beastie Boys once in her goddamn life before now?

4. Lacey's face. Yeah, Aaron was a new person now. But that didn't make his past body-shaming remark hurt any less.

5. Spinelli's face. I didn't know how much Spinelli knew about the List—or if he knew anything at *all*—but upon seeing his

name in lights, his face contorted into a catacomb of emotions. It was impossible to tell whether they were good or bad.

6. There wasn't a moment when people weren't laughing. If the video hadn't made such a crippling case against Aaron and the List, even *I* would have thought it was hilarious. But as it was—and this leads us to Thing Number 7—

7. —we were kind of fucked.

The lights flickered on. At the podium, Esther interlocked her fingers and smiled.

Seriously. That smile. It was so smug, she might as well have been cradling a trophy.

"There's so much I can say," said Esther. "*Sooooooo* much. But since I have one more speech to give...I don't know about you, but I'm rather eager to hear what Neanderthal—oh, I'm sorry—what *Clifford* has to say. He sure was scary, wasn't he? Do you think he beat up Niko because he's black?"

Esther turned and winked at me. Then she curtsied to both sets of bleachers—yes, *curtsied*—and sat down.

The audience roared with applause and cheers.

That, in and of itself, was loud. Almost deafening. But it didn't speak with *near* the volume as the single student who stood up, awkwardly navigated his way out of the bleachers, and veered to the west exit.

It was Noah.

Even from where I sat, I saw despondency carved in every line of his face. It wasn't just sadness; it was the look of giving up. Apparently he wasn't interested in seeing me make a fool of myself.

To be fair, I wasn't keen on it, either.

As he exited, the west door closed slowly, eased by its hydraulic damper. Nevertheless, the sound it made was sharp and resounding and irreversible. An echo, rippling across the universe.

Esther's mouth curled with smugness.

I glanced nervously at the projector—*still* occupied by only four nerds. Jack—the fifth and final nerd—was nowhere in sight. Julian offered a sympathetic shrug. And nothing else.

And that's when the east gymnasium doors—the ones opposite of where Noah exited—swung open. Jack came running in.

Relief came roaring through the floodgates.

I mean, it was *sort of* running. Actually, it was more of a ragged, breathless jog.

Except Jack wasn't running to the projector. He was running to me.

He didn't look happy.

When Jack reached me, he collapsed with his hands on his knees. "It's"—wheeze—"gone."

"The flash drive?"

"The flash drive, the backup . . . *everything*. Someone hacked into our shit and deleted *all* of it."

My jaw was hanging by the sinews.

"Please tell me you have something to say," said Jack. He looked almost as distressed as me. "We can't let Esther win this."

It meant a lot to me that Jack was concerned about our success in the Sermon Showdown. I could see it in his eyes—that he truly, deeply *cared*. But I didn't know what to tell him. Because I literally had *nothing* to say. There was so much nothing, it was suffocating. Like I was trapped underwater, and the only thing I could accomplish by opening my mouth was letting water into my lungs.

Jack seemed to sense that.

So he walked past me and took the podium.

"Um, hi," said Jack. "My name is Jack Halbert. I was working with Aaron and Cliff to make a really cool, weird film-slash-documentary thingy. Unfortunately, *someone*"—Jack directed a brief, meaningful glance at Esther—"stole it."

"Excuse me?" said Esther—loud enough for most of the gym to hear.

"But whatever," said Jack, hands in the air. "It doesn't matter. Because, as Esther already pointed out, you were *there*. You were *in* it. And I'd like to think that I'm not the only one who felt something. Look, I don't want to get into a discussion about whether there is or isn't a God. Really, it doesn't matter. What *matters* is that Cliff and Aaron have done more good for this school then anyone I've ever known. And the List—wherever it came from—is the source of that. If that's crazy, then I hope this school gets all the crazy Aaron and Cliff can throw at it."

Jack left the podium. And as he did, the room became quieter. But it wasn't a bad or awkward quiet.

It was the sort of quiet that meant something.

When Jack reached his friends at the projector, Julian was grinning and raised his hand for a high five. They slapped hands.

Julian, however, interpreted this in the context of tag team wrestling, because he immediately veered to the podium. Waltzed up to the mic like he was about to host the Academy Awards.

"Hey, hey, hey!" said Julian. "I'm Julian—Jack's best friend. Aspiring CIA field agent. So here's the thing: Jack's the smartest guy I know. And if Jack believes the List is legit, than I do too."

Julian flashed a peace sign and strutted back to the projector.

It was the start of a shock wave.

Niko stood up in the bleachers. He didn't walk to the podium, but he didn't need to. He had everyone's attention.

"Niko," he said. "And I'm not black."

This elicited possibly the largest explosion of audience laughter yet. Esther seemed to shrink in her chair a little bit.

"I'm Polynesian. Also, Aaron and Cliff are all-right guys. And I believe in the List too."

Frankie stood up. "Hey. I'm Frankie fuckin' Robertson."

"Language, Frankie," said Spinelli.

"Frankie freakin' Robertson," said Frankie without pause. "And Cliff Hubbard taught me that family is more important than anything. Even when your family is broken and messed up. And I just wanna let Tegan know—"

His voice faltered. He sniffled and wiped his eyes.

Holy shit sandwiches. Was Frankie crying?

"—I want her to know that I'm sorry," said Frankie. "And I believe in the List too."

Tegan stood up. "My name is Tegan fuckin' Robertson—"

"LANGUAGE!" Spinelli exclaimed. "FOR CHRIST'S SAKE."

"Freakin'—whatever," said Tegan. "And I accept Frankie's apology—but only because he cried like a baby in public. And I believe the *shit* outta the List. Also, I dunno about y'all, but I came here to hear Cliff speak. Anyone else with me?"

She didn't even wait for a response before she started chanting: "Cliff! Cliff! Cliff!"

Tegan was a wildfire. Her manic chanting spread.

"CLIFF. CLIFF. CLIFF."

Feet were stomping. Fists were pumping. It was like a rock concert, and the crowd was demanding an encore. Except they never got the show they paid for to begin with. So basically, the anticipation was through the roof. I thought I would be nervous. But I wasn't. I couldn't even explain it—this thing washing over me, breathing fresh air into my lungs, soothing my nerves.

"CLIFF. CLIFF. CLIFF."

I stood up. The crowd cheered.

There was this tingling sensation all across my skin as I made my way to the podium. (The entire five-foot commute.) I had no clue what I was going to say. But for reasons beyond my comprehension, I wasn't too worried about it.

Standing there, staring at so many faces, my only concern became this:

What do I do with my hands?

Like, do I move them while I talk? Do I let them just hang there? I did not even *remotely* comprehend the art of hand movement in public speaking. If I just winged it, I was worried I'd panic and start doing the Macarena or the YMCA. But if I did nothing—just let them hang there—they felt like a pair of fifteen-pound trout dangling from my shoulder blades. And that was just weird.

I resolved to shove my hands in the pockets of my lucky hoodie and leave them there for the duration.

That's when I discovered the colossal hole Lacey had burrowed in the pocket of my hoodie. If my lucky hoodie was a planet, this would be the hole where all the Mole People dwelled. My fingers splayed inside, gauging just how big the hole really was.

My middle finger brushed the corner of something thick and papery. What the . . . ?

It was wedged deep within the inner fabric of my hoodie—practically at the waist—but I managed to pin it between my index and middle fingers. Removed it slowly. It was a folded-up sheet of paper, slightly yellowed with age.

There, in front of a captive audience of four hundred people, I opened it and read silently.

I only had to read one paragraph—in Shane's perplexingly neat handwriting—before realizing that life was indeed a door, and in this moment, it was wide open. All I had to do was step through.

> *Dear Cliff,*
>
> *Happy Birthday! Also, congratulations on finding my secret note! Sorry your hoodie had a hole in it, by the way. I swear, it's brand-new, and it was like that when I bought it. (But hey, secret notes, right?) This is the real present anyway. Because I'm about to bestow upon you all of the wisdom and knowledge of my sixteen years on this Earth. Remember the three rules to high school that I taught you? Well, this is like the opposite of that. You should get McCaffrey to call an assembly and read it in front of the whole goddamn school. Are you ready?*

I was ready.

"This is a letter from my brother, Shane," I said. Somewhat timidly, I raised the creased, handwritten sheet of paper for all to see. My mouth opened, hesitating to preface this with something else. Then I decided against it.

I turned my eyes to this message from the Other Side of the Door, and read aloud.

> "*There are three rules to high school irrevocably inscribed within the interstellar fabric of the universe.*
>
> "*Rule number one: It's hard, but it's worth it.*
>
> "*I mean, it's really hard. Sometimes, it's so hard,*

I don't even know if I'm going to make it. I can barely survive the self-loathing inside my own head. How the HELL am I supposed to survive in a world that gives me even MORE reasons to doubt and hate myself? High school practically pops those reasons out like Skittles from a candy dispenser—and hey, they're color-coded for my convenience! Lucky me.

"And yet, there are moments.

"Moments between the giant dumps that life takes on your head. Moments between those fierce, plunging spirals into despair. Maybe they're not even moments of happiness. They are, however, moments of peace. Moments of understanding. Moments where we realize that life is so much more than happiness and sadness and the labyrinth in between. It's about the people who navigate that labyrinth with you.

"Which leads me to the second rule of high school: People are good.

"I know what you're thinking: People AREN'T good. People are actually kind of evil sometimes. They're narcissistic, hate-filled creatures whose only concern is themselves and their own shallow agendas. They'd sooner make a staircase of the corpses of their peers to get what they want than stop and give someone a helping hand, just because they can.

"At least, that's how I feel sometimes.

"But then I stop. I look around, and I see all these people. Each and every one of them is experiencing this lucid and enigmatic thing we call life, but through their own eyes. To them, this is their story—complete with its own plot twists and heartbreaks, hopes and devastations. Maybe life is shitting on *their heads, too. Maybe they hate themselves—and that, in and of itself, is a battle they're scraping to survive. Maybe I'm just a secondary character—maybe even an extra—from that one scene when they needed help from someone. Anyone. But I didn't help them because I didn't know them, or maybe I didn't even care.*

"Maybe that moment would have made all the difference.

"Which brings me to high school rule number three: Be the difference.

"I'm not going to sugarcoat the situation. High school is messed up. Life is messed up. But that doesn't mean you can't do something about it. And even WHEN you can't, that doesn't mean you shouldn't try. Always try. Because the alternative is a world where people don't. A world where people see no good, and they have no hope. They exist because that is the default state of life, and then they die because that's what happens next. All the while, they let the world rot and fall apart around them.

"But life is more than just existing. And it's more than just a door with death and nothingness on the other side. Life is a <u>series</u> of doors. Every moment, every decision, is a door. And by opening them and stepping into the unknown, we are expanding and illuminating a world that we never knew existed. But if we don't open those doors? If we stay put? We'll be living in a world of walls.

"Don't you want to know what's on the other side?"

I should have stopped reading there. There was a space before the following paragraph, indicating that what he had to say next was a separate thing. But I was so swept up in Shane's words, I couldn't stop.

> *"P.S. If I'm not alive when you read this, know that I am so sorry."*

The words were like fishhooks, ripping my throat open from the inside. The auditorium reacted as if my mouth were actually bleeding—a swell of gasps and whispers.

I kept reading aloud, even as my voice quivered.

> *"It must sound hypocritical of me to say all this when I don't even know if I'm going to make it. When I don't even know if I'm strong enough. But please know, Cliff, that you are. And that I'll never stop being your big brother.*
> *"Sincerely,*
> *"Shane Levi Hubbard"*

If there had been any hope of me walking away from this Sermon Showdown without crying, it was underwater by now. I sniffed, swept a heavy sleeve across my burning eyes, and blinked the wetness away.

Carefully, I folded Shane's letter, and I inserted it in my lucky hoodie pocket.

"I don't know why Shane killed himself," I said.

I inhaled and exhaled—deeply—like I was giving away a piece of myself. Carving it right out of my soul.

"It seems unfair," I said, "that someone can take their own life, and not tell you why they did it. As if they somehow expect it to not torture you every day for the rest of your life. But that's all that Shane left me—questions with no answers. And somehow, I'm supposed to make the most of it. Well, that's what I intend to do. Maybe I don't know why Shane killed himself, but I'll tell you what I do know: Happy Valley High School sucks."

Several students laughed. It was short-lived, however, when it became clear in my expression that I was not joking.

"Three years I've been going to school here," I said, "and all I've ever seen is a bunch of teenagers being awful to each other—cliques and gossip, bullying and harassment, prejudice and hate. I don't know about you, but I refuse to accept the idea that that's just how people are. Maybe there isn't an easy fix. Maybe the answer is way more complicated than some hokey to-do list. But maybe the answer is easier than we think. Maybe we just need to *try*. Maybe Aaron's List isn't *the* answer, but it *is* something. Christ, if we had all *tried*? If we all had *done* something a long time ago? Maybe Shane would still be here. Maybe. Who knows. It's useless torturing ourselves over the past. Ruminating over the what-ifs. But it's not too late for someone else. I don't know who else may be struggling like my brother was—who may be silently hurting like he was—but I think the List is for them."

I cast my gaze like a fishing line across a sea of eight hundred eyes. Four hundred faces.

And possibly one girl named Haley.

"I think the List is for you," I said.

That was it.

I had said everything I had to say.

I was done.

A vacuum of silence filled the auditorium—oppressive and crushing. The sort of silence that makes you wonder if your wildest nightmares have come true, and you've somehow become naked in public.

After a quick downward glance—still clothed, thank God—I nervously retreated to my chair, and sat down with my hands in my lap.

What happened next was like a hydrogen bomb, but with less radioactive fallout, and more clapping and cheering.

"Fuck yeah!" Tegan somehow managed to scream over everyone else. Her hands became twin pistols that she pointed in a downward V, pretending to shoot the bench in front of her. "That's my fuckin' boyfriend, yo!"

Spinelli shook his head. "I'm going to pretend that I didn't hear that." But then he turned, smiled, and—I swear—he actually winked at me. "Good job, kid."

Even Zeke Gallagher was clapping! He was still standing by the projector—awkwardly—with Jack and Julian and the others. Although I only really noticed this because of what happened next.

"Are you kidding me?" said Esther. "Are you freaking KIDDING ME?"

She noticed Zeke first. And her volume trumped Tegan's by a couple hundred decibels.

Zeke slow-clapped to a halt—hands frozen together, like he was praying for his life.

Esther stood up. Marched right over to him, causing him to back against the nearest wall.

She attacked.

"YOU'RE—SUPPOSED—TO—BE—ON—MY—TEAM!" Esther shrieked with each blow—slapping, kicking, even going for a throat punch.

"*Urp. Gluck. Blechh*," Zeke gurgled.

"Holy hell," said Spinelli. Scrambling out of his chair, he made a feeble attempt to pry Esther off Zeke's soon-to-be corpse. "Help! Can I get some help?"

The Sermon Showdown kind of dissolved on that note.

"I did not lose!" Esther screamed. "A captain can't lead an insubordinate ship! I demand a rematch! I DID NOT LOSE!"

She screamed this declaration to the four hundred students who passed the main offices where she was being "detained" on their way out. One school security officer was trying to get her to calm down. Another was on the phone with Mr. and Mrs. Poulson.

Technically speaking, Esther was right. Because she never gave her rebuttal speech, there was no clear-cut winner of the Sermon Showdown. Spinelli called it an "incomplete debate."

But he also added, "I think you can decide the winner for yourselves."

As far as incomplete debates go, I couldn't have been happier with the results.

I didn't waste a moment. The moment I cleared the deafening chatter of the crowds, I called Aaron.

There was a staticky shuffle on the other line, and then Aaron's voice. "You better have some good news."

"You're alive!"

"Is that what they're calling it these days?"

"What's going on? Is your brain okay?"

"Well, I've officially been diagnosed with epilepsy."

"Shit."

"Dude, it's fine. Basically all that means is that I've experienced two seizures from the same brain injury. Maybe I'll experience more, maybe not. Some epileptics go months or even years between seizures. The worst part is that football is definitely out—probably forever. Unless I want to play Russian roulette with my brain."

"Shit," I said again.

"But it's *fine*," Aaron reemphasized. "They x-rayed; there's no bleeding. No damage at all."

"How are you feeling?"

"Impatient. I'm just sitting on a hospital bed playing *Plants vs. Zombies* until they tell me I can go home—which may be never. I thought I'd never get tired of this game, but right now, I hate it so much. Now the real question—HOW'D IT GO?"

Up until this point, the weight of Shane's letter had been pretty heavy on my chest. Like my lungs had been replaced by vacuum bags and were now filled with dust and debris and shit. A year later, and Shane's death still felt raw and fresh.

But here, on the phone with my best friend, I gave myself permission to take a deep breath, set the pain aside, and completely lose it.

"AAAaaaaaAAHHHHHHhhhhhhhHHHHHHhhhHHHHH HHHhhhhh!!!" I said.

"Whoa, whoa. Is this a good *ah* or bad *ah*?"

"Good *ah*! Very good *ah*!"

"We *won*?!"

"Well . . . sort of?" I said, physically and emotionally breathless. "But not exactly."

"Huh?"

"It kind of ended before it was officially over."

"What? It did? But the film was a success, right?"

"Actually, someone stole Jack and Julian's flash drive, hacked their shit, and deleted all copies of the video. So we never played it."

"WHAT?"

"But it's cool. It all worked out."

"How is this a good *ah*? This sounds like the worst *ah* ever!"

I recounted every detail—from Jack, Julian, Niko, Frankie, and

Tegan injecting their two cents, to discovering Shane's secret letter in my lucky hoodie, to Esther *literally* attacking Zeke because he had the audacity to clap after my sermon.

Aaron's response was appropriate: "AAaaaaAAHHHHhhhhhh-HHHHHhhhHHHHhhhh!"

Somewhere in the background, I heard frantic footsteps and a nurse freaking out. "Doctor? Doctor!"

"No, no, I'm okay!" said Aaron. "Christ, I'm okay!"

FORTY-ONE

The Sermon Showdown was a big event, no doubt. But what it sparked was something even bigger. A craze. A pandemic, even.

Everyone had contracted Shane fever.

A year after his death, Shane had become a posthumous celebrity. There were posters of his likeness everywhere—8.5-by-11-inch print-outs of his last yearbook photo with the caption *Shane Forever*. Outside the main offices, one girl was selling "Forever Shane" bracelets. Judging from the actual line to purchase them, and an extra-large pickle jar stuffed with dollar bills, they seemed to be selling like hotcakes made of gangbusters sprinkled in stardust.

The digital world was even worse. Aaron and Tegan showed me on their phones. There was a hashtag—#ShaneForever—taking the Happy Valley social networks by storm. Suddenly, every photo anyone had ever taken with Shane—every experience they had ever shared with him, no matter how small—was paraded online like the latest Internet challenge. Judging from each individual post, you'd think that Shane was this person's best friend, and they had just now come to terms with this great and devastating loss.

I appreciated that Shane was being remembered.

Really, I did.

But at the same time, it felt like Shane's memory was being appropriated and sensationalized. Like his name and face were a trend and nothing more.

"Is this weird?" I said. "Tell me this isn't weird."

I noticed both Aaron and Tegan—absorbing the Shane craze with me—inconspicuously glance down at their brand-new Forever Shane bracelets. Tegan, visibly embarrassed, managed to slip hers off with one hand and tuck it into her pocket.

"It's a bit much," Aaron admitted. "But it is cool, right?"

Exploitation aside—I guess it was kind of cool.

The coolest thing was how Esther was taking it. (Hint: it wasn't well.) As if to counterbalance the Shane craze, she made a big show of reiterating how "not over" the Sermon Showdown was. But it was only the façade of a pump-up speech. At its core, it was a *This is your fault* speech.

"A leader is only as good as her followers," said Esther. "And let me tell you, my followers are *not* as good as they could be. In fact, I even struggle to call you *good*. I want you to take a long, hard look in the mirror. I want you to ask yourselves: What have you done for the JTs lately? What have you done for *me*? Because I can tell you, I'm sick and tired of giving you *my* everything and getting nothing in return. I'm sick and tired of your disloyalty. Your half-*assed* dedication. So, this is your moment of truth. I want you to either pledge your *full* loyalty to the JTs, or I want you to get the hell out of here. We have no room for you here."

The JTs were *humongously* not into this. Disbelieving glances were exchanged. Eyes were rolled. And then—for the first time ever—a JT walked out on her.

It was Zeke.

"Hey!" said Esther. "Where do you think you're going?"

"Getting the hell out of here," said Zeke.

Others were quick to follow. Not all of them. Not even most of them. Probably a solid twenty or so—give or take—but with a great many others who seemed severely on the fence. Enough to make it blatantly clear that the JTs were no longer what they once were.

This was more than just a schism. It was an awakening.

All day, I experienced something of an existential crisis. Something big had happened with the Sermon Showdown—something bigger and flashier than a mere "victory"—and I didn't know how to process it. Let alone, do school. Like, what *was* school anyway? How does one "go back to school" after an event like the Sermon Showdown?

Well, I started by going to Ms. Allmendinger's World History class and actually paying attention. She talked about World War I and the nine million soldiers and the seven million civilians who died as a result of the war. Maybe it was the vastness of the death that stunned me. Sixteen million people—dead. I thought about the families and loved ones who received letters or had soldiers showing up at their door, informing them that their father/husband/brother/son was dead. And how that father/husband/brother/son was just a number to some general, moving little figurines on a war room table, preparing the next strike. But to the people whose doorstep was visited, that father/husband/brother/son was Everything.

Even now, people all over the world were dying in wars, and we were seeing it on the news while our parents drank coffee and we got ready for another day at school, and they were even less than numbers. They were background noise.

But they weren't. To someone, somewhere, those lost people were Everything.

This pattern of listening and thinking followed me to second-period Algebra, where—according to Mr. Gunther—math was the language of the universe, to third-period Physics, where matter and motion formed the fabric of space and time.

On my way to fourth period, exchanging textbooks in my locker, I noticed Zeke confronting Robin Dunston.

Okay, in my peripheral, it *looked* like a confrontation. So naturally, I rolled up my soft-cover Spanish workbook until it was an indestructible tube of kick-ass.

But Zeke stopped a safe and respectable distance away from her. His lanky, wristband-laden arms dangled at his side—fidgety and awkward. When Robin turned from her locker and noticed him standing there, her entire pixie body tensed up.

"I'm sorry," he said.

Robin was frozen, clearly waiting for the part where this turned into another malicious prank.

Except it wasn't a prank. Zeke's eyes were somber orbs of apology.

"What I did was messed up," he said. "And I can't blame the JTs for what I did. They were my own actions, and no one else's, and I'm just . . . I'm really sorry."

Robin still wasn't moving. It was hard to decipher her thought processes, other than the fact that they were processing hard.

"Is there anything I can do to make it up to you?" he asked.

Robin's eyes shifted up in thought—mulled for a brief, silent moment—then met Zeke's gaze.

"You work at the Bookshelf," she said.

"Huh?"

"The Bookshelf—that bookstore in Kalispell. You work there, right?"

Zeke's confusion seemed to melt rather quickly, leaving his face with nothing but a big, dopey smile. "Yeah, that's right. I've seen you there, haven't I?"

"You've probably checked me out a few dozen times. Anyway, I like free books."

Zeke nodded, barely suppressing a chuckle. "Okay, okay. How about this? I give you unlimited access to my employee discount—twenty percent off—and your first book's on me?"

Robin extended a hand to shake on it. "You got yourself a deal, Gallagher."

Zeke laughed, took her hand, and shook it firmly.

By the time the lunch bell rang, my brain was in hyperdrive, and it felt kind of weird getting excited that today was chimichanga day.

Aaron and I claimed our usual seats at lunch. And then Tegan appeared, holding her lunch tray, pretending to glance apprehensively at the empty seat next to me.

"Just so you know," she said, "I am *way* too attracted to you right now. So if I happen to grab your ass, I refuse to take responsibility for the consequences. Is that seat taken?"

My mouth lost motor function, so I just shook my head.

"Gag me with a spoon," said Aaron. "You realize I'm sitting right here."

Not a moment later, Jack and Julian sat down beside us. Tegan glared at their blatant cock-blocking, because *clearly* five was a crowd.

"Mind if we dine with you?" said Jack. "Our table started talking about which My Little Pony they would bang, and we just couldn't do it anymore."

"Yeah, it's so stupid," said Julian. "Everyone knows that Twilight Sparkle is the only pony worth banging."

Jack and Julian sat across from each other, next to Aaron and me, respectively. Lacey joined our table shortly after, flanking Aaron's other side.

"Good job on the Sermon Showdown," said Lacey, offering me a high five—which I reciprocated. She then glanced around the table. "I guess I should be congratulating everyone. Well, everyone except for Aaron."

"You could congratulate me for not *dying*!" said Aaron. "Thank you very much."

I proceeded to wolf down my chimichanga, and Julian politely informed me that chewing was a general function of higher life-forms, and Jack added that it was also a good tactic for not choking and dying, at which point I stuffed the whole damn thing in my mouth and flipped Jack and Julian off with both fingers. Lacey laughed, nearly spewing her milk.

And then I saw Frankie.

He was standing a good forty feet away, with tables and students and noise between us like a glass wall. His lips were pinched into an oddly timid line.

Tegan met his eyes. Then she smiled and waved him over.

"What are you waiting for, an invitation in the mail?" said Tegan. "Get your ass over here. We got room—even *with* Cliff and his chimichangas."

"Hey, leave my chimichangas out of this," I said.

Frankie laughed as he sat down.

"Where's Noah?" said Jack. His head rotated, scanning the cafeteria.

"I haven't seen him since he walked out of the Sermon Showdown yesterday," said Lacey.

"He *missed* it?" said Aaron. "He's been fighting for this longer than any of us. I can't believe he missed it."

I couldn't believe it, either. In fact, the sheer injustice of it made me kind of dizzy. I whipped my phone out of my pocket and hastily texted him.

Hey, are you at school today? You walked out of the Sermon Showdown right before we WON!!!

Okay, we didn't really win. But it was close enough. I consider it a metaphysical victory.

Noah texted back almost instantly:

i left after first period. wasn't feeling well. and yeah, robin told me about it. she said you read a letter from shane. sounds like it was really good.

And then:

although esther doesn't seem to think she lost.

I texted back:

Dude, it doesn't even matter. She's basically the ONLY person who doesn't think she lost.

Noah:

classic esther. too bad shane wasn't there to say those things in person. he may have sucked at math, but he was quite the orator.

Actually, that was an understatement. Shane never gave a formal speech that I was aware of, but when he wanted to, he had a bizarre eloquence. He made the words come alive, made them perforate your every pore, made them stir up your insides until you were ready to *viva la résistance!*

Yeah. I texted. *It's too bad.*

Just mentioning Shane, and the irrefutable fact that he was no longer here, almost brought me down. But then Julian said, "You know, maybe I would bang Fluttershy," and Jack said, "Dear god," and Lacey complimented Tegan's Gorillaz shirt, and Tegan said Lacey's shoes were "bomb," and I was just grateful to God or Morgan Freeman or whoever for friends.

———

As poetic justice would have it, my perfect day ended in a confusingly imperfect way. I was almost home—hadn't even made it up the front steps yet—when I heard the screaming.

It wasn't my dad.

I hesitantly opened the front door like it was a Pandora's Box.

"Like, who are you?" said my mom. "I don't even know anymore! I'm done. I'm done with your alcoholism, your unemployment, the fact that you have absolutely *no* aspirations in life. None whatsoever! Unless, of course, bullying our sons is an aspiration! Jesus Christ! Do you ever wonder if *you're* the reason Shane killed himself? Because I do. I wonder that every fucking day. And I wonder if *I* killed him because I *let* you treat him the way you did. I have to *live* with that guilt. Well, guess what? Not anymore. I'm—"

She screeched to a halt, midrant, when she noticed me in the doorway. With a mental flip of the switch, her muscles and jaw relaxed. She swallowed hard, like she was digesting pure hate. And just like that, it was gone.

She ran a hand through her hair and smiled. "Hey, sweetie. How was school?"

I cast a timid, indirect glance at my dad. He was standing—something he only did when he was angry. But he wasn't angry now. Right now, he was cowering, shoulders hunched, with his hands buried deep in his pockets.

"Uh...good?" I said.

My mom kept smiling. It wasn't even a fake smile, and I didn't know how that was possible. "Could I have a word with your father in private?"

"Sure...?" I said.

"Thanks, sweetie."

I walked slowly into my bedroom. Closed the door. It was a moment or two before my mom continued her rant—several notches lower than before. But what she lacked in volume, she made up for in venom.

"Give me a reason," she said. "Give me one, and we'll be gone before you can get your ass out of that fucking chair."

I thought those words would make me happy. I thought I would feel victory.

Instead, all my brain could process was a single memory—one that I had all but forgotten.

Shane's seventh birthday.

I remembered us—*all* of us—going out for pizza and ice cream. I ordered a chocolate ice-cream cone, and Shane got cookies and cream—although we switched halfway through because that's what brothers do, and what are germs anyway? Shane opened his present—an official Grizzlies football. (Shane secretly hated football, but he never told my dad that until years later—in a fight that left Shane with a broken tooth.) Instead, he grinned and acted like it was the greatest present in the world. We drove to Meyer Park, and all four of us played catch until the sun sank beneath the trees. Shadows stretched across the park, but we kept playing until we couldn't see anymore. Because that's what Shane wanted.

FORTY-TWO

The next morning, I woke up to the Apocalypse.

It was delivered to every student and faculty member in his or her HVHS e-mail. The subject line read: "The End is Coming" and it contained a single website link:

happyvalleyapocalypse.com

Naturally, I clicked on it. We all did.

Fortunately for our dumb asses, it wasn't some all-powerful computer virus with the capabilities of breaking the Internet. Instead, the Happy Valley Apocalypse website was a plain black screen with only two features: (1) a timer that was actively ticking down from 22 hours, 53 minutes, 18 seconds and counting, and (2) a video.

The video thumbnail was the iconic camera lens eye of HAL 9000 in *2001: A Space Odyssey*. Glowing neon red. Watching endlessly.

It didn't take a detective to know who was behind this.

Naturally, I pushed Play. We all did.

There was no video component—only audio to the static image of HAL 9000. But that didn't make the message any less disturbing. HAL (or Haley, as I knew her) was using a voice distortion tool to mask her voice. She sounded like a genderless robotic drone.

This is what she said:

I am HAL.

Up until now, my hacks and pranks have all been in good humor. My better half always liked to make people laugh. Unfortunately, that part of me has been gone for a while now. And in the interim, I've discovered something about myself.

I really don't like people.

Students and faculty alike—I kind of hate you all. And I mean that in less of a My Chemical Romance way, and more of a V for Vendetta way. In the immortal words of V, "Love your rage, not your cage." Therefore, I've spent the better part of a year collecting things. Private messages and texts, pictures and videos—all the things you've never wanted anyone to see. The secrets. The lies. The truth. When this timer reaches zero, that information will go public. What happens next—who knows? When the masks all drop, and we see ourselves for who we really are ... well, sometimes a little anarchy is the best means of purging the filth.

We'll see who survives the Apocalypse.

The video ended.

"What do you think?" said Aaron.

He had showed the video to me (and Tegan) on his phone. Tegan had already seen it, but judging from her face, it didn't seem any less unsettling the second time around. I was now staring at the end-of-video replay option, and the timer that was tick-tick-ticking away. All the while, in an alternate reality at the back corner of my brain, I was staring at the fifth item on the List.

Find and stop HAL.

Tegan was on the same page.

"Do y'all even have a clue how to stop this clown?" she asked. "Or how to *find* him, even?"

"Her," I said. "Her name's Haley."

"Her, whatever. Jack and Julian told you that there *isn't* a Haley who goes to school here. So I'd say you're at ground zero."

"Yeah, but she was in a relationship with Shane. *And* she dropped off Shane's journal on my doorstep."

"So?"

"So I think she *wants* me to figure out who she is. I mean, she gave me her *name*! Why would she do that?"

Tegan pursed her lips skeptically.

"I think she knows why Shane killed himself," I said.

"Also, it's on the List," said Aaron. "So *obviously* we're gonna find and stop her."

Tegan rolled her eyes. "You and your goddamn List."

"I think you mean god-*given* List," said Aaron, winking.

At that moment, my phone vibrated. I fumbled to pull it out of my pocket. It was a text from Jack.

Julian and I just did something. You need to see this.

———

Jack and Julian were simultaneously hunched over the same computer. Jack had commandeered the mouse, scrolling slowly. Julian's jaw was steadily dropping. At one point, they scrolled past something that almost caused Julian to have an anime-fan-service-level nosebleed.

"Sweet baby Jesus in a manger," he said.

Jack spotted us in the doorway.

"Oh, thank god," he said, and immediately jumped out of his seat to greet us. Sort of. It was more of a passive-aggressive Secret Service greeting, planting a hand in the middle of my and Aaron's backs, forcefully guiding us to the computer of interest. Tegan followed awkwardly.

"I knew you guys would want us to try to hack HAL's countdown site—what with the List and all," he said. "So I took the liberty of getting a head start."

We crowded around the computer.

"Well. We cracked it."

There were dozens upon dozens of open windows scattered across dual monitors. I leaned forward and absorbed them all. I determined that they could essentially be broken down into three categories: (1) screenshots of achingly private conversations, (2) embarrassing and/ or incriminating videos and pictures, and (3) lots and lots and *lots* of nudes.

"We're only inside the cache," said Jack. "I haven't managed to disable anything yet. It was encrypted, but not very well. Like HAL decided to code this thing overnight. Which is weird because he obviously spent a lot of time collecting this dirt."

"Damn," said Tegan. "I've never seen so many tits in my life."

"Alas, the ghost of Snapchats past," said Julian.

"We need to shut this thing down," I said. "Like, ASAP. Can you guys do that?"

Ding.

A message box popped up in the bottom right corner. All six of us leaned forward.

HAL9000: *do you like what you see?*

Ding. Another message.

HAL9000: *i've spent a long time collecting these skeletons. saving them for a rainy day.*

Ding.

HAL9000: *a day of reckoning.*

Everyone stared absently at the messages. Exchanged blank glances with each other. Said nothing.

I shoved myself between Jack and Julian, and seized the keyboard. (It helped that they were both on rolling chairs. My girth sent them careening.)

"Whoa!" said Jack.

"Hey!" said Julian.

I typed desperately and hit Enter.

LaDy_KiLlAh: *You don't have to do this.*

"Lady...Killah?" said Tegan.

"Yeah, Gibson, my man!" said Julian, clapping his hands. "That's rad. I especially like the alternating caps and lowercase. Very edgy."

Ding.

HAL9000: *i don't expect you to understand.*

Ding.

HAL9000: *sorry, cliff.*

That's when I noticed the webcam light—but only as it flickered out.

HAL was spying on us.

Before any of us had a moment to adequately WTF, the screen disintegrated, obliterating into a million disjointed pixels.

"No," said Jack. He stood up, cradling the monitor gently by the sides. "No, no, no, no, no. Don't you die on me. Don't you die!"

The system crashed. When the fritzing and spazzing came to an epic cease-fire, all that was left was a blue screen, a frowny-face emoji, and a message that essentially said: *Your PC ran into a problem that it couldn't handle, and now it's fucked.*

That's not *actually* what it said. But we all knew that's what it meant.

FORTY-THREE

HAL was a bigger threat than Aaron and I knew how to handle. There were so many factors working against us, we didn't even know where to start. Such factors included:

1. We had no idea who Haley was.
2. We had no means of contacting her.
3. Time was an unstoppable force working against us. (The countdown was set to end tomorrow morning at 6:00 a.m.)
4. Jack and Julian refused to let us use another computer in the lab.
5. Even if we *found* another computer on which to hack happyvalleyapocalypse.com, Jack and Julian refused to help us.

"HAL's a better hacker than us," said Jack. "The only reason we got in is because HAL *let* us in."

"Not to mention the fact that we don't wanna piss HAL off," said Julian. "I've got so much dirt HAL could pull on me. For example, there was this one time Jack dared me to stick my dick in a toaster, and he recorded the whole thing, and it was on his computer for a whole year because every time he had a bad day, he would watch the video of his BEST FRIEND HURTING HIS DICK IN A TOASTER, and while I'm glad that I brought so much joy to my best friend in times of hardship, I'm not gonna lie, that's a seriously messed up thing to do."

Jack was laughing his way into critical condition. "Oh my God. Thank you for bringing that up. I feel so much better now."

In conclusion, Aaron and I had no clue how to find and stop HAL.

Aaron offered to drive me home, but I was too distracted by the utter hopelessness of our situation.

"No thanks, man," I said. "I think we both just need time to think. Brainstorm. You know?"

Aaron bit his lip and nodded. "Oh. Okay. Yeah."

I walked home. And as I walked, I racked my brain harder than it had ever been racked before. Searching for some clue. Some puzzle piece I had overlooked.

Why did Haley hate everyone so much?

Why did she give me Shane's journal?

What was Shane keeping from me?

Something was missing. Something so big, it left a chasm in the picture.

Without it, I was building half a puzzle.

———

When I left school, I thought I was leaving the Apocalypse behind me—if only temporarily.

Instead, I came home to it.

The first things I noticed were the three trash bags stacked by the front door. Then I heard the voices in the bedroom. Actually, it was just a single voice—my dad's—but instead of yelling, he was participating in a desperate, pleading, one-sided conversation.

Somehow, that only made the tension worse.

"Don't do this, baby. Please don't do this to me. Goddammit, *please!*"

I didn't need to see his face to know he was crying. Which was weird, because I'd never even heard him cry before. Not once in my entire life.

My mom barged out of the bedroom. Except it wasn't my parents' bedroom. It was *my* bedroom. She was also carrying a fourth and final trash bag—one that I realized was filled with *my* stuff. The sleeve of one of my long-sleeved shirts was hanging out of the top.

When my mom saw me, there was only a moment—a split second—of hesitation. "Grab a trash bag, Cliff. We're leaving."

My dad followed after her, and he looked even worse than he sounded. His raw, tear-stained eyes shifted to me.

"Cliff!" he sobbed. "I'm sorry! Tell her I'm sorry!"

My mom was doing a stellar job of ignoring his existence. Instead, she brushed past me, walked out the open front door, and yelled, "CLIFF. TRASH BAG. NOW."

I stared at my dad. Sad and pathetic. Broken and defeated.

Then I grabbed a trash bag and followed my mom out the door.

It took us three whole minutes to pack the car with four trash bags (poor-people luggage) and a few miscellaneous items my mom had failed to pack: *Speaker for the Dead*, a half-eaten box of Pop-Tarts, *2001: A Space Odyssey*, not to mention the most important document ever written—Shane's journal.

When we climbed inside and shut the doors, my dad was at my mom's window, crying harder than ever.

"I can change!" he said. "You always believed I could change, didn't you? Don't you think I can change?"

"I don't care anymore," she said.

My mom started the car, and we drove off.

She didn't look in her rearview mirror. Not once.

———

We were driving to a Motel 6. My mom informed me of this the moment we pulled out of Arcadia Park, and we'd been driving for ten minutes now.

We hadn't spoken a word since.

I wasn't trying to give my mom the silent treatment. God, I *wanted* to say something. But what? I'd been waiting for this moment for years—longing for it, fantasizing over it—and now here it was. It was supposed to be the happiest day of my life. So why did my stomach feel like it was being knitted into a scarf?

My mom didn't look victorious at all. She just looked stressed out.

Burned out.

Done.

I watched the houses and trees and shadows of sunset slip by in a sleepy haze. They were just moving things, and I was moving, and time was moving, and God, I wished that for one moment it would all just stop.

"How are things?" said my mom, finally.

"Things?" I said. "How are *things*?"

"How are *you*?"

I opened my mouth. Closed it. Bit my lip and shrugged. "I don't know. How should I be?"

"This sucks," she said. "It shouldn't suck. But it does." She peered over at me, digging for a sign. "Am I close?"

I shrugged. I didn't really know *what* to think anymore.

"Okay, how about this?" said my mom. "Finish this sentence: Life is . . . ?"

"Problematic," I said.

She nodded. "Okay. I can get behind that. Life is totally problematic. Heck, life is so full of problems, it makes me want to scream sometimes."

"But you don't."

"Well, you don't see me when I'm driving in the car by myself. I could have an alter ego in a screamo band."

I couldn't help chuckling.

"Would you like some motherly wisdom?" said my mom. "No? Well too bad, here it is: The problem is not the problem."

"The problem is not the problem," I repeated. "Ah. Okay. That literally makes no sense."

"Problems happen. That's just life. The real problem is when we run away from our problems."

"Um. What are we doing right now? Isn't this running away?"

"Sometimes staying in the same place is running away from the problem. Sometimes facing the problem means walking away from someone you used to love. But even though you're walking away, it doesn't mean that you're giving up on them."

I bit my lip. Lowered my head quietly. Studied the passenger's-side floor mat.

"How are you, Cliff?" she said. "Really."

"I feel like . . ." I said. But I couldn't seem to find the right adjective.

Maybe the right adjective didn't exist. "I feel like the End of the World is happening. And I'm supposed to save the world somehow, and I don't know how to keep my own life from falling apart, so how can I help anyone else?"

"Uh-oh. You're not secretly a superhero, are you?"

"Definitely not."

"Because I could *totally* see you as Peter Parker. And I'd be a really hot Aunt May."

"Maybe I'd be Peter Parker if he was the size of Juggernaut and couldn't stop eating Pop-Tarts."

"Peter's a high schooler. I'm sure he's never had a balanced breakfast in his life. And since he's always on the go, he probably eats Pop-Tarts for breakfast, lunch, and dinner."

I was laughing and shaking my head. "Okay. Whatever. You win."

"Yeah," said my mom, nodding. "You're *totally* Peter Parker. High schooler by day, crime fighter by night. And all you want is to save the world and be a normal teenager at the same time. Is that too much to ask for?"

I was smiling uncontrollably—a side effect of having an awesome mom.

"Now I've got a question for you," said my mom. "How does Peter Parker do it? Save the world and keep his own life from not falling apart at the same time?"

"Um . . . with . . . great . . . responsibility?"

My mom smirked. "Nice try, Uncle Ben. But I like to think there's more to his success than just responsibility."

"So what's his secret then?"

"He tries," said my mom. "And he keeps trying. And he never stops trying."

"He *tries*?"

"Even when the odds are stacked impossibly against him. Even when the world comes crashing down around him. Even when he loses the people he loves."

"He never stops trying," I said.

This time, my mom smiled. "In my opinion, you can never *truly* defeat someone who never stops trying."

———

I'd never stayed at a Motel 6 before. (Or any motel, for that matter.) I always had this stereotypical image in my head that Motel 6s were flea-infested, disease-ridden brothels. Where the fungus was alive, the pillows were stuffed with heroin needles, and the cockroaches performed musical dance numbers in the manner of *Joe's Apartment*. So I was kind of surprised when I discovered our second-floor room was about a billion times cleaner than our house, and just as big (or small, depending on perspective). It was a quaint little thing with bright orange walls, sharply tucked bedspreads, and a shiny hardwood floor.

"Wow," I said. "Fancy."

"Oh my God," said my mom. "My son just called a Motel 6 fancy. This is what my life has become."

"I think I could eat off this floor!"

"Please don't."

———

My mom went to bed almost immediately. It was just one of those days. But she *did* let me use her smartphone to connect to the Wi-Fi with only one stipulation—that I not wake her up. If I woke her, so help her God, I would be sent to the gallows.

My mom had a BBC costume drama problem. Sometimes she talked in turn-of-the-century British.

So as my mom fell asleep, an arm draped dramatically over her face, I lay wide-awake—staring at the Happy Valley Apocalypse countdown screen as the seconds ticked by.

Occasionally, I mixed it up. Playing HAL's apocalyptic monologue over and over again (with headphones), scraping for clues. Surfing the Internet for people named Haley. (Yes, the *whole* Internet. That was about as successful as you'd expect.) Texting Aaron.

> *Aaron, tell me you have an idea.*

an idea? does it have to be an idea
about how to find and stop HAL?

> *That would be preferable. But ideas*
> *on solving world hunger are always*
> *welcome too.*

nope. no ideas. but i think i learned
how to solve a rubik's cube.

> *A rubik's cube.*

i thought learning to solve a rubik's cube
would make me smarter and my mind
would expand and, by default, i'd have
an epiphany of how to find and stop hal.
no dice.

In retrospect, texting Aaron was probably less successful than googling "Haley."

By 3 a.m., I was still nowhere. But all was not lost, because I *did* find the video Aaron and I made for the Sermon Showdown.

It was in my e-mail.

That's right. Seth might have deleted the video in Jack's Sent box—along with damn near every other copy in existence—but Aaron and I still had final copies in our in-boxes. It was both maddening and hilarious.

I titled the video "What Is the Meaning of Life?" and decided to put it on YouTube. Lost in a sea of makeup tutorials, video game walk-throughs, and cat videos. And yet, there for the whole world to see.

I was just about to click the Upload button when I was interrupted by a phone call from an unknown number. My phone was on vibrate, but it proceeded to rattle noisily against the nightstand.

"Shit, shit, shit," I hissed and answered it. "It's three in the morning. Who is this?"

The thing on the other line sounded like a robot crying.

"Is this some kind of joke?" I said.

"I . . . I'm sorry for calling so late," said a voice that I realized *wasn't* a robot. It was a voice distorter.

"Haley?" I said.

"Yeah," said Haley, and it was clear she was still weeping. "It's me."

I tiptoe-ran across our motel room like the world's largest ninja, shimmied out the door and onto the cold, exposed balcony, and closed the door behind me.

"What are you doing? No. Scratch that. *Why* are you doing this?

"I'm doing this because Shane is dead," said Haley. "And someone needs to pay for it."

"So you've spent the past year collecting shit on everyone, just so you can plaster it all over the Internet?"

"Don't tell me you're not disgusted with these people. Forever Shane? The posters and the hashtags and the bracelets? They know *nothing* about Shane. They never gave a shit about him. They're just a bunch of pigs shoving their noses in the same pile of slop. Getting it while it's hot. A week from now, they won't even remember he existed."

"So the whole school needs to suffer?"

"Cliff...I *loved* Shane. I'd think you, of all people, would understand."

"Have I met you before? I mean, do I know you?"

"It's not important."

"It's important to me."

"No, Cliff. What's important to *you* is finding and stopping HAL."

"You know about that?"

"Come on, Cliff. *Everyone* knows about that. Honestly, I was surprised when I first heard number five on the List. At first, I wasn't even sure *what* it was you were supposed to be finding and stopping. I thought giving you the journal might make things more clear—for both of us. And maybe it has. All I know is that the most important thing to *me* is hurting the people who hurt Shane in ways that they'll never understand. Tell me, Cliff: Do you know what causes people to become cruel?"

"Huh?"

"Comfort," said Haley. "Comfort brings out people's cruelty. People become comfortable with themselves. They feel like they're untouchable. The only way to end cruelty is to rip off their costumes and expose them to the world. It's impossible to be cruel when you're naked among your peers."

"You sound awful sure of yourself," I said. "So why are you calling me?"

"Because if anyone can change my mind, it's you."

I leaned over the balcony railing and stared out across the ghost town of Happy Valley at three in the morning. Asphalt gleamed beneath lonely streetlamps, illuminating the emptiness.

"You *want* me to change your mind?" I said.

"*If* you can change my mind," said Haley, "then I at least want to give you the chance to try."

There were a lot of things I could have said. Things that were obvious to me. Obvious to *most* people. But somehow, I knew that my truth didn't apply to Haley.

I snuck back into the motel room, saved Haley's number in my mom's phone, uploaded "What Is the Meaning of Life?" to YouTube, and sent Haley the link.

"What's this?" said Haley.

"It's something that Aaron and I made," I said. "Just for you."

"For me?"

"We just didn't know it at the time."

Haley didn't seem to have a response to this.

"If this doesn't tell you what you need to hear," I said, "then there's nothing I can say to change your mind."

Again, silence. Finally, Haley hung up.

I thought the anticipation would kill me. But it didn't. Somehow—against all reason—I felt okay.

I crawled into bed, pulled the covers up to my neck, and sleep washed over me, like a silky wave across an untouched shore.

FORTY-FOUR

If you were to go on YouTube at this moment and search "What Is the Meaning of Life?" you would discover, several results pages back, a video posted by CliffLovesPopTarts. A video with a single view. Maybe two views now that you're watching it.

It went something like this:

Aaron Zimmerman stands in front of HVHS's main entrance. I'm behind the camera (my only camerawork in the entire video), angling it so you can see the chiseled letters that form the words HAPPY VALLEY HIGH SCHOOL.

"So," I say, offscreen, "what is the meaning of life?"

"You're kidding, right?"

"Nuh-uh. What is it?"

"What the hell makes you think *I* know what it is?"

"Well, you saw God, right? He gave you the List. So—"

"Dude. It's subjective, don't you think?"

"Subjective?"

"Well, yeah. I think the *point* is to find it for yourself. And maybe what *you* find is totally different from what *someone else* finds."

"So what you're *saying* is I need to ask everyone at school what the meaning of life is to *them*."

"What? No. That's not what I—"

The video explodes into a cinematic montage—accompanied by Diego's soft electronic sound track. Alternating shots of Jack and Julian following Aaron and me around HVHS, inside and out. Crowded hallways, sidewalks, classrooms, fields.

JED: Is this a trick question?

ROBIN: The meaning of life? Is that even a real thing?

CARLOS: Easy. One word: aliens.
CLIFF: You think the meaning of life is . . . aliens?
CARLOS: The truth is out there.

TEGAN: Sex, drugs, and rock 'n' roll.
CLIFF: Tegan!
TEGAN: Just kidding. About the drugs, I mean. Drugs are for pugs. But sex is good!
CLIFF: Tegan . . .
TEGAN: And rock 'n' roll is life. Don't you dare tell me it isn't.

AARON: Not a trick question. In your honest opinion, what is the meaning of life?
JED: I s'pose it's being with the people you care about. Like friends and family.
AARON: Which is more important—friends or family?

JED: I don't think you can say one is more important than the other. You need a lot of things in order to survive.

AARON: If it *was* a real thing, what do you *think* it would be?

ROBIN: Um. I suppose it starts with having a dream. And then chasing it. You chase after it like your life *depends* on it. In a sense, I guess it does.

AARON: What sort of dream?

ROBIN: Any sort. It doesn't matter what it is. The only thing that matters is that you want it from the deepest part of who you are, and you chase after it with everything in you.

AARON: What happens when you get it?

ROBIN: I feel like dreams are never that two-dimensional. You never just "get it." The more you chase, the more your dream expands. It's like, the more you know, the more you realize you *don't* know. Every step you get closer to your dream, the more the world around you crystalizes into something you never knew it was.

AARON: Wow. That's really eloquent.

ROBIN: Thanks. I read books.

CARLOS: Okay, in all seriousness, life is like ET.

CLIFF: The . . . Extra-Terrestrial?

CARLOS: Yeah. Little dude. Squatty legs, arms like a monkey, ugly as hell.

CLIFF: (*sighs*) Okay, I'm listening.

CARLOS: *We're* ET. We're all lost. We're all tryna make our way home, except we have no way of getting there. Not without some help. And then there's Elliott. We all got an Elliott in our life—this person who we're just *connected* to. It just happens, and there ain't no breaking that connection. They didn't choose each other. They just collided into each other's lives, and suddenly there's no going home without each other's help.

CLIFF: So what's the point?

CARLOS: The *point* is find your Elliott, man! You need each other like you need air. Your destinies are intertwined.

KYLE: Football.

AARON: The meaning of life is football.

KYLE: Yep.

AARON: Damn, I'm screwed.

KYLE: (*laughs*) Okay, maybe not just football. But I feel like there's always that one thing that makes you feel alive like nothing else does. For me, that's running around on a field, intercepting balls, and getting tackled to the ground. There's something about it that just wakes something up inside of me. I don't even know what it is. It's a moment. It's passion. Maybe that's what life is about: passion—and whatever draws it out of you.

ROBIN: Wow, Kyle. Did you actually find an articulate way to talk about football?

(*Kyle laughs, grabs his little sister's head, and pushes it offscreen.*)

KYLE: Get out of here! You already had your turn!

Jack captures a stunning shot of Lacey, standing at the far corner of the football field, watching the cataclysmic beginnings of a sunset. The oranges and the pinks and the purples span and swirl like acrylic paint, floating on a body of water. Clouds soak up their hues like cotton swabs.

LACEY: (*voice-over*) I'm not really a spiritual person. But when I see stuff like this...? I feel like there's something out there. Something bigger than life as I know it, just waiting to be discovered. Waiting for *me* to discover it.

(*Lacey brushes a lock of hair behind her ear and looks at the camera. Her eyes reflect the sky, radiant with wonder.*)

LACEY: (*voice-over*) I feel like there's a sense of meaning in the unknown. It's life's way of telling you to go out. Explore. Try something new. Learn something that contradicts the world as you know it.

Julian sets up a series of shots in Spinelli's classroom, focusing on random classroom fixtures—old, scratched-up desks, stacks of writing assignments waiting to be graded, a whiteboard with a Hemingway quote: *Now is no time to think of what you do not have. Think of what you can do with what there is.*

SPINELLI: We can't even begin to understand the universe. And even when we *think* we know things, the truth as we know it often changes. Suddenly, the Earth isn't flat, it revolves around the sun, and *neither* of these are the center of the universe. The universe has always been, and always will be, a mystery—unfolding slowly, surely, but never completely. It will always store secrets in its infinite hiding places. So to say that you don't *believe* in something because you don't *understand* it is a fallacy. I find that the things I believe in the most are the things that I don't fully understand—whether it be God, or the love between partners, or the fact that there's a goodness in mankind that will *always* transcend the bad.

NIKO: I think the point is to not be afraid. Honestly, I've spent most of my life being afraid.

CLIFF: You? *Afraid?*

NIKO: Yeah, man.

CLIFF: Afraid of *what*?

NIKO: Everything. Afraid of the past, afraid of the present, afraid of the future... Afraid of people who are *different* than me, afraid of people who are the *same* as me... Man, sometimes I'm afraid of myself.

CLIFF: Yourself?

NIKO: Yeah, man. I scare the *hell* outta myself sometimes. I feel like a moving car, and my brakes just went out, and I don't know how to stop myself without crashing and dying. So I just keep going.

CLIFF: So how do you stop being afraid?

NIKO: I think I'm mostly afraid of people letting me down. I've had a lotta people let me down. People I trusted. And the only way I knew how to stop people from letting me down was to stop trusting them. But I think that's a bad way to live. Sometimes, you just gotta trust people. Even when you're afraid. Maybe es*pecially* when you're afraid.

NOAH: Some days, I don't want to believe in a God. Other days, I just... I *need* to believe. Horrible things happen, all over the world, every day. We ask ourselves: Why would God let this happen? And we want an answer to that question so bad, but there is no answer. Instead, there's just this... hope. This hope that, somehow, things can be right in the end. And I pray every day that it's true.

FRANKIE: I was just a toddler when my mom walked out on us. It was just my pops, my baby sister, and me, and it was hard. I was just a toddler, and I can still remember how mad I was at my baby sister. I thought it was her fault my mom left. I mean, everything was good until she came into the picture. So I decided I was gonna march my toddler ass into the baby room, get up on my potty stool, and yell at that dumb-ass baby in her dumb-ass cradle. Tell her how much I hated her. So I dragged my potty stool in there, climbed up, and glared into that cradle.

(Frankie's voice breaks. A tear trickles down his cheek. He sniffs and wipes it with a tattooed finger.)

FRANKIE: But in that cradle was the most beautiful thing I have ever seen. And somehow, in that moment, I knew that little girl came from somewhere special. They say you can't remember stuff when you're that young, but I remember, man. I remember.

TEGAN: Okay, all jokes aside . . .

CLIFF: Please.

TEGAN: I think we all just need to take a deep breath.

CLIFF: Take a deep breath.

TEGAN: Yeah.

CLIFF: And then what?

TEGAN: And then do whatever you want! But stop first. Take a deep breath. We live in a world where everything is instant, and the Internet shoves it in our faces, and suddenly we're worried about all the hate filling our news feeds, and countries having dick-measuring contests with their nukes, and why does everyone else's lives seem so much more happy and perfect than mine? And it's suffocating. It's like someone is holding my head underwater. I'm worried about so many things at once, I can't even function, and Christ! I just . . . I'd do *anything* to shut it all off!

(Tegan follows her own advice. Stops. Inhales deeply. Lets it out like she's releasing a piece of herself.)

TEGAN: We're all gonna die. And we only have so many fucks we can give in a lifetime. So give a fuck about the things that matter most. Maybe you don't know what those things are right now. Maybe 'cause you're too busy *worrying* about the fact that you don't know what matters most to you. So stop. Take a deep breath.

(Tegan grabs Jack's camera.)

JACK: (*voice-over*) Whoa! Hey!

She holds the camera away from herself—at selfie length—angled so it captures both her and me, Cliff Hubbard. She grabs me by the collar and pulls me down, simultaneously lifting herself on her toes. Then, she kisses me.

Caught completely off guard, my arms flounder aimlessly for a moment. And then they fall, slowly, onto her waist.

Our lips part. Tegan angles the camera on herself.

TEGAN: Sometimes the things that matter most are right in front of us.

FORTY-FIVE

I woke up to a strange text message. It was Noah. The fact that it was almost six in the morning only amplified the strangeness. He texted:

If you could tell Shane one thing, what would it be?

I might have responded sarcastically if I was more than half awake. But I wasn't, and, in a sleepy haze, I considered my answer just a little too seriously. I replied:

I would probably ask him why he made me think I knew everything about him, when really, I didn't know anything. I would also tell him that I love him and that killing himself was a dick move.

There was a long pause before Noah's next text. I may or may not have dozed off, but the buzz and the bright flash of the screen woke me up again.

I would tell him that everything's going to be okay from now on.

I stared at that for a long moment before one plus one equaled *Holy shit!* Today was the anniversary of Shane's death.

And then I fell back asleep.

I woke up to a number of things—my phone vibrating, my mom yelling/groaning/burbling my name, but mostly, I woke up to the pillow that flew across the room and hit me in the face.

"Who? What?" I said.

"Your phone!" My mom was still lying in bed with an arm draped over her face. "It's been going off for the past half hour. *My* alarm is set to go off in fifteen minutes. If I don't get to enjoy those fifteen minutes in peace, either you or that phone will die."

My mom didn't seem concerned with an answer as she rolled over sideways, curled into a ball, and smothered her head with a pillow.

I grabbed my phone, walked outside, and answered it without glancing at the caller. "Hello?"

"Cliff, where are you?" It was Aaron.

"Uh..." I had to think for a second. "Motel 6?"

"Motel 6? Why are you at a Motel 6?"

So, for the next several minutes, I explained in detail why I was staying in a Motel 6. It was a deeply uncomfortable conversation.

"Damn," said Aaron. "The Motel 6 on Gleason?"

"Uh. Yeah?"

"Okay." Aaron hung up.

I stared at my phone, trying to figure out what the hell was going on. When the pieces failed to come together, I gave up and started getting ready for school. I was halfway through the most wonderful shower of my life—God bless Motel 6's Niagara Chrome showerhead—when I remembered the Happy Valley Apocalypse countdown.

I stumbled out—waging battle with the shower curtain in the process—wrapped a towel around all seventeen acres of my ass, and ran out of the bathroom, soaking wet. I fumbled with my mom's phone until I navigated my way to happyvalleyapocalypse.com.

The countdown was gone. The audio clip was gone. The website was completely empty, except for a single quote:

"You wear a mask for so long, you forget who you were beneath it."
—Alan Moore, *V for Vendetta*

And that was it. No blackmail. No extortion. No nudes or embarrassing/incriminating messages, pictures, or videos.

I did it. I stopped HAL.

The elation of this moment was disrupted by a knock at the door.

I glanced at the door. I glanced at my mom, who was practically in cryostasis. Then I glanced at my big, wet, naked self.

After dressing myself in Guinness World Record time, I answered the door.

It was Aaron and Tegan. And Tegan was holding a four-pack.

"Is that beer?" I started to ask—but Aaron and Tegan were already attacking me in a vicious group hug.

My confusion lasted for only a moment. "Is this about the Apocalypse countdown?"

Aaron and Tegan released me from their covert hug assault.

"That *is* amazing news," said Aaron. "But no."

"I remembered that today was the anniversary of..." Tegan hesitated. "You know. Shane."

Oh.

Oh!

How had I forgotten that?

"We wanted to get him flowers," said Tegan, "but the grocery store flowers were lame and wilty, and I realized that Shane would probably hate flowers anyway, so I stole some beers from my dad's garage stash."

"So *now*," said Aaron, "before school, the three of us are going to pay Shane a visit. The fourth beer is for him."

I could already feel the waterworks coming—like a great tsunami in the back of my eyeballs. I attempted to hide it by returning the hug attack, pulling each of them in with an arm.

"You guys are the best friends ever," I said.

"Um, *friend*?" said Tegan.

"Girlfriend, best friend, whatever. You guys are the best."

———

"Whoa, whoa, whoa, what is this?" I said.

The "this" I was referring to was Aaron sitting in the backseat of his Camaro, and Tegan—who did not have a driver's license— climbing behind the steering wheel.

"Oh, I'm not allowed to drive for the next couple weeks," said Aaron. "You know, in case I have another epileptic seizure. Doctor's orders. So Tegan offered to be the wheelman."

Tegan winked at me.

"She never earned her driver's license!"

"About that, Cliff . . ." said Tegan. "I may have told you a slight untruth. I didn't want you to think I was a bad person."

"Oh my God."

"I *did* earn my driver's license. I just had it revoked when I accidentally T-boned an ice-cream truck."

"Tegan!"

"But the driver was okay!"

"How do you *accidentally* T-bone an ice-cream truck? It's a car the size of an ambulance that plays 'Turkey in the Straw' from a megaphone!"

Aaron shrugged. "You don't have a license, either. I don't care who drives as long as it's not me."

Tegan's hands fastened on the steering wheel. "You already drove once. I've got dibs."

I surrendered the argument, climbed into the passenger seat, and buckled my seat belt. I even tugged on the buckle, just to make sure it was secure.

It was a quiet drive. But not a sad one. This was mostly due to the fact that I was monumentally distracted. I couldn't think about Shane because I was too preoccupied with HAL.

Aaron and Tegan, meanwhile, might as well have been mannequins. They were probably trying to pay their respects—which I appreciated—but right now, there was a cyber-terrorizing elephant in the car that needed addressing.

"HAL called me last night," I said.

Tegan nearly swerved off the road, and Aaron exercised the incredible versatility of the F-word. After a brief moment of zigzagging, and everyone's lives flashing promptly before their eyes, Tegan reined us back into the correct lane.

"Holy shit," Aaron concluded.

"*You* stopped HAL?" said Tegan.

I recounted my entire phone conversation with HAL—every detail—leading up to me texting her the link to our video. The moment I mentioned the video, Aaron's mouth splintered into a crazed smile.

"The *video* stopped HAL?" said Aaron. "*Our* video?"

"As far as I can tell."

"We did it! We found and stopped HAL! The List is complete!"

"But that's the thing. We *stopped* HAL. But we didn't find her. We still have no clue who she is."

Aaron's hysteria boiled down to a simmer. "Huh."

"Oh, c'mon," said Tegan. "I don't think God was being *that* literal. The List is *done*. You guys did it! Right, Aaron?"

I glanced back at Aaron. He looked just as unsure as me.

And then Aaron's eyes widened. "Oh shit."

"What?"

"Is there a quiz today in Algebra?"

I rolled my eyes. "Who do you have?"

"Mr. Gunther."

My eyes shifted up in thought. "Yeah, there's a quiz. But it's easy stuff—quadratic polynomials."

"Easy?" said Tegan. She snorted and laughed.

Aaron grabbed his skull. "What the hell is a *quadratic* polynomial?"

He didn't even wait for an answer. He pulled his backpack onto his lap, unzipped it, and sifted through the contents.

"Shit! I don't even have my book!"

"Would you like to borrow mine?" I said.

"Oh my God, yes, please."

I unzipped my own backpack and pulled out my textbook—an ancient hand-me-down from Shane. Technically it was school property, but Shane never returned it. He never had the chance to.

"We can postpone this," I said, handing him the book, "if you need to study."

"No, no, no, no, no," said Aaron. "No postponing. This morning's for Shane. Lemme just cram on the way to the Monolith."

Aaron opened the front cover. Paused. "Why do you have Noah's textbook?"

"Huh?"

Aaron lifted the book with the front cover open for me to see. A name was scribbled in the top left corner:

Noah H. Poulson

I knew why I had Noah's textbook—because he tutored Shane in Algebra, and it seemed like an easy mistake for textbooks to get shuffled in the process.

But then there was the initial between Noah's first and last name.

I stared at that *H* for an infinity compounded into mere seconds.

I fumbled to pull my phone out of my pocket, scrolled through the contacts, and called Jack. He answered after the second ring.

"Hey, Cliff," said Jack. "What's up?"

"I need you to look up Noah's middle name for me."

"Noah? Why?"

"Just do it!" I paused before adding, "But don't bother with the school directory. It's not there."

"What do you want me to do? Hack the private student files?"

"Can you *do* that?"

"Well, yeah, but—"

"Yes. That. Do that."

"Okay..."

Tegan eyed me from the driver's seat, clearly confused. Aaron pulled the textbook back into his lap, returning his attention to Noah's name. Out of the corner of my eye, I saw him go breathless.

"No way," said Aaron.

There was silence on the other line. An occasional click or scroll of the wheel button on a computer mouse.

"No. Way," said Jack, finally.

"What is it?"

"Haley," he said. "Noah *Haley* Poulson."

It was a good thing I wasn't driving because this was the part where we would have crashed and died.

"Holy shit," said Jack. "Does this mean Noah is HAL?"

It meant much more than Noah being HAL.

It meant that Noah and Shane were in love.

Fragments of Shane's journal were flashing in front of me. The dots were connecting.

. . . I started liking Hal, but I didn't fess up to it, because Hal REALLY wasn't my "type."

We haven't had sex yet, and frankly, having sex with her kind of scares me, which probably sounds weird, but if you knew her, you'd understand.

And then the kicker:

It seems like I've told you a lot, but I really haven't told you anything.

I am a liar. The truth is that I don't know how to tell the truth, to you or to anyone.

I've been freaking out a lot lately, and I've been taking it out on Hal. Which isn't fair. It's not her fault I'm in love with her. At first I was asking myself how I could love someone so much and hate them at the same time. But now I realize that she's not the person I hate.

I hate myself.

Shane was gay. Or maybe bisexual. And he had lived in a cesspool of homophobia. Between the JTs—who infiltrated nearly every social sphere—to my dad, Happy Valley was certainly not supplying him with reasons to *love* himself.

My mind was a spinning top, and the rotational inertia was just getting started.

If Noah was Haley, that meant that *he* was the one who left Shane's journal on my doorstep. Which meant that he knew about the lie in the journal. He knew that Shane had crafted this fake version of their story, turning Noah into a girl named Haley. Shane couldn't even tell the truth to a journal!

Realization struck me like a line drive to the face—a texting conversation I had only hours ago. It had been all but a forgotten dream. But now, in this moment, reality sucker-punched me awake.

If you could tell Shane one thing, what would it be?

Why would Noah ask me that?

I would tell him that everything's going to be okay from now on.

Oh my God.

"Cliff?" said Aaron. "Cliff, are you okay?"

I ignored him. "Jack?"

"Yeah?"

"I need you to find Principal McCaffrey *right now.*"

"What? You're not going to rat Noah out, are you?"

"Listen, there's no time—"

"C'mon, Cliff. Noah stopped the countdown. There's nothing on that List that says you need to throw Noah under the bus like—"

"DAMMIT, JACK. *I think Noah's going to kill himself.*"

That shut Jack up. "What?" he said, eventually.

"WHAT?" said Aaron and Tegan, simultaneously.

"I don't have time to explain," I said to Jack. "Find McCaffrey and see if she can find him. . . ."

"Okay, okay, I'm going!" said Jack. "Shit." And he hung up.

"Cliff, what's going on?" said Tegan.

"Do you know where Spruce Forest Drive is?"

"Where the Poulsons live?"

"Yes! YES! Do you know where they l—?"

Tegan didn't wait for me to spit out another syllable. She simultaneously hit the brakes and turned the steering wheel hard, flipping the bitchin'est U-ey ever flipped.

"Jesus, Tegan!"

Two seconds and 180 degrees later, we were nearly doubling the speed limit in the opposite direction. Apparently, shit had just gone from bad to Biblical because the Seven Seals of Revelation were unraveling, and man and machine were becoming one. In that moment, Tegan and Aaron's '69 Camaro Z28 RS transformed into the Fifth Horseman of the Apocalypse.

"So this is how I die," Aaron mused.

"Confession," said Tegan. "In first grade, Esther and I used to be best friends. You know, before she discovered Jesus, and I discovered sociopaths."

"WHO ARE YOU?" I said.

"Hey, we were six, and we liked Bratz dolls! Back off!"

This revelation could be digested later. Right now, I was already dialing Noah's number. I listened to the ringback tone and told myself I was overreacting. Noah would answer. He would wonder why I was freaking out and tell me he was just planning on visiting Shane's grave later this afternoon. That I had fabricated this whole suicidal innuendo in my head. McCaffrey would be pissed, Jack would be irritated, and Noah and I would have a great big laugh about the whole thing. Everything would be okay.

No one picked up. Instead, it went to Noah's voice mail.

"Fuck!" I hung up and began hyperventilating into my hands.

"Noah is Haley," said Aaron, breathless. "Isn't he?"

"What?" said Tegan.

I took a deep breath and let everything out. "Long story short: Noah and my big brother, Shane, were...uh...in love apparently, but now Shane's dead, and today's the anniversary of his death, and Noah texted me something vaguely suicidal last night, and his voice mail is...Oh shit, this is bad."

"Oh my God," said Aaron.

"Holy fuck," said Tegan.

My phone rang—causing my heart to do Cirque du Soleil in my chest. Please let it be Noah, please!

It was an unknown number. I answered, "Hello?"

"Cliff, what's going on?" It was McCaffrey.

"Principal McCaffrey!" I screamed into the receiver. It wasn't until after the screaming that I thought better of it.

"Cliff," she said, unfazed. Her voice was dead fucking serious. "Jack just told me that you said Noah might be planning to commit suicide."

There was no way I could convey the urgency of the situation to her without spilling the details. So I did, because Tegan had no intention of slowing down, and I felt like I needed to be doing something besides sitting my fat ass in the passenger seat. I explained Shane's journal, and the story of Haley, and Noah's text messages, and his voice mail.

McCaffrey had never been so silent. When she finally spoke, her voice was heavy and sharp. "I'm sending some staff to look for him. If he's here, we'll find him. Where are you?"

The car stopped—brakes screeching like a banshee giving birth. It was a good thing I was wearing my seat belt, otherwise my head might have made a new hole in Aaron's glove box. My gaze darted from the elaborate half-moon driveway we were parked on, to Tegan turning off the car, to Aaron jumping out the back door.

"We're at the Poulsons' house, gotta go," I said.

"Cliff, wait. What are you—?"

I hung up.

Aaron, Tegan, and I raced up the concrete path to the front door of—holy shit!—the biggest house I had ever seen. In person, at least.

It was like the Playboy Mansion had given birth to a baby mansion that was promptly baptized. A tiny brass Jesus was being crucified on the front door, right above the knocker. I didn't bother with the knocker; I raised my fist and *whaled* on the door, FBI-style. I didn't stop knocking until it opened. It was Esther.

"Cliff?" she said. "Aaron? TEGAN? What are you—hey!"

I brushed right past Esther, storming through the entryway. A crystal chandelier gleamed over me, illuminating a miniature Jesus gallery with crosses and pictures of Jesus doing Jesus-y things, and framed plaques of warm, fuzzy Bible-gibberish phrases.

"What the *hell* do you think you're doing?" said Esther.

"Where's Noah's room?"

"You think you can just barge in here? I'm calling the police."

"Jesus Christ, Esther, your brother is going to kill himself! Where's his fucking room?"

Esther's eyes widened, and her pupils became specks. You could see it in her gaze—she was falling. Gravity had toppled sideways, and she was falling backward into endless sky.

"Uh . . . u-u-u-upstairs," she said—suddenly, frantically. "Second door on the left—"

I was already barreling up the staircase, two steps at a time. The second door on the left had an aluminum sign with the biohazard symbol on it. I practically blasted through the door.

Contrary to the biohazard warning, Noah's room was obnoxiously neat and clean. Especially considering all the rock posters on the wall, everything from the Rolling Stones to the Red Hot Chili Peppers. There was an obsessive-compulsive symmetry to their arrangement.

And no Noah.

"No," I said. I glanced from his empty bed to his empty desk—all perfectly arranged, picturesque, and desolate. "No, no, no, no, NO!"

I punched the nearest wall, which hurt like hell, and also left a fist-shaped crater in the drywall.

"Where is he?" said Tegan, close behind me.

"Esther," said Aaron, "do you have *any* idea where your brother could be?"

"I...I don't know," said Esther, who had apparently followed us upstairs. Her face was sucked of color, her eyes and mouth shuddery. "We haven't talked lately."

Of course they hadn't.

"He's...kept to himself."

Of course he has.

"What's going on?" said Esther. "Why do you think Noah...? Why would he...?"

I wanted so badly to scream in her face. To tell her that while she was busy bullying in the name of Jesus, her brother was dying. But it *wasn't* her fault. Not entirely, anyway. If anyone was to blame, it was Shane. By killing himself, Shane had inadvertently killed a part of Noah too.

And that's when I saw it.

The Door of Life.

I walked slowly—hypnotically—across Noah's room, staring at the wall. I stopped directly in front of a poster. I could feel everyone's gazes burrowing disconcertedly into the back of my skull.

"What are you doing?" said Tegan.

It was the only poster that wasn't a rock poster. It was a movie poster. It was *2001: A Space Odyssey*. On it was a simple black rectangle—the Monolith.

Shane's journal was screaming in my head.

I took Hal to this old, abandoned building we call the Monolith. I guess I was acting kind of flirty, and she was too, and our hands touched on the stairway railing, and then we got really close, and I told her how not into her I was, but I said it really soft, and she said she didn't know what I was talking about, and she said it even softer. And then we kissed.

They shared their first kiss there. And Shane killed himself there.

I flew past Aaron and Tegan, out the door, and down the stairs.

"Cliff!" Tegan yelled.

"Where are you going?" said Aaron.

I suppose it was notoriously stupid to run off without the guy with the car *and* the girl with the car keys. Fortunately, he and Tegan were chasing after me.

"The old, abandoned building on Gosling and Gleason!" I shouted. "That's where he is!"

We were out the door and in the Camaro in seconds, Aaron and I hurtling into the passenger side, Tegan sliding into the driver's seat, and then . . .

"Whoa," said Aaron.

"Um . . ." said Tegan.

I twisted around to find Esther also in the backseat beside Aaron. She ignored our stares and buckled herself in. When she finally made eye contact, she returned our incredulous looks tenfold.

"What are you waiting for?" said Esther. "Let's go!"

We couldn't argue with that. Tegan pounded the gas in reverse, we squealed out of the half-moon driveway, and we were off.

"Why would my brother want to kill himself?" said Esther.

Tegan was focused on the road. I was ignoring Esther out of spite. I could only imagine what Aaron was doing in the backseat.

"Cliff Hubbard, why does my brother want to kill himself?"

"You know, it's really funny that you should care," I said.

"I didn't ask for your social commentary. Why does Noah want to kill himself? Don't I deserve to know that much?"

"You know what? You *do* deserve to know. Your brother wants to kill himself because he lost Shane. *My* brother. They were secretly dating and then Shane killed himself. There you go. I hope that makes you real happy."

Esther looked anything but happy. The evidence glistened in the corners of her eyes.

"That doesn't make me happy," she said.

I ignored her.

"I love my brother," she said.

"Well, you have a hell of a way of showing it."

Esther sank into a mire of silence.

The peak of the Monolith broke free of the horizon like a black knife, cresting behind trees and houses. Tegan made several sharp turns, veering around cars going the speed limit and doing anything but stopping at stop signs. At last, we arrived at the corner of Gosling and Gleason, careening into the empty, weed-ridden lot on the west side of the Monolith. With the sun rising in the east, we were completely immersed in the blanket of its shade. Tegan had barely come to a halt when Esther and I jumped out of the car.

"Oh no," said Esther.

My eyes followed her gaze up, up, all the way to the near-peak of the building and its gaping mouth. The unfinished balcony. My and Shane's spot. Probably Noah and Shane's spot too.

Noah was standing on the edge.

"Oh my God, oh my God," said Aaron.

I ran.

I plowed through the broken doorway, dodging through planks and plywood and discarded construction equipment and debris. I sailed up the stairs, telling my dying lungs to shut the hell up. Noah obviously knew I was coming up. He could jump at any moment. I would certainly know when he did. I could only hope and pray to God—any Great Omnipotent Something out there—that he hadn't.

Please, oh please, give me just a few more seconds.

I emerged from the stairwell, and there was Noah, on the ledge, a silhouette against a hemorrhaging sunrise.

"STOP, NOAH, PLEASE!" I screamed.

Except the moment I barged into the room, Noah was stepping *away* from the ledge. He was also holding a bouquet of flowers—very nonlethal looking. There was a look of deep concern on his face.

That concern seemed to be directed at me.

It was about at this point that I realized I had made a dire miscalculation.

"Whoa, hey," said Noah, raising his hands *and* the bouquet. "I don't think I'm doing what you think I'm doing."

This was the part where I was supposed to feel really stupid and embarrassed. Leave it to Clifford Hubbard—emotionally damaged psycho for life—to make a mountain out of a very nonsuicidal mole-hill. However, I was physically incapable of feeling anything but relief—the sort of relief that crushes your chest, burns your eyes, and makes you fall apart completely.

I started crying.

"Oh man, uh . . ." said Noah. "Sorry. I didn't mean to . . ."

He sort of trailed off because what was there for him to be sorry for? That his friend had unaddressed PTSD that automatically made him jump to the worst conclusions imaginable?

"Do you need a hug?" he asked.

I attempted to nod, but I was crying so hard, it was difficult to operate my head properly. So my head just bobbled in a semivertical manner.

Noah seemed to get the gist of it. With the bouquet still in hand, he wrapped his arms around my big, trembling form. Squeezed me tight, without a hint of letting go.

"It was you," I said in between sobs. "You were Haley."

Noah sighed. "Yeah. I'm Haley."

And then he sniffed. I felt an emotional reaction in every muscle of his body.

"I knew you'd figure it out," he added.

"Why didn't you tell me?"

Noah shrugged. "Shane didn't tell you. It wasn't my secret to tell. Not directly, anyway. I figured Shane's words were the only ones that mattered."

"So you left his journal on my doorstep."

"Yeah."

"Noah . . ." I said. "I'm so sorry."

"No, Cliff." He pulled himself away. Grabbed me by the shoulders and looked me in the eyes. "*I'm* sorry. I knew that Shane needed help. I tried to get him to see someone—to talk to a professional or something—but I . . . I didn't try hard enough. This is my fault. It's my fault he . . ."

Noah's lip quivered. His entire face trembled, threatening to break.

"Noah," I said. "It's *not* your fault."

And it wasn't. Shane made a decision. Maybe it was impulsive, maybe it was well thought out. But the door he stepped through was a permanent one. A one-way destination. The moment he stepped through it, the door slammed shut behind him. The cosmos rippled with his sudden, inexplicable exit from the universe. Those of us who loved him were left to deal with the consequences.

Noah dropped roughly to the concrete. I kneeled beside him and pulled him close.

"I miss him," said Noah, between choking sobs. "I miss him so much."

"I know," I said. I grabbed Noah's head, and I wept into his hair. "Me too."

Aaron, Tegan, and Esther must have been waiting out in the stairwell because they stepped out now, slowly. Tegan's eyes dropped to the bouquet, still clutched desperately in Noah's hand.

"Damn," she said. "I knew we shoulda bought flowers."

Tegan had her arms around Esther. The moment she let go, Esther stepped forward. Each step was slow and heavy, like she was trudging through mud.

The moment Noah saw her, his eyes inflated. "Esther?"

Esther lost all control of herself. Her face crumpled, wringing out tears, shaking her head softly. Her lips moved, soundless, mouthing the words, "I'm so sorry, I'm so sorry…"

Noah let go of me. Stood up. Approached Esther.

"It's okay," he said, and he hugged her.

Esther squeezed him in her arms like he was the last thing she would ever hold.

Gazing past the tops of everyone's heads, I watched the sun rising over Happy Valley, shedding its warmth and light, unveiling the lies and illuminating the secrets.

It was a new beginning.

FORTY-SIX

We paid Shane a magnificent tribute. The five of us drank four beers in Shane's honor. (Esther volunteered to be designated driver.) We shared stories, played Shane's favorite songs from our phones, and offered silence. Once we were sufficiently tardy—and buzzed—we went to school.

After school, I went home.

Where was home?

Not Arcadia Park anymore. Not Motel 6 either.

My mom and I moved in with my aunt Sadie in Kalispell—which was a city, apparently. Population: 22,000. I kind of hated it. Fortunately, Happy Valley was only ten miles north—a twenty-minute drive. (Seven if Tegan was driving Aaron's Camaro, God help us.) And Principal McCaffrey agreed that I should finish my junior year at HVHS. We'd "talk" about senior year.

School went on, and I continued cramming knowledge into my brain.

In between Physics and Spanish, Aaron leaned against the locker adjacent to mine and asked, "How do you know if you're in love with somebody?"

"In love?" I said.

"I mean, is it like spiritual enlightenment? Like nirvana? Where your chakras align, and your chi is unlocked, and you just know?"

"Nirvana?"

"The Buddhist concept, not the band. No disrespect to Kurt Cobain, may he rest in peace."

I scratched my head. "What are we talking about?"

"Am I in love with Lacey?" said Aaron.

"You're asking me?"

"Well, yeah. You're the resident expert."

"What?"

"You and Tegan, dummy!" said Aaron.

I stared back at him with a special sort of cluelessness.

"You guys *have* dropped the L-bomb . . . haven't you?"

"The . . . L-bomb?"

" 'I love you!' " Aaron exclaimed, rather loudly.

This garnered a significant amount of attention from the students occupying the surrounding lockers.

"Oh, c'mon. *Context, people!*" Aaron shouted for everyone to hear. Several staring faces returned their attention to their lockers and textbooks and backpacks. Aaron dropped his volume several notches. "You haven't told her you love her?"

"*Should* I have?" I said, slightly alarmed.

"Well . . . not necessarily," said Aaron. "I was just under the impression . . . I mean, how comfortable you guys are together? And how honest you are? It's like there's nothing you two can't say to each other. It's all on the table, and that's awesome. And the way you *look* at each other? God, it's like you're making love with your eyeballs."

I continued to stare at Aaron. My mouth was definitely open.

"You know what?" said Aaron. "Forget I said anything. You and Tegan have such a good thing going on. No need to overthink it and complicate things."

"Oh my God. Am I in love with Tegan?"

Aaron began moonwalking backward, waving his arms like noodles. In a voice that was part ghost, part hypnotist, he said, "*Youuuuuuu didn't hear anyyyyyyyythiiiiiinnnngg.*"

"Aaron? AARON. Dammit, Aaron!"

But he kept moonwalking—down the hall, around the corner, noodles for arms all the way.

———

It was the ironic process theory in action. Dostoyevsky told me not to think about the polar bear, and suddenly, the damned polar bear was the only thing I could think about!

Did I love Tegan?

I determined to settle the matter through a simple yes-no table chart. I spent most of fifth-period English mapping out the complicated layers of Cliff Hubbard's "feelings."

Am I in Love with Tegan?

Yes	*No*
• She's the most beautiful human being I know.	• I'm sixteen.
• Holding her hand is my favorite thing in the world.	• She's my first girlfriend.
• I can't stop smiling whenever I think about her.	• Everything I know about love I learned from *Titanic*. And we all know how that ended.
	• We haven't had sex yet.

	Yes		No
•	She's like a human antidepressant.	•	What is love anyway? A mere construct of ideals perpetuated by social norms and mass media to ensure societal order? A formality for sex, but really nothing more than a mammalian drive, sugarcoated in fairy tales and lies of a happily ever after to appease the pathos? Like, is love even real?
•	She can probably beat me up. (And just thinking about that turns me on.)		

As Spinelli paced up and down the aisles and desks, reading aloud a Walt Whitman poem called "A Glimpse," I failed to notice him reading over my shoulder. Not until he stooped down and wrote an answer to my question, *Is love even real?*

He wrote: *Just because it defies logic and comprehension, that doesn't mean it's not real.* And then he just kept walking and reading aloud:

"There we two, content, happy in being together, speaking little, perhaps not a word."

———

After English, I saw Tegan in the hallway. I marched right up to her, put my hands on her hips, and kissed her like I meant it.

"I think I'm magnetically drawn to you," I announced in a moment of profound enlightenment and social stupidity.

"You're so strange," she said, shaking her head. But her voice was soft and breathless.

"I think I love you. Like, the real thing."

Tegan didn't seem to know what to say to that.

"Also, I want to ask you on a date. Like, a *real* date—dinner, a movie, the whole shebang. Have you seen *Plan 9 from Outer Space*? They're showing it for Throwback Thursday at the dollar theater. It's absolutely terrible. I love it."

Tegan continued to stare at me. This was approximately ten times more awkward than I thought it would be.

"Or we can watch something else," I said.

"You . . . love me?" said Tegan.

Okay, words. Words were good. I could do words.

"I think so, yeah," I said. "I mean, I know that's kind of a taboo phrase when you haven't been dating long, and I don't expect you to say it back to me, it's just, it's the only word I can think of to explain how I feel about you, and—"

Tegan grabbed my collar and pulled me down. Her lips met mine. I absorbed her, breathed her in, and nothing had ever felt so right.

Tegan finally pulled away, but her lips lingered close. "Tell me more about this terrible movie."

I turned down Aaron's standing offer to drive me home. I wasn't ready to go. Not yet.

Instead, I walked to the Monolith.

I had made this walk so many times, but right here, right now— this was something else. The streets might have been empty, but there was life everywhere. In the boughs of tall trees, rippling and swaying like an ocean above me. In the cicadas singing their invisible symphony.

In the anxious beating of my heart.

Why was I anxious? Because I was alive, and it was exciting—if slightly terrifying. But whatever lay ahead of me, I had a feeling I could handle it.

When at last I reached the Monolith, I navigated the labyrinth. Stepping through trash, winding around old construction materials, climbing the winding stairwell until I reached the top.

Someone had beaten me there.

Noah sat cross-legged at the edge of the concrete overlook. A gentle breeze nipped at his Flaming Lips T-shirt, sweeping his hair out of his eyes. He turned his head at the sound of my footsteps.

"Oh hey," he said.

"Hey there," I said. "Come here often?"

Some people try to think of the most awkward things they can possibly say. For me, it just came naturally. It was a gift.

Noah laughed softly. The humor faded into a sigh. "Not enough."

He turned back around and gazed off into the panorama. I joined him. I sat with my legs dangling over the lip, casually kicking the wide-open emptiness.

"What was he like?" I asked.

Noah blinked and looked at me. "Who? Shane?"

"Yeah. I mean, I thought I knew him better than anyone. But now I feel like maybe I didn't know him at all."

Noah shook his head. "No, you knew him, all right. He was exactly the guy you remember."

"But—"

"Just because he had a secret, that doesn't make him any different. He was awesome and insecure and hilarious and obnoxious. Really, he was kind of a marvelous dickhead. But I think that was part of his charm."

"What did he talk about?"

"You."

"What? Really?"

"Oh yeah. Shane *loved* his big-ass little brother. It was kind of insane."

If Noah was just trying to make me feel good about myself...

...he was doing a *really* good job of it.

In that moment, the Monolith lived true to its namesake—an anomaly independent of space-time. I found myself gazing into the Memories of the Past. The Mysteries of the Future.

And Now.

Now was everywhere. It was everything. So many doors, so many possibilities, intertwining and reaching infinitely.

"What do you think's gonna happen?" I asked.

"What do you mean?"

"I mean... everything's different now. Like, I *think* it's a good thing... but it makes me nervous. I feel like I just pounded three energy drinks in a row, and my heart is about to explode."

"I think that's normal. Everyone is afraid of change. That doesn't mean it's bad."

"But how can you be sure?"

"You can't," said Noah. "That's kind of the whole point."

"Huh," I said.

I resolved to shut up. Talking was just making me feel stupid.

"Esther disbanded the JTs," said Noah.

What the...? I tried to blink the dizziness out of my head. "You're shitting me."

"Oh, it gets better. She actually attended a GSA meeting."

"YOU'RE SHITTING ME. YOU'RE SHITTING MY ACTUAL PANTS."

"Nope. True story."

"How'd it go?"

"She actually sat through the whole thing without saying a word. Just listened."

"No. Way."

"I mean, she looked like that blueberry girl from *Willy Wonka*—like she was about to explode at any moment—but still! All things considered, it was kind of a watershed moment for her."

Noah smirked, and I laughed.

I stared out into the small forever that was Happy Valley. The river was still there, dividing the north and south parts of town, and the mountains encompassed it all in a cereal bowl. But it was *far* from Shitty Puffs. Buildings and houses and streets and trees of every shape and size—old and new—came together. Misfit puzzle pieces clicking into place. Paintbrush strokes blending into one. All part of the Masterpiece.

Part of me wished that Shane was here to see it.

The other part—the greater part—felt him here with me.

He might have died, but he was far from dead. He was a part of me. And he was *everywhere*. I could see his footsteps—his fingerprints—in every facet of my universe.

And there were so many doors ahead of us.

ACKNOWLEDGMENTS

First, I should thank my agent, Jenny Bent. She is not only Master of What She Does, but she's a genuinely good human being. If you want evidence, find me at a book signing or a Taco Bell or somewhere and ask me how she became my agent. She's also the only person I know who loves Girl Scout Cookies as much as I do. Secondly and coequally, my editor, Laura Schreiber, who is a true visionary and is also mind-blowingly ambitious. I'd be lying if I said I wasn't totally skeptical about the major editorial change she wanted to make with *Neanderthal*. (It somewhat resembled raising Lazarus from the dead.) I'd also be lying if I said the book wasn't a million times better as a result. I am grateful to her entire editorial team, Hannah Allaman and Mary Mudd, for their thoroughness and awesometacularness, and for the little meta-jokes in the margins that legitimately made me laugh. And a special thanks to all the wizards and ninjas in the background who made this book an actual, successful book: Frank Bumbalo, Emily Meehan, Dina Sherman, Elke Villa, Holly Nagel, Cassie McGinty, Phil Caminiti, Mary Claire Cruz, Sara Liebling, and

Guy Cunningham. And lastly, the two most important people in my life. First, my mom, who gave me terrible parenting advice such as "follow your dreams" and "be a writer." And lastly, my very own Tegan—Erin Rene. She's basically cooler than me in every way imaginable.